MARI HANNAH

DEADLY DECEIT

PAN BOOKS

First published 2013 by Macmillan

This edition published 2013 by Pan Books
an imprint of Pan Macmillan, a division of Macmillan Publishers Limited
Pan Macmillan, 20 New Wharf Road, London N1 9RR
Basingstoke and Oxford
Associated companies throughout the world
www.panmacmillan.com

ISBN 978-0-330-53996-8

1 3 5 7 9 8 6 4 2

A CIP catalogue record for this book is available from
the British Library.

Typeset by Ellipsis Digital, Glasgow
Printed and bound by CPI Group (UK) Ltd, Croydon, CR0 4YY

Visit www.panmacmillan.com to read more about all our books
and to buy them. You will also find features, author interviews and
news of any author events, and you can sign up for e-newsletters
so that you're always first to hear about our new releases.

DEADLY DECEIT

Mari Hannah was born in London and moved north as a child. Sponsored by the Home Office, she graduated from Teesside University before becoming a Probation Officer, a career cut short when she was injured while on duty. Thereafter, she spent several years working as a film/television scriptwriter. During that time she created and developed a number of projects, most notably a feature-length film and the pilot episode of a crime series for television based on the characters in her book, the latter as part of a BBC drama development scheme. She lives in Northumberland with her partner, an ex-murder detective. In 2010, she won the Northern Writers' Award. *Deadly Deceit* is her third novel.

www.marihannah.com

By Mari Hannah

The Murder Wall
Settled Blood
Deadly Deceit

For my parents
Marie & Gordon

Twelve forty-five a.m., Thursday, 24 June 2010. Another hot and sticky night. Standing in the shadows, the girl peered into the darkness. Not a soul about. Several streetlights were out thanks to a couple of local yobs who possessed an air rifle each and no more sense than they were born with. She had to admit, the conditions were perfect for someone with murder in mind.

Just metres away, in scenes reminiscent of the end of World War Two, the scruffy back lanes of Newcastle's West End had been transformed. Red-and-white bunting blew in the breeze, criss-crossing Victorian terraces. Beneath it, trestle tables laid end to end stretched the full length of the lane where she lived.

If anyone could actually call it living.

With the eyes of the world on South Africa, the Brits were behaving like wankers celebrating a one–nil win over Slovenia after a piss-poor start to their World Cup. The party had begun at noon, a knocked-off flat screen rigged up outside so everyone could watch the match and get smashed in the sunshine. Paper plates were piled high with enough sandwiches and crisps to feed a small nation, crates of cheap booze stacked against one wall, a barbeque as big as Texas built just

for the occasion, a karaoke system laid ready and waiting for the really sad fuckers.

One of the guys had organized a mini football tournament, clearing wheelie bins away and drawing makeshift goalposts on the gable end of the next terrace down. Before coverage of the big game began, he'd exhibited his ball skills with an impressive number of keepy-ups to the delight of the kids. As they ran towards him cheering, he'd dribbled the ball past one, past two, and scored a goal before running off celebrating through a rotting wooden gate that was hanging from its hinges, returning minutes later with prizes: water pistols and catapults. Perfect choice for the next generation of fuckwits unlucky enough to grow up round here.

But that was nearly twelve hours ago.

Leftover food, gone stale in the heat of the day, littered the ground, blown there by the wind. Kids were tired and fractious, many of their parents drunk and incapable – none of them remotely interested in putting their bairns to bed. They'd spent the last few hours with beer goggles on, bigging up the game: *Terry was awesome, Upson too, Milner outstanding – we can go on and win the tournament now. Bring on Germany!*

Yeah right: only yesterday they were accusing the England team of bottling it, choking under pressure – their manager, Fabio Capello, of ill-considered tactics. In the pre-match build up, TV commentators had talked of the courage required to play for your country. *Bollocks.* Her brother was in Afghanistan fighting for his. That took courage. Not kicking a ball round on a patch of grass for an hour and a half, a group hug at the end to show their solidarity. Footballers

were only good for two things: shagging or fleecing – and not necessarily in that order.

The smell of barbequed food reached her. That would be the kid three doors down – twenty-two years old and thirty stones in weight – never more than three metres from a burger, two if there were chips and curry sauce on the go. It seemed like everyone was involved in the street party.

Except one.

A raised voice broke through the laughter. A bottle flew through the air and landed in the street a few metres away, smashing into a million pieces. They were off, the neighbours from hell. It would all end in tears, probably at the General Hospital, their second home. Pissheads, both of them. Deserved each other. Wouldn't know a good time if it ran up and bit them on the arse. Still, with neither of them working, there was a whole day ahead to sleep it off. Or so they thought.

But then *they* didn't know what *she* knew.

2

Within hours, the place would be a crime scene crawling with emergency personnel: medical, fire, forensic teams and cops. Locals rounded up. Statements taken. Those too pissed to cooperate locked up for drunk and disorderly, assaulting the police, breathing the same air – mutual disrespect the order of the day.

Then it really would be game on.

A snotty-nosed kid in Ben Ten pyjamas – no more than four years old – wandered out into the middle of the road. Kai, his mother called him. Poor little bastard hadn't long been home from the care of the local authority after a non-accidental injury resulted in a place of safety being sought by social workers concerned for his welfare. Where the hell were they when he needed them, eh? Or the divvies he called parents, come to think of it?

The boy blinked – dead on his feet – the epitome of neglect.

Winking back at him, she stepped into the shadow of the doorway, stubbing her fag in the wall as his mother arrived, totally gone, vodka bottle in hand, no shoes. Just an England shirt and red leggings on pins that looked like they were on upside down. Her face was grotesque, smeared with the remains of a flag of St George. Unaware she was under

scrutiny, she took hold of the young 'un by the scruff of the neck and dragged him kicking and screaming up a side alley and back to the party.

The front of the terrace fell silent again and her attention shifted to the house across the road, lights inside dimmed, a wall-mounted TV reflected in the mirror in the living room. In her mind's eye she saw the fire before it was even lit. A smile formed on her lips as it ignited for real, small at first – barely a flicker – then building in strength as it licked its way silently up the stairs, raging out of control, fast and more furious now.

Dense, acrid smoke drifted beneath the door. Windows exploded. A scream from inside. Him not her? It was a sound so chilling it made her shiver. The male voice surprised her. He was persona non grata in that house, supposed to be at his pad looking after their kid. Had she misheard? Maybe she'd got it wrong. It looked like Maggie had gone away and he was house-sitting, not babysitting.

Oh God! Now she had a decision to make.

A fire alarm went off but no one came running. In the lane behind her, The Killers' 'Mr Brightside' blasted out as someone turned up the volume. Even without the music, elderly neighbours not at the party would write it off as just another bloody false alarm, cover their heads with pillows to drown out the din. Many of them too scared to venture out at night in an area where it paid to mind your own business.

And still the elements of fire, oxygen and heat combined to create a mini inferno, so intense she could feel it burning her suntan from where she was standing. Deep down, she felt guilty. But not for long. No sweat. He'd have scarpered out

the back door for sure. Anyhow, this was an opportunity she couldn't afford to miss. Pulling out her mobile phone, she switched to camera mode and took her shot, wondering if the image she'd captured could do her any good. They say knowledge is power. Well, knowledge was money in her world.

3

Thursday, four a.m. Thunder rumbled overhead. On the southbound carriageway of the A1, a driver braked suddenly and then lost control. His lorry slewed across the road, fish-tailing as he tried to correct it, then hit the central reservation and literally took off. It flipped, rotating as it travelled through the air in slow motion, before crashing to earth with an almighty racket, sparks flying everywhere as it continued on its roof for several metres.

The tail-gating driver behind couldn't stop in time. His car aquaplaned on the wet surface and then ploughed into the back of the first car with a low crunching sound, throwing its unbelted rear passenger through the windscreen on to the underside of a third car.

Her body began to cook on the red-hot exhaust.

A third vehicle joined in the madness with an almighty crack, its engine seizing on impact, steam billowing from beneath the bonnet. Then another, and another, in a con-certina of mangled metal. An HGV in the nearside lane had no chance. Jack-knifing as its driver swerved to avoid collid-ing with the others, it took out two cars in the fast lane, pushing one over the central reservation into the path of oncoming traffic.

Metal crumpled like bits of paper, puncturing fuel tanks

that spewed a lethal mixture of petrol and diesel on to the road. Glass and bones shattered simultaneously, rupturing internal organs, soft tissue ripped away. A swift death for some. Unimaginable pain for others as their bodies fought to survive. Misery for all concerned.

The road was blocked in both directions. And still vehicles added to the chaos, emerging through the torrential rain at high speed, colliding with upturned cars, resulting in multiple casualties, horns going off, and fire as one car burst into flames.

One minute there was lots of noise . . .

The next, a deathly quiet.

Local stargazer David Hedley was certain the death toll would be high as he looked down at the carnage from the balcony of his third-floor flat. The rain was welcome after days of dry weather but the sudden downpour had caused mayhem. Wrecks with their headlights still illuminated were strewn across wet carriageways, on grass verges, two straddling the central reservation. In utter disbelief he watched motorists emerge from cars, some crawling on their hands and knees, collapsing as their bodies succumbed to horrific injuries.

A flash of lightning lit up the gory spectacle.

One man had a limb missing, a flap of skin hanging loose where his arm once was. Blood pulsed from a main artery and he fell to the ground as two of the walking wounded went to his aid. Dazed and pale. Numb. Unable to take in the full horror in front of them. How anyone had survived at all was a mystery to David. The golden hour would be critical: the difference between life and death. He called the emergency services before rushing out to help.

4

Detective Chief Inspector Kate Daniels swore under her breath. If she hadn't made a detour to Wideopen to pick up her DS from a mate's house she'd have been at her crime scene by now. An urgent callout had summoned her to work, interrupting her sleep for the second time in as many days. A case of arson, according to the control room, an accelerant, most probably petrol, poured through the letterbox of a terraced house in the West End. The resulting inferno had claimed two lives.

As duty Senior Investigating Officer she couldn't complain about her work schedule. In recent weeks there had been an unprecedented lull in murder enquiries. That would change now summer was here. As the temperature rose, so would crime. Guaranteed every year. But she was going nowhere in a hurry tonight. Traffic had ground to a halt in front of her, stretching into the distance as far as she could see. Sirens wailed and blue lights flashed in her rear-view mirror. A tell-tale beam of light pointed down from the sky on to the road ahead. The police helicopter – India 99 – had been deployed. With budgets in every department being squeezed, that meant only one thing: the incident was serious, if not fatal. People were out of their cars, engines left running, keys dangling from ignitions. Abandoning their vehicles and their

belongings, drivers were walking up the dual carriageway in between car lanes, chatting to strangers or talking on mobile phones, all craning their necks to see what was going on, putting their own lives at risk.

She picked up her radio. '7824 to control.'

'Control to 7824, go ahead.'

The familiar voice of Pete Brooks, the radio controller, woke her sleeping DS. Hank Gormley opened one eye, peering through the windscreen at a long line of tail lights. Daniels could smell alcohol, but Hank wasn't pissed by any stretch of the imagination. He knew better than to hang one on a school night. He was a bloody good investigator, her professional partner for almost a decade, a man she respected and cared for a great deal, a valued friend and colleague she couldn't do without.

'What's going on?' he said, through a gaping yawn.

Daniels touched her lip to silence him in favour of her radio. 'Pete, I'm southbound on the A1. Could you advise the fire department that I'm delayed? Tell them I'll be with them ASAP. I'm stuck in a long tailback. From the looks of it, I'm not getting out of here anytime soon.'

'That's received.' There was a tap-tapping sound as Brooks accessed his control room computer. 'Multiple RTA ahead of you, Kate. Total gridlock, according to air support. First responders en route. You may as well send out for pizza, 'cause you're gonna be a while.'

Shamefaced, Gormley apologized for dragging her out of her way.

Daniels shrugged. 'Hey, don't worry about it. You're entitled to a life.'

'Really?'

'No, not really! That's a warrant card in your pocket . . .' A loud explosion made them duck. They waited for another. When it didn't come, they raised their heads. The beam from the helicopter was highlighting a huge plume of smoke through a curtain of pouring rain. Daniels went back to her radio. 'Things are kicking off approximately quarter of a mile in front of us, Pete. Speak to Traffic. Tell them we're stuck and ask if we can be of any assistance.'

'Senior officer is Mike 7295. Shall I put you on talk-through?'

'Please.' Mike 7295 was the call-sign of an officer Daniels knew well. What he didn't know about traffic accident management wasn't worth knowing.

The radio again. 'Control to 7295. Take talk-through with 7824?'

'Affirmative.'

Another voice. Low and controlled. Mr Cool. 'This is not a good time, Kate.'

For either of them, Daniels thought. '7824. Two officers. Plain clothes. En route to serious incident. Southbound. Approximately five hundred metres. Sounds like you need a hand. Anything we can do?'

'If you've got a couple of high-viz jackets, we need all the help we can get.'

'Roger that.'

Gormley looked at Daniels. 'It's raining stair-rods!'

'Don't be such a wuss, Hank.' She swung the wheel to her left, blue light and siren engaged. 'You can swim, can't you?'

Pulling on to the hard shoulder, Daniels edged her way

forward, weaving in and out of traffic that had no business being there, dodging pedestrians who'd rushed out of their homes with blankets, torches, anything they thought might assist the dead and dying. None of them remotely aware of what they were letting themselves in for.

5

At the epicentre of the accident, pandemonium reigned. First responders included police, fire, medical personnel, but not in the numbers needed to cope with such a large incident. Motorists were bloodied, some screaming, some sitting on the grassy bank by the side of the road. Others wandering aimlessly away, causing more problems for those trying to help them. Still more casualties lay injured in their cars.

For some, the pain had already gone.

In one car an elderly couple were trapped and in a very bad way. As the man lost his fight for life, his wife, Ivy Kerr, wept, her summer dress drenched in his blood. It was getting light now. The scene out of the window was nothing like the road she knew. It was more akin to a breaker's yard she'd seen on American TV. The car closest to her, a green Peugeot 205, looked like it had been in a crusher; its driver slumped over the steering wheel, dead as a post. A woman's slender arm was lolling out of the rear side window. Blood trickled down her ring finger and dropped on to the wet road, zigzagging across the uneven surface and pooling in a shallow pothole, turning rainwater red.

Ivy shivered. In her head, she could still hear the screeching of brakes, the shattering of glass, the sound of metal

crunching on metal, the screams of trapped motorists – the whoosh of a fire close by.

And now she could smell petrol.

Fear ripped through her.

Was she going to die too?

Ivy closed her eyes and then opened them again as a hand reached out to her. Not her husband's, rough and hard from tending his garden, but smoother, much younger skin altogether. The familiarity of a soft Geordie accent cut through the sound of panic going on around her – the voice of the person who'd come to help her.

Ivy's relief was overwhelming.

'Don't worry about me. Help him,' she pleaded, unaware of the mantra going through the heads of the rescue personnel flooding into the area as fast as they were able.

Faced with such a chaotic situation, certain decisions had to be made and made quickly. The dead were beyond help. And silent casualties caused fewer problems than those screaming for assistance, even though they were most probably more seriously injured. Prioritizing medical attention was the key to saving lives. And Ivy *could* be saved if they could get her to hospital quick enough.

If they could extricate her from the car . . .

If the car didn't burst into flames . . .

If was a very big word.

'What's your name, love?'

Ivy said her name in a voice that sounded like someone else's.

'Well, don't worry, Ivy. The ambulance will be here soon. You're going to be fine.'

Ivy wept again. 'I . . . I told him it was madness.'

'Here, let me try and make you a bit more comfortable. Told who, love?'

Ivy's eyes shifted to her husband, his glasses skewed on his face like they always did when he fell asleep reading in bed, a frequent occurrence in the last few years. Maybe he wasn't dead after all, just knocked out having banged his head.

'Husband, boyfriend or fancy man?' The soft Geordie voice again.

'Husband . . .' Ivy managed a little grin. Feeling too calm for the circumstances, she looked down at legs she couldn't feel, feet she couldn't see. 'It's our Diamond Anniversary in August.'

'Wow! Congratulations! You in any pain at all?'

Ivy nodded.

'Whereabouts?'

Moving her hands to her pelvis was an effort for Ivy.

'OK, let's have a look shall we?'

Ivy thought she might vomit as efforts were made to free her. Once more, her eyes drifted towards her husband. He was in a bad way. But at least he couldn't see the mayhem surrounding them. Or the blood. He'd been squeamish all his life. He'd turn his eyes away or make an excuse to leave the room rather than sit through a gory scene on TV. In all the time they'd been married, Ivy had never let on that she'd noticed. Instead, she allowed him to maintain the pretence of being the stronger partner when he was really nothing of the sort.

'Try not to worry, pet. He's just unconscious, take my word for it. He looks to me like a tough old bugger. You'll have come through a lot worse than this together, I bet.'

Tears welled up in Ivy's eyes. Her husband was indeed a survivor. They'd known each other since primary school, lived in the same street in Byker in the East End of Newcastle as kids. They'd started seeing each other when they were fifteen years old, nearly seventy years ago. He'd worked in the Tyneside shipyards where his father worked before him and was also in the Territorial Army. One of the first to be called up when war broke out. His departure in May 1941 from Newcastle – along with hundreds of other Northumberland Fusiliers – had been heartbreaking for Ivy. She feared she'd never see him again.

She couldn't lose him now.

6

'Stay with me, Ivy . . . Ivy? Can you open your eyes for me?'

The voice seemed further away than before. Straining to do as she was asked, Ivy's eyelids refused to obey her command. There was that flutter in her chest again, like a large bird was trapped there. And still her eyes felt as if they were stuck together with superglue. It was as though she was sinking, down and down further, to a place beneath the level of the road. John was there too, smiling at her, encouraging her to keep her chin up as he'd done in 1941 – the first and only time they'd been separated.

He'd been in Cyprus when she sent word she'd given birth to their only daughter, a letter sent through the free postal service run by the British Red Cross. People were so kind back then. Instead of moaning about hard times, they looked out for each other. Like the couple from Benwell in the city's West End who used to listen in to Vatican Radio and write down the names of POWs. They took it upon themselves to write to Ivy and tell her that John was among them, captured in North Africa by the Italians. Their kindness averted heartbreak for Ivy who, the very next day, received a letter from the War Office telling her that John was posted: missing, presumed dead.

Like the person helping her now, the Benwell couple were

good people. Salt of the earth. Not long after they had made contact, Ivy received a pre-printed postcard for war prisoners with a red cross stamped on it and bits crossed out where appropriate. Ivy was so shocked to receive it, she could remember the words by heart . . .

(post mark date)
(Data del timbre postale)

My dear, *Ivy*

I am alright (~~I have not been wounded~~ (or) I have
Sto bene (non sono stato ferito (o) sono

been slightly wounded). I am a prisoner of the Italians
stato ferito leggermente). Sono stato catturato dagli Italiani

and I am being treated well.
e mi trovo bene.

 Shortly I shall be transferred to a prisoner's camp and
 Nel prossimi glorni saró transferito in un campo di

I will let you have my new address.
Prigionieri del quale vi comunichero l'indirizzo.

 Only then will I be able to receive letters from you
 Soltanto allora potró ricevere la vostra corrispondenza

and to reply.
e rispondervi.

 With love *John (signature)*
 Saluti affettuosi (firma)
 J. Kerr

The word *wounded* worried her sick. Just how wounded *was* wounded? That was the question she'd asked herself in the weeks and months that followed. But, with telegrams arriving daily for less fortunate soldiers' loved ones, knowing John was alive was of great comfort to her and his extended family. He ended up in Stalag 18, near Wolfsburg in Austria when the Italians capitulated. He stayed there until peace was declared, working on a farm, being cared for by equally good people. He'd always wanted to go back there, find the family and thank them for all they had done. Only he'd never had the means, until a few hours ago when an opportunity to return to Austria had fallen in his lap. He'd seized upon it without a moment's hesitation before it was too late.

That's how much it meant to him.

They were separated for nearly five years in total. They went to live with Ivy's mother when John came home until they could afford to rent a place of their own. Times were tough. They were practically strangers when he returned. He never talked about the war but she knew he'd seen bad things. He wasn't the same afterwards. They married for their daughter's sake, but it was a rocky relationship at times.

Ivy loved him so much, even though she suspected he'd fallen in love with an Austrian girl when he was away. Not that it mattered any more. He'd come home to *her*. Married *her*. Been a good father to Annaliese, the name he'd chosen for their daughter. Forcing her eyes to stay open, Ivy tried to focus straight ahead and not on John, who still hadn't moved or made a sound. He would survive. He had to. If only to make that trip.

'He hates the sight of blood,' Ivy said, as if her rescuer had been party to her memories.

'It's a good job he's taking a nap then. You're doing *really* well, Ivy. I'll have you out of there in no time.'

The wind had changed direction and rain was bleaching through the open window. Ivy felt cold. *So cold.* 'He will be all right, won't he?'

'Try not to worry, love. Let's concentrate on you for now.'

Words of comfort couldn't console Ivy in 1942. And today was no different. What was taking so long? Wasn't anyone else coming? There were no trenches here but the place looked like a war zone nevertheless.

What terrors must John have seen all those years ago?

'We were arguing when he lost control . . .' Ivy confessed, a pang of guilt niggling deep inside her – making her feel partly responsible. 'I wanted to delay 'til morning but he insisted there was no time like the present. Said we'd be in London by mid-morning. Our daughter doesn't even know we've gone.'

'I'll take care of that, pet. Soon as you're both out of here. Going on a trip, were you?'

Ivy nodded. Glancing at John, she began sharing the secret he'd insisted she keep to herself.

7

'*Jesus!*' DCI Daniels said, as they stepped from the Toyota.

Gormley linked his fingers and put his hands on his head. They had attended serious road traffic accidents before but this was something else. Body parts and cars were strewn across both lanes for several hundred metres. There were dozens of vehicles involved. Two fatalities they could see as they walked towards the worst of it. Many serious injuries and lots of walking wounded. On the periphery of the incident blue strobe lights converging from all directions as police, medical personnel and fire crews battled to reach the scene.

Smoke drifted from a tanker lying on its side and there were casualties everywhere they looked: sitting on barriers, shaking heads, crying and getting upset. Apart from the dead and injured, there were upwards of twenty-five civilians running back and forth, some involved in the incident, others trying to administer aid – an investigative nightmare for the traffic department.

The police helicopter hovered overhead, sending vibrations through their feet. Suddenly they were in its spotlight. Daniels looked up, shielding her eyes from the rain, wondering if the pilot was a mate of hers, a civilian witness in her last case who'd received a commendation for services to the police and had since been employed by them following a

recommendation from her. The spotlight blinked on and off letting her know Stew Cole was watching over her.

He'd heard her on the radio to Mr Cool.

A young man walked towards her. He had spiky hair and piercing blue eyes, was dressed in jeans and T-shirt with a film spotting logo on the front and blood – real blood – smeared across it. He was wearing flip-flops. Sensible footwear for the surface water they were standing in, Daniels thought, her eyes homing in on the rainbow effect of spilt diesel on the road. A biker's nightmare, even after the rain stopped.

'You police?' The man was a little breathless.

Drenched, cold and thoroughly miserable, Gormley looked down at his high-viz jacket. Daniels thought he was about to say *What do you think?* So she nudged his arm and he restrained himself.

'You hurt, sir?' he said instead.

'Me? No. I wasn't involved in the accident. I'm just doing my bit.'

Daniels didn't think the man was injured. She noticed a heavy camera bag slung over his shoulder. 'Name?'

'Steven, with a v, not a p h.' His eyes were like saucers. 'I counted *three* fatalities so far. But the body count will rise, there's no doubt about it. And that's just this side of the road. I haven't been on the other side yet. Oh man! I've never seen anything like it! Who needs special effects?'

'That'll be Spielberg then, will it, Steven with a v?' Gormley didn't bother trying to hide his contempt. Flipping a pad open, he took a pen from his pocket. 'Stop pissing about, son. I need a surname. An address. Then you can sling your hook

and go back to your movies. People are in pain here. Show some bloody respect, why don't you?'

Gormley wrote his details down and then told him to move along.

They watched him slope off, his bag bumping against his thigh as he walked.

'What a dick!' Daniels rolled her eyes and lifted her radio to her mouth. '7824 to 7295. Now on scene. Your six o'clock. What d'you want us to do?'

The senior traffic officer turned towards her, calm in a crisis as she knew he would be.

'Can you walk up the line, Kate? I need a rough sketch. Reg numbers. Position. Details of occupants where possible. Appreciate your help. See the bus?'

Daniels' eyes scanned the scene. A single-decker was right side up but half its windows were out. Red-and-white flags flapped through gaping holes where the glass was missing. Its passengers peering out from within, all of them ashen, some with superficial injuries, gawping at the chaos in disbelief.

'Yeah, I see it.'

'Thirty plus on board. En route to the airport, apparently. I've instructed the driver to keep the doors shut, but they're whingeing to be off. They could use a little encouragement to stay put, Kate. I need more casualties wandering round like a hole in the head.'

'Consider it done.'

Daniels led Gormley away from the film buff, who was still hanging around enjoying the spectacle, behaving like an arse. She didn't have time for him. They had serious work to do.

8

Ivy Kerr was much more comfortable now with less pressure on her pelvis. She thought she'd seen John move a minute ago. But maybe she was mistaken. As her eyes slid over his face, she noticed, bizarrely, that the white hairs in his ears needed a trim. He would hate that. He'd always taken such a pride in his appearance.

She'd tease him about it when they got home.

More rescue personnel had arrived. Strobe lights from emergency vehicles flashed non-stop and there was frantic activity as professionals took over from civilians. A couple of plainclothes police officers with high-viz jackets walked by as the rain began to ease off. Despite the chaos all around her, the woman appeared calm, confident and businesslike. She stopped making notes in order to direct medics to a particular individual in distress. The man with her, a large man with a pleasant face, looked at Ivy through the car window.

'You guys in there OK?'

Gormley waited for a response. Hours ago, on a rare night off, he'd been watching footie with unmarried police mates. Take-out Indian food. A few jars. A few laughs. Time away from marital disharmony. And then all hell broke loose: three mobiles rang out simultaneously in the middle of the night,

three ringtones competing with each other to interrupt deep, alcohol-induced sleep. Even for coppers, for all of them to be called out was unusual. An omen of what lay ahead. And now he was surrounded by death and destruction in the middle of a traffic nightmare in the pissing rain, with no bloody idea why Daniels had agreed to get involved.

Who was he kidding? She couldn't walk away from a lost dog.

He didn't approach the vehicle, just ducked beneath the height of the car roof, raising his voice over the din of sirens and screams and the noise inside his head. 'Need any help in there?'

A young woman grabbed his arm, begging for help. He led her to the nearest paramedic and then turned back to the car. Gormley knew a dead body when he saw one. The driver was a fatal by the looks, the old lady being worked on not much better. A front passenger, she looked proper poorly, her green eyes paling to yellow in the early morning light as they strained to meet his. She reminded him of his mother, or what she might look like in a few years' time, should she live that long. The same stamp: heart-shaped face and short-cropped, silver hair. He gave her a reassuring smile.

Ivy was comforted by his caring face. As the big man in plain clothes moved off, her rescuer smiled at her, far too busy cutting off her seatbelt to turn around and chat.

'We've got it covered here, haven't we, Ivy? You're a star, aren't you, love?'

'Nice of him to ask,' Ivy managed in return.

She was relieved to hear that her rescue was proceeding

well. It meant she *would* live long enough to make that trip. God forbid she'd meet anyone called Annaliese in Austria. Another glance at John. Those flapping wings in her chest again. It was time she learned to trust him. She took his hand in hers, praying he'd survive his injuries and make a full recovery.

Ivy looked out the window. The big man had caught up with his female colleague. They were heading in the direction of a busload of passengers Ivy could see in the distance. In the foreground, a young woman suddenly appeared in front of her. She'd crawled out from beneath a load of boxes that had spilled from the back of a four-by-four, blood streaming down her face, rendering her sightless. She walked towards Ivy, hands feeling her way, oblivious to her surroundings.

'Help! Help me,' she cried. 'Is anyone there?'

Ivy never saw the object that struck her, or the torch illuminating her bag. Never felt the hands searching her pockets, or the gap in her cleavage where the item was nestled between her breasts. She met her end holding her dead husband's hand, with police and medical personnel metres away, a blind girl looking straight at her. And she certainly never heard the shout go up as her damaged brain stopped functioning.

'Over here! I need help over here!'

9

Haunted by images of blood and mangled flesh, Daniels and Gormley left the crash site to continue their journey. They had done what any police officers would in similar circumstances, given assistance to the living before attending to the dead, remained at the crash scene until the incident management team had everything under control and they were no longer required.

Gormley glanced at his watch. It was just gone five.

'You think the dash-and-splash will still be there at this hour?'

His pet name for the fire department was an attempt to lift Daniels' mood. But it would take more than that, the way she was feeling. She gave a shrug, driving a little slower than usual tonight. Turning left, she entered Ralph Street where the alleged arson had taken place. A hundred metres ahead, a large white tent had been erected around the front door of a terraced house to keep prying eyes out. A fire engine was standing by, as well as a number of panda cars and Forensic vans. She drove towards the scene, steeling herself for more misery to come.

They got out of the Toyota and stood for a moment viewing the scene. There was a media scrum behind police tape: reporters, photographers and local television crews all

jockeying for position, capturing what they could through telephoto lenses. Some elderly neighbours were in the street too, offering tea to their unexpected guests. Just then a man in a forensic suit emerged from the crime tent to greet them. He ushered them inside so they could talk freely without fear of being quoted chapter and verse on breakfast news.

Fire Department Investigator Geoff Abbott was a man they knew well, a professional highly regarded in his field of expertise, as serious about his job as they were theirs. That didn't stop him going tit for tat with Gormley over their poor response time.

'Take the scenic route, did you?' he said.

Gormley gave him a wry smile. 'Don't tell me you're complaining about the ovies hitting your pay packet this month. Rumour has it your lot spend most of your service in bed. Why shouldn't we? Figured we'd stop off for coffee and croissants on the way. The boss was feeling a bit peckish.'

Daniels was feeling anything but. The accident had sickened her and food was the last thing on her mind. She turned to Abbott. 'What's the story here, Geoff?'

'Control room got a 999 call at one-o-four. We received a Persons on Premises call seconds later. Officers attending found two dead: believed to be Jamie Reid, ten months, and his father, Mark Reid. The house is leased by the boy's mother, Margaret Reid. She'd been out for the evening, leaving her ex to babysit. The building was well alight when she came home.'

'*She* called it in?'

'Yep. And there are no other witnesses – at least none that have come forward since I got here. I'll check with my lads.

Call me a suspicious old git, but that sounds iffy to me. According to elderly neighbours, that way –' Abbott pointed to his left – 'the couple are still married. They get on fairly well, despite no longer living together since the baby was born. Reid kept in regular contact though, so I'm guessing the child was his. As far as the neighbours are concerned there was no animosity between them.'

'Reason for their split?'

'Same old, same old. Extra-marital is the word on the grapevine.'

'His affair or hers?' Gormley asked.

'Didn't say, didn't ask. That's your remit, not mine.' Abbott eyeballed Gormley, his expression hard. 'Don't want to tread on anyone's toes after what happened in December, do I?'

The venom in his voice was not lost on Daniels. In a previous arson case, inaccurate information provided by fire crews had been acted upon by a Murder Investigation Team – thankfully not hers – causing red faces all round. Inter-agency cooperation was all well and good, but intelligence still had to be checked out. It was as much the fault of the police for not covering the bases. It happened sometimes in the heat of the moment when resources were stretched. Nothing to fall out about.

Gormley eyeballed him. 'No one blamed you, Geoff.'

Abbott bristled, holding his gaze. 'That's not what I heard—'

'Hey, you two, cut it out!' Daniels shot them both a look. 'I'm in no mood for a punch-up. It's old news. For God's sake, move on!' They didn't need telling twice. She glanced

towards the house. 'Appreciate what you've given us, Geoff. Can we take a look?'

'Be my guest. But I have to tell you it's not pretty. You'll be pleased to hear the young 'un's been taken away already, recovered from his cot upstairs by officers first at the scene. They tried to revive him but . . .'

He broke off. Daniels could tell from his expression that he'd witnessed the rescue attempt and she was relieved to have escaped the immediate trauma of seeing the child herself. She had no kids of her own, or any intention of ever having any, but she got on with children and hated to see them hurt. The gruesome post-mortem would come later. Her promise to Detective Constable Lisa Carmichael that the next PM was hers would have to be broken. Lisa would have to wait a while longer. This one would be far too distressing.

Unzipping the holdall she'd brought with her from the car, Daniels noticed a heavy medical bag at the entrance to the premises, the initials TWS engraved on the side. It belonged to Home Office Pathologist, Tim Stanton. She wondered how he'd got there. His Range Rover wasn't parked outside.

'Kit off, Hank,' she said.

Gormley's shoulders fell. 'You've got to be kidding me!'

Daniels was already down to her underwear. 'Come on, don't be shy.'

Gormley dropped his pants. He was wearing a pair of Union Jack shreddies his wife had bought him – his lucky World Cup shorts she called them – an infrequent gesture of affection these days. He'd felt obliged to put them on. It was either that or face more argy-bargy from Julie when he got

home. He hadn't figured he'd be sharing the spectacle with his female boss and the fire investigator.

'Where's that camera?' Abbott laughed. 'Got to get this for *The Burning Issue.*'

Daniels grinned at his reference to the fire and rescue bi-monthly magazine.

'Move and you're dead meat,' Gormley warned.

10

A camera flashed as they picked their way into the hallway where crime scene investigators were doing their bit. Tim Stanton looked up from the body as they walked through the door, greeting them with a nod. The house hardly resembled a house at all. Everything was black and smouldering, the air heavy with the nauseating stench of burning flesh – like barbequed meat left on too long. Ceiling tiles had caught fire, melted and dropped down igniting furniture below. There was a gaping hole above their heads and the sky could be seen where the roof once was. A body, unrecognisable as man or woman, was lying on what was left of the staircase, beaten back by the flames, its hand fused to the metal pin securing the charred remains of a banister.

Another volley of shots from the CSI camera.

Beneath her mask, Daniels tried to breathe. It was like a manifestation from hell. She'd seen enough death and destruction for one day. But as horrific as the scene facing her was, the accident she'd come from had been much worse. Dead bodies were dead bodies, whereas people alive and in pain really got to her. She could avoid the eyes of a corpse, but never those of the living. Helplessness in a situation like that was what kept her awake at night.

Psychologically wrung out, she stared at the body on the

stairs, her mind drifting back to the RTA. One casualty, Bridget McCabe, a pretty girl of about eighteen, had clung on to her, begging her to ring her dad, himself a policeman on nightshift. Though the DCI didn't know the officer personally, it made her feel sick to think of him going about his business not knowing his daughter had come to harm.

In her years in the force, she was used to dealing with the fallout from major road accidents. But somehow it seemed more personal because this was a fellow officer's child. As Bridget was finally lifted into an ambulance, she'd contacted Hexham station to break news of the accident to Sergeant McCabe, hoping his daughter would make it to hospital.

11

When she got home, Daniels stripped off her clothes at the front door. She carried them straight to the laundry room, dumped them in the washing machine and set it to a hot cycle. Then she walked upstairs to the shower, keen to wash away the muck and the grime from her body, wishing she could do the same thing to the images in her head. Had her mother still been alive, she'd most probably have called her for a sympathetic ear. She always did that whenever she felt unwell or down or just pissed off. Sadly that was no longer an option.

As the water pulsed from the shower, Daniels checked the diver's watch her mother had bought for her thirtieth birthday. Six-thirty a.m. She needed to get a wriggle on: a quick change of clothes, a coffee to go, and then a race back to the Murder Incident Room before the troops arrived – an opportunity to get her shit together on the drive into town.

As she stepped from the shower, her landline rang. That would be Gormley checking on her. Something he'd done frequently in the past few months, aware she had no one at home to offload on after a day like today. He was a little overprotective sometimes.

The phone stopped ringing.

Daniels hated living alone. Her former partner, Jo Soulsby,

had moved on and so must she. That was easier said than done when the woman was the department's Criminal Profiler, still part of her world, working alongside her, eating in the same bate room – tantalizingly close and yet a million miles away.

The phone rang again.

Gormley was such a softie.

He knew all about her nonexistent love life and the reasons behind it. He seemed to know when she was feeling rough and tried his best to comfort her. Once or twice he'd gone too far, attempting to play Cupid between her and Jo, interfering in matters that didn't concern him. Smiling, Daniels dried her hands, threw herself on her bed and picked up.

'I'm fine, Hank. But thanks for asking . . .'

A woman's voice came on the line, one she didn't recognize.

'Am I speaking to DCI Kate Daniels?'

'You are.' Daniels' stomach tightened.

'My apologies, I thought you might have been someone else.' Palming her forehead, Daniels listened. 'Yes. Yes I did . . . OK, no, I didn't know her personally. Yes, tragic . . . Thank you for taking the trouble to call.'

Replacing the handset gently on its charger, a sob caught Daniels' throat.

Bridget McCabe hadn't made it.

12

The RTA and the fire played second fiddle to World Cup football on the radio, the sporting achievements of eleven men dominating the news headlines. Daniels had watched the game alone at home, unmoved by the hysteria that was going on in the rest of the country. Not that she didn't like sport. She did. But she could've done without the hype beforehand. Her team had talked about nothing else for weeks. The tournament hadn't lived up to its billing – not by any stretch of the imagination.

A murder enquiry was well underway by the time Daniels reached the incident room, launched by her new boss, Superintendent Ron Naylor. She could feel the tension in the office the minute she walked in. She was expecting that. The nature of the crime, the death of a young child, affected everyone. But like the components of a well-oiled machine, each member of her team had a part to play and it was business as usual.

She watched them from the doorway, brooding on her visit to Bridget McCabe's home on her way in. She'd gone to offer comfort to the girl's father, not knowing if she'd be welcome at such a difficult time. He was a widower, a single dad of three girls, who'd lost his wife to a malignant brain tumour a year ago.

Poor sod!

In a moment of confusion, Daniels' jaw had dropped when Bridget opened the door. Except it wasn't her at all. It was her identical twin, Becci.

McCabe had come to the door, pulling the surviving twin inside. 'Fuck's sake! What is wrong with you people?'

The DCI had shown her badge to reassure him she wasn't press. Inside the house, she'd managed to convey, she hoped, a sense that Bridget had no idea of how poorly she was, that she was conscious, joking even – that she wasn't alone. Mick McCabe appreciated that. There was nothing more to be said.

Such traumatic situations made Daniels question her decision to join the force. But then the opposite was also true. Those same events compelled her to remain in the job for as long as possible. Nevertheless, at the McCabes' front door she'd had a sudden urge to run and keep running, not to get involved, let the traffic and welfare departments do their jobs. It was their remit to support bereaved police officers, not hers. But she liked to think that her timely intervention had made a difference in some small way.

Gormley looked up, probably wondering why it had taken her so long to dash home, shower and change. She thought of offering an explanation but then decided not to get into it. They both needed their minds on the job. They had an arson case to solve and, as brutal as it might sound to the wider public, Bridget McCabe was history. Reflection was a luxury Kate couldn't afford. It was time to move on.

Her DS looked weary. He'd not gone home, hadn't wanted to disturb his wife – at least, that's the reason he gave. Instead, he'd opted for a shower in the men's locker room.

Like the rest of the team, he kept a change of clothes there for such an eventuality. Daniels' attention shifted to a nearby desk.

The squad rookie, Detective Constable Lisa Carmichael, was a bright and bubbly twenty-five-year-old with more nous than her age would suggest. A whizz-kid on the computer, she was an officer of exceptional talent, ripe for promotion and tipped for the top. A young woman keen to put a recent setback behind her, having been slipped a Mickey Finn by some freak in a nightclub on the team's last, her first, under-cover operation.

Right now, she was entering data into the HOLMES system. As she typed, information was updated automatically on a state-of-the-art murder wall, a digital, touch-screen facility in the relatively new murder suite. The identities of victims Nominal One and Nominal Two – Mark and Jamie Reid – were highlighted, along with their ages, dates of birth, relationship to each other. Daniels had instructed Carmichael to upload only images of Mark and Jamie Reid alive. She didn't want civilian typists seeing the harrowing crime-scene photographs displayed. More importantly, she wanted her officers to relate to the victims as people, which was difficult to pull off if badly burned corpses were constantly in their faces. It was a skill, knowing how to get the most from her team.

Carmichael was scratching to find information to input at present. A video of the crime scene would be shown at the briefing later. But there was a lack of witness statements coming in from the house-to-house team. Unbelievable in a street where most of the residents had been up when the fire

began. Daniels' guts were telling her that the person she was looking for would be among them, or else not so very far away from Ralph Street. Only time would tell if she was right in that assumption.

Carmichael logged off. She'd just removed her warrant card from its slot when her landline rang. She took the call, gesturing to Daniels not to move away. She obviously needed a word. After a moment or two, she thanked the caller and put down the phone. 'That was Tim Stanton,' she said. 'He needs to get an early start in view of the unprecedented number of bodies lying in his morgue. You heard about the RTA?'

'Yeah, I heard.' Daniels explained that she and Hank had been delayed by it on the way to the fire. 'Tell Stanton I'm nipping back to the crime scene with Hank and then I'll be with him.'

Carmichael's face dropped. 'But you said the next one was mine.'

'Don't whine, Lisa. I know what I said. Trust me, this isn't the right one for you. You don't want to go there. Post-mortems are gruesome, more so when the cadaver no longer resembles a human—'

Carmichael looked at Gormley, a plea for support.

'What?' Daniels said. 'You got something to say, Hank? Spit it out!'

'You did promise her. No point putting off the evil day.'

The DCI listened carefully as he made a case for Carmichael. It reminded Daniels of when she was starting out. Keen to experience a murder enquiry down to the last detail, she'd pleaded and cajoled, using every trick in the

book in order to tick all the boxes and impress her senior officers. Countless times, her former boss and mentor, Superintendent Bright, had warned her she needed to walk before she could run. But did it make a difference? *Did it hell!* As far as Daniels was concerned, she knew best. From the begging expression on Carmichael's face, her DC thought *she* did too.

Daniels had to hand it to her: the girl had guts. Problem was, she didn't know what she was letting herself in for. But, knowing how protective of their protégé Gormley was, the DCI knew he'd given the matter serious thought and not jumped to a decision they'd all live to regret. If he reckoned Carmichael was ready, that was good enough for her.

'OK,' Daniels relented. If the truth were known, she was too tired to argue. 'I'll drop Hank off and pick you up in half an hour. Get yourself some mints.'

'Mints?' Carmichael queried.

'That's what I said.' Daniels walked away.

13

The newspaper reporter took out his pen, flipped open his notepad and made a beeline for a group of kids milling around the crime scene. They were making fun of a puny bouquet and a teddy bear tied to the black railings outside number twenty-three. Chantelle Fox glared at them. She'd stolen the flowers from a neighbour's garden and wrapped them in paper that was entirely inappropriate. But it was all she could manage at such short notice.

Improvisation, she called it.

It was another fabulously sunny day. Yet most of the curtains in the houses were drawn, the neighbours still half-cut from the party the night before. A team of police officers at either end of Ralph Street obviously hadn't heard of letting sleeping dogs lie. They were working their way from house to house, banging loudly on doors, refusing to take no for an answer. They'd get to her eventually. Not that Chantelle had anything to say. Not to them, anyhow. Or to the young journo who was eyeing her from across the road.

He gave her a smile, testing the water.

A lad not much older than herself, he was wearing a shiny suit and open-neck shirt. Couldn't be very important if he didn't warrant a photographer. Chantelle looked away. What was this? Some kind of a joke? She'd tonged her hair to

within an inch of its life, put on her slap and made herself presentable. So where were the nationals, the TV crews and stuff? Probably stuffing their faces at a café on Westgate Road. Best fry-up for miles around. As much toast as you could shake a stick at – white not brown – with lashings of butter and mugs of watery tea to wash it all down. Lovely.

'Miss, have you got a moment?'

The skinny journo had arrived at her side, News Desk written on his press badge.

Divvi. Did she look like she was in a rush?

Chantelle didn't answer. She spat her chewy on the ground to show some respect as a handheld recording device was pushed under her nose. Deciding to make him sweat a little longer for her comment, she put on her saddest face and wiped away an escaping tear. It wasn't just an act either. Torching a house was one thing. Killing the folks inside was something else, an innocent kid especially. Chantelle dropped her gaze and hung her head in shame, knowing full well that a phone call from her might've saved them. She felt really bad about that. But what was done was done. It made her snaps all the more newsworthy.

Sensational even.

She could name her price.

The journo turned away as a car approached. Across the road, a Toyota pulled up behind a fire engine on standby in case any embers in the house should reignite. The same cool lady cop who'd arrived in the middle of the night got out with a fat fucker in tow. Cameras flashed as they ducked under the police tape. Suddenly there was a riot of activity as the press surged forward, seemingly out of nowhere. The

journo ran too, leaving Chantelle standing on the pavement like a spare part. Affronted didn't quite cover it.

Damn cheek!

'Well, piss off then!' she yelled, almost stamping her feet. 'And don't come crawling back to me! You'll get fuck all from her!'

14

George Milburn drew himself away from the grim scene beyond his blackened window. As the curtains settled back in position, a million dust particles hung in the air forming silver streaks across the room where the sun streamed in through the living-room window.

He sat down for a moment to think.

Word on the street was that two had died in the fire, a man and a young child. *Tragic.* In the forty-odd years he'd been living there, bad news had been a frequent visitor. Even so, this event set a new low that sent him spiralling into a deep depression. Draining his tea, he carried the mug to the kitchen sink where he rinsed it under the tap. He dried his hands, opened the kitchen drawer and took out a Philips screwdriver. Then he walked upstairs, got down on his hands and knees, and pulled back the bedside rug.

Unscrewing the floorboard, he lifted it out and reached inside for the plastic bag, hell bent on giving the contents away. He couldn't think of a finer recipient than his grandson, Elliot. A great kid. Always lent a hand down the allotment when George wasn't feeling up to the heavy stuff. Never asked for so much as a red cent for the hours he spent there.

Counting the cash into hundred-pound bundles took George a while because his hands became stiff. He kept losing

his place and had to start all over again. When he was satisfied he'd calculated the total amount correctly, he bundled it up in a brown paper parcel and called Elliot, arranging to meet him within the hour at the Ford garage on Scotswood Road where his daughter once worked. There was a car there, in good condition with a manufacturer's warranty, according to the lad. Only the price tag was too steep. *Well, not any more.* Not if George had any say in the matter.

'I've decided to help you out, lad. Call it an early nineteenth-birthday present.'

'What?' Elliot was excited. 'Why? Are you sure?'

'You want the money or not?' George asked. 'You can pay me back in spadework.'

'I will, Granddad. Every weekend, I promise.'

'Aye, that'll be reet. You'll be too busy driving the bloody thing. I'll probably not see you for dust. Can you meet us off the ten-past bus?' George realized he'd have to get a move on if he was going to reach the bus stop in time. 'It's a secret, mind, Elliot. No telling your dad.'

'Are you OK, Granddad?' Elliot's excitement faded. 'We heard the news. Mum and I were worried about you. You should have called. I would've come round.'

George felt his anger rising. There was no mention of his son being concerned for his welfare following the fire next door. Some things never changed. The bastard wasn't interested in anyone but himself. Wouldn't know how to show affection if his life depended on it. He was like one of them psychopaths George had read about in the papers. Hard on the outside. Same on the in.

'I know you would, son. That's why I never asked.'

George put down the phone. Pulling his jacket and cap down from a peg on the wall, he put them on, then picked up his parcel and left the house. As soon as he closed the door, he was mobbed by reporters wanting to talk to him, get his take on things, probably after some dirt on the folks next door. A community beat officer held them back, allowing George to scurry off.

Three-quarters of an hour later, Elliot met him off the bus as it pulled into the stop. They crossed the road, then the boy set off towards the showroom as if he were in a race to get there. George toddled along behind. His pins weren't so good nowadays. Bit of arthritis in his hips and knees made him waddle like a duck. He'd considered getting one of them motorized scooter things but decided against. He figured it would make his legs even worse than they already were.

'Use 'em or lose 'em,' his GP had told him.

They entered the yard round the back where the garage stored the second-hand trade-ins.

'Show us which one it is then,' George said.

Elliot's face dropped. The car he'd set his heart on had gone. It had been parked near the perimeter fence yesterday. Now only a space remained. They looked around for another but couldn't find one he liked for the price they were willing to pay. Reluctantly they agreed to wait a week or two and try again. The boy seemed to accept that. If it was worth having, it was worth waiting for.

15

The morgue was only a few streets away from the station. Carmichael sat in silence looking out of the side window. Having second thoughts, Daniels suspected. She had no time to chivvy her along. The young DC had made her bed. Now she'd have to lie in it. Her own thoughts were on the fire. The most likely scenario, assuming the dead were actually identified as Jamie and Mark Reid, was that the father had been watching the game, had a few beers and fallen asleep, only to wake too late to save his son.

In most murder enquiries, crime scene investigators would lift forensic traces of hair, blood and skin. But the fire had been so intense such evidence had been destroyed. Daniels didn't need telling that there'd be very little to go on. Arson, with or without intent to endanger life, was a senseless act, an offence most right-minded people would baulk at. But then Daniels knew she wasn't dealing with right-minded people. You had to be switched wrong to set fire to a house with people inside.

So who was she dealing with?

And what was the motive?

A scare tactic, perhaps? A random attack carried out by idiot kids? A drunk from the party in the back lane last night? A joke that went horribly wrong? It wouldn't be the first

time. The crime scene was bang smack in the centre of the area most visited by the city's fire service, if recent reports were anything to go by. She'd read once that nearly forty per cent of fire-setters were aged between ten and seventeen. Of those, the majority were male. But she couldn't afford to make that assumption. So was it the house or the person inside who was the target? Maggie Reid was the tenant. The dead man no longer lived there.

By the time they reached the morgue, Mark Reid's identity had been confirmed by dental records faxed to the pathologist, Tim Stanton. The victim's name was being withheld from the press and public until his extended family were informed. Both his parents were alive. But given the state of their son's body, they wouldn't be asked to view it. There was really no point. Mark Reid was unrecognisable as the man he once was.

'With no dental records to go on, the child's identity is more difficult to establish,' Stanton told her. 'I've sent his DNA for analysis, although it's almost a foregone conclusion that it is Jamie Reid.'

Daniels nodded, her eyes drifting past him to a bank of freezer units along the far wall, each one containing a cadaver. In cases where identity had not yet been established, they were assigned a number; the rest were labelled with the name of the deceased – Bridget McCabe among them.

A few feet to her left, Carmichael was finding it difficult to drag her eyes away from the charred remains laid out in front of her. She'd never seen anything like it before and never wanted to again. Daniels' argument that this one would be

too harrowing a case for her was proving to be spot on, though she would be the last to admit it.

Harsh words, spoken by Gormley during her very first involvement in a murder enquiry almost a year ago, echoed in her head as she stood there now. A dressing-down, uttered in anger to curb her over-exuberance back then: *Murder victims are people, Lisa . . . flesh and blood, like you and me . . . it's not a game.* At the time, Carmichael had slunk away to a quiet corner to lick her wounds, taken aback by the harsh tone of his voice.

How right he was.

In her wildest dreams, she could never have imagined her first post-mortem would be like this. The gruesome corpse she was looking at was but ten months old, someone's treasured child, nephew, grandson. His father lay on the next slab along, a hero in Carmichael's eyes, dying in a heroic attempt to save the boy from harm. The fingers on his hands fused together as he'd attempted to mount the stairs of 23 Ralph Street.

Carmichael looked away as a wave of revulsion hit her.

'You OK, Lisa?' Daniels had seen more experienced officers than Carmichael buckle at the sight of victims far less horrific than the ones in front of them now.

The DC nodded, probably scared to open her mouth in case no words came out. Daniels had known she wouldn't learn much from this post-mortem. Normally, forensic examination could aid detectives in so many ways. It could identify the size, type and shape of a weapon, shotgun or handgun, if a firearm was used. How tall or short an offender

might be, based on the angle of a wound. It was even possible to deduce whether the assailant was left- or right-handed. But this case was very different. From what Stanton was telling them, there was no physical contact between victim and perpetrator . . .

'No obvious wounds to inspect,' he concluded.

Carmichael breathed a sigh of relief as Stanton put down his scalpel and declared that he was done. He moved to a stainless steel sink and scrubbed up with a stiff brush, rinsing his hairy arms under a running tap, which he expertly turned off with his right elbow. He dried his hands and pulled down the sleeves of his scrubs.

His findings were conclusive and said with confidence.

'Cause of death, smoke inhalation and nothing more. No evidence that either victim has sustained any pre-mortem injuries. I'm sorry, Kate. That's all there is. There is absolutely no evidence here to suggest an attempt to hide or disguise an alternative cause of death.'

16

Minding the gap between the platform and the step-board, a tall redhead entered the first-class carriage of the 13.28 Newcastle to King's Cross train with only one minute to spare. A young male porter showed her to her seat. He smiled, handed back her ticket, and wished her a pleasant journey, then scurried off with a big fat tip burning a hole in his pocket.

The redhead sat down, conscious of eyes turned in her direction.

An attractive man followed her on: white shirt, red tie, good watch. Removing his jacket, he hung it on the peg provided, then took the seat opposite, his nose twitching as he picked up her scent, a smile playing on his lips that said: *I'd like to fuck you right there in your seat.*

She smiled at him with her eyes as well as her mouth.

He took out a MacBook and began work, concentration etched on his face. She wondered how long he could keep up the pretence. As a little girl she'd always been the centre of attention, always been told that she was special. Too special for her own good, her mother used to say; a comment that was usually accompanied by a good hard slap.

She settled back for the boring journey south, leafing through magazines and then staring blankly out the window at the lush green countryside, the occasional church steeple

in the distance, a row of terraced houses close to the track, unsettled by thoughts of her unhappy childhood. A ticket inspector interrupted her reverie before they reached Durham, where three Japanese men boarded the train, one wearing a face mask like they do in Tokyo.

Takes all kinds.

'Any refreshments, Madam? Sir?' a young woman asked as they got going again.

She ordered coffee and her admirer did the same. Someone close by ordered lunch. The redhead's hunger had nothing to do with food. The man opposite looked up, the sexual chemistry between them now crystal-clear. She moistened her lips, allowing her tongue to linger a little longer than was necessary. It worked every time. The guy was practically drooling.

Melting under her gaze, he loosened his tie, placed his hands on his laptop to make out he was working. *Pushover.* He was hers for the taking. And there was still a whole two hours and – she glanced at her watch – forty-eight minutes to go until they reached their destination.

Her phone rang.

Saved by the bell.

She took the call but didn't speak. 'Is everything OK?' the Cypriot said.

'Why wouldn't it be?'

'Any problems, you bail.'

'Relax, I told you the matter is in hand.'

The redhead hung up, looking back at her new friend. Shame she had better things to do today than having sex with a stranger, albeit a very attractive one. In just under

four hours, she'd enter the lion's den and face the most important meeting of her entire life. Question was: *could she pull it off?*

17

It was getting on for two as they left the morgue. Carmichael's phone rang, a request from Gormley that they stop and pick up Dene's Deli sandwiches on the way back to the incident room. When they got there, Daniels went to brief their guv'nor while Carmichael handed out refreshments to the team. But she was picking at her lunch when the DCI returned.

'OK, you lot. Mobiles off!' she said. 'Hank and I are expected elsewhere.'

Daniels sat down, surrounded by core members of the squad, all eyes turned in her direction. Hank Gormley took a seat by her side, directly opposite DC Andy Brown. Andy was mid twenties, built like the scrum half, his ruddy face topped with a mop of strawberry blond hair. He was a great bloke whose parents were employed at either end of the lifecycle – his mother a midwife, his father an undertaker – which Brown always said equipped him well for the brief interlude in between. He was Daniels' obs man, the detective she used whenever there was a need for surveillance. He had the capacity to sit still for hours and could survive with very little sleep.

Sitting next to him, as always, was Lisa Carmichael. They had joined the squad together and were the best of mates. She was about to bin her lunch when DS Neil Maxwell

reached out and took it from her. Large, lazy and lethargic, he was nicknamed Sicknote by the others. He had a fondness for women and soft porn, in any order, and both at the same time if he could possibly manage it. He'd been forced upon the squad, arriving under a cloud on a final warning. Considered the weak link in the team, he'd shown significant improvement after a choice word in his shell-like from Daniels, a true believer in three strikes and you're out.

And lastly, DS Paul Robson, Robbo for short. A skilled detective but a man whose popularity had plummeted following mistakes he'd made recently that reflected badly on the team as a whole. A new father with a gambling addiction he'd not yet come to terms with, he still looked like he had the weight of the world on his shoulders.

Daniels got straight down to business, giving a brief case review to kick-start the enquiry. The consensus among the team was pretty clear-cut. If Mark Reid was last seen alive by Maggie Reid at around seven-thirty when she put Jamie down for the night – the same woman who'd dialled 999 nearly five and a half hours later – that in itself was highly suspicious.

'Then again . . .' a voice at the back said, 'the West End shite wouldn't call the police if the aliens had landed—'

'I need evidence, not innuendo,' Daniels countered. 'Having talked to the woman myself, I'm not convinced she's anything other than a grieving mother.' She looked at her watch. 'I'll let you know when I've seen her again. Hank and I are due there in twenty minutes.' She eyeballed the smart-arse at the back. 'Remind me never to recommend you for Community Crime Prevention.'

A titter went round the room.

Daniels allowed them their moment of fun, naming Robson as statement reader before moving on to specific actions she wanted carried out immediately. 'Lisa, look into Mark Reid's background. Find out who his friends are, talk to his work colleagues, try to build a picture of the kind of man he was.' Her gaze shifted to Brown. 'Andy, until we know more, I want covert surveillance of that street in case there's a pyromaniac on the loose. Fix it up with Technical Support. Tell them it's an urgent job, no excuses. Then liaise with the Search Coordinator. Drains and rubbish bins are to be searched before the next collections in case evidence was dumped by the perpetrator fleeing the scene. Neil, canvass all local petrol stations. Make a note of anyone buying petrol in a can of late. And seize CCTV where you think appropriate.'

It was a start, of sorts.

Daniels left the station with Gormley. Leaving the city centre, they headed up the West Road passing the motorcycle garages where the DCI spent a lot of her off-duty time. A little further up the hill a fight was going on outside the bowling alley, two uniforms getting stuck in. She slowed the car in case they needed a hand. Satisfied that they had everything under control, she picked up speed again passing the City West Police Station on her left where she once worked, a challenging location for any officer on the force.

As she drove by, she thought of the staff there with affection. In the bate room at the back, you could see all the way to the Angel of the North. It was the place she'd first met Gormley. She drove on, counting down the streets. Police officers were taught to associate a saying with streets abutting

a main road. For example: Fair Lady Hampstead stood for Fairholme Road, Ladykirk Road and Hampstead Road. It made it easier to recall them if you needed to get there in a hurry.

They dropped down on to Elswick Road, still heading west, then down again on to Armstrong Road where Maggie Reid was being cared for by her sister-in-law, Nadia Turner. They were shown into a tidy living room with views across the river to Gateshead's Metro Centre. A uniformed officer stood up as they walked in, explaining that Maggie's parents were too traumatized to look after themselves let alone their grieving daughter and so Nadia had volunteered to do so until alternative accommodation could be found.

Nadia offered them tea, telling Daniels that no Family Liaison Officer had yet arrived.

This news angered the DCI more than she could possibly show. 'My apologies . . .' She glanced at the PC. A silent message to sort the FLO. And then to Nadia. 'We'll take care of that right away.'

The officer and Nadia both made themselves scarce.

Maggie Reid was sitting hunched over in a chair by the picture window, but the vista across the Tyne was completely lost on her. She was in a hell of a state, hardly registering their presence as they sat down to talk to her, spaced out on sedatives the doctor had given her before they arrived. Her eyes were dull and lifeless and she was still dressed in the same clothes she'd gone out in the previous night, blue streaks in her blonde hair matching her smudged eyeliner.

'I'm very sorry for your loss, Maggie . . .' Daniels said gently. 'And for intruding on your grief at this difficult time.

But I'm afraid I must ask you some questions. Is that OK?' Reid nodded without making eye contact. 'When exactly did you make arrangements to go out last night?'

'Ages ago . . . couple of weeks, maybe . . . Mark was good and stuff, but he liked plenty of notice to babysit.' She looked up, trying to hold back the tears. 'It's his birthday today. We were going to celebrate as a family, like we used to. I made him a chocolate cake yesterday, his favourite . . .' Her voice trailed off.

'Who else knew he was at your house?'

'What do you mean?'

Daniels rephrased. 'Who else knew Mark was looking after Jamie?'

'Me mam. What difference does it make?' Maggie looked puzzled. Her hands shook as she tore at a bunch of tissues Nadia had shoved on her lap before leaving the room.

'Can you think of any reason why someone would want to harm Mark? Or you, for that matter?' Daniels didn't mention the child this time. Maggie didn't respond and hadn't yet twigged what she was getting at. 'Maggie? I need you to think very carefully. Any idea who might have a grudge against—?'

'No! Despite our differences, Mark's a lovely guy. Ask anyone, if you don't believe me!' The woman's face paled further. She pawed at her throat, fighting back vomit, almost choking on her words. 'He wasn't supposed to be there . . . him or the bairn! Mark usually has Jamie at his and me mam picks him up to give me a lie-in and that when I go out clubbing. It's usually late when I get back. She can't keep him at her place overnight coz me dad's got special needs and Jamie

doesn't sleep. It's too much for her to look after them both at the same time.'

Daniels caught Gormley's unease. He was standing a few feet away, stroking the stubble on his chin. He raised an eyebrow. This was certainly an interesting development. Responding to the silence in the room, Maggie looked up, her gaze flitting back and forth between the two detectives. Her eyes grew big as the penny dropped.

'You saying they were after *me*?'

'We don't know.' Gormley's tone was flat. 'We were hoping you could tell—'

'What did you mean, they weren't supposed to be there?' Daniels said, interrupting.

'Jamie had a nasty cold. Mark and I decided he'd be better off at mine.'

'You changed arrangements at the last minute?'

A nod was Maggie's answer.

'You on Facebook, Maggie?' Gormley asked.

It was a good question. When Maggie didn't reply, Daniels repeated it, adding other social networking sites in case she'd mentioned her change of plan publicly. People were cavalier in their attitude to giving out personal information these days. They rarely thought through the consequences. But Maggie was in a bad way, too wired to answer. With a flick of her head, Daniels sent Gormley off to ask Nadia if she had a Facebook page or Twitter account.

Seconds later, he was back in the room, shaking his head.

Daniels turned to Maggie again. 'So where did you go last night?' she asked.

'I told you, I went clubbing.' Maggie sniffed. 'With a mate.'

'We'll need a name,' Gormley said gently. 'Of the person you were with and the club you visited. You'll understand why.'

Maggie Reid just looked at him. Blurting out the name Stella Drew, she ran from the room.

'The sudden change of arrangements could be highly significant,' Daniels said as they left the property and got back in the car. 'Assuming for one moment that Maggie's an innocent in all this, either the offence was totally random, or she *was* the target, or someone very close to one or both of them knew they had altered their plans.'

'She's lying, boss!'

'Makes you say that?'

'You saw her reaction when you asked her who she was with last night. She was sweating like a Geordie on a spelling test.'

Daniels grinned. 'You don't think her grief is genuine?

'I've seen others fake it better. Do you?'

Daniels waggled her hand from side to side. The jury was still out on that one. She started the engine and moved off as a crash of thunder brought more rain. 'Much as we might like to think so, we have no idea what she's going through. She doesn't know what she's feeling or thinking, let alone saying. And where the *hell* is the FLO?'

Gormley shrugged.

'Well, find out! And put your bloody seat belt on.'

18

The redhead stared at the last dregs of countryside as it flashed by. In the seat behind her she could hear a couple of guys arranging a game of golf. Someone had ordered a late lunch and the chink, chink of cutlery on china was beginning to annoy her. She'd never understood why people ate on trains: in half an hour or so they'd be nearing the outskirts of London with hundreds of brilliant cafés and restaurants at their disposal.

She flinched as a train whooshed by, going in the opposite direction, vibrating the carriage as it sped past. She wondered what lay ahead and wished it were over. Should she take a cab from King's Cross or walk? Yes, *definitely* walk. She needed fresh air in her lungs, needed to oxygenate her brain and concentrate. Everything depended on her memorizing her script by heart. She opened the browser on her phone, then closed it again, remembering she had an app to guide her to her destination. Pressing the menu key, she scrolled to it in readiness to type in a postcode. The device wasn't playing.

'Bloody technology!' She rolled her eyes as her prosperous admirer looked up. 'Of all the times to go walkabout . . .' Sighing, she put the phone back in her bag. 'The mapping system appears to be down. I can't live without it now. How about you?'

'Same here . . .' The man took off his Prada glasses and smiled at her. That sexual tension again. 'I was considering a glass of wine. Would you like to join me?'

She was all set to decline – she needed her wits about her today – but then a frosty woman sitting diagonally opposite who'd boarded the train at York gave them a filthy look. The redhead had been watching her too. She'd been reading *The Stock Trader* by Tony Oz. Its strap line: *How I Make a Living Trading Stocks.* Obviously thought she was a player. Didn't the silly cow know she was in the company of the best in the business?

'I'd like that very much.' The redhead grinned.

Picking up the menu, the man held it out to her.

'Anything but Sauvignon,' she said, ignoring the menu. 'Do you fuck too?'

She didn't bat an eyelid when a number of passengers turned to look at her. Appalled, the woman across the aisle hid behind her book.

The man stuck out his hand. 'I'm Ben . . . Foster.'

But the redhead already knew his name, his date of birth, his home address. That he was a professor at Newcastle University. She'd read the passport application he'd been fiddling with since the train pulled out of the Central Station of her home city. She also knew that he was on his way to the University of California, Berkeley, in the not too distant future and that the trip involved an international conference.

It never ceased to amaze her how many people laid themselves open to identity theft. She could read upside down almost as well as the right way up after years of practice. If she were so minded, her interesting stranger would be

begging for his life back in a matter of weeks. She was a class act.

He had no fucking idea who he was dealing with.

'I'm Liv, short for Olivia . . .' Taking his hand, she looked deep into his eyes. 'Delighted to make your acquaintance.'

Ben held her gaze. 'You always this direct on a first date?'

'Only when I see something or someone I really like.' She glanced briefly at the *Stock Trader* book cover being held in front of a stranger's face. 'Then it's no holds barred and I don't stop until I get what I want. You?'

'Same, pretty much.'

Yeah right. Who was he trying to kid?

'Where you from?' he asked. 'No, let me guess. South of the river, certainly. Low Fell? Springwell? Am I at least warm?'

The redhead wasn't happy. She'd spent time and money trying to lose her accent – trying to have no discernible accent at all – and this joker had nailed her good and proper. Her elocution coach was toast. Must try harder, she thought.

'I'm a linguist . . .' Ben said, filling in the silence. 'Accents are my business.'

'Is there a Mrs Ben?'

'Indeed.'

'Of course there is. But what she doesn't know, right?'

'That about sums it up . . .' He blushed like a schoolboy. 'My father told me if you play with fire you'll eventually get burnt. You think I should listen to him?'

The redhead swallowed down the bile that rose in her throat, shivering as a ghost crept over her skin. She was somewhere else entirely, back in that dark, dark box room.

She knew all about being burnt: she still bore the scars under her very expensive clothes. She could feel them now – tight where the skin had healed itself – puckered pockets of ugliness.

Hideous.

She forced a smile.

As the train rattled on she rubbed her shoeless foot up and down Ben's inside leg. She loved playing games with men she didn't know. Loved fucking with their heads, seeing how far she could push them. Over the years she'd found that even the most devoted of husbands came round to her way of thinking. *Eventually.* Of course, she'd wait until they were absolutely besotted before making her play. A lucrative play it had been up to now.

Shame.

There would still be men like Ben.

But she was going to miss the rest of it.

19

It was gone four by the time Daniels and Gormley reached Mark Reid's flat. The property was much more upmarket than the one he'd shared with his former wife. Situated in Jesmond, it occupied the second floor of an end terrace, south facing with a view over a parcel of land known locally as the Little Moor. A green space other city dwellers could only dream of.

Gormley gave an impressed whistle. They were standing in a hallway stuffed with original features: an elaborately carved staircase, ornate cornicing and stained-glass windows. Daniels followed him upstairs into Reid's flat, the leaves of a pot plant brushing her right hand as she entered the living room. A woman's touch was her first thought as she scanned the interior – one with an eye for the good things in life, from the look of it.

'You reckon it's his?'

Gormley glanced up from the desk drawer he was about to search. 'This place?'

'Yeah. No offence, but nothing in here tells me it belongs to a man. It's really tasteful, not the sort of place I imagined at all.'

'Hey! Men can do taste . . .' He scanned the room. 'I see what you mean, though.' He pointed at a designer lampshade

suspended from the ceiling like a big diamond swirl. 'He didn't buy that, for a start. No bloke I know would clean that thing.'

His words prompted a smile. '*He* doesn't clean this place. No way! See if you can find a cleaning contract, mortgage docs, rent book . . . There's something about our Mr Reid that doesn't add up.'

Daniels left him and went to explore the rest of the flat. The kitchen and the bathroom were similarly tidy and well equipped, the first bedroom she came to likewise. She opened a cupboard, finding Reid's own kit in one side: a mixture of suits, jeans, shirts, underwear. In the other side, there was some women's clothing, enough to cement the impression that he was in a relationship, but not nearly enough to make her believe that he wasn't the only one living there. Daniels knew clothes and these were bloody expensive – too expensive for *her* police salary. She checked the labels. Size 14. Either Reid was a pint-sized transvestite who got his kit from high-end boutiques, or he was seeing a high earner who knew how to shop.

The last room she came to took her breath away. A child's nursery: a magical space filled with brightly coloured toys, mobiles, a frieze of nursery rhymes stencilled on the walls. On the far wall, a cot was crammed with soft toys, its bedding lovingly chosen with Jamie's name embroidered in the centre. On a chair, a pair of child's pyjamas and a nappy sat ready for a little visitor who had never arrived.

Daniels turned away, trying her best to blank out the image of a dead child that was forcing its way into her head. She wouldn't let it. She couldn't bear to look at it again. She

just couldn't. Carmichael wasn't the only one suffering from the experience. You never got used to something like that.

There were no personal photographs on display in the room. But stuffed inside a drawer beneath children's clothes was a framed photograph of Maggie and Mark Reid in happier times. Entwined in each other's arms, Maggie heavily pregnant, presumably with Jamie. Daniels wondered if they were planning to get back together. Was that what all this was about? Maybe someone didn't want that to happen. But who? Was she looking for a jealous other half?

If that was the case, was it his or hers?

Gormley shouted from the living room, interrupting her train of thought. She retraced her steps and found him by the window with his notebook out. He pointed at the landline. The display showed the correct date and time as well as two new calls, but no SMSs. A flashing light indicated that one of the callers had left a message.

'One's from a local dialling code – East End, if my memory serves: Wallsend? North Shields? Somewhere near the coast. Call came in at eight-o-six p.m. on Wednesday. Someone listed in the phonebook as Dave. The other is a mobile number. Call timed in the small hours, at one twenty-three a.m., to be precise. Caller is listed as Judy. I've taken a note of them both. You want to listen to the message?'

Daniels picked up the handset and dialled 1571. An automated voice hit her ear: *Welcome to BT answer 1571. You have one new message. First new message. Message received at 1.23 a.m. on Thursday, 24 June.* A woman's voice came on the line. Fairly young, Daniels thought. There was a lot of background noise, laughing and chatting, as if the caller was in a pub or

at a party: *Hi, babe. Tried your mobile. Assume it's on charge. Hope I haven't woken Jamie. If you get this message, call me.* The line clicked off.

Then BT bollocks again: *To return the call, press—*

Daniels hung up. She looked at Gormley, wondering if she'd stumbled upon Reid's girlfriend. 'We need to find Judy,' she said.

20

George Milburn tripped and put a hand out to steady himself. He sat down on a wall to rest for a moment, pulled off his cap and wiped his brow with a handkerchief already damp with sweat. It was a stifling midsummer day, the hottest he could remember for a very long time. No breeze either. Just baking hot sun. OK for the young'uns, but he couldn't cope with it any more. Maybe not the best of days to spend at the allotment with Elliot.

He'd been thinking about his grandson all the way home, feeling his disappointment as if it were his own. The lad's face had dropped when he realized the car he'd set his heart on had been snapped up by someone else. It was a setback, not the end of the world. George had attempted to cheer him up while they worked, joking that the motor was probably an old banger and not worth half the asking price, if truth were known. No doubt it was clapped out somewhere, steam billowing from beneath the bonnet, its new owner beginning to realize he'd been sold a bag of shite and wasn't quite the petrol-head he thought he was.

Elliot's mood had lifted slightly. There would be other motors. Other days to spend their hard-earned cash. Though George suspected a lingering wish to possess that car, Elliot had managed to cover it well. He'd heard the words *crying*

and *spilt milk* often enough over the years for them to have some meaning. Unlike his peers, he'd always listened respectfully to what George had to say. Even if sometimes they ended up agreeing to disagree. Only once had he gone off on one, his frustration boiling over at having to repeat himself. George had forgotten some minor detail of his first days at school. The name of his teacher, he seemed to recall.

Miss Proctor, Granddad. I already told you . . . three times!

Giggling, he'd leapt on to George's knee and given him a great big hug – his way of saying sorry for yelling. He was only four then. These days he was more forgiving of his grandfather's senior moments. And for his part, George was grateful to have the ear of someone so young. Their relationship was one to be cherished. It gave George a reason to get up in the morning.

His smile disappeared when he saw Chantelle Fox grinning at him from across the road. She never listened to anything other than her own voice. The girl was a complete fantasist. She'd told him once that her dad was a diplomat. He knew her father well: he was a dipper not a diplomat; a man who'd rob his granny for her eyes and come back for the sockets – and a pathological liar to boot. But she wasn't all bad. She'd helped George at times when he needed errands run and Elliot was at work. Wasn't her fault if she came from a family of wasters. The lass's heart was in the right place.

But it wasn't *her* heart that was bothering him. The pain in his chest had been coming and going since the fire last night. From the looks of it, a police presence in Ralph Street looked set to continue for some time yet. Mark Reid's wailing as he tried to reach Jamie would stay with George for ever.

Unfortunately for George, for ever was right now. The old man hit the deck before he had chance to call out to Chantelle. There was a flash. Then everything went black.

21

Carmichael's enquiries into Mark Reid's background had yielded a lot of new information. As a consequence she had the floor of the incident room as well as the attention of her peers. The team already knew that Reid was a joiner by trade and worked for a local firm: Albright's. But his parents had told Carmichael that a year ago he'd got lucky and his life had really taken off, an event his former wife had failed to mention when questioned earlier. Hardly surprising, given the death of her only child, Daniels reminded them.

No one argued.

Lisa checked her notes before continuing: 'Reid's skills so impressed the MD of the Malmaison hotel chain he was taken on permanently, pissing off his former employer and losing him a lucrative contract to boot. He went into bat for himself, was self-employed at the time of his death, earning good money too, by all accounts. Good enough to pay off his parent's mortgage.' She paused for breath. 'Colin Albright, on the other hand, has been pushed over the edge during the recession. His company has recently gone into liquidation.'

'This all makes sense.' Daniels described Mark Reid's home. 'His belongings are not those of a common-or-garden joiner. It's obvious he's come a long way since leaving Maggie,

assuming he left her and not vice versa. The question is, did his newfound success lead to his death?'

'Albright's place is something else. A real fuck-off pad, but it's up for sale.' Carmichael gave an address at Runnymede Road, Darras Hall, an affluent suburb out past the airport in the village of Ponteland. Everyone knew how posh it was. Even Alan Shearer had chosen to live there. 'Took me an age to get in. Bloody place is like Fort Knox.'

Gormley glanced proudly at the DCI. Carmichael had done well.

'What's he like?' Daniels asked her.

'Albright? I wasn't feeling the love, if that's what you mean. His wife is a right pain in the arse. Bet she's a real piece of work behind closed doors. Drinker, too. I could smell the whisky soon as she opened the front door.'

'Describe her.'

Carmichael looked perplexed.

'Humour me, Lisa.'

'Stick thin, good clothes, too much make-up—'

'Please tell me they call her Judy.'

'Denise. Why?'

'Hank found a message on Reid's answerphone.' Daniels nodded to the recovered item. 'Have a listen in. See if you recognize the voice.'

Carmichael stood up, walked over to the device and did as she was told. Then she turned it off and shook her head. 'Nah, that's not her.'

'What size is she?' Daniels asked.

'Eight, possibly even a six.' Carmichael sat back down.

'OK, so she's not the owner of the clothes in Reid's

wardrobe. What did the Albrights say about Reid? Anything of interest?'

'No love lost. They blame him for their current predicament, the business going tits-up. Denise Albright admitted that the For Sale sign is a front. The house isn't for sale, it's being repossessed.'

DS Robson whistled. 'That's quite a motive.'

'She's livid.' Carmichael was referring to Denise Albright. 'The business was set up entirely with her money. I spoke to the administrator, too. Colin Albright's not a savvy managing director by any stretch of the imagination. His wife had bailed him out before, standing guarantor for large loans he'd been forced to take out at the bank.' Carmichael turned to Brown. 'Andy, you want to say something about the restaurant?'

Maxwell interrupted. 'They own a restaurant too?'

'No, but I made enquiries in the village. Albright's a bit of a gobshite, not well liked outside of his own set. There was an altercation in front of the Rendezvous one night between him and Reid. Not the behaviour people round there see very often, I imagine. Not something easily forgotten either. It drew quite a crowd. By the time our lot turned up, they'd all pissed off.'

'Handbags at dawn then,' Gormley said.

'Kinda. Albright got all defensive when Lisa asked him about it. And when I told him Reid was dead, he nearly shit himself. Unlike his wife. She said, quote "I'm glad" unquote.'

Daniels' interest grew. 'Where were they last night?'

'Slaley Hall,' Carmichael's enthusiasm diminished. 'Golf tournament. Charity Fundraiser. Anyone who's anyone was

there, including the Chief. Denise Albright was almost smirking when she told me that.'

'Shit!' Daniels sighed. 'Thought it sounded too good to be true.'

'There's better news . . .' Carmichael said finally. The team held its collective breath. 'The Albrights weren't the only ones to lose out when their business folded. Four others lost their jobs and as far as I know they're still on the dole.'

22

Chantelle slipped her phone back in her pocket as she watched the ambulance disappear. No lights or sirens. Too late for that now. It was horrible, seeing George drop like a stone to the pavement right in front of her. He was a canny old man. A stingy old git. But he'd always been kind, especially when her parents threw her out – a frequent occurrence over the years. She felt guilty for what she'd done. Still, George was past caring, why should she bother?

When her neighbours had wandered away, Chantelle had hung around watching the polis work on him. The daft sod hadn't twigged that there were three outstanding warrants for her down at the nick – unpaid fines going back years. Then again, he'd been rather busy trying to revive the old man.

George's demise had drawn the attention of the journo she'd yelled at that morning. Having photographed the disappearing ambulance, he was hurtling towards her from across the road, one finger raised in the air to catch her eye, his man-bag bumping against his legs as he ran. She knew he'd come crawling back sooner or later. DCI la-de-da Daniels had sent him packing with his tail between his legs earlier.

What a divvi!

He smiled, apologized for leaving her high and dry.

She shrugged. 'S'oright . . . wasn't ready to talk to you then anyhow.'

'You know the old man?' he asked.

'No, never clapped eyes on him.'

'Really? You seem upset.'

'Hay fever.' Chantelle wiped her eye. She nodded at the shell of the house across the road. Chancing her arm, she asked, 'What's in it for me if give you the heads up on stuff round here then? An exclusive, I mean.'

'Depends what you know.'

Chantelle knew plenty. And she could spot an opportunity from a hundred metres. Her pissy part-time job at a second-hand phone dealership wasn't going to make her rich, was it? She was going to have to create her own luck. Lay her hands on a bit of cash some other way. By fair means or foul – she wasn't arsed which. She was prepared to take her chances wherever and whenever they appeared. But the journo wasn't taking her seriously.

Realizing how transparent he was, all of a sudden he started being nice. Offering to take Chantelle's picture. Maybe even get it into the *Evening Chronicle* if she came across with what she knew.

Loser.

'We could help each other out,' he said. 'C'mon, I need something special for my editor, something that might give us a handle on who started the fire.'

'A snout, you mean?' Chantelle laughed. 'Do me a favour. Posh boy like you would be hard pushed to find one of them

round here. I do have something, as it happens, something that would make your eyes bulge . . . but I'm not givin' it to you, so get lost.'

He walked off in a huff.

23

Tim Stanton looked at his watch, saddened by the thought that he'd not managed to finish in time to get home for his son's fifth birthday tea in the garden. He exhaled loudly. He'd promised his wife he'd be there *no matter what*. But with two of his colleagues on leave, the urgent demands of his job required his presence here.

The pathologist and his associates were busier than they had ever been. Eleven sudden deaths in the space of twelve hours was unprecedented: a young woman hit by a bus while crossing the road; six fatalities from an accident on the A1; two from the scene of a suspicious fire; a motorcyclist who'd failed to take a sharp bend. And now, an old man who'd keeled over in the street on his way home from a family visit – probably a heart attack, aneurism, or some other catastrophic condition.

Promising himself he *would* get home in time to kiss his son goodnight at least, Stanton looked down at the examination table where Ivy Kerr's body was laid out.

'Turn her over please, Sally.'

Bright, and with a Scottish accent, his assistant was in the final stages of a postgraduate course in forensic medicine at the University of Edinburgh. Stanton had taken his own qualifications there and was now an Honorary Lecturer. Sally

had been working with him for the past three months and had proven she was capable and committed to her job. He registered her reaction almost before it had formed fully on her face, alerting his curiosity, bringing with it a sinking feeling as reality dawned.

There was little chance his kids, Edward and Maddie, would see their Daddy tonight.

His eyes followed Sally's, homing in on her concern immediately. Something was very wrong here. At that moment, his duty of care to the dead woman became his one and only priority.

'Tell me what you see,' he said.

Sally pulled a magnifying lamp towards the body, angling it slightly. She leaned in, peering at the mess of matted blood and hair at the back of Ivy's head, taking her time before answering. 'Acute haematoma caused by penetrating trauma to the back of the head, cerebral contusions and brain matter—'

'Which are?' Stanton said, interrupting.

'Inconsistent with injuries in any road traffic accident victim *I've* ever seen.'

'How can you be so sure?' Stanton was playing Devil's Advocate now. He wanted her to justify her statement. 'We have no way of knowing what heavy items she might've been carrying unsecured in the back seat of her vehicle. Maybe something shot forward at the point of impact, striking this lady, entering the brain and causing her death.'

'No . . .' Sally shook her head confidently, her eyes showing no doubt. 'These injuries suggest repeated bludgeoning with

a heavy object, something with a rounded edge. Looks to me like a ball-peen hammer or suchlike. This unfortunate soul didn't die of injuries sustained in the crash. She was murdered.'

24

Back at the MIR, the seven o'clock briefing was already underway. Detectives ate at their desks, conscious that home-time was a long way off. The first twenty-four hours of any murder enquiry often produced the best results. If you found a perpetrator within ten minutes, likely as not they would still be wearing the same clothes. Ten hours, they might not have got round to washing the clothes. Ten days, trace evidence may well have been lost for ever.

The squad had been tossing around a number of scenarios in an effort to find what in police terms was called *motive to victim*. Why was this particular house set on fire? And who was the intended victim? Discounting the child as the target, they were left with only three possibilities: Mark Reid, Maggie Reid, or the person who lived in the house before them.

'There is a fourth,' Daniels chipped in.

'You think they got the wrong house?' Maxwell asked. He was sitting on a desk directly in front of her, a can of Coke in one hand, a half-eaten bacon stottie in the other.

'It's not the first thing that springs to mind,' Daniels said. 'But it *is* a consideration. Without forensics, we start with the victim and go from there.'

Questions came thick and fast from the floor. What was

Maggie not telling them? Gormley was convinced she was hiding something. Who knew Mark Reid was in the house? Whose clothes were hanging in his wardrobe? Who was Judy, the woman on the phone? Mark Reid's professional success had unwittingly upset people: the Albrights, their staff, maybe his ex. According to Carmichael, several Albright employees had lost their jobs. They needed tracing and eliminating as a matter of urgency.

Daniels instructed Maxwell to check out the Albrights' alibi. 'I want confirmation that they stayed over at Slaley Hall. I want times, names of other guests they might've seen, including when they turned in and what they had for breakfast. Don't save the horses – and time your journey, starting at the crime scene. If they slipped out to start a bonfire, whatever route they took, there are too many cameras to get there and back without detection. It's what? Twenty-five miles, tops?'

Maxwell nodded. 'About that.'

'The Albrights seem to think they're home and dry with the Chief there,' Carmichael said. She got up and handed A4 sheets to everyone. 'These are the people that lost their jobs when Albright's company went bust.'

Having speed-read the list, Daniels looked up. 'Names ring any bells with anyone?'

Heads shook and no one spoke.

'OK, run them through the database, Lisa. See what gives. Do it now, please.'

Carmichael was already on her feet and heading for her computer, DCs Neil Maxwell and Andy Brown watching her leap into action. Daniels smiled. Either Carmichael was

totally unaware of the effect she had on these two or she chose to ignore it. She had only one thing on her mind, and it wasn't getting her rocks off with fellow officers, on or off duty. She'd been burned once and there was no way it was happening again.

'What else have we got?' Daniels asked. 'Any news from the search team?'

'Sure is,' Brown said. 'A petrol can dumped in a wheelie bin three streets from the crime scene, along with a singed rubber glove. The householder has been interviewed, gave a statement claiming *she* didn't put it there. She seems pretty genuine, according to the reporting officer.'

'Make sure the items go off for urgent forensic examination, marked for my attention.'

'Already taken care of, boss.'

The team were buoyed by this potential new lead. Daniels was too. However, her enthusiasm was replaced by annoyance as her mobile phone rang out. If it had been anyone else but Stanton calling, she'd have ignored it. It must be important for him to interrupt her during a briefing. And *important* from a forensic pathologist usually wasn't good.

What he had to say depressed her.

'Are you sure?' Daniels' mind raced back to the A1 crash: the rain, the mayhem, the dead and the dying, *Bridget*.

'We wouldn't be having this conversation if I wasn't, would we?' He sounded hacked off.

It wasn't like him to snap. It made Daniels realize that her team weren't the only ones in the criminal justice system working flat out. The incident room suddenly came into sharp focus, like a scene fading up on a movie screen. Faces

were turned in her direction, inquisitive expressions on all of them, Stanton's voice bringing her attention back to the phone.

'. . . despite the massive injuries, even at her age, I'm certain this lady *would* have lived, given the necessary medical intervention. I'm afraid you've got yourself another murder case, Kate. One of the worst I've come across in all the years I've been practising.'

'What about her husband? The other crash victims?'

More worried stares from around the room.

'So far, so good.' He didn't sound entirely convinced.

'What does that mean?'

'I'm about to examine the last one. They were all unlucky, but this lady in particular, murdered when she was at her most vulnerable.'

25

The redhead had practised all day yesterday. Nothing written down. Just a script she'd created with the Cypriot, learned by heart by the time she stepped from the train and set off for that all-important meeting equipped with the relevant documentation. The meeting went the way she'd planned it. Word perfect, in fact.

It had been quite a while since she'd been in London and she was filled with excitement as she woke early in a sumptuous king-size bed in a suite where immaculate attention had been paid to the last detail: bespoke furniture, heavy drapes, those little touches that made a difference between a good and mediocre hotel. She didn't ever want to get up, except – cliché or not – today was the first day of the rest of her life.

Arching her back, she yawned, stretching her arms above her head. For a moment she just lay there thinking of Ben, the stranger she'd met the day before. No longer such a *stranger* after a quick shag on the train – *quick* being the operative word. It was over in a flash, a sordid fuck in a confined space with a man she'd never see again. Never speak to. No need. He'd served his purpose, filled in a bit of time on her boring journey south.

On the pretext of helping with her luggage, he'd followed her dutifully from the first-class carriage. As they'd passed the

lavatory, she opened the door and manhandled him inside. It was a small space. Big enough. But even in first class there was water – or something worse – on the floor.

Shoving him down on the seat with some force, she had undone his flies, lifted her skirt and straddled him. She was born to take risks. It was what made her tick. Made her feel alive. She took him deep inside her, his hands on her hips as she worked her magic. But he disappointed, came way too soon, before she'd even got started. And afterwards, he couldn't get out of there quick enough.

Blushing as he reached the comfort of his seat, he didn't know where to put himself as the eyes of fellow passengers turned in their direction, the financial wizard's included. The redhead knew she'd smell sex on them. It was the sole reason she'd fucked him – to shove that dirty look right back in the woman's frosty face. Maybe next time she'd think twice about looking down her nose at people.

When the train pulled in, Ben had guided her through the station, turning left and out into the sunshine to find a cab. Walking to her meeting wasn't an option after all. It turned out to be twenty miles from central London, *a monumental pain in the arse*. So she had joined a long queue of business-men, tourists and locals who'd opted not to take the tube, Ben insisting on keeping her company while she waited. They stood there, making small talk, until a black cab arrived. He even kissed her goodbye before she climbed in.

Fool.

Didn't he realize that women like her never looked back?

Now, in the comfort of her hotel suite, she wondered if he'd hung around where she'd agreed to meet him. Her

mobile suddenly rang out. Mark, probably. *Took him long enough.* She rolled over and answered the phone.

'Mission accomplished?' The Cypriot wasn't one for chatty conversations.

'Free and clear. Forward the assignment in the usual way.'

The line went dead.

The phone rang again almost immediately, this time a number she didn't recognize. It certainly wasn't the Cypriot. Or Mark. Or boring Ben. They hadn't exchanged numbers. No. This same number had called her yesterday, twice while she was on the train, opting not to leave a voicemail. Intrigued, she sat up in bed and pushed the receive key without speaking.

'This is DS Hank Gormley, Northumbria Police. Who am I speaking to, please?'

Damn. The redhead hung up. Removing the SIM card from the phone, she inserted another she took from her purse. Yesterday she'd pulled it off. Now she had to be careful.

26

It was only eight a.m. and yet the Murder Investigation Team were already at full stretch as the DCI entered the MIR in search of Gormley. He was sitting at a desk in the centre of the room in relaxation pose, legs outstretched, feet crossed at the ankles, a phone nestled in the crook of his neck. She was about to spoil his day.

'Hmm . . . that's odd,' Gormley pocketed his mobile.

'What is?' Brown asked.

Gormley didn't answer. He was deep in thought. Ignoring Brown, he picked up his desk phone, redialled the same number and listened as it rang out. Seeing his concern, Daniels wandered up to join him, still stewing over the latest developments. Stanton's call the previous evening had been followed by an unscheduled meeting afterwards that lasted late into the night, a meeting her team didn't yet know about.

Ivy Kerr's murder was an incident so serious it would be deemed a category A – the worst possible kind – on a par with the arson MIT were already dealing with. Superintendent Naylor had hinted as much and had asked her to run both enquiries.

No problem.

She'd done so before and could do so again. In fact, she'd told him she'd work round the clock to find whoever was

responsible. Daniels shuddered at the thought of a defenceless old lady being trapped in her car at the mercy of a killer. It was hard to imagine who'd do such a thing. Two scenarios played out in her head. It was either a civilian who'd raced to the scene or someone sent to rescue her. The second was unthinkable. Whoever it was, she'd take great pleasure in putting them away. First, however, she had to break the news to Hank.

'That was a number Mark Reid called regularly from his landline,' Gormley said, as he hung up the phone. 'There was no answer at all yesterday. Then just now, I thought I'd got lucky, but as soon as I introduced myself the bastard cut me dead.'

Daniels' interest grew. 'Judy?'

He stopped chewing his pen. 'Not unless she has two different mobiles. I don't even know if it was a man or a woman. They hung up without speaking.'

'Put an action out to trace who it belongs to,' Daniels said. 'And check with Reid's parents to see if they recognize it. Actually, before you do, I need a word, Hank. My office?'

Gormley threw his chewed pen on his desk. Gathering up his phone and car keys, he stood up. They were almost at Daniels' office door when Carmichael approached, practically blocking their entry into the room. The expression on her face told them she had something important to share.

'Am I interrupting?' Her cheeks were flushed. 'I am, aren't I?'

Daniels wanted to say yes, but instead said: 'No, Lisa. What is it?'

'Three of the four of Albright's staff who lost their jobs are now working. They all have alibis and are giving statements

as we speak. But the fourth might be of interest to us.' She looked down at the sheet of paper in her hand. 'David Matthews. Single. Pre cons for Section Eighteen: Wounding with Intent. Served a year at Castington two years ago.'

'Of interest' was putting it mildly. Castington Young Offenders Institution had since merged with Acklington prison to form HMP Northumberland. If Matthews had form, Daniels wanted to know a lot more about him. She gestured to an empty desk; they pulled up a chair each and sat down, then the DCI nodded for Lisa to carry on.

'That's all there is, boss. He took a course in bricklaying while he was there. His probation officer managed to talk Albright into hiring him. God knows how. As I told you, the man's a prick. Didn't you say someone called Dave phoned Reid on the night he died?'

'Does he live in the East End?' Gormley asked.

Carmichael nodded. 'On the Meadow Well Estate.'

Robson looked up from his desk. 'That's all we need.'

Daniels took in the clock on the wall. This new development excited her, but she was pushed for time. She had things to discuss with Gormley and a murder file to submit. Not to the Crown Prosecution Service, as would usually be the case, but to the Force Crime Manager at headquarters, her former boss, Detective Chief Superintendent Bright. The perpetrator of her most recent case – a vengeful father who'd killed a young student – had poisoned himself in custody and taken his guilt to the grave. His death had left her with a real headache. Not to mention an investigation by the Police Complaints Authority to contend with. Even though the man was dead, the Murder Investigation Team still had to prove

his culpability beyond reasonable doubt, in exactly the same way they would've done had he been prosecuted in a court of law. Her Majesty's Inspectorate of Constabulary demanded nothing less. It had taken weeks to assemble a full file.

On top of that, she had back-to-back meetings for the rest of the morning. But she didn't want Carmichael heading out to the Meadow Well alone. Almost twenty years ago, the estate – formerly The Ridges – had been the scene of violent riots after a police chase of a stolen vehicle ended in the deaths of two youths. The place was no longer a no-go area – thanks to residents and community groups who'd worked hard to repair the estate's damaged reputation and give local youngsters a better start in life – but there was still some lingering anti-police feeling.

'OK, check out Matthews,' she said to Carmichael.

Carmichael nodded. 'Beats a PM hands down. Remind me to take your advice next time.'

It was the first indication that Lisa was willing to share her anxieties and admit when things bothered her instead of bottling them up. Officers who didn't grasp the concept of *the debrief* often took on too much. Many ended up with the force psychologist banging on their doors. Or worse. There had even been one or two suicides over the years.

Daniels caught Brown's eye. 'Andy, go with her in case he gives her any humpy.' She shifted her gaze back to Carmichael. 'That's no reflection on you, Lisa. There's a lot both of you don't know about the Meadow Well and I haven't got time to fill you in. Suffice to say you'll be glad of the company.'

Carmichael and Brown had received the warning loud and clear.

27

Daniels waited until Gormley had followed her into the office then shut the door. He went and sat near the open window, waiting patiently as she made them both a coffee and took it over to him. Not entirely sure where to begin, she sat down at her desk and chose the indirect route.

'I've been thinking,' she said.

'Does it hurt?' Gormley joked.

'You know, sometimes it actually does.' She was stalling, not wanting to give him the bad news about Ivy Kerr, knowing how he was likely to react when he heard what had happened to her and when. 'This old guy who lives next door to the crime scene, George Milburn? Anyone managed to see him yet, take his statement?'

'Only Stanton . . .' Gormley said. 'The *old guy* is as dead as a post.'

'What?' Daniels put her coffee down, a worried look on her face. 'When did this happen?'

'Yesterday afternoon. Heart failure, according to Stanton. He did the PM first thing, rang me when he noticed the address was so close to our crime scene.' Gormley sighed. 'Coincidence, I reckon. Just his turn to go. Either that or the upset of the fire killed him. Unless of course he's a dab hand

with a petrol can. You think it's possible to die of a guilty conscience?'

'You serious?' she said, looking worried. She glanced down at the murder file she'd just completed. Another dead perpetrator would finish her off.

'Why not? Elderly doesn't mean incapable of murder. I've met some grumpy old gits in my time. My old man, for starters. He'd have killed me with his bare hands if he thought he could get away with it. Was that why you wanted to see me? About Milburn?'

He waited.

It was obvious she was holding back.

'You don't miss much, do you, Hank?' And still she hesitated. 'We've got another murder case on our hands: Ivy Kerr, woman in her late eighties.'

The name meant nothing to him. Why should it? A crash site in the pissing rain was hardly the place to get properly acquainted.

'When did that come in?' he queried. 'There was nothing on the incident log this morning. I looked.'

'I withheld it, wanted to talk to you first.'

Hank's face paled as she filled him in on the grim details of Ivy Kerr's death. He didn't need accident investigators to draw him any pictures. He'd witnessed the mayhem with his own eyes. Daniels had worked out who Ivy was from the ages of the victims on the RTA report. There had been no other elderly women involved. Ivy had to have been the old lady she'd seen Hank speaking to at the scene.

The news hit him hard. At first he didn't seem to grasp what she was saying. Then, as the information began to sink

in, it was as if he'd been punched, a body-blow from some-one twice his size. His head went down and his shoulders slumped. When he looked up, his jaw bunched and his eyes were filled with hatred, not all of it directed outwards. It was obvious he blamed himself for Ivy's fate. He couldn't get over the fact that he'd actually been standing metres away, probably only minutes before she was bludgeoned to death.

'It's despicable,' Daniels said.

'She was alive,' Gormley said. '*Alive.* She looked at me, Kate. Smiled almost, relieved that someone was helping her, except they weren't, were they? Jesus Christ, what kind of animal could do such a thing?'

He lit a cigarette, took the smoke deep into his lungs and stared across the room at her. She didn't ask him to put it out. By the look on his face, he needed it. For a while they sat in silence, instinct reminding them of an impossible task ahead. Apart from those directly involved in the accident, scores of people had gone to the casualties' aid. Dozens of emergency service personnel: police, fire, medical. Then there were the civilians who'd left their homes and cars. To help. To gawp. Probably a bit of both. No forensics had been retained. To make matters worse, Ivy's car had caught fire and had to be hosed down by the fire service, which meant it would be doubly difficult to find any evidence.

'What a 'mare.' Gormley flicked the cigarette butt out the window.

'Everyone at the crash site needs interviewing,' Daniels said, trying to drag him from his reverie and propel him into action. 'The car's gone off for forensic examination, for what good it'll do. I've got a feeling this one's going to run and run.'

'Not if I have anything to do with it,' Gormley snapped.

She knew he meant it. It was unlike Hank to let a case get to him. But this was no ordinary case. He'd work day and night to take this bastard down. Draining her coffee, she signed off on the outstanding murder file and called Robson's extension, asking him to collect it from her desk.

'Make sure it's transported in a police car directly to head-quarters,' she told him. She hung up, checked her watch. *God! She was jaded already and it was just gone ten*. She stood up. 'We'd better get going, Hank. The guv'nor's waiting and I need to brief the squad.'

'I'll be right along.' Gormley picked up her phone. 'Long story. I've got to call my mum.'

28

Chantelle glared at the back of her boss's baldy head as he walked away. *Fat bastard*. He'd given her a right royal rollicking for coming in late. Said he didn't care if Jesus Christ had showed up in her street, she was on a final warning and that was that. Where did he get off, showing her up in front of her mates?

Well, screw him.

She hated the man. Hated the stupid job, had only taken it 'cause the Social said they'd stop her benefits if she didn't – same reason she couldn't hand in her notice. The best she could hope for was the sack. Slipping off her five-inch platforms, she kicked them under the counter, put on a pair of flat glittery pumps and waited near the till for the hordes to arrive. Lizzie, the new girl, unlocked the door and threw it open, but no one was waiting outside. Hardly surprising. It was boiling again. Oppressive. The continuing heatwave meant no one wanted to shop.

Another mind-boggling day of boredom to look forward to.

The boss was too tight-fisted to put in air conditioning. God forbid he'd invest any of his considerable wealth on his staff. The place hadn't seen a lick of paint in years and was stained brown with nicotine from when he allowed

customers to smoke. The staff had never been allowed, of course, even in the back yard that housed the netty, bog, loo, john, WC – whatever form of words you cared to use. Chantelle hated going in there. Spiders were like tarantulas. They waited until you sat down before making an appearance. Same with the rats. The first time she'd seen one, she'd run outside with her knickers round her ankles, straight into Baldy's path.

Only time she'd seen the dickhead smile.

The evil twat took great delight in docking her pay for any misdemeanour under the sun: being late, texting, flirting with customers, eating, chewing gum, generally having a laugh. If he couldn't think of a reason, he'd make one up. Breathing was allowed, but only just. He didn't mind her showing her tits though, did he?

Wanker.

Chantelle sighed. It was her day off tomorrow and she planned to go to Whitley Bay, check out the beach and top up her tan. She deserved a little fun after the mayhem of the last thirty-six hours, what with the press and all.

The boss stuck his head out of his office, checking they were all getting on with their work. Omar was sniggering in the corner, pretending to dust the phones, Chaz on window-cleaning duty making a right mess.

And still Chantelle waited behind the counter. Had everyone died? Where the fuck were the customers? She waited some more and then checked her phone. No messages. Keeping one eye on the office door, she texted a couple of mates:

wot u up 2 the morra? metro to coast ok? got hods of nwz'll blow yr mind.

Seconds later, she received a reply from Tracy, her best mate from school: *oh yeah?*

And another from Karin: *like wot Shell?*

pure gold! meet us at mine – not 2 urly – tell u then. Xx

Chantelle enjoyed being a tease.

Staring through the open door, she pocketed her phone. The sex shop opposite was doing a roaring trade. A sign in the window said: *70 per cent off – Midsummer Sale.* She might pop over at lunchtime if Baldy went out. It wasn't Harrods or Harvey Nicks, but they had some good lingerie in there for very special occasions. The way she figured it, she'd be celebrating soon.

'How much is this one?' Omar's voice interrupted her day-dream.

He was holding up a Motorola at least ten years old. *Bless.* Chantelle walked round the counter and dropped her voice, telling him not to waste his money. If he really wanted it, he should nick it tonight before they closed and she'd look the other way. She'd done it hundreds of times and never been caught. But he looked at her affronted, dubious about her plan. Problem was, he'd been brought up, not dragged up, and he was far too nice.

'Just call it staff discount!' she whispered.

Omar backed away.

'Oh, for God's sake!' she said. 'Shy bairns get nowt!'

Still he wasn't convinced.

Chantelle made a face. 'Doh . . . you're on the minimum wage!' Then she went back to her dreams, annoyed by his hacky look. Give a person advice, the very least they could do was take it. She was pleased she didn't have his scruples. He

was too honest to be trusted, that was his problem. No way would she share her secrets with him. Having an appetite to better yersel' wasn't a crime, was it?

Chantelle thought about this for a moment. Her father didn't think so. He'd taught her never to look a gift horse in the mouth. He was a good dad really, when he was around. Always gave her the benefit of his advice. She could practically hear him from the grave: *As one door closes, another slams in your face!*

Well, not this time . . .

Chantelle had plans and couldn't wait to execute them. She'd stumbled upon an opportunity and was hell-bent on making the most of it. Catching her reflection in the glass cabinet to her left, a tingle of excitement ran down her spine as she imagined herself transformed. In a few weeks' time she'd have new clothes, new hairdo, totally new image. New identity? Nah. Well, maybe. Nah. She liked the name Chantelle. It had a certain amount of je-ne-sais-quoi, as her French teacher used to say. She didn't know what it meant, but it sounded posh.

God is good, Chantelle thought, a*nd the Devil's not bad either.*

29

Their new guv'nor, Detective Superintendent Ron Naylor, ordered them to sit. He was angry. Not quite as much as Gormley, but angry nevertheless. And who could blame him? It wasn't even coffee time and Daniels had briefed him on yet another suspicious death, the circumstances of which were unimaginable. And that was only the half of it. There were numerous suspects but no bloody crime scene. If there was one thing they didn't need right now it was another public relations nightmare.

'Let me get this straight.' He was almost yelling. 'There was little evidence recovered at the scene of the crash and – because it wasn't a murder from the outset – we're left scratching around in the dark for any tangible leads as to the identification of the person or persons responsible for Ivy Kerr's death.'

Daniels nodded. 'That's about the size of it.'

'Was she DOA at the hospital or declared dead at the scene?' he asked.

'A paramedic pronounced her dead at the scene at four-fifty a.m. I'm seeing him later this morning.' Daniels looked down at sketchy notes she'd cobbled together thus far, so little intelligence she'd managed to scribble it all on half of an A4

sheet. 'It might be an idea to have someone from the accident investigation team attached to the squad during the enquiry, don't you think, guv?'

Naylor answered with a nod. 'I'll sort that for you.'

'I've instigated enquiries with all of the emergency services. There's quite a bit of friction because of the implied suggestion that one of them is a vicious murderer. And lots of speculation I'd like to nip in the bud. The cause of the accident was a lorry losing control. At this stage there doesn't appear to be a link between the RTA and the murder of Ivy Kerr. It was entirely opportunistic, I'm sure of it. A case of wrong time, wrong place.'

Naylor placed his elbows on his desk and cradled his hands. 'What day is pension day?'

'Wasn't that obvious, guv,' Daniels said. 'Ivy's bag was recovered at the scene: pension book, credit cards and over three hundred pounds in cash that it would appear she'd recently withdrawn from a hole in the wall near her home. I understand that the receipt was still in her bag.'

'That doesn't make sense! If theft wasn't the motive, what the hell was? She wasn't alone, you say—'

'No, guv. But her husband didn't make it—'

'You sure his injuries were caused by the crash?'

Daniels nodded. 'He had massive internal damage, according to Tim.'

'What were they *doing* out at that time of night?' Gormley said to no one in particular. 'I mean, they were a bit old to be tripping the light fantastic until dawn weren't they?'

'I was wondering the same thing.' Daniels wafted a fly away from her face and watched it drift out of the window.

'I assume they were either headed somewhere special or returning from holiday. My guess would be the former.'

Naylor looked at her. 'What makes you say that?'

'Their house is north of the accident and they were travelling on the southbound carriageway. But, hey, we both saw the road, guv. It was impossible to tell which way was up, wasn't it, Hank?'

Gormley nodded soberly. He rose to his feet, itching to get going. 'Mind if I start the ball rolling, guv? I'd like to speak to Ivy's neighbours, her family, see if I can get a starter for ten. Unless either of you want me for anything else?'

Naylor and Daniels both shook their heads.

Gormley made for the door, stopping short when Daniels called him back.

'You don't have to do this, Hank,' she said. 'Why don't I send—'

'No, I need to do this. Someone must know where they were heading, what they were doing out at that time of night.' He hesitated, his hand on the door, his focus on Naylor. 'Guv, you need to reassure the public that we're working round the clock to sort this one. When it gets out that Kate and I were actually there, we're going to be in for a lot of stick.'

'It wasn't our fault, Hank,' said Daniels. 'Stop blaming yourself.'

'Yeah, well, you never looked into her eyes, did you?'

As the door closed behind him, Naylor sighed. 'Anything I should know about?'

'No, guv. He's fine. You want me to update you on Ralph Street?'

'If you must. But stick to Ron when it's me and you, OK?'

Daniels nodded, an idea popping into her head. Since Naylor's transfer from Durham Constabulary he'd been complaining about being chained to his desk. Same job. Different force. But infinitely bigger area geographically, which meant more time spent in the office, a situation he wasn't entirely happy with.

'You want to get out of here for an hour, guv?'

'Depends.'

'On?'

'Whatever it is you're cooking up in that head of yours.'

'Your management style is similar to mine, guv.' She grinned. 'I thought it was time you got your hands dirty for a change.'

His face lit up. 'What did you have in mind?'

'If you could drag yourself away from that desk, I'd appreciate your input at the crime scene – I can update you on the way.'

30

They left the station and headed out to Daniels' Toyota. Naylor was very quiet as they drove off. She wondered if the press conference scheduled for later was bothering him, an appeal for witnesses to the A1 crash. Or maybe the possible amalgamation of the Durham and Northumbria forces, a report on which had landed in her in-tray that morning.

What bright spark thought that one up?

If implemented, it would affect them both, scuppering his plans to return to the Durham force as Chief Constable one day, the reason he'd made the sideways move to Northumbria in the first place. It would diminish her own chances of promotion too. Right now, though, she didn't have the time or the inclination to indulge that thought.

'You're not going to like this, Kate.' He turned in his seat to face her. 'I'm having second thoughts about you running the A1 incident. I think you should step away from it, you and Hank both. I vote we split the squad up. You two stay on the arson with Robson. I'll act as SIO on the A1 incident with Carmichael, Maxwell and Brown.'

'Hank won't like that.'

Daniels meant she wouldn't. She'd like to run both incidents herself. Already she was beginning to regret involving him. If he got a feel for the hands-on approach, knowing

Naylor, he'd get used to it. Friends or not, she didn't want him to cramp her style.

As she glanced sideways, he turned his head away.

He knew she was rattled.

'I'm afraid Hank will have to lump it, Kate.' He stared out of the side window, avoiding her eyes. 'We need to be above reproach on this one and you were both present at the scene. Potentially, you could end up as suspects, as ridiculous as that sounds. At the very least, you're material witnesses. Hank is, anyway. He actually saw the woman alive, you said so yourself.'

Something outside of the car caught Daniels' attention. She jabbed the heel of her hand on the horn.

In front of Ken's Motorcycles on Westgate Road a couple of petrol-heads they both knew were chewing the fat over a fag and a take-away snack. One was an off-duty motorcyclist from Traffic, someone they often rode with in the Cumbrian countryside at weekends. He waved at Daniels, delighted *he* wasn't on duty. But all she managed was a slight nod in return.

Naylor waved as they drove by and then swivelled in his seat to face her. 'Come on, Kate. You know it makes sense. We can run both incidents from the same MIR. I have no problem with that. All the other rooms are busy anyway and the one downstairs is still in the throes of redecoration. We need some demarcation, obviously, but we can handle that.'

'You're the boss.' Her tone was chilly.

She drove past the bowling alley and the West End nick. Naylor was about to say something more but his voice was drowned out as an ambulance passed them travelling in the

opposite direction, its lights and siren engaged. She watched it disappear through her rear-view mirror, noticing that it was the very same vehicle that had taken poor Bridget away from the scene of the RTA. The siren faded to nothing as the ambulance cleared the traffic lights and turned left into the General Hospital heading for Accident and Emergency.

'Kate?'

'Sorry?'

'I asked you about the arson?' he said pointedly. 'We any further forward?'

'Maybe . . . fire investigators found a small fragment of yellow rubber glove caught on a nail in the kitchen cupboard at Maggie Reid's house, the area least affected by the blaze. It's identical to the one the search team recovered from a bin a few streets away. I'm waiting for a match report from Forensics. It's too early to tell if it was an inside job or not. Can't see it myself. Maggie Reid is too badly traumatized and I don't think she's faking it. Hank would have you believe otherwise. He's convinced she lied about where she was and who she was with at the time the fire started.'

'You talk to her alibi yet? The woman she claims she was with.'

Daniels shook her head. 'Stella Drew is keeping a low profile. I have people out looking for her.' She glanced at Naylor. 'It bothers me that Maggie was the one who called the Fire Brigade, of course it does, especially in light of the party going on across the road. She claims she had better things to do, but that in itself was unusual.'

'How so?'

'A neighbour three doors down told the house-to-house

team it was unheard of for Maggie to miss out on a big do, let alone a full-blown street party. She's the life and soul apparently, into karaoke, footie too, I believe, both of which were on offer that night.'

At a zebra crossing, two Asian women in traditional dress hurried across in front of the car. Their saris looked colourful and cool on such a baking hot day. Daniels watched them safely to the other side and then set off again. She took a sharp left, narrowly missing a scrawny kid who'd rushed out into the road after a ball. When she tooted her horn to let him know she was there, he pulled up sharply, dropping his head as they drove by.

'You watching the footie tonight?' she asked.

'Why don't you join me? I could rustle up a few beers at my place.'

'Think I'll pass. I'm going to work late.'

He didn't take offence, just suggested they must do something together soon. Daniels suddenly felt guilty. She'd not seen much of him socially since he'd moved to Newcastle. He'd bought a house near Heddon-on-the-Wall, a dilapidated farm cottage he planned to upgrade, and had recently invited the whole squad to christen it in the adjoining barn, a celebration she'd missed.

'I'm sorry, Ron.'

'For what?'

'Want a list? And don't tell me you didn't notice me getting arsy about your involvement either. You're right, obviously . . .' She grinned, covering her embarrassment. 'I've not been much help to you since you moved here, even

turned down your invitation to your house-warming party. I'm sorry.'

'You should've come. It was a good do.'

'Never known you to throw a bad one.'

They had reached the crime scene. She parked the car a little way up Ralph Street and they sat for a while discussing the case. Daniels didn't know why she felt compelled to take him there. Just a case of two heads most probably. She was finding it hard to imagine anyone starting a fire with so many people partying nearby. Why risk being seen? Unless the risk was greatly reduced because the perpetrator was local – no one would bat an eyelid then, would they?

They got out of the car. Locking it, she led Naylor to the terrace opposite in order to view the blackened building from across the road. They stood in silence for a while. For her part, she was trying to imagine the place in darkness with a noisy party going on in the lane behind her. Offences she'd dealt with as part of the Murder Investigation Team and before that in the Serious Incident Squad floated in and out of her head. *Motive. Opportunity. Means.* She couldn't decide if the arson was a prank gone tragically wrong or an offence that had been carefully planned, executed in cold blood with calculated intent to cause death.

'First impressions?' she said.

Naylor was thoughtful a moment. 'What would Jo make of it, I wonder?'

It was a good question, one Daniels didn't immediately answer.

'More importantly,' he added. 'What advice would she give?'

'She'd tell me to think like an offender, get inside their head, be their shrink. She'd point out that arsonists can be habitual, remind me there's often an element of voyeurism associated with such offences, a thrill-seeking element too, no doubt. Hard to imagine, I know, with a baby in the house.'

She fell silent, trying to stem images of Jamie Reid's body on a cold slab in the examination room of the morgue. Closing her eyes, she brought to mind the picture of the child on the murder wall: a happy snap of a little boy with dimpled cheeks and a mass of dark, curly hair. That made her more depressed but all the more determined to catch his killer. She looked past Naylor, her eyes locking on to something on the wall over his right shoulder. He turned to see what had caught her interest, homing in on a blackened mark where a cigarette had been stubbed out. Its residue was still embedded in the brickwork. Beneath it, a single cigarette butt lay on a concrete flagstone.

It hit them simultaneously.

Had someone been watching the place burn?

31

Identifying his grandfather's body at the city morgue hit Elliot Milburn hard. It was a task no grandson should ever be asked to perform, one he'd been dreading all day. His mother was too upset and his father was working away, too busy and too selfish to do this one last thing for his own flesh and blood. It was common knowledge that the two men hadn't got along and Elliot wasn't entirely sure why.

Neither one would talk about it.

The morgue assistant was a compassionate woman, softly spoken, with caring eyes. She'd insisted on keeping Elliot company while he waited to view the body, supporting him and yet still managing, somehow, to allow him the silence he craved. He was staring at the green door opposite, willing it not to open. Inevitably, after a while, it had. Elliot froze. Without saying a word, the assistant gently touched his elbow, eased him to his feet and into the viewing room to go through the motions of identification.

It was sad moment; the worst of Elliot's life so far. He found it incredibly hard to be there in that room. His grandfather meant everything to him. He idolized the man. Who would give Elliot guidance now this wise old man was gone? Even though he'd had a good long life, they had so much

more to do together. This was to be their very last meeting and yet Elliot couldn't bring himself to look at him.

But then he realized he had to.

It was the sole reason he was there.

Raising his eyes from the floor, they came to rest on the old man's weather-beaten face. He looked so peaceful, like he did on a sunny Sunday afternoon in his garden at the allotment where they'd go after lunch, where he'd fall asleep in his deckchair, his belly full of roast beef, Yorkshire pud and veggies he'd grown himself.

Giving George a final kiss goodbye, he turned away in tears.

Outside, in the anteroom, the old man's belongings were handed to him in a transparent plastic bag: the clothes he'd been wearing the last time they saw each other; his ancient watch rendered useless as a timepiece, its numerals blurred by deep scratches on the face from handling brambles in the allotment; his rose gold wedding band, soft and smooth with wear; a few quid and some loose change.

Not much to show for nearly eighty years of exemplary life.

It's not much. They were his grandfather's very words when he held up the brown paper parcel at the garage with his money inside. *It's not much but it's all I've got, lad, and I want you to have it.*

Elliot suddenly got to his feet, panic rising in his chest. The morgue assistant looked genuinely shocked when he asked her where the rest of the money was. Taken aback by the question, she asked him to sit down while she rechecked the property log, specifically the entry made when his grand-

father's body was transferred to the morgue from the hospital emergency room.

She shook her head. 'I'm sorry, Mr Milburn. I'm afraid that's all there was.'

'No! That's not right!' Elliot tried not to display his anger after the kindness she'd shown to him earlier. 'My granddad had over a thousand pounds in his pocket, his life savings. I want it back.'

Taking the only avenue open to her, the assistant referred him to the police to make a formal complaint of theft. He'd been stewing over it ever since. It wasn't the money that worried him but the thought that his grandfather may have been murdered for it. Had he been mugged in the street? There were no obvious signs of injury on his person, no bump where he'd fallen – or so they said. Cause of death had been determined as sudden cardiac arrest according to the medical examiner. Not suspicious in nature, just plain old natural causes.

But that didn't quite cut it for Elliot. Cardiac arrest could've been brought on by shock, couldn't it? If his grandfather had been attacked, or even threatened, it might well have contributed to his death. In his mind, that was tantamount to murder. No different to that of a thief plunging a knife into the old man's chest. And if foul play was even suspected, then, much as it pained him to do it, he would insist on a second post-mortem.

Poor Gramps.

Elliot took out his handkerchief and blew hard, choking back a flood of tears he still had left to shed, wondering how he'd

fill the void left by his grandfather's demise. The clock on the wall opposite ticked forward a notch to three-fifteen. He'd been waiting for ages to see Detective Chief Inspector Kate Daniels, the woman in charge of the Murder Investigation Team. He'd asked for her by name but was told she was dealing with a major enquiry, which he presumed was the arson in Ralph Street. He'd seen her on the television many times appealing for witnesses or talking to the press. She'd always impressed him as a compassionate human being, a person determined to seek justice for victims of crime. Not like some of the tossers you get on the box nowadays, only interested in getting their sound bites in, their main aim to look good in front of the camera in order to attain the next rank.

A big man appeared through a security door marked *Staff Only Beyond This Point*. He crossed to the counter and talked in low whispers for a second to the desk sergeant, who pointed at the bench where Elliot was sitting. Then the big man turned to face him, giving him a sympathetic half-smile as if somehow he knew about his grandfather and understood exactly what he must be going through.

'Mr Milburn?' he said. 'I'm DS Gormley, Murder Investigation Team. I understand you've been waiting to see DCI Daniels.'

Elliot nodded cautiously.

'I'm sorry, but she's been delayed. Please come this way.'

32

The redhead's eyes widened. Of all the people in a city this size, she had to run into *him*. Even though she didn't know Ben Foster well, she clocked his unmistakable profile immediately: his sharp jawline, short cropped hair flecked with grey, those thick dark eyelashes.

Sensing her presence, he turned.

She looked away. Had her scent alerted him? Did the smart arse possess ESP? Her own insights were telling her to avoid him like the plague. She'd had her fun but didn't intend, or want, to see him ever again. She had to shake him off.

The tube lights flashed off, then back on.

Oh fuck! He was making his way towards her, squeezing his body through tightly packed passengers. Closer. Closer. Ever closer. The last thing she needed was complications now. She felt the tube slowing as it neared Goodge Street station. But not quick enough. Ben was already by her side.

'Hello again . . .' His eyes slid over her. 'You must think I'm a waste of space. I'm sorry I missed you last night. Got held up at the conference and couldn't get away. By the time I reached the restaurant you'd gone. Am I forgiven?'

The redhead was profoundly hacked off. Not only had the bastard stood her up – and that didn't happen often! – but he'd told a train-load of fuckwits all about it. Just who the

hell did he think he was? Did he really think she'd been wait-ing there, hoping he'd come, like some drooling schoolgirl with a crush on an older man? That would require feelings. And feelings were in short supply in her particular box of tricks.

'I'm sorry?' She smiled at him, a mixture of puzzlement and embarrassment. It was time to show the pathetic loser who was boss. 'You have me at a disadvantage. Do I know you?'

He just looked at her, incredulous, a deep furrow on his brow. 'You are joking, right?'

'I don't think so!' She scanned his face, pretending to search her memory in an effort to remember where – if – they might have met before. Then she shook her head, bemused. 'I really think you must've mistaken me for some-one else.'

'This another one of your games, Liv?'

'Now I know you have me mixed up,' she said. 'My name isn't Liv.'

The jerk was still smiling. 'You like playing games, don't you? Well, so do I.'

The redhead looked around her. People crammed into the carriage were earwigging their conversation. One in particular was glaring at Ben. A young guy: mid-thirties or thereabouts, body-building type, fair-haired, six-two, square shoulders, military crew cut, a man who looked like he could handle himself. Her eyes pleaded with him to intervene. He didn't need asking twice . . .

'Pardon me, ma'am.' He sounded like a New Yorker. 'Is this guy bothering you?'

'No, well . . .' She flashed him an innocent smile. 'I'm sure he made a genuine mistake.'

'Oh, please!' Ben Foster looked at the Yank. 'She's winding me up! She's pissed with me for not turning up last night.'

The redhead was wide-eyed. 'I've never seen this man before!'

'Back off, buddy!' The Yank leaned into Ben, his dark eyes sending him a message: Don't-mess-with-me-if-you-know-what's-good-for-you. 'The lady isn't interested.'

Ben stood his ground, furious now. 'Will you mind your own business?'

Thanking the American, the redhead excused herself politely and moved towards the door, easing herself through a muddle of bodies as fast as her long legs would carry her. The tube screeched to a stop. Once she was off the train, she looked over her shoulder. The doors were still open, allowing passengers on. Ben was about to follow her when the American guy put a hand against his chest, preventing him from getting off. As the train doors closed, the redhead smiled, relieved to be free of him.

33

The minute Daniels stepped through the front door of the station, Hank Gormley caught her eye, sending a clear message that something was up. The exchange was so brief, Naylor didn't appear to notice. But when Gormley said he needed her ear, the Super narrowed his eyes.

'Something I should know?' He was no fool.

'Long story . . .' Gormley flicked his eyes in the direction of four civilians waiting to be seen: two middle-aged women, an elderly guy in a wheelchair, and a skinny young man who looked a little distressed. Dropping his voice to a whisper, Gormley said, 'Mind if I grab the boss a mo, guv? I'm sure she'll fill you in later.'

Naylor held his gaze. 'This isn't trivial office politics, is it?'

Gormley shook his head. 'No, sir. It's not.'

Rolling his eyes, Naylor didn't argue. Without another word, he spun on his heel, punched a number into a keypad and pushed open the door, disappearing along the main corridor and into the labyrinth beyond. When he was out of sight, Daniels turned toward her DS, a question in her eyes. Gormley nodded to the interview room and then followed her in, closing the door quietly behind them.

'George Milburn,' he said.

Pulling out a chair, Daniels slumped down on it and crossed her arms. 'What about him?'

'The young lad in reception is his grandson, Elliot.' Gormley let out a worried sigh. 'He claims the old man was rolled, possibly even murdered. Apparently he was carrying a large amount of cash on him and now it can't be found. Had the old man collapsed on any other street, I'd have offloaded the job to another incident team, Kate. I'm sorry—'

'You don't need to explain. I made it perfectly clear I wanted any activity within that beat area logged and brought to my attention.' For a moment, she stared at him, processing this new information. No wonder he was worried. They already had two murder cases to deal with. Yet another complication was the last thing they needed. The very thought of it sapped her energy. 'What exactly did he tell you?'

Gormley had spent quite a while with the lad, he told her. The interview had thrown up more questions than answers, but it had proved useful too, given him a fresh perspective on Ralph Street. Crime pattern analysis was all well and good, but if you really wanted to know what went on in a particular area, nothing could beat talking to locals. In that sense, policing hadn't changed in decades.

'He said a lot of residents complained about being disturbed at night, being sworn at, called names. George did too, even rang the police on occasions, asking to remain anonymous in case he was singled out as a grass. The lad claims it's gone on for months and our lot have done sod all to stop it. You know the area, Kate. Kids round there couldn't give a stuff about a blue uniform. They laugh and stick a finger up if challenged. Community Support can't cope, simple as that. They move them on and ten minutes later they're back, giving the old folks even more grief for calling the law. It's a vicious circle.'

He was right of course and it made the DCI angry. The police service was not the one she had joined. It had been undermined by politicians obsessed with cutting costs. They had pushed through a succession of measures, recruiting community support personnel at the expense of real police officers, to the detriment of both the force and the communities they served. In Daniels' opinion, the Home Office needed to stop the rot before the situation got any worse, take a step back and think about the consequences of their actions, support her force to do its job, revert to the in-depth training her generation of recruits had been given. The Police Federation's concerns had been voiced and discounted by a succession of Home Secretaries who'd sold them out. Morale was lower than it had ever been.

It was a depressing thought.

When George Milburn suddenly collapsed, Gormley had raised concerns that there might be a connection between his death and the fire. At the time, Daniels hadn't taken it too seriously, but now her mind was all over the place. Could the old man have started the fire? He lived so close, it would have been easy to slip out and back without being seen. Maybe he hadn't known the child was inside. Had the shock of finding out precipitated his heart attack? Or perhaps he witnessed the arson but was too scared to come forward for fear of reprisals, the stress of that playing on his mind.

Daniels placed her elbows on the table and made a steeple with her hands, her thoughts turning in a different direction. 'You think the old man was in some kind of trouble?'

'Like what? Elliot says he was a nice old man who wouldn't hurt a fly—'

'He would say that, though, wouldn't he?'

'Why d'you ask?'

'Either these two incidents are purely coincidental or they're not. If they are, fair enough. But if there is a connection, could it be that Maggie Reid's house was mistaken for George's?' Daniels didn't wait for an answer. 'What's Elliot like?'

Gormley thumbed toward the interview room door. 'Breath of fresh air, compared to the low-lives normally frogmarched in here.'

'This missing money bothers me,' Daniels said. 'Is he absolutely sure?'

'One hundred per cent. George took a grand to the garage yesterday to buy the lad a car but it was already sold. They spent some time together at the old man's allotment and then Elliot put him on the bus. A witness saw him get off the bus and he goes down like a bag of hammers. That was less than half an hour before an ambulance took him to hospital. He couldn't have spent the money and there were no banks on his way home. Elliot says he wouldn't use one anyway 'cause he kept his money in the house under the floorboards.'

'And it's not there now?'

Gormley shook his head.

Something didn't smell right in Daniels' view. Had someone relieved him of the cash on the bus? she wondered. She discounted that. Too risky. Buses had CCTV nowadays. Anyway, George would surely have raised the alarm with the driver. She asked, 'Where did the money come from, Hank?'

'Life savings.'

'Who apart from Elliot knew about it?'

'Not another living soul, according to the lad.'

'What did you say to him?'

'What could I say?' Gormley hesitated. 'OK, I said we'd get to the bottom of—'

'Hank! There's no evidence George Milburn was murdered!'

'I know and so does he now . . . I told him I knew the pathologist who carried out the autopsy and that he wasn't a man given to mistakes. I stressed that there was no doubt his granddad died from natural causes, but I had to accept the possibility that he may – and I stressed *may* – have been threatened or robbed before that happened. What else could I say?'

Daniels stood up, gathering her bag from the floor. 'Bet that went down well.'

'Actually, he accepted it.' Gormley stood up too. 'I told you he's a nice kid.'

'You did right, Hank.' Daniels patted his arm as she walked past. 'Tell Elliot we'll look into it. But make sure he knows that further enquiries will have to be made and that'll take time. You better brief the guv'nor too.'

'Don't you want to do that?'

'In a word, no.' Grabbing the door handle, she turned to look at him. 'You did good with Elliot. But you're not the only one with news, Hank. Naylor wants a word.'

'What the hell does that mean?'

'You'll know soon enough.'

34

Daniels returned to her desk and slipped her warrant card into the slot in her computer in order to access the report on George Milburn's death. Bizarrely, it had taken place not only in the same street, but literally metres from Maggie Reid's front door. As she waited for the incident to pop up on screen, she sat back wondering if the old man was somehow involved in her current case, either as the arsonist – as Gormley had suggested initially – or as a lucky target because the fuckwit that started the fire had got the wrong address. With his body lying in the morgue, it was going to be difficult to prove either way.

Scrolling through the incident report, she noted that a call had come into the control room from a female member of the public. MAN COLLAPSED is all it said. The first responder to the subsequent callout from the control room was recorded as PC4576 Dixon, an officer standing guard outside Daniels' crime scene.

Small world.

She read on . . . Dixon had given mouth-to-mouth and called the ambulance. The case was then referenced off, having been handed over to the ambulance service. There was a note of a number of witnesses to the event, locals who

lived on Ralph Street, and a list of names taken. None of them rang any bells with Daniels.

Picking up the phone, she dialled the West End nick. After a few minutes the desk sergeant answered. She explained who she was and asked to speak with PC Dixon, but neither he, nor his supervision, Sergeant Terrance Smith, were currently in the building.

'B Rota is on days off,' the desk sergeant said.

'OK, make sure either one calls me as soon as their shift comes back on duty.'

She hung up as someone knocked on her door. Looking up, she saw it was Gormley. He had a face like thunder. Assuming Naylor had told him he wouldn't be working the A1 incident, she beckoned him in, ready for a fight. He slung himself down in the chair opposite but before he had chance to open his mouth she held her hands up in surrender as if he'd pulled out a gun.

'I know what you're going to say, Hank. And, for what it's worth, I don't like it either. But that's the way it is. Believe me, I want to get the nut-job that killed Ivy Kerr as much as you do, but it isn't going to happen, so you may as well get used to it. Besides, I need you on the arson with me.'

'Can't I swap with Carmichael?' He was practically begging. 'You could have a word with the guv'nor, he'll listen to you. You know he will.'

'No, he *won't*. I've already been there. Besides, he's got a point, Hank. You're too emotionally involved. Too close to the case to be objective. You know as well as I do that situations like those rarely, if ever, prove fruitful for the case or the officer concerned. Naylor's right. We should stay out of it.'

'Thanks for your support. You could've at least warned me.'

'There's no good sulking about it, Hank.' She studied him for a moment, letting him sweat. 'What exactly *did* you see anyway . . . at the crash site, I mean?'

'I thought you said we should both stay—'

'That was the official line.' She grinned. 'Unofficially, I've spoken to Carmichael and asked her to produce a computer-generated image of the A1 accident from the rough sketches I drew up at the time. I made contemporaneous notes of the walking wounded and what cars they belonged to, so we should get a pretty clear picture when she waves her magic wand. Lisa has agreed to feed back anything we need to know at the end of each day – confidentially, of course.'

'You are some piece of work, Kate Daniels!' Gormley beamed at her. 'And if Naylor asks Carmichael what she's doing?'

'She'll be using her initiative, as always.'

'If he catches on, I hope you know you'll get your head in your hands to play with.'

Daniels was resolute. 'We were there first!'

'Did I ever tell you how much I love working with you? Your epitaph should read: "Insubordination for the good of the cause." You're my Jack Bauer.'

She grinned. 'That makes *you* my Chloe.'

'I'm on it, Jack. How can I help?'

Laughing at his Kiefer Sutherland impression, she responded in kind: 'I think we should talk about what you saw. The President is depending on us. We can't let him down.'

'Since when was Jack Bauer Irish?'

They chuckled, the tension leaving them both.

Dropping the accent, Daniels said. 'Get your thinking cap on. The guv'nor wants a statement from you right away.'

'I know, he told me.' Gormley's expression darkened. 'I've been wracking my brains, but the simple truth is I'm not really sure what I saw.'

'You must have some idea! The person attending Ivy – was it a man? A woman? Police, fire officer, paramedic . . . ?'

Gormley looked at her. Of his own admission, he'd had a skinful that night, having spent the evening drinking beer and watching the match. Probably shouldn't have been working, if the truth be known. It was tanking down when they'd arrived at the crash site. So much going on. It was entirely understandable if he couldn't recall everything in minute detail.

But he had to.

And he would – eventually.

'I just remember Ivy's face . . .' He palmed his brow. 'Jesus! Those eyes will haunt me for the rest of my days. Someone wearing a high-viz jacket was crouched down beside her. I never saw their face, I swear.'

'A high-viz jacket means fuck all,' Daniels reminded him. 'They're two a penny at Amble Market. I nearly bought one myself last Sunday.'

'Yeah, but I was concentrating on her. Seeing *her*. Then a kid came up to me, nasty head injury. I turned away to find some medical help before I got an answer.'

'Can't you visualize the person with Ivy? Why don't you walk yourself through a cognitive interview in the same way

you would any other witness?' She didn't need to remind him that the mind does funny things to people when they get stressed out. Often shuts down in order to protect a person's sanity. 'Come on, Hank. Your evidence might be all we have. Did you speak to them at all?'

'No, yes . . . I asked if they needed a hand.'

'They?'

'Figure of speech.' He shook his head, disappointed not to have been able to tell her more. 'I'm sorry, that's all I recall.'

Daniels was disappointed too but didn't let it show. He was beating himself up enough without her giving him any more grief.

35

The evening briefing began at seven o'clock sharp. The MIR was full to bursting and Naylor had the floor. He'd informed the Murder Investigation Team of his intention to split them up, half remaining on the arson, the rest working the A1 incident under his leadership as SIO. Detectives were unhappy about the situation. Daniels could see it in their eyes. She was hardly jumping up and down about it herself. The handover had come at the worst possible time as far as she was concerned. Naylor's assurance that other officers would be drafted in to assist either enquiry as and when the need arose didn't exactly fill her with joy. They may not be perfect, but this was *her* team. A bunch of detectives who worked well together as a unit, not some hastily arranged hotchpotch that didn't know their arses from their elbows. Still, she had no choice in the matter. Officially, at any rate. She'd have to get on with it.

As Naylor elaborated on his plans, she thought about the arson case. Progress was slow. She was still waiting for forensic results on the rubber glove recovered from the wheelie bin and the fragment found in Maggie Reid's house. *A match now would certainly float her boat.* Colin and Denise Albright appeared to be in the clear. There was no evidence to suggest that either had made a journey from Slaley Hall to the West

End of Newcastle in order to carry out a revenge execution in the dead of night. But lab technicians had managed to identify residue from the petrol as Shell. Maxwell had spent the afternoon following that up, visiting garages within a three-mile radius, trying to establish how many punters had bought petrol in a can recently. So far, he'd covered Scotswood Road, Denton Road, West Road, down to nineteenth-century landmark The Big Lamp, and all points in between. He was now on his feet telling them what he'd discovered.

Sensing where he was taking them, Daniels gave him a nod of encouragement, even though it was a long shot. This was flaming June after all, the beginning of summer, a month when people frequently bought fuel to store at home in case they ran dry – gardeners and motorcyclists being two obvious examples. Such purchases would be time-consuming to investigate. And petrol used to start the fire could easily have been months old, stored in someone's garage or lock-up.

Still, anything was worth a try.

'Had it been winter, it would've been a much simpler . . .' Maxwell was almost verbalizing Daniels' thoughts. 'I came up with fifteen purchases made over the three days prior to the arson, out of which eight have already been identified by garage staff as local people known to them. They're being seen as we speak and actions have been raised to trace the others.' He paused for breath, before adding, 'But there is one CCTV image that bothers me . . .'

Daniels met his eyes. 'How so?'

'Punter was acting weird, boss. Medium build and height. Boiler suit and baseball cap. Being really careful not to look

directly at the camera.' He pointed at Carmichael. 'Lisa has uploaded the tape.'

'Was it a Shell station?' Robson asked.

Maxwell nodded.

Daniels looked at Carmichael. 'Show me.'

Carmichael ran the footage on the electronic murder wall. The room went quiet as detectives watched Maxwell's weirdo fill up a can and walk, head bowed unnaturally, into the cashier's desk to pay – in cash, Daniels noted – before making off on foot.

'Bing-bong,' Gormley sung the words like a doorbell. 'He's our guy.'

'Could be local too, if he didn't drive there,' Brown offered.

Daniels was still peering at the screen. 'Not necessarily. If he *is* our man he'd hardly bring his car on to the forecourt, would he? He'd have left it parked in the street to avoid detection. Run it again please, Lisa.' Carmichael quickly rewound the tape and set it running with dozens of pairs of eyes fixed to the screen as they took a second look. 'Freeze it there!' The DCI turned to face the squad. 'Anyone else think "our guy", as Gormley so eloquently put it, walks like a girl?'

There was a chorus of: possibly, maybe, not sure.

Looking back at the murder wall, Daniels wondered if the shapeless boiler suit had been worn as a partial disguise. It could mask several layers underneath: added bulk to make the punter appear bigger than they really were. The victim's wife, Maggie Reid, popped into her head. Her alibi – the elusive Stella Drew – still hadn't turned up or answered repeated calls to her mobile and Daniels had the distinct impression that she was staying out of the way on purpose.

'Boss?' 'Boss?' Brown and Carmichael said in unison.

Carmichael gestured for Brown to go first. He smiled and did the same. He was a good detective, less vocal than some at MIT but an essential part of the squad. Their surveillance specialist, he liked working in the background. He had taken a shine to Carmichael. They'd joined the squad together and, when they worked as a twosome, she was almost always the spokesperson.

Carmichael took her cue to proceed. 'We just got back from the Meadow Well Estate. You'll be pleased to hear we had no humpy from David Matthews, the lad I told you worked for Albrights firm, the only one with a CRO number. He wasn't quite what we expected, was he, Andy?' Brown shook his head and she moved on. 'He was a quiet lad, salt of the earth, actually, despite his appearance. No neck and tats,' she explained. 'Looked like your average thug, but he was *really* helpful. Considers himself one of Mark Reid's mates in spite of losing his job when Mark put Albright's firm out of business.'

'Easy to say after the event,' Gormley reminded her. 'Reid's not around to confirm or deny it, is he?'

'True,' Carmichael acknowledged. 'But he seemed pretty genuine to me.'

'They continued to see each other afterwards?' Naylor asked.

'Yes, guv. Matthews was gutted to hear of Reid's death. Even more upset about the boy. Read it in the newspaper, apparently. He was also up front about his conviction and expecting our visit, I reckon—'

'I agree with that, guv,' Brown said. 'The lad was in tears

at one point, not bolshie in the slightest. Comes from a hard-working family. Parents both in employment. Mother has some involvement with the Meadows Neighbourhood Centre. Father's a postie. I've not had time to check, but I'm guessing that means he has no form. Both parents seem determined to give their kids a better start in life than they both had.'

Robson looked up from the notes he was taking. 'Where was he between seven-thirty p.m. Wednesday and one a.m. yesterday?'

'Same as most people, insensible after the match. We're checking that out, but we're probably wasting our time. Reid was taking Matthews on. He was due to start work for him on Monday. Claims that's why he rang him, to cadge a lift to the site. We saw the offer of employment and it was dated last week.' He looked at Daniels. 'There's a copy on your desk.'

'Why bite the hand?' Naylor said to no one in particular.

'That's what we thought, guv.' Carmichael glanced at Brown to check he had nothing to add. 'Matthews claims Reid was having an affair but was being very secretive about it. Don't know if it means anything, but he thinks the woman was a security guard.'

'Just thinks?' Daniels queried. 'Don't suppose he knew her name?'

'No, boss. We were hoping he might have thrown some light on Judy, the woman who called Reid the night he died. Anyway, Matthews only saw the girlfriend once but he did notice she was wearing a white shirt under a civvi jacket. Could equally have been a prison officer, I suppose. Or a WPC, for that matter, though he didn't seem to think so.'

Carmichael and Brown both smiled, enjoying a private joke. 'When Andy pushed him on it, Matthews said growing up on the Meadow Well you get a kind of sixth sense about the police. We're easy to spot, apparently, in or out of uniform.'

A chuckle went up in the room.

Daniels thought for a moment. 'The female kit I saw in Reid's flat doesn't fit with my idea of ill-paid security guards. When this Judy woman called Reid there were people talking in the background, so maybe she's a shift worker. The call is timed at one fifteen and she asked him to ring her back, which would suggest she wasn't hitting the sack right away. It's certainly something to bear in mind . . .' Daniels shifted her attention to Maxwell, commending his diligence in following the petrol trail. She pointed at the frozen image on the murder wall. 'Neil, concentrate your efforts on this one. Does anyone else have anything to add before we wrap it up for the night?'

There was a collective shake of heads.

'Right . . .' She began packing up her stuff. 'Those of you no longer working the arson make sure you hand everything over tonight. From tomorrow morning, you're officially off the case. Thanks a lot, guys.'

As everyone disbanded, Daniels caught Gormley's tired eyes across the room. It had been a long day – a long week in fact – and they were both exhausted. In the coming days, possibly even weeks, they'd be working at full stretch with half their usual complement with a double murder to solve, the A1 murder to occupy their minds and the hopes of Elliot Milburn weighing them down. Things couldn't get much worse.

36

Kate left the MIR immediately, making her way down the stairwell and out of the station via the back door. Force of habit. Suddenly remembering where she'd parked her car, she turned towards the entrance gate, slinging her bag over her shoulder and giving Gormley a wave as he pulled away. Turning left, she dug her hand into her pocket for her keys and came to a sudden stop, her eyes searching the street.

'Shit!' *Shit, shit, shit!*

The Toyota wasn't there.

With her heart thumping in her chest, she walked up the road a bit, making sure that tiredness hadn't confused her. She passed a number of cars: an Audi A4, a VW Passat, Vauxhall Corsa, Land Rover Discovery, the old type – but no black Rav 4. The Corsa had its offside front light smashed. Fragmented glass lay on the floor beside it. No prizes for guessing what had happened there.

As she stood in the middle of the road with her hands on her head, a car tooted behind her.

Robson's voice broke through her trance. 'Boss? Why are you staring at the pavement?'

'Some bastard's nicked my car!' she yelled, almost breaking into a run.

An hour later, having filed a report – for what bloody good

it would do – she hailed a taxi and went home. Angry with herself for having parked the Toyota on the road outside the station in her rush to get into work, she decided that even if she got the car back she wouldn't keep it, not after some arsehole had been raking it around doing God knows what inside.

No chance.

If a burglar had been in her bed she wouldn't want to sleep in it again, would she?

There was a pile of mail on the floor in the hallway as she entered the house: several utility bills, a letter from her cousin in New York and a postcard from Venice that, despite her black mood, brought a smile to her face. It was unsigned but in the same handwriting as the other three she'd received that week. It contained just four words:

Are you hungry yet?

It surprised her how much she'd thought about Fiona Fielding in the past few weeks, how tempted she was to ring and say hi. But on each occasion she'd lifted the phone, something had happened to stop her: yet another emergency cropped up, one of her team needed her ear, or Jo Soulsby leapt out of the shadows, pushing any thoughts of Fielding to the back of her mind.

How sad an excuse was that?

Fielding was a successful artist – a witness Daniels had interviewed on her last murder enquiry – an attractive woman with a raspy voice and deep blue penetrating eyes. She was very outspoken and had the world at her feet. Not a hang-up in sight. No worries *she'd* be held back in her chosen profession because of the way she chose to conduct her life.

She was free to do whatever she wanted, *with* whoever she wanted.

Rereading the postcard, Daniels could feel her cheeks burning as she recalled meeting Fielding for the first time – an unforgettable encounter. If she was being honest, it was the same inexplicable feeling she'd had when she'd first met Jo, a spark between two people too powerful to ignore, something that went much deeper than physical attraction. In the space of half an hour or so, Fielding had somehow managed to get under her skin. Then she'd disappeared, never to be heard of again. Or so Daniels thought, until the postcards began arriving. She'd kept all twenty-eight.

The woman was relentless.

Putting the postcard in a drawer with the others, she wondered if her feelings for Fiona were stronger because she reminded her of Jo. She too had disappeared off the scene as quickly as she'd arrived, allowing Daniels to put her on a pedestal to idolize from afar. Until one day she materialized as the new criminal profiler.

Daniels sighed. *What a fucked-up mess her life was.*

She couldn't go there again.

Why was she pretending she could?

Despite the late hour – it was almost ten and getting dark – she changed her clothes and went for a run in Jesmond Dene, her favoured circuit, a draw for locals and tourists alike. A haven of tranquillity on the edge of a busy city, it had a certain stillness she craved after a long day in the office, particularly late at night when her head was crammed with multiple problems. It gave her the opportunity to think

things through, then file stuff away until morning and get a good night's sleep.

Entering from the top road, she took a steep path down into the wooded valley past the pet cemetery and Pet's Corner – a small city farm – keeping the stream on her left. She ran on, crossing the bridge, pausing a moment or two to listen to the refreshing rush of the waterfall, then peering over the stone wall to watch the water crashing into the moonlit stream below. Hard to imagine she was less than three miles from Newcastle City Centre on a Friday night.

When she got home, she showered and fell into bed.

But her run hadn't done its job. Her sleep was filled with images of death and destruction: the Rav 4 racing through the streets, crashing through the security barrier at the station with Bridget and Ivy inside, banging on the windows like patients in a lunatic asylum; her running upstairs to get help – her heart almost bursting with the effort – and not being able to find any; the ear-splitting noise of a fire alarm.

She woke with a start, fighting her way from beneath her duvet, drenched in sweat. Confusion subsided as she lay there in the dark. The doorbell was ringing. *Shit!* She looked at the clock by her bedside. Eight-fifteen. That was OK. Naylor had asked her to stay clear of the office while he got the A1 incident underway and marked out their respective territories.

Jumping out of bed, she hurried to her bedroom window. It was a glorious day and Jo was at the door with newspapers, a carton of milk, and what looked suspiciously like a bag of fresh croissants. Daniels flung on a robe and rushed downstairs, her heart pounding from the nightmare still running in her head.

Jo was casually dressed in a pair of cut-off shorts and her favourite faded khaki T-shirt. She'd worn it the first time they'd gone out together, but with jeans and killer heels that made her even taller than her normal six feet. They had met up at Francesca's, an Italian restaurant not a million miles from where they both lived. Jo had had her back to the door, chatting to a staff member, her distinctive laughter filling the air when Daniels walked in. Then, sensing a presence behind her, she'd swung round, her eyes sending a secret message across the room: *You are so special.* It turned Daniels' legs to jelly.

Still did, even now.

'Hey . . .' Daniels' tone was flat. She kissed Jo lightly on the cheek. 'Am I glad to see you?'

'You don't sound it. I nearly didn't knock when I saw no car.'

'Some bastard stole it.'

'No! When?'

'Last night. I was going to call you, but to be perfectly honest I couldn't be arsed.'

'I noticed your bedroom curtains were drawn. You feeling OK? You look awful.'

'Could've done with a better sleep, but I'm fine.'

'You sure? I rang the office and they told me you weren't due in till twelve.' Jo stepped into the hallway, squeezed past the Yamaha motorbike, turning to face Daniels when they reached the kitchen. 'If you want the truth, I came round because I was curious to know why you were taking time off in the middle of a murder enquiry. You're the SIO on the arson in Ralph Street, aren't you?'

Daniels nodded.

'You're not ill, are you?'

'No . . . I'm involved in two cases, Jo. But therein lies the problem. In one of them, I'm a witness and possibly even a suspect—'

'What?' Confusion flashed across Jo's face.

Leaving nothing out, Daniels briefed her on the death of Ivy Kerr, the fact that she and Gormley had been on the scene at the time, the whole sorry mess. She also mentioned Naylor's insistence that she stay out of the MIR until the lines were well and truly drawn between the two incidents . . .

'He's covering our arses so that further down the line no barrister or judge could accuse us of any impropriety or conflict of interest.'

'Sounds sensible,' Jo said.

Daniels locked eyes with her.

'What?' Jo said. 'You're unhappy with that?'

Pointing at the bakery bag in Jo's hand, Daniels sidestepped the question. 'What you got there?'

'Kate? Don't do it . . . This will not end well.'

Daniels wasn't listening. Splitting the team was a sound idea, but that didn't stop her feeling aggrieved. OK, she had Robson and Gormley to investigate the fire, but Carmichael had skills they didn't and she'd be unable to utilize them while her DC was working for the Super. Besides, she'd promised Hank they would do a little digging themselves and she didn't feel inclined to let regulations change her mind.

'Fine!' Jo said. 'If you insist on getting fired you need to eat before going in.' Jo held out two Danish pastries, a warning in her eyes. 'You, coffee. Me, eggs.'

Daniels put on the coffee, excused herself, then ran upstairs and jumped in the shower. Had Jo not been there she'd have skipped breakfast altogether and gone into the incident room in spite of Naylor's insistence that she stay away. But now she had an invitation to spend time with Jo, maybe for once she'd actually do as she was told.

Jo tried to talk Daniels out of her maverick tendencies but she wouldn't listen, so they took their coffee outside into the sunshine and sat in her back yard like an old married couple, scanning the morning papers the way they used to, *light years ago*.

'Stop it!' Jo said.

'Stop what?' Acting innocent, Daniels lowered the *Guardian*.

'You were staring at me!'

'No I wasn't!' Daniels pointed at Jo's Serengeti sunglasses. 'Anyway, how can you possibly tell with those on?'

Jo tapped her right lens and then lifted the glasses on to the top of her head. 'With these I can see straight into your heart. There's no escaping my powers!'

Daniels laughed out loud.

She began reading again, grateful still to have Jo in her life, albeit it not as close as she'd like. Ironically, the job that had pulled them apart now bound them together as friends and colleagues. She didn't have to like the situation to accept it as a fact. But on that beautifully sunny morning – surrounded by ugly brick walls on all sides and no view whatsoever – she couldn't think of a single thing that would spoil that moment.

Then the phone rang.

38

Daniels paid the driver and leapt out of the cab. Gormley looked hot and bothered as he hurried towards her, cutting her off from entering the station via the back door. Grabbing her upper arm he led her around the side of the building, guiding her to a quiet spot where they could talk without fear of being overheard.

'We've got to stop meeting like this,' Daniels said. 'People will get the wrong idea.'

'Very funny. What's with the taxi?'

'You haven't heard then . . .'

Daniels wondered if her Toyota was still in one piece or lying burnt-out somewhere, along with the kit she'd left in the back. Thankfully, none of it official or traceable to her home address. Just a few personal items, including a tyre pressure gauge and bike lock she'd only just bought.

Bastard joy riders.

Gormley looked confused. 'About what?'

'Never mind. This had better be good, Hank.' She tried not to sound put out, even though her morning had been spoiled by his phone call. Jo would still be eating breakfast alone in her sunny back yard, the first quality time they'd spent together in ages. 'I wasn't due in for a couple of hours and neither were you. Mind telling me what the hell we're doing here?'

'Long story . . . won't bore you with the details.'

'Oh, good. We're both speaking in code!'

'I couldn't sleep. That's all you need to know.' Gormley pointed towards the perimeter fence where a number of police vehicles stood idle. Next to them was a flat-back lowloader carrying a smashed-up vehicle. 'I spotted it arriving as I parked my car. Recognize the Honda Jazz? That's Ivy's car. Thought you'd like to take a look before the CSIs offload it. They've gone for a late breakfast in the canteen, hence the urgency. You haven't got long if you want to examine it before Naylor does.'

A couple of uniformed officers walked by and said hello as they passed. Acknowledging them with a nod, Daniels watched them get into a panda car and drive away. Glancing up at the second floor of the station, she homed in on the windows of the MIR. The low loader was visible from there. If spotted tampering with the car she knew she'd be in deep shit with her new boss – friend or no friend.

Gormley picked up on her anxiety. 'Don't sweat,' he said. 'Naylor's busy launching his enquiry. You know what that's like. He'll be tied up all morning.'

She shook her head. 'Too risky, Hank. Can't be done.'

'Yes, it can! Carmichael promised to keep him occupied 'til I give her the heads-up that we're finished.'

'That sounds rather like a conspiracy. Er, Naylor? Me? What bloody difference does it make who examines the vehicle? We're on the same side, remember?'

'Please, Kate. Just take a look. And hurry, or I'll need another shave.'

Daniels punched his arm and then set off towards the lowloader as naturally as she could, Jo's warning ringing in her

ears: *This will not end well.* Gormley followed, reminding her that officers not party to last night's briefing wouldn't give them a second glance. They were murder detectives, after all, even if they weren't behaving like it. As they neared the recovery truck, he bent his knee for her to use as a step, feigning a groan as she propelled herself on to the vehicle.

Daniels looked around her. Gormley was right. No one was paying her any attention. Ripping off her scarf, she used it as a glove and opened the door of the Jazz. A set of keys were still dangling from the ignition; there was blood everywhere, a shallow pool of which had congealed on the rubber matting in the driver's footwell, enough to make her think that Ivy's husband had bled to death in his seat. Leaning in, she turned the ignition key a notch and nearly jumped out of her skin as the computerized voice of the satnav filled the car:

'Turn round. Turn round.'

Letting out a sigh, she glanced up at the MIR again. Naylor was standing with his back to the window. Praying that he wouldn't turn round, she took in Gormley's apologetic expression which suddenly morphed into a plea for her to continue. This is crazy, she thought. Returning her attention to Ivy's car, she quickly accessed the satnav, checking the device's saved locations, scrolling down to the last entry which was nothing more than a postcode: WD18 9RN. She read it out and told Gormley to write it down, then leapt to the ground, hoping it would lead to something because they had sod-all else right now.

39

In Chantelle's opinion, Whitley Bay wasn't the place it used to be. Nowadays, disappointed tourists came looking for Spanish City and found nothing resembling the fairground it once was. A place so iconic that its Tunnel of Love had inspired a song by Mark Knopfler, no less. She had binned the idea of spending a day there, opting instead for Seaton Sluice a couple of miles north up the coast, talking her mates into going with her. It had the same fabulous golden sands but no cafés, candyfloss or chips, just miles and miles of beach fringed with sand dunes where they could smoke a spliff without being seen, or strip off naked if they wanted to.

'cept not one of the bottleless mingers did.

'Who needs St Tropez, eh, Shell?' Tracy said.

Chantelle didn't answer. She was too busy gawping at Leigh and Daisy, who already had fabulous tans on account of the fact that they were out of work. Thinking she had a lot of catching up to do, Chantelle watched Tracy get her kit off, revealing a lush polka-dot bikini underneath. It showed off her superb figure and left nothing to the imagination. She worked in a knocking shop on Elswick Road, and had once taken Chantelle there for an interview – if that was what giving the owner a blow-job was called these days. But the nobber said she didn't have quite the right qualifications.

What he meant was, she was a little larger than his other girls.

Tosser.

Chantelle would never tell Tracy, but the experience had dented her confidence and made her all the more determined to show them she didn't have to be a slapper to earn her keep. Anyhow, she was better than that. Classier. No need to lie on her back and think of England for some married, hairy-arsed polis, judge, accountant, looking for a bit on the side. She had a brain in her head and intended to use it.

Starting tomorrow.

Maybe then she could bag herself a footie player and realize her dream of becoming a WAG. Chantelle stroked her stomach. She'd lost weight lately and had spent all morning brushing up on Celebrity Biggest Loser on the net. Poring over their weight-loss stories, picking up tips: what worked, what didn't. More of the divvies seemed to be going up than down this week, which made her feel a little less inadequate.

Spraying her legs with Tesco suntan lotion, making sure she covered the bits round her knees that always got burnt, she bristled as she noticed a bottle of Piz Buin sticking out of Tracy's bag. Knocked-off, obviously. She couldn't afford to buy it, not with a kid at home to look after, no matter how many tricks she turned. Couldn't pronounce it neither, prob'ly.

That was Tracy in a nutshell: *all the gear, no idea.*

But they were great mates – had been since starting school. They had fallen out numerous times, but never for long. If Chantelle was being honest, Tracy was the one person in the world she could trust, the only one who was there for her

through thick and thin. Mostly thin, now she came to think of it.

A kid screamed as he entered the shimmering water. Chantelle watched him run back out and kick sand in his sister's eyes, making her cry. Little twat reminded her of her brother, whose real name was Todd but who was referred to as Samantha by his mates – a nickname that stuck with him when he entered the military. He took great pleasure in her discomfort. There was a posh word for that, so his social worker said. German, if Chantelle recalled right. Chardonnay? Sommat like that, at any rate. Why didn't folks speak plain English?

'Evil little shit' worked just as well.

There were no adults in the sea. And who could blame them? Chantelle had dipped her toe in the water when they arrived and watched as it turned blue. She could swear it was degrees warmer when she was a kid than it was today.

'Global warming, my arse!' she said out loud.

'Eh?' Tracy looked up from *Grazia* – the fifth-birthday collector's issue she'd half-inched from a mate's house the night before. The magazine was well thumbed, its pages curled at the corners. It had a picture of Lady Gaga on the front, the celebrity she most admired.

Pulling a face, she threw a baseball cap at Chantelle.

'Better put that on,' she said. 'Either you've had too much sun or too much dope!'

Chantelle ignored the hat, repeating Tracy back to herself, mimicking her broad Geordie accent, which was far more pronounced than hers. She'd always tried to talk proper on account of the fact that she was going places, the only one

trying to better herself – the only one working, for that matter. The only one with a plan.

Out of the corner of her eye she noticed an unhappy boy lying on a towel, his father ignoring him completely in favour of the phone in his hand. She wondered who they were, why they had bothered to come down to the beach together. The lack of interaction between them made her feel sad. She wanted to go over and speak to the kid, do something to brighten his day. Being ignored was the worst thing that could happen to anyone. She knew all about that. No wonder she craved the limelight.

She laid down and suddenly there was no wind, only baking, relentless sun. Gulls flew right overhead in a clear blue sky, a rare sight in the north-east. There wasn't a cloud to be seen, just acres of blue, reminding her of trips to the beach with her mam and Todd. He always insisted on bringing a cricket bat and stumps, a bottle of water and jam sandwiches to last a whole day. But Chantelle was watching her weight, so lunch was a little more sophisticated nowadays: potted spread, BBQ crisps and Red Bull.

Smashing.

Chantelle suddenly sat up again.

'Fucking Gobi Desert down there,' she said. Turning around to face the water, she scanned the beach. Apart from the lad who was being ignored, there was maybe half a dozen families, no more than that, paddling, sunbathing, some of them reading, cool-boxes and bottles of pop everywhere. The water looked so inviting.

Sighing, Chantelle glanced at her mates. 'Anyone fancy a plodge?'

Nobody moved.

Chantelle laid back down. She could hear the wash of the sea on the shore, the laughter of children playing on the beach and some dozy cow yelling like a banshee for a dog called Roly. Chantelle didn't like dogs, having been bitten by a terrier when she was four. Little twat sunk its teeth right into her arm and she still bore the scar to this day. Let sleeping dogs lie, her father had always told her. But did she listen? *Did she shite.*

Turning her head sideways, Chantelle saw that her mates were all fast asleep, their faces lifted towards the sun. Tracy's mouth was wide open and she was snoring like a horse. *Very* attractive. Chantelle wished she could do the same, but she was so tense. So restless. She had far too much on her mind. In the immediate wake of the fire, you couldn't get shifted on Ralph Street as scores of police officers flooded the area. She'd thought it best to keep a low profile until the excitement died down. Two days on and the house was boarded up, the street empty of police now they'd gone back to headquarters to investigate the case. Maybe it was time to make her move.

Unable to keep a secret for very long, Chantelle had told the only one she knew she could trust. But her plan hadn't gone down well; Tracy had tried laying a guilt trip on her as soon as she heard. In the end, Chantelle warned her to keep her mouth shut if she knew what was good for her, or Wannabe Lady Gaga would end up looking like someone had chopped sticks on her face. That shut her up good and proper; she hadn't mentioned it again.

Right now, Chantelle wished Todd was there to talk to,

even if he did kick sand in her face. Her brother understood the concept of looking after number one. He'd once told her that, in order to be first over the hill, you had to tread on the necks of others or get trampled in the stampede.

Chantelle smiled and shut her eyes. *Necks it is then.*

40

The tall redhead smiled at the female receptionist as she entered through a revolving door. Ignoring the young woman's offer of help, she wandered away, her fuck-me high heels clicking on pristine floor tiles, each step echoing around the cavernous showroom. It felt great to be back in Newcastle on a Saturday, perfect timing for a shopping spree in a busy showroom selling high-end cars.

There were some glass display cabinets on her left with good kit inside. Accessories for those who could afford them, boys toys mainly, with the Porsche brand-name emblazoned across them: jackets, hats, key-rings, watches and leather goods, including a mini golf bag that would fit perfectly into the limited boot space of the bigger toys on sale. Each one of the cars was a genuine piece of precision engineering, design classics made with the discerning motorist in mind.

Although sufficient daylight flooded in through floor-to-ceiling windows, spotlights suspended from the ceiling were perfectly positioned to highlight the sleek lines and stylish interiors of the vehicles on display. The place even smelled classy – a mixture of polish and expensive leather – everything about it said quality. Inhaling deeply, drinking it in, the redhead drew an odd look from a balding fat man who was sitting at the service desk. He looked right through her before

handing a set of keys to a young woman dressed more like a senior bank official than an automotive admin clerk.

'Can I help you, madam?' a voice behind her said.

Madam? The redhead liked the sound of that. She wished her late father had been there to hear it spoken so deferentially in such an upmarket dealership. Fast cars were the only thing they had in common. He'd once told her she had designs above her station and should remember where she came from. Well, she had news for him. She wasn't arsed where she'd come from. It was where she was going that interested her.

She had no idea if it was true, but someone had once told her that a tiny percentage of the people possessed a disproportionate amount of the nation's wealth. Well, she was on her way to join them. She turned towards the voice, almost expecting a salute, and came face to face with the bluest eyes she'd ever seen under a mop of tousled blond hair. The young sales executive had a striking resemblance to her father's hero, the late Formula One World Champion, James Hunt, who had retired from racing in 1979 – the year she was born – and died fourteen years later aged forty-five.

Living in the fast lane had its pitfalls.

Hunt flushed up under the intensity of her gaze. 'Is it the basic 911 that interests you?'

'Do I look like I do basic?' she countered, her eyes flirting with him. 'I was rather hoping you'd help me choose.' She scanned the showroom. 'I'm torn between models and colours: the Carrera 4S versus the convertible—'

'The cabriolet is a beauty,' he corrected her.

The redhead bristled. So Porsche didn't call them convertibles. She didn't need a little prick who worked in a garage to remind her of that.

Taking in her reaction, the sales executive flushed up and changed the subject to cover his gaffe. 'In terms of colours, we have speed yellow over there . . .' He pointed to a car near the front of the showroom. He waited for a reaction which she didn't supply. 'We also have ruby red metallic due in later today, if you'd be interested.'

'Tacky,' the redhead pulled a sour face. Turning her back, she stared off into the distance, her eyes sliding over the models, and spoke without turning round. 'No, I was thinking more platinum silver with red leather interior. Failing that, I'd consider black.' She pointed to one particular machine parked at a jaunty angle near the door. 'That one I do like very much.'

'That one is sold, I'm afraid.'

'Perfect, isn't it?' a man's voice said. 'Seems I pipped you to the post.'

The redhead turned. The bald man from the reception desk had his chubby hand out. She ignored it. Taken aback by her rudeness, he stomped off in a huff. She wandered away in the other direction, with Hunt hot on her heels. 'One of your best customers, I assume?' she said, as he caught up with her.

'Yes, buys new every year without fail.'

Of course he does. 'Why don't you show me what you've got available? I have other cars in mind and I'm in rather a hurry. I want something I can pick up on Monday at the very latest.'

Hunt looked stunned. 'Monday might be cutting it fine, madam. I—'

'I don't think you understand,' she interrupted him. 'I'll be paying cash.'

'I'm happy to ring round other dealerships if our shipments don't suit your requirements. I'm sure we can accommodate you.' He held out his hand, inviting her into a second showroom which was as impressive as the first. 'I take it you're looking for a new car?'

'Is there any other kind?'

He stifled a grin. 'Any idea on spec?'

She waited a beat. 'I think the accepted term is "fully loaded".'

'Yes, madam.' Hunt rushed off to make enquiries.

41

For a Saturday lunchtime the station canteen was pretty empty. As a rule, there were more officers and PSOs on duty at weekends per head of population than at any other time, mainly to police the cultural and social activities on offer in the city centre, but also to counteract an increased level of criminal activity. There were more fights, for a start. More drink or drugs consumed. More arseholes emerging from their hovels to take advantage of decent folks flocking to Northumberland Street and Eldon Square, Newcastle's shopping heart.

Summer always brought out its fair share of shoplifters and pickpockets. An offender's paradise, Daniels thought as she watched Gormley tucking into an all-day breakfast: egg, bacon, sausage, mushrooms and beans. They were sitting at a table near the open window discussing her find in Ivy's car when her pocket began to vibrate. Putting down her coffee cup, she pulled out her mobile phone.

The display showed Robson calling.

He didn't introduce himself, just apologized for disturbing her break and launched straight in, telling her that Maggie Reid's alibi, Stella Drew, had resurfaced within the last half-hour. 'To be honest, I don't think she's been anywhere at all . . .' he said. 'The uniform I sent round said she's not the

travelling type, unless you include space exploration. I'm told she's well out of it. Anyway, you said you wanted to know if we found her. You want me to chase that up? I'm happy to—'

'No, sit tight, Robbo. Hank and I are done here. Is she at home now?'

'At home might be stretching it, boss.' He chuckled. 'She's in a bad way, apparently, but the attending PC told her to stay put until you'd spoken to her. Whether she does that is another matter entirely.'

Robson's upbeat chat pleased the DCI no end. It was like having an old friend back after a prolonged period of absence. His gambling addiction had caused him enormous personal problems and he hadn't been himself in a while. Maybe things were finally working out for him. She hoped so. She'd missed him.

'You got an address for me?'

Taking a pen from her pocket, she looked around for something to write on but there was nothing available. Napkins, never mind notebooks, were a luxury item that had passed by the attentions of those running the staff canteen. Instead, she accessed the memo pad on her BlackBerry and typed a note as he gave her the details.

Thanking him, she rang off.

Gormley asked her about the call.

'C'mon, tell you on the way,' she said. 'OK if we use your car?'

Twenty minutes later they arrived at the address Robson had given her. Stella Drew didn't answer their knock so they followed the racket coming from round the back of the

property. A wrought-iron gate led them to a garden littered with rusting trikes and toys. On a barren patch of grass, an indoor sofa the colour of Chicken tikka masala took centre stage. Stella Drew was slumped on it, almost horizontal. Awake, barely. Three scruffy-looking boys – the oldest about three years old – clung on to her, all talking at once, all vying for her attention. The youngest child's legs were covered in an angry rash, his sodden nappy hanging around his knees with the weight of the urine inside.

A snarling Rottweiler took exception to the presence of the detectives. It barked incessantly, straining to be free from its chain, saliva drooling from its jaws.

Jesus Christ! Daniels couldn't hear herself think.

Stella Drew was oblivious to the din. She was painfully thin – anorexic thin – probably weighed less than six stone wet through. Robson's joke about space exploration was spot on. In the crease of her left arm there were track marks, evidence of recent drug abuse. She had dark, greasy hair tied back in a ponytail and wore no make-up. On heavily tattooed arms were the names of at least three males. Wondering if they were the names of the children or their respective fathers, Daniels tried to rouse the woman and explain why they were there. But her eyes were dull. She clearly wasn't in. And when she did manage speech, it was hardly what they wanted to hear.

'Leave me alone,' she whined, switching her attention from Daniels to the kids. She shoved them away. 'You'n all. Go and play or sommat.'

Her words were ignored.

Daniels raised her voice over the children. 'You can't hold

out for ever, Stella. We need that statement. Just tell us where you were on Wednesday and Thursday and we'll be on our way.' Getting no answer, she turned to Gormley. 'I've got a headache, Hank. Either get rid of the rug-rats or entertain them while I talk to their mum.'

'Mind telling me how?'

'I don't know! Pretend you're Mr Tumble or something!'

'Who's he when he's around?'

'Big guy, acts the fool on TV. You've got a lot in common, I'm sure you'll find a way.'

Reaching into his pocket, Gormley drew out a Nestlé Kit Kat. Homing in on the sound of the red-and-white wrapper coming off the chocolate biscuit, the three little ones stopped screaming instantly, let go of their mother's legs and ran towards him. Six hands, ingrained with muck, reached up like starving beggars being offered charitable aid. He gave them a finger each and threw the last piece to the dog.

'Silence is golden, isn't it?' he said, licking chocolate from his fingers.

Drew scowled at him. 'The bairns haven't had their lunch!'

Or breakfast either, Daniels thought. *Like you'd care.*

'Sorry . . .' Gormley crumpled up the wrapper and put it in his pocket. 'You should've said.'

'I just did!' Drew growled, looking to her left. 'And you can fuck off too!'

It was a ferocious attack on her next-door neighbour, a woman with spiky blonde hair who'd peeked over the fence. She was hanging out her washing, craning her neck to see and hear what was going on. Her presence prompted Stella Drew to haul herself up off the sofa and go inside. Daniels

and Gormley followed her indoors through a chaotic kitchen and into the living room, where she sat down on another sofa, this one less threadbare than the one outside. Sweeping a rogue hair from her face, she lit a cigarette and blew a cloud of smoke into the air. The kids were back, inhaling her poison and eyeing Gormley's suit pocket.

'Stella, do yourself a favour and tell us what you know,' Daniels said. 'I'm in no mood to play games. I've got a long list of stuff to do and not enough time to fit it all in. We can do this here or we can do it at the station. It's entirely your choice.'

'I'm going nowhere and you can't make me,' Drew bit back. 'I done nothing wrong.'

'No one is suggesting you did. But I can spot a lie when I hear one. Were you or were you not out with Maggie Reid on Wednesday night?'

'Why's it so important?'

'Don't play dumb.' Daniels bent down and picked an unread newspaper off the table. She held it up, tapping the front-page headlines with the back of her hand: *Inferno Kills Father and Son.*

Stella Drew remained silent – took another hit of nicotine.

'Well?' Daniels waited. Then chose her words carefully so as not to alarm the kids. 'I'm in the middle of a major enquiry, Stella. That means I haven't got time to mess about. So if you know anything that might be important to us, get it off your chest now. Don't put yourself out for Maggie Reid. She's probably not worth it.'

'Get the fuck out of my house. I told you, I've done nowt wrong!'

'I'm pleased to hear it. Now answer my question. Where were you Wednesday night?' Again Daniels waited for what seemed like a very long time. Then she let out an exasperated sigh. 'OK, I've had enough of this. You've had your chance. Got a neighbour who can watch the kids? Or do I contact Social Services?'

'Good idea . . .' Gormley put his head on one side. For Daniels' benefit, he pointed at something on the floor beside Stella's feet. 'If you're going to kick a hypodermic under the couch, you should make sure you do it properly.'

Drew's face paled but still she kept shtum.

Daniels glanced at Gormley. 'Make the call, Hank.'

'No, listen—' The end of Drew's Marlborough dropped on to the greasy armrest of her chair as she spoke. Brushing it away, she stubbed out the cigarette in the ashtray and stood up to face them, her eyes flitting to each of her kids before finally coming to rest on Daniels. 'Whatever you think of me, my kids are all I've got. They mean everything to me. I'm trying to get clean, I swear to you. I'll tell you all I know if you don't tell the Social.'

'I want to believe that . . .' Daniels made a mental note to phone Social Services as soon as she got back to the office. The kids were at risk, whatever their mother might say. You could tell that by looking at them. 'If you cared that much you'd put them first and get rid of the gear for good.'

The *Scotswood stare* is a colloquialism for an intimidating glare: an angry look, a glower, hard eyes. Whatever description a person cared to use, it was impossible not to know when you'd received one. Stella Drew's were degree standard, a mixture of hatred and despair thrown in for good measure.

Her eyes fixed on to Daniels' like lasers. 'What would you know?' she said.

'Very perceptive . . .' Daniels gave a half smile. 'You're right, I'm not a mother. But even I can see when kids are being neglected. These little ones deserve more than you're prepared to give, Stella. But that's not why we're here. Tell us what's going on. We're going to find out anyway.'

'No Social? Promise me . . .' Drew pleaded. Her eyes misted up when Daniels didn't answer. 'I agreed to cover for Maggie, right? But I don't want to get involved now that . . . now that her kid . . .' She broke off, wiping snot from her nose with the back of her hand. 'We weren't together that night. She asked me to lie 'cause she's got a boyfriend, a married one. Lives local. But I don't know who he is, I swear. She wouldn't tell me. I think she's scared of him.'

Daniels had what she came for. Stella Drew would cough sooner or later, but for now she refused to be drawn any further. At least they knew Maggie Reid was lying about being out with her on the night of the fire. And if she hadn't been clubbing, then where the hell had she been? Maybe the boyfriend wasn't the only thing she'd lied about, Daniels mused on the way back to the MIR. Maybe the child wasn't Mark Reid's at all. Maybe the mystery boyfriend was the father, but not quite ready for fatherhood. There were always a million maybes.

When they pulled into the station, Gormley seemed preoccupied. Daniels followed his gaze to the perimeter fence. The low-loader was gone, Ivy's car nowhere to be seen. She got out and looked at him across the roof of the car, the postcode she'd lifted from Ivy's satnav pushing its way into her thoughts.

'That postcode I gave you? You got it with you?'

Gormley stuck a hand in his pocket, pulled out a bit of paper and waved it in the air. Daniels took it from him, got out her phone and keyed it into BlackBerry maps. Her eyes were like saucers as the result popped up on the tiny screen. Raising her head, she looked at Gormley for a long moment, her heart banging in her chest, her hands shaking as she pocketed the phone.

'Get on to the search coordinator,' she said. 'Tell him I want to see him right away.'

Gormley frowned. 'What's up?'

'Just do it!' Daniels yelled.

42

The search coordinator shook his head, a concerned expression crossing his face. He leaned on a pool cue, one leg crossed over the other at the ankle. They were in the recreation room surrounded by officers making the most of their tea break. By the looks of them, they weren't too happy about the interruption.

'You going to be long, boss?' one of them asked, impatient to resume his game.

Daniels shot him a dirty look. She eyeballed the search coordinator, a man she trusted implicitly to tell her the truth. 'You're absolutely certain that no lottery ticket was found on either body or in the car?'

'One hundred per cent, boss,' he answered confidently. 'Searched it myself.'

Gormley and Daniels exchanged a look.

'Is there a problem?' he queried.

'No, no problem,' Gormley said. 'Sorry for holding up your game.'

Daniels pulled a fifty-pence piece from her pocket and placed it under the pile of coins already there. 'Next game's on me,' she said, then walked away with Gormley following close behind.

They headed straight for the MIR, excitement giving way

to anxiety as they reached the second floor. Stopping at the head of the stairs, Gormley was breathing heavily as usual, chuntering about losing weight again.

'So greed is the motive for Ivy's murder,' he said.

'Looks like it.' Daniels sighed. 'That's assuming she bought a ticket.'

'Of course she bought a ticket! Their satnav was—'

'Programmed for Lottery HQ, I know. But without the ticket we have no proof. We need to talk to Ivy's family, Hank. Find out if she was in the habit of buying tickets and, if so, when and where from. If we can pin down a particular retailer, maybe we have a chance. Right now we need to spill the beans to Naylor. He's not going like it that we've been meddling in his case.'

Gormley stared along the corridor towards the MIR. 'OK, here's what we do,' he said. 'Just blame me, like it was all my idea—'

'Ahm, it *was* your idea.'

'Don't split hairs! Anyway, what's he going to do, sack me?'

'I've seen him can people for less.'

'Nah. He's one of the good guys! That's never going to happen.'

Daniels wasn't too sure.

'You think?' Gormley made a crazy face. 'So we took a peek at Ivy's car, so what?'

Daniels wasn't really listening.

'It's hardly a hanging offence!' Gormley added when she looked back at him. 'Just tell him it was—'

'He expressly told us not to involve ourselves, Hank. That's direct insubordination in anyone's book. Maybe sacking's a

bit strong. But think of it from his point of view. He's relatively new in post and one of the first orders he gives is ignored. You can't expect him to be happy about—'

'You got a better idea?'

She didn't answer.

'Didn't think so . . .' Gormley stroked his chin, searched his brain for inspiration, not finding any. 'Well, we can't sit on what we know. Someone needs to follow it up with Ivy's family right now, not when the B Team get their arses into gear.'

'Hope that wasn't for my benefit, Hank.'

Detective Inspector Roger Wallace had reached them on the stairwell, a big man with eyes too close together and really thin lips that made him appear bad tempered even thought he was actually quite jolly. Gormley glowered at him. For some reason these two gentle giants had never got along.

'You shouldn't creep up on people,' Gormley growled.

'Sorreee!' The DI feigned surrender, both hands in the air. 'Didn't mean to interrupt. You two sound like you're having a domestic. Like me and my lass . . . on a good day. I give her grief. She gives me earache. It's what the guv'nor calls a lively exchange of views. If I were you, I'd kiss and make up.'

'If I were you, I'd piss right off,' Gormley said.

The DI walked away grinning.

43

The saying 'walls have ears' is true of all police stations. Detectives worldwide earwig other people's conversations and take an interest in their business, invited or not. It's all intelligence gathering, after all – a skill drummed into them at training school. Once Wallace was out of earshot, Daniels checked the stairwell to make sure others weren't listening in. Two officers lurking on the floor below looked up. Seeing her peering over the top of the handrail, they scurried off, and she turned back to Gormley in time to catch his dumb idea.

'Why don't you suggest to the guv'nor that he treat Ivy's car as an absolute priority?' he said.

'Oh, that'll work!' She grabbed his arm. 'Come on.'

Entering the MIR ahead of him, she did a double take as she passed over the threshold. Naylor had completely reorganized the place. Because she had wanted to stay in touch with the A1 murder case, the idea of sharing the incident room sounded great when he had suggested it. But in reality she could see it was going to be a total nightmare: desks pushed together haphazardly, filing cabinets moved, no rhyme or reason to the arrangement. Clearly, aesthetics were not his strong point.

Carmichael flashed them a dubious look. Swivelling her

chair round to face them, she asked what they thought of their new home. It was obvious she didn't like it. Daniels didn't either, but she ignored the question.

'Is the guv'nor in, Lisa?'

'He was a moment ago.'

'Alone?'

'Last time I looked. Something wrong?'

'A bit of Feng Shui wouldn't go amiss.'

Lisa burst out laughing. 'Reminds me of the old room downstairs—'

'What's wrong with it?' Gormley interrupted. 'It's not supposed to be cosy. It's an office!'

'Well, I don't like it,' said the DCI. 'Hank, you'd better make yourself scarce. I'll let you know when you can come back out to play.'

Carmichael gave them an odd look.

'Don't ask,' Daniels said.

She went straight to her office, shut the door, and logged on to her computer. She needed some quiet time to think things through; time to come up with a strategy before she told Naylor the ugly truth that she'd gone behind his back. For once, she was delighted to see that her inbox was full of emails requiring an immediate reply. She dealt with those, then turned her attention to a hastily scribbled Post-it note from Harry Graham, the receiver: I NEED AN URGENT WORD. IT REALLY CAN'T WAIT.

Thank you, God!

But when she phoned his office, Harry told her he'd already spoken to Hank and had his question answered. Sod it, she thought, looking at her watch. Six-fifteen. Her desk

and in-tray were clear of anything resembling work. With nothing else to distract her, she went to 'fess up.

She found Naylor in his office surrounded by files. On one side of his desk was a large white binder – the ACPO Murder Investigation Manual – the office bible. He'd been brushing up, though she couldn't imagine why. What he didn't know about running a major incident she could write on a postage stamp. Propped up on one elbow, he was eating a salad from a transparent plastic bowl.

'This isn't just food,' he said. 'It's M and S food.'

Daniels smiled. His attempt at mimicking Dervla Kirwan, the voice of the Marks and Spencer ad campaign, was dreadful.

He held up the bowl. 'You're eyeing my grub. Want some?'

'Not for me thanks, guv.'

'No appetite for good food? You'd better sit down then. It must be serious.'

He knew her too well.

'I'm not hungry,' she said. Her stomach rumbled audibly.

'Doesn't sound like it.' Chasing a cherry tomato around the salad bowl, he eventually managed to spike it with a white plastic fork and popped it into his mouth whole. 'Is there something specific I can help you with? Pull up a perch.'

'I was wondering how Ivy's case is going.' She remained standing, acting like she was just passing the time of day – normal office chat. 'Got any definite leads yet?'

'Eh?' Naylor carried on eating. 'I know I'm good, Kate. But I'm no miracle worker. How did you get on?'

'Maggie Reid's alibi collapsed. I need to interview her again.' She rubbed at the back of her neck, playing for time,

feeling hot and hoping it didn't show. Then she lost her bottle altogether as guilt crept into the equation. Naylor wasn't just her boss. He was a good mate too and had been for as long as she could remember. She smiled weakly. 'I'd . . . better get on.'

She hadn't reached the door when his voice caught up with her. 'This got anything to do with what you found in Ivy's car?' he asked.

With her back to him, she froze. Pressing her lips tightly together, she turned to face him. His eyes were smiling – a good sign, she thought – then they weren't. She found she couldn't read him. There was an awkward silence for a moment. Out of the corner of her left eye, she caught movement in the office outside. Carmichael's cheeky face popped up at the internal window, then Brown's, Maxwell's and finally Robson's, fanning out like cards. They were doubled up laughing.

Daniels blushed as they walked away. Anticipating a bollocking, she tried to find a reasonable explanation for involving herself in *his* case. Direct disobedience of an order was a situation she'd been in before and one she'd vowed never to repeat. On the last occasion it had been a different boss, but all the same . . . Here she was again, keeping things from her guv'nor, digging herself a bloody big hole. Why oh why couldn't she play it straight for once?

'Pull another stunt like that and I'll be forced to put you on the naughty step,' Naylor said.

'I won't, Ron. I promise.' She sat down and pulled her chair closer to his desk. 'You're not going to believe what I found—'

Her attempt to leave Gormley out of it failed.

'I know exactly what you found and who you were with when you found it. But don't you worry. The B Team will sort it.'

Daniels cringed. That bastard Wallace had grassed them up. 'We really *were* rumbled, weren't we?'

'Spectacularly.'

The guv'nor sat back in his chair, enjoying himself at her expense. Same old Naylor she'd known at training school: happy to roll with the punches and not averse to bending the rules himself.

'Where is the big man anyway?' he asked.

'Powdering his nose.'

'Is that a euphemism for hiding?'

'Something like that, but under my direction. Guv, please leave Hank out of this. I take full responsibility.' Her plea brought no response. The result of the postcode search barged its way into her head: *Camelot Group plc*, an address at Tolpits Lane, Watford, Hertfordshire. She was desperate that Naylor take immediate action. 'You going to get on to Lottery HQ? Winners are the only ones who make that trip.'

His triumph dissolved. 'Carmichael's already been on to them.'

'And?'

'There were five winning jackpot tickets on Wednesday night. Only one was bought in the north-east. All winners have been authenticated and prizes paid out.'

'Already?' Daniels was shocked. 'Surely not?'

''Fraid so. A cool 1.1 million each.'

Daniels whistled. 'We're not looking for someone who just

searched a bag and found a lottery ticket, are we? Not if they knew where it was bought and when. And they had to have done, to make a claim without raising suspicion—'

'Indeed,' Naylor said. 'Ivy must've told her attacker everything.'

'Silly, silly woman . . .' Daniels paused. 'Which also means she trusted them. Either that or she was forced to reveal the information under duress. What can Camelot tell us?'

'Not a great deal. They have contacted the winners. Four are happy to talk to us if we can guarantee discretion. Their identities are obviously a closely guarded secret and they are anxious not to have personal details disclosed to the media—'

'That's a given, guv. And the fifth? I assume that's the winner from this region.'

Nodding, he glanced at a sheet of paper on his desk. 'Jennifer Rankin: tall, mid to late twenties, redhead, described as well dressed and respectable with looks to go with her newfound wealth. She produced everything they asked for: when and where the winning ticket was purchased; the fact that she used the same numbers every week, as well as passport, driving licence, rent documents, utility bills and bank account details. She had the lot, Kate. There was nothing suspicious about her.'

The Super leaned back in his seat, placed his elbows on the arms of his chair, linking his long fingers, his eyes sending her a message that there was more to it than that. Daniels had seen that look before. If she was reading him right, she figured that the news wasn't good.

'I'm nearly afraid to ask,' she said.

'Rankin declined assistance with money management, opting for no publicity. Winners are offered an advisory panel of legal and financial experts but she wasn't having any of that. She told Camelot staff that she was an entrepreneur with her own team of financial advisors who'd take care of that side of things for her.'

'I bet she did. The money transfer went through?'

'Worse than that. The cash has since been transferred again and again from the destination account to offshore accounts all over the knot end. Ones that have been set up for months. Rankin's address is an empty flat. Andy said it hasn't been lived in for months.'

'Fuck!' Daniels' jaw tightened. 'It's totally clean?'

''Fraid so.'

That meant only one thing.

They had a major player on their hands.

44

Daniels was confused. She'd had the motive for Ivy Kerr's murder pegged as an opportunist theft. But if the money was being transferred from account to account all over the world, who the hell was she dealing with? Mulling this thought over, she made her way to her office. Detectives were already putting the MIR back to normal – *thank God* – before the mother of all briefings Naylor had scheduled for later. With three murders to solve, the next few days and possibly weeks would be taxing for all concerned.

Those who knew she'd been rumbled by Naylor grinned at her as she walked by, grins she was certain would evaporate when she told them there was no longer even a small chance of them watching England's next World Cup game, due to be televised tomorrow. Gormley had come out of hiding. He was standing near his desk looking sheepish. It was clear that he knew Naylor had been wise to them all along, turning the tables on Daniels, payback for trying to pull a fast one. She rolled her eyes as she approached him, flicking her head in the direction of her office. He scooped up his mobile phone and followed her in, shutting her door behind him.

'Lisa filled you in?' she asked.

He nodded and sat down.

'Does it make sense to you?'

'None at all . . .' Gormley took off his tie. 'I assume we're back in the mix?'

Daniels nodded. 'All hands on deck for both incidents. He can justify that to Bright, now we're no longer suspects. Lottery HQ confirmed that a young posh bird collected Ivy's win.'

'Ah, that *does* makes sense . . .' Gormley kept a straight face. 'Young bird rules me out totally. And posh? Well, need I say more?'

'This is serious, Hank. The money trail could take months.' Crossing her legs, Daniels leaned back in her chair. 'The woman calls herself Jennifer Rankin, but I'm betting that's an alias. What was the name of the guy who called in the accident? David somebody?'

'Healey? Hedley? Something like that—'

'I think we should start with him and go from there.'

'Why?'

'It's as good a place as any.'

'You said it was a woman collected the win.'

'Yeah, well, maybe our Mr Healey or whatever his name is has a girlfriend. Apart from the walking wounded, he was the only person on the scene until the first responders arrived. I'll put Lisa on it. I'd like you to find that other little scrote: the one we spoke to at the scene, the film buff, remember him? Steven with a v, not a p h.' Her mobile rang. She fumbled in her jacket pocket with the intention of silencing it, then changed her mind and decided to take the call. 'DCI Daniels.'

'It's PC Dixon, B Rota, West Area Command. You wanted to speak to me, ma'am?'

'Hold on a second . . .' She covered the phone with her hand. 'Sorry, I need to take this, Hank. Can you make sure the room is put back exactly as it was before Naylor's re-organization? I know it's an office, but I can't possibly work in there.'

Gormley nodded, got to his feet and headed out, leaving her to take the call. Of all the times, this was probably the worst for PC Dixon to ring her. She had a double arson to solve and now Ivy Kerr's murder too. But she'd promised Elliot Milburn she'd look into his grandfather's missing money and felt duty bound to follow it through.

'PC Dixon?'

Dixon answered in the affirmative.

'I need to see you ASAP.'

'About?'

'Anything I damn well please!' she barked.

There was a short pause.

'Sorry, ma'am. I mean, is there a problem?'

'I'll explain when you get here . . .' Logging on to her computer, she listened as the anxious constable made all sorts of excuses why he couldn't get there. He was beginning to irritate her. 'No, *now*! . . . Don't worry about that, OK? I've already cleared it with him. Take my word for it.'

Ending the call abruptly, she pulled up the accident report. David Hedley had called the incident in on a mobile phone. Making a few notes she went back to find Carmichael in the MIR, checking the murder wall for any news as she entered the room. On the right side of the digital screen there was a box – a screen within a screen – a kind of newsflash arrange-ment that flagged up new developments so that no member

of the Murder Investigation Team missed anything significant if they'd been conducting enquiries out of the office.

Nothing was listed.

Scanning the room, she found Carmichael back in her usual spot. Sensing Daniels' gaze, Lisa glanced up attentively, looking fresh and alert, despite having been at work since the crack of dawn. Her inclusion in the team had a made a real difference. She was well liked by everyone, especially on days she brought in her famous lemon drizzle cake, as she had done that morning. The empty plate on her desk was evidence of that – not a crumb in sight.

'I want you to interview David Hedley,' Daniels said. 'Be subtle about it though, Lisa. We've got nothing on him, but I checked the PNC and he's got form. The 999 call came in from his mobile. I want to know if he rang from his flat or from the road. The background noise from the control-room recording will probably tell us that, but be sure to ask him anyway.'

'OK . . .' Carmichael tapped on her keyboard to bring up David Hedley's address, scribbled it down on a Post-it note and shoved it in her pocket. Collecting the keys to her 3 series Beamer, she stood up. 'Anything else you're after – specifically, I mean?'

'Yeah, try and find out if he recalls seeing Ivy's car or anyone around it. And ask if he's in a relationship. I'd like you to report back at the evening briefing, so don't hang about. Just get what we need and get back here.' Daniels thought for a moment, while the young DC gathered her things together. 'You're into films, aren't you, Lisa?'

'I go to the Tyneside Theatre a lot, if that's what you mean.'

'You know much about writers? I'm thinking scriptwriters in particular.'

'Not much . . . I know of one group that meets at the Lit and Phil once a month. A mate of mine goes occasionally. Northern Screenwriters, I think they're called, but don't quote me on that.'

'Would such a group operate on Twitter and Facebook, sites like that?'

'Absolutely. Why?'

'There was a film buff at the scene. He was a bit of a weirdo, excited rather than horrified by the spectacle. He told Hank he was a film maker. A writer/director, I think he said. I want him checked out discreetly. When you get back, give your mate a call. Ask around. See if anyone knows him. His name and address are on the system. When you've done that, tell Andy to get over there and take a full statement. I want the clothes he was wearing seized and any stills he took. He had a camera with him.'

'Consider it done.'

Daniels returned to her office. Ten minutes later, Gormley was back, this time with a red-faced PC Dixon in tow. He was in his mid-thirties, older than she expected for someone not long out of training school, an officer with obvious potential, according to his supervision. He looked like a poster boy for the force as he assumed the position on the opposite side of her desk, almost standing to attention as if he were on parade. He was extremely nervous. Something to hide, she wondered, or anxious about being questioned by a senior detective he hadn't met before?

More like a Spinetti than a Dixon, the probationary con-

stable had chiselled features, olive skin and smoky eyes. He wore his jet-black hair slicked back off his forehead and seemed immensely proud of his immaculate uniform. Her eyes slid over it, taking in his bulled shoes and pressed shirt. His uniform trousers had been taken in a little further than regulations allowed, showing off his toned physique, no doubt adding to his pulling power.

Reminded of her mother's meticulous care over her own uniform, Daniels guessed Dixon still lived at home and hoped to God she was wrong about him.

She got straight to the point: 'PC Dixon, a serious allegation has been made. A considerable amount of money has gone missing from an old man you rendered assistance to on Thursday morning following his collapse in the street.'

The absence of a reaction troubled Daniels. Her eyes left the rookie, settling on Gormley, who took that as his cue to speak.

'Constable Dixon? Do you have anything to say?'

Dixon pointed at his chest. 'Allegation against me?'

'Do you *know* anything about it?' Daniels was irritated.

The PC shook his head. 'I did assist the old guy. Gave him mouth-to-mouth, actually. How could I forget? It was my first time. He was barely alive when he went in the ambulance. It was only later that I heard he didn't make it. I didn't see any money though.'

'Did you search him for ID?' Gormley asked.

'No!' Dixon's eyes flitted back and forth between the two detectives. 'I was too busy and, to be honest, I had no need to. There was this gobby cow standing over me the whole time. She knew who he was and where he lived. She was with him when I arrived.'

Guilty people often try and shift the blame. Daniels wondered if that was what Dixon was doing or if he was telling it straight. Time would tell, she supposed. The truth almost always came out in the end. She pushed a little further . . .

'This gobby cow? She the one called the control room?'

Dixon shrugged. 'Dunno.'

Gormley tutted. 'Did you get a *name*?'

'No, sorry . . .' The PC was sweating. 'Look, she refused to give it to me. I know I should've insisted, but I was in a hurry to get back to your crime scene. I was supposed to be guarding it . . .' He looked at Daniels. 'That's how come I was first to respond when the call came on the radio. I was right there, y'know. I did what I could and then let the ambulance crew get on with it.'

'What did the girl look like?' Daniels asked.

'She was a tart, boss. Short skirt, lots of slap and bling. She had a tattoo of a seahorse on her upper arm, if that's any use to you. She lives close by, I know that much. She's been hanging around the crime scene, talking to the press and stuff.' Dixon came over all apologetic. 'I wasn't away from the crime scene long, ma'am.'

'That's not important.' Daniels was quiet for a moment. 'You did the right thing and used your initiative. Making accurate judgements is what being a copper is all about. That's what I want you to do now. Do you understand?'

'Not sure I do, ma'am.'

'Let me put it another way then. What you do and say in relation to this matter is vitally important to your future in the police force . . .' Her eyes never left his. '*Now*, do we understand each other?'

Dixon nodded, his face frozen with fear.

'OK . . .' Daniels searched for the right words, ones she hoped might elicit the truth. Ones that stopped short of a direct accusation. 'Did you take possession of anything for safekeeping when you attended George Milburn?'

'I don't like what you're implying, ma'am.'

Gormley intervened. 'We're not *implying* anything.'

Daniels sighed. Gormley's timing was off. He'd reacted a little too quickly for her liking. She'd have preferred to let the officer sweat a moment longer. She stared at Dixon, trying to read him. Anxiety and guilt were often difficult to separate when accusations were being made. He certainly looked uncomfortable, but then so would she in similar circumstances. That didn't mean he'd done anything wrong. The burden of proof was on her.

'It's a simple enough question,' she said, finally. 'One that requires an answer.'

'No, boss.' Dixon eyeballed her, a flash of anger creeping in. 'I *didn't* take possession of any items for safekeeping, *never* saw any money and *wouldn't* have touched it if I had. I can assure you, I—'

'Thank you,' Daniels said. 'You can go.'

Dixon didn't move, despite the dismissal.

'That'll be all,' Gormley said.

The constable stared at them both, then turned on his heels and left the room, not bothering to close the door behind him. They watched him walk the length of the incident room, no haste in his step, his head held high. He didn't look back, just let himself out through the door at the far end.

Daniels tapped her teeth with her pen. 'What do you reckon?'

'Hard to say.' Gormley looked at his watch. 'Tell me to wind my neck in, but with three murders on the slate, have we got time for this?'

'We're making time, Hank. I gave my word to Elliot Milburn. If that means working even later than usual, then so be it. There's something fishy going on here and I've got a feeling it's about more than a few missing pound notes.'

'You telling me the old man's death wasn't coincidental?'

'You already theorized that he set the fire—'

'Which you rubbished, as I recall! Look, I changed my mind, OK? Everything Elliot told me about Milburn points to him being a decent old man—'

'What if he saw who set the fire, Hank? What if he was being paid to keep his mouth shut? Elliot thinks the money was his granddad's life savings, but we've only got his word for it. It may not have been.'

'Anything's possible, I suppose.'

'I entirely accept his death was from natural causes. Stanton's clear on that score. There was no evidence whatso-ever that he was mugged. Assuming for one moment that he *did* see the arsonist and was paid for his silence, maybe the stress of it all is what killed him. Maybe the arsonist took her money back.'

'The girl with the tat you mean?'

Daniels just looked at him.

45

It had to be said, they weren't feeling the love. Chantelle Fox had refused them entry at first, until Gormley used his own gentle powers of persuasion, pushing past her into the house while she demanded to see his non-existent search warrant. There was a nauseating smell in the room, an odour Daniels couldn't easily identify. It was sweet, like baby sick. Surreptitiously, she popped a mint in her mouth to mask the stench.

Chantelle rounded on them. 'I called the ambo, yeah. But that's all!' The girl's eyes shifted back and forth between the two detectives and then she restated her innocence. 'There was no one near him when he went down, I swear! So it was either the copper or the medics that robbed the old bastard. Don't try pinnin' it on me! I might be shite but I'm honest shite.'

'Oh yeah?' Gormley questioned. 'Like father like daughter, I heard.'

His comments only served to wind her up. 'You've got the cuffs on me already, haven't you?' The girl's voice grated on her visitors' ears, like chalk across a blackboard. 'Well you're not putting me in the cells. No way, José! If my arsehole of a father taught me one thing it was to be sure you can get out the back when you got a knock at the front door. Only I didn't run, did I? Know why?'

'Because I stuck my size ten in the door before you slammed it in our faces?' It was a rhetorical question from Gormley. 'We could get a warrant, if you insist.'

'No! I didn't run 'cause I've nowt to hide!'

Daniels ran her eyes over the girl. Not only did she sound like her old man but there was a physical resemblance too. The same pale complexion and gap in her front teeth. The same big mouth, both literally and figuratively. Arthur Fox was a well-known villain, a prolific thief, philanderer, an all-round waste of space she'd locked up on numerous occasions. He died in a fatal car accident when he was forty-nine years old. Tampering was suspected but never proved, because of the poor condition of the car, which had worn tyres and dodgy brakes. He certainly had enemies though.

Daniels glanced at the seahorse tattoo on Chantelle's arm.

'Take a good look, why don't ya?' The girl stopped chewing the skin around her right thumb and wiped her hand on her tight-fitting dress. She checked her watch. 'Fuck! I'm going to miss my bus now!'

'They run every ten minutes,' Gormley said. 'We're not finished with you yet.'

'Oh, I get it. I don't stand a hope in hell, do I? Your lot always close ranks when someone gets caught with their fingers in the till . . .' Chantelle picked up a thick black patent-leather belt from a side table. Clipping it round her waist, she slipped on shoes to match, a woeful attempt at the 'wow' factor. The five-inch heels gave the impression that she'd have to work really hard to avoid toppling over. Keen to hit the party city, she looked in the mirror, checking her appearance, teasing out dull, lifeless hair which she covered

in a foul-smelling spray until every last strand was glued to the next. Then she turned to face them. 'It's my word against his, right? Yeah, that'll work. Tell you what, you bring the thieving git here and I'll get the truth out of him.'

Daniels tried not to get angry: bent coppers were scum as far as she was concerned. They gave decent officers a bad name and turned the public against them. If Dixon had done wrong, she'd take great pleasure in stripping him of his pristine uniform and putting him before a court of law. No ifs, buts or maybes – he'd get what was coming to him.

'You listening to me?' Chantelle carped. 'I'm not having it, OK? So you can fuck off and find yourselves another patsy. Anyway, do I look like I've got money?'

Daniels scanned the room. Despite the odious smell, which she still couldn't identify, it was a tidy house filled with bright-coloured fabrics and no clutter. Ikea influence, she thought. Apart from the carpet, which was old and worn, everything in the living room looked new, perhaps a little too new. The furniture seemed odd and it took her a moment to figure out why. There was a definite symmetry to it all, as if it had been deliberately staged. Cushions plumped up on a sofa that had never been sat on. Celebrity magazines scattered across a coffee table artificially, as if a tape measure had been used to align them just so – *Hello*, *OK*, *Grazia* and *Look* among them.

'You are some nosy cow!' Chantelle bellowed, lifting a sparkly bag off the floor. 'I know what you're thinking, but you're wrong. I won a few quid on the lottery, that's all.'

Daniels and Gormley exchanged a look, mention of the lottery worrying them both.

'How much is a few quid?' Gormley said.

'Two-fifty, not that it's any business of yours.'

'Thousand?' Daniels asked.

'Yeah, right!' Chantelle cracked up. 'Call yourselves coppers? People round here would kill for less.'

Gormley glared at her. 'That's an unfortunate choice of words.'

'Didn't mean nothin' by it,' the girl said. 'Hey! What you accusing me of now?'

'Calm down, Chantelle.' Daniels tucked her hair behind her ear, logging the girl's anxiety. She would hardly have mentioned the lottery if she'd had anything to do with Ivy's death. She might be from a long line of wasters but the one thing she wasn't was stupid. 'I take it you meant two *hundred* and fifty?'

Cocking a sneer at Gormley, Chantelle nodded.

'Any proof?' he pushed.

'You never give up, do you?' Chantelle applied her lippy in the mirror, glowering at Gormley's reflection as she did so. Then she swung round to face him. 'Ask at the Paki shop, the one on the corner . . .' She thumbed to the right. 'It's their biggest win this year. I'm a bit of a celeb round here, as it happens. Now if you don't mind, sling your hook!'

Daniels walked into the hallway, her eyes seizing on a dark baseball cap hanging on a peg near the door. It had no motif and was similar to the one worn by the shy man or woman Maxwell had drawn her attention to, the one buying petrol from a garage nearby. She turned towards Chantelle, sizing her up, wondering if she could have been that figure.

'Where d'you buy your petrol?' she asked.

'There's only one place you buy petrol round here. Down the road at the Shell garage.'

Shell, eh? Daniels opened the front door. 'Cheers. We might need to see you again.'

'Not if I see you first.'

Daniels smiled and stepped outside.

Gormley followed her out, flinching as the door slammed behind them. 'That was a lowballer,' he said.

'Just thought I'd throw it in . . .' Daniels looked across the street where crime-scene tape flapped in the breeze outside Maggie Reid's house, the windows all boarded up to keep the local kids out. Then she glanced at Chantelle's front door. 'She's hiding something, Hank. I don't know what it is, but I can spot a liar when I see one. That mark there . . .' She pointed at a black smudge on the wall. 'That's where I got the cigarette butt I sent off for forensic testing.'

'You think she's the arsonist?'

Daniels' expression was impenetrable. 'I think we need that result.'

46

DC Lisa Carmichael knocked at the door and waited. There was music coming from inside the flat, Snow Patrol: 'Chasing Cars'. Great choice. She had the album herself and liked it a lot. The door was opened by a thin wiry man, mid twenties, dressed casually in combats and a faded T-shirt. His hair was wet and he smelled of good aftershave.

'David Hedley?' Carmichael showed ID.

The man nodded. 'This about the accident?'

'Yes, I need to ask you a few questions, if it's convenient.'

'OK.' Hedley opened the door a little wider but not quite wide enough for her to squeeze through. 'If it's not a daft question, what's a murder detective got to do with a car crash?'

Carmichael was impressed. Not many folks bothered to look closely at police identification, despite repeated warnings in the press to do so. They just saw the shiny badge and assumed it was genuine. Most had never heard of the offence of impersonating a police officer.

She pointed into the flat. 'Can we talk inside?'

Hedley took a step backwards, allowing her in this time, killing his iPod as he followed her into the living room. Carmichael was immediately drawn to the window. She walked towards it and looked down at the A1 trunk road. It

was busy in both directions, cars nose to tail on the north-bound carriageway, the route to the best beaches in the country in the opinion of anyone who'd ever seen the Northumberland coast. Mile after mile of golden, empty sand, the county's – possibly even the country's – best-kept secret.

Carmichael wished she was joining them.

On both sides of the road were POLICE ACCIDENT signs, asking witnesses to come forward. More or less routine after a fatal. On the grass verge, there were some wilted bouquets, and on the southern carriageway someone had placed a makeshift cross. It was sticking out of the ground, waiting to impale the next poor motorcyclist unlucky enough to come off their bike there.

Did people ever stop to think?

'I told the accident investigators everything I could remember,' Hedley said as he came and stood alongside her, sighing loudly, staring down at the traffic below. 'What is it you want to know?'

Carmichael hesitated long enough to put him on edge. 'Your statement—'

He glanced sideways. 'What about it?'

'You were first to arrive at the scene. Is that right?'

Hedley nodded, his left eye twitching.

'How long did it take for the emergency services to arrive?'

Staring off into the distance, a sad expression crossed Hedley's face as he searched for an answer, reliving a memory she suspected he'd rather forget. It took him some time to speak. 'Five minutes maybe. Felt like hours . . .' When he looked back at her, his eyes were misted up. 'It was mayhem on both sides of the road. I didn't know what to do.'

'I understand,' Carmichael said gently.

'Do you? I don't think so. It's different for you. You've had training and stuff.' He dropped his gaze, fighting to hide his feelings. 'I felt so helpless. I don't suppose I'll ever repeat the experience, but I've signed up for a first-aid course in case. I never want to feel like that again.'

Carmichael allowed him a moment to compose himself.

'What do you do for a living, Mr Hedley?' she said eventually.

Hedley pulled himself out of his trance. 'I work for the local authority Parks Department. Boring administration, but someone has to do it. That's why I took up astronomy.' He pointed to a large telescope aimed at the sky through the picture window. 'There's nowt new on the box these days and it's a fascinating subject. Keeps *me* occupied, anyway. Means getting up in the middle of the night but I don't mind that. I've always been a light sleeper and this recent heat-wave hasn't helped. There was nowt to see Wednesday night . . .' He lifted his eyes to the sky. 'Up there, I mean. I was on my way back to bed when I heard a loud bang. Now I can't sleep at all.'

'Isn't it too light here to get a good look at the stars?' Carmichael asked.

Hedley suddenly perked up, pleased that his visitor was taking an interest. 'Are you an enthusiast, yourself?'

Carmichael shook her head. 'Not personally, but I do know a little about it.'

'Figures . . .' For the first time since Carmichael arrived, Hedley managed a smile. 'The subject bores the pants off most people. When I talk about it to colleagues at work I can

see their eyes glazing over. Doesn't bother me though. They don't know what they're missing.'

Carmichael smiled back. 'I have an uncle who's really into it. Has been for years. He lives in the sticks, near Kielder.'

'Lucky man.' Hedley paused. 'Did you know it's the darkest place in Europe? There's an observatory up there, open to the public. You should check it out. It's absolutely magic. Unfortunately I don't have the means to move and commute fifty miles a day to indulge my hobby. Who does these days?'

The person who stole an old lady's lottery ticket might. Carmichael forced another smile. She scanned the living room; a man's taste, she thought. 'Do you live here alone?'

Hedley nodded, his enthusiasm fading.

'No girlfriend round that night?'

'No girlfriend, period.'

'Any recording facilities – for the stargazing, I mean?'

'No, why?'

'No reason . . . I know this must be difficult for you when all you want to do is forget, but I'd like you to cast your mind back. I'm interested in one car in particular: a Honda Jazz with an elderly driver and front-seat passenger. Can you recall seeing that vehicle?'

Hedley shook his head. 'Doesn't ring any bells.'

'Maybe I can help you.' Carmichael pulled a diagram from her bag. Unravelling it, she took it to Hedley's dining table and flattened it out, holding the ends down with her car keys and phone. 'Your flat is here, with a good view of the carriageway obviously.' She pointed to one particular spot. 'Front door is here. How did you make your way to the roadside?'

'That way –' Hedley indicated the north side of the building. 'Out the front door, across the mound here. I scaled the fence. There's no other way. It has to be blocked off in case the little kids run on to the road.'

'And that's when you dialled 999?' She watched him closely for a reaction.

'No, I did that from here. Soon as I could. Then I grabbed some clothes and legged it. I'm afraid to say I froze when I got there.'

Hedley's expression darkened as he relived the nightmare again in all its gory detail: the blood, the despair, the terrible injuries sustained by the casualties. Carmichael knew that some of them had been horrendous, even in the opinion of the most hardened of professionals. It had only been a few days since the accident but she'd heard on the grapevine that one fire officer had gone sick with post-traumatic stress. Emergency services personnel who'd attended the scene were still talking about it. Gormley, on the other hand, wouldn't. And she couldn't fathom why.

'I'm sorry . . .' Hedley said, regaining her attention. 'I'm absolutely useless with blood. Always was. I saw this bloke with an arm missing, staggering along the road, a stream of blood gushing, squirting from . . .' He shuddered and closed his eyes – a genuine reaction, she thought. 'I'm sorry, after that I hardly remember a thing.'

Carmichael nodded. It must've been a hell of a thing to see in the middle of the night. She imagined Hedley in his pyjamas, looking down on the scene from the window, maybe not hearing their screams but seeing their pain, sharing their shock.

'The man you saw did survive,' she reassured him. 'And that's probably down to you.'

Carmichael knew that the badly injured man's car was one of the first vehicles Hedley would've come across if he joined the road at the point he described. And Ivy's car was metres away. Was he telling her the truth? Daniels had alluded to a conviction for deception. But did Hedley have the capacity for violence? Did he have it in him to whack an old lady over the head for a lottery ticket?

In all honesty, she couldn't say.

She decided to leave it there for now.

47

Daniels was really pissed off. Her day had begun so well having breakfast with Jo but had since turned into a 'mare. They'd not spent quality time together for ages. Hadn't been able to catch up before Gormley's call dragged her away, let alone finish talking about something they'd both been dancing round for weeks. When they last spoke privately, Jo had dropped a bombshell: she'd been offered a secondment in a local prison to work alongside a friend she'd gone to university with. The psychiatrist, Martin Stamp, had asked her to join him on a research programme studying the characteristics of serious sex offenders and the effects of custody upon them – a subject close to her heart.

In Daniels' considered opinion there was an easy answer to that: sex offenders were a waste of space. They hardly ever admitted culpability and didn't like being locked up. What was to research? And who the fuck wanted to work in a prison anyway?

Staring blankly out of her window, she wondered whether Jo would accept the job and hoped to God she wouldn't. The programme was due to start at the end of the year and would last for twelve months. The psychologist originally chosen for the project had baled. Emily McCann – a lovely woman Daniels and Jo both knew personally – had recently lost her

husband and didn't feel able to take it on in addition to a demanding caseload. And who could blame her? She'd not only lost the love of her life, but she had a teenage daughter at home grieving the loss of her father and giving her mother a seriously hard time.

Daniels sighed.

If Jo took Emily's place it would mean suspending her work with Northumbria Police. For personal reasons, Daniels had tried to talk her out of it. But she knew that if Jo's mind was made up, there wasn't a hope in hell of changing it. She could be as stubborn as two-year-old when she wanted to be. The only saving grace was that she wouldn't be moving away.

Grateful for small mercies, Daniels scooped up her phone to call her. Her finger hovered over the call button for a second. Then she hit the return key and chucked the phone on her desk, deciding that what she had to say was best said in person.

Or was it?

In her back yard earlier, she'd wimped out. With the warmth of the sun on their faces and the faint smell of suntan lotion in the air, they were having such a good time, it felt like they were still together. It was magical while it lasted. Not wanting to spoil the moment, Daniels had avoided the thorny subject of Jo's leaving, hoping it would sort itself out – which, of course, it was never going to. Finally Jo had broached the matter herself, but then duty called and Daniels had to leave in a hurry.

Same old, same old.

Daniels felt guilty now, an emotion that turned to depression as a horrible thought dawned on her. If Jo was getting

itchy feet, maybe the research project would lead to other positions that would take her away from Newcastle for good. When she'd come into Daniels' life, never in her wildest dreams did she imagine her leaving again. *But now* . . . Picking up the phone once more, she dialled that all-important number and waited.

Jo picked up on the third ring.

Dispensing with a cheery Hello, it's me, or even Hiya, Daniels decided that this was no time for small talk. She went straight for the jugular. 'Will you at least think about what I said this morning?'

'You said something this morning?' Jo was teasing her. 'I was under the impression you were checking me out when you thought I wasn't looking. Could be wrong, but I was half expecting you to rip my clothes off right there in the yard. I seem to recall you have previous for it.'

Daniels laughed. She had this thing about getting up close and personal in the open air and remembered the experience vividly. Thankfully her neighbours both sides were away on holiday at the time. Other memories crowded in on her: making love in the middle of an oilseed rape field at dusk; on an empty beach in Crete, unaware that an ocean liner had sailed into the bay and dropped anchor. The expression on Jo's face when she sat up and saw several pairs of binoculars trained on them was priceless.

'I'm serious, Jo. I don't want to lose you.'

That sounded so lame.

'There are other profilers,' Jo said.

'Not like you, there aren't.'

'Are we still speaking professionally?'

There was a short pause. Jo was angry and had a damn good right to be. Had they been in the same room, Daniels would have reached out, taken her in her arms and begged her not to go, or at least tried to say something that would make her stay.

'Remember what I said to you, first time I took you to Hartside Pass?' she said.

The line went dead.

Daniels sighed. Hartside Pass was her fuck-off destination, her favourite place in the whole wide world, a place where she went to mull stuff over and get things into perspective. A wilderness in the middle of nowhere, long since abandoned to the elements. A summit from where it was possible to see right across the Solway Firth to Scotland, as well as Great Gable and Skiddaw in the Lakes. A place she only ever visited alone.

With one exception.

Redialling, she willed Jo to answer.

She picked up, but didn't speak.

Daniels took a deep breath and tried again.

'Please don't hang up. Just tell me you remember . . .' An icy silence followed. 'OK, then don't. Just believe me when I say that I meant what I said, Jo – every word of it.'

'You ready to share that with anyone else?'

Daniels looked at the ceiling. This was so difficult for her. She had vowed to win Jo back, whatever it took. But she was asking such a lot. Asking her to give up the chance of making it to the very top of a career she'd poured her life and soul into. No matter how many people told her otherwise, she couldn't – wouldn't – risk jeopardizing that. In a blinding

flash she realized she wasn't ready to make their relationship public and probably never would be.

'That's what I thought.' Jo's words were clipped. 'You're full of shit, you know that?'

'What do you want me to say? That our break-up is down to me? That I'm willing to accept responsibility for it? I do. It's *all* my fault. Don't you think I know that? Don't you think I wake up alone every morning wishing things were back the way they were?' Daniels paused. 'I'm crazy about you.'

'That's never been the issue.'

'Exactly! So what does it matter who knows, who doesn't?'

'It matters, OK? I'm not living my life as your secret!' A phone rang in the background. Jo's get-out-of-jail card. 'Look, Kate, I've got to go.'

'Don't hang up! Listen, you'd hate being locked up in a prison. You've always said so. Imagine having to be there every single day. It'll drive you insane. Besides, who else would I argue with?'

'I haven't yet accepted the post – not that it's any of your business.'

Jo excused herself and hung up. Daniels sat for a long moment, realizing she'd made matters ten times worse. She pocketed her phone and stood up. It was time for the evening briefing.

48

Detectives from several departments were milling around the MIR, anxious to get the briefing underway. Even civilian indexers whose hours matched those of the Murder Investigation Team were in attendance, despite grafting since the crack of dawn. They all looked jaded, keen to get the meeting over and done with so they could go home. Daniels knew how they felt. For the second time that day, a telephone call had prevented her from explaining herself to Jo. She'd been a fool not to tackle the subject of her leaving earlier. She should've told her the truth, begged her to stay and persuaded her not take the damn job. Instead she'd reverted to type and let the matter fester, until Jo forced a confrontation. Inevitably, what Daniels *had* said had come out wrong.

It was standing room only. And still detectives piled into the room, their conversations ranging from the long hours they were keeping to England's chances of progression in the World Cup. The next game was scheduled for tomorrow, a game they now knew they'd miss 'live' on TV.

Acknowledging them as they passed her by, Daniels' mind was on promises she'd made to Jo. Empty promises, as it turned out. As people, they were poles apart. They wanted different things of a relationship. A free spirit, Jo deserved a partner she could introduce to friends and family. Daniels,

on the other hand, didn't see the need. As long as they were happy together, all the rest was unimportant. She feared being alone and craved the special kind of relationship her parents had enjoyed. But she was her own worst enemy in achieving this. Even before Jo came into her life, she'd failed to balance home and work successfully. And it wasn't only the job that was holding her back. Her father's disapproval was also eating away at her. She hadn't even told Jo about that yet.

Another secret.

God, will you ever learn?

Daniels hated that she needed her father's approval. It had taken such courage to bare her soul to him and he'd reacted as if she'd fallen in love with a woman just to piss him off. Maybe she had: payback for not being there for her when her mother died. He'd been at pains to point out the obvious: that all of her former relationships had been *normal*. That really went down well. He'd since tried apologizing, vehemently denying any homophobia on his part, citing several gay acquaintances.

She noted he didn't say *friends*.

As far as Daniels was concerned, the hurtful comments that came out of his mouth could never be unsaid. They were out there for ever and she had no intention of forgiving him. She glanced at her watch. It was already nine-thirty and the troops were getting restless. *Hardly a time for psychoanalysis.* Besides, she didn't want to think about Jo any more. It would sap what little energy she had left. No matter how much she wanted to go home and sort her life out, the job she prized so

highly kept getting in the way. And that meant leading by example with her mind focused on the job.

Later . . . I'll call her later. One more stab at explaining how she felt wouldn't go amiss.

The door to the MIR opened. Maxwell walked in, last to arrive as usual. Apologizing for keeping them all waiting, he slid into the crowd out of sight. Conversations immediately died down and all eyes were turned in Daniels' direction.

'Right, if everyone is ready, we'll begin with the fire and then move on to the A1 incident.'

A hand went up. Officers parted so she could see who it belonged to. DC Andy Brown wasn't the tallest detective in her team. He edged his way forward to stand near the front, his eagerness to contribute raising her expectations. She knew exactly what this was about before he opened his mouth, but asked the question anyway.

'You got something for me, Andy?'

Brown nodded, turning to address his colleagues. 'I was checking the force-wide incident log earlier and noticed a domestic disturbance at the home of Nadia Turner, Maggie Reid's sister-in-law. Officers from West Area Command attended the scene, reporting a row between two females. A fight ensued, but no further action was taken in view of the recent family bereavement. I just spent the last hour following it up.' He paused for breath. The room was heavy with anticipation as he took out his notebook, flipped it open and found the appropriate page. 'Maggie and Nadia were still rowing when I got there. I spent some time calming them down and then questioned Maggie about the rubber glove we recovered. The boss thought it might scare her into telling

the truth. But she didn't bat an eyelash, said she buys them in Tesco – a new pair every week.'

'She's got a point,' Robson commented. 'The wife's got some like it at home.'

Brown glanced at Daniels. 'She's still off her face on medication, boss. Had absolutely no idea what I was alluding to. I then tackled her unsafe alibi. Told her Stella Drew had coughed that they weren't together when she said they were. At this point Nadia got really agitated. I'm guessing that's what they were arguing about in the first place. She then blurted out the name of the mystery boyfriend.' He glanced at the scribbled note he'd made. 'A man by the name of Charles Milburn, known locally as Charlie.'

Milburn? Mention of the name set alarms bells ringing in Daniels' head. Gormley had homed in on it too. They glanced at one another, hoping that Brown had stumbled on a break in the case.

'Is he local?' Daniels asked.

'Very . . .' Brown scanned his notes. 'Unemployed welder, forty-five, married with one son, lives less than two streets from the crime scene. Bit of a hard man, by all accounts. He's been pulled in a time or two.'

'How old is the son?' Gormley queried.

Brown's enthusiasm wavered. 'Didn't ask. Sorry.'

'You got a name though?' Daniels pushed. 'For the son, I mean.'

The tension and urgency in her voice made Brown and the rest of the Murder Investigation Team sit up and take notice. No one in the room – bar Gormley – had a clue why the son might be of interest to her. Brown shook his head, tripping

over himself to apologize again. He glanced frantically at Carmichael and gave her an address. Her fingers were already on the keyboard. The room fell silent as she accessed the council's electoral role. Milburn was a common name up north. Daniels had relatives so called. But she had a feeling that this particular Milburn might be highly significant. From the start, an old man's sudden death in the same street as her crime scene had played on her mind. If her instincts were right, then Maggie Reid was seeing the old man's son – Elliot Milburn's father, Charlie.

A few seconds later, Carmichael confirmed it.

Daniels was silent for a moment, considering this new information. Then she swung into action, outlining what she knew about the Milburn family so far. She left nothing out, including the bad feeling between George and Charlie and, of course, the money Elliot had reported missing.

'If George Milburn had knowledge of the affair with Maggie, it gives him motive, maybe not for murder but for arson, certainly. It also explains his estrangement from his son. He lived next door. Plenty of time to nip out in the dead of night and set fire to the property. Maybe he knew Maggie was going out for the evening with Charlie and thought he'd cause them some aggro. I'm speculating here, but he might even have known the child was due to stay with his father.' Daniels glanced again at Gormley. 'Hank had a theory that the old man might somehow have been involved. Initially, I thought it a bit far-fetched, but it looks like he may very well be right.'

'No one likes a smart arse,' someone said.

A ripple of laughter went round the room.

'If the old man stopped speaking to his son because of the alleged affair, maybe he did something about it and threw a wobbler when he realized his mistake had caused the death of a child,' Carmichael offered.

'That's a real possibility,' Daniels said. 'Unfortunately, dead or alive, we still need to prove the case.' She paused, before reminding them how difficult it was to do this without a live suspect to bring in for questioning. 'What I'd like to know is, why has Charles Milburn not come forward? I want him in here first thing tomorrow morning.'

49

Excusing those not involved in the second incident up for discussion, Daniels thanked everyone and broke off the meeting to allow the rest a ten-minute break in which to stretch their legs, grab a coffee, or have a quick fag. The fire escape was the last remaining hiding place for the nicotine addicts among them since the smoking ban was imposed a few years back. Naylor and a couple of civilian indexers nipped out for a hit, the smell of cigarettes following them in as they returned to the MIR.

With the arson filed away, for the time being, their thoughts were entirely on the A1 case as they got back down to business. With fewer bodies in the room, the temperature had dropped to an acceptable level and there was enough space for everyone to sit comfortably. Robson, who had interviewed Ivy Kerr's only daughter, was first up. He looked positively upbeat as he began précising what he now knew and the rest of the team didn't.

'Annaliese Ridley is a sixty-eight-year-old retired head teacher. Really nice woman. Totally shattered by her parents' deaths and still in shock, as anyone would be. She lives with her husband in Whickham . . .'

Robson's voice became lost, drowned out by thoughts running through Daniels' head. Her heart went out to the poor

woman he was describing. Losing one parent was bad. Losing two at the same time must be devastating. Although she'd never met Annaliese Ridley, she felt empathy with the woman. Daniels had lost two parents also, even though her father was still alive. They had had very little contact with each other in the past few years. She was a mug to think she could involve him in her life, and knew that he'd consider it a weakness to reach out to her now. Result? Their relationship was deadlocked: both waiting for the other to make the next move.

Robson paused for breath.

The resulting silence broke Daniels' daydream.

'Was her mother in the habit of buying lottery tickets?' she asked.

Robson nodded. 'Always at Tesco Extra at Kingston Park. Always on a Friday, the day she collected her pension. She played the same numbers every week and kept the repeat slips in a writing bureau at home so she didn't have to write them out each time. I accessed the house and found these, right where Annaliese said they'd be . . .' He raised his arm. In his hand were three credit-card-sized transparent plastic folders, familiar to almost everyone in the room. Inside were little pink tickets bearing barcodes of Ivy's chosen numbers. 'These three slips represent Wednesday, Friday and Saturday draws.' He dropped his arm down by his side. 'Our Camelot contact claims that the barcode on Wednesday's winning ticket proves *without a shadow of a doubt* that it was bought with the corresponding one of these—'

'Good work, mate!' Gormley said.

Others in the room echoed the sentiment.

Daniels was pleased to see Robson on top of his game after a period of uncertainty and a struggle to put his gambling behind him. 'I presume they were also able to ident the retailer where they were bought?'

'Time, date, the works.'

'You've requested the CCTV?'

'And sent someone out to pick it up.'

'Now we're getting somewhere.' Naylor sounded impressed.

The Super had been quiet up to that point; so quiet Daniels had forgotten he was in the room – an unlikely situation had Bright still been her guv'nor. She had great respect for both men, but their styles of leadership were poles apart. She turned her focus back to Robson, who was waiting patiently to resume.

'Anything else we need to know?' she asked.

'Only that Mr Kerr was a secretive man. Annaliese was adamant that the trip would've been his idea. She said Ivy would've been desperate to share the news of their good fortune but that her dad made the rules and her mum generally followed. It came as no surprise that he'd taken off for London without telling her where he was going. It's the way he was, apparently. Not cold exactly. Just a man who played his cards very close to his chest, a man with hidden depths.'

Gormley had a wry smile to himself. Daniels did her best to ignore it. He'd asked her earlier if she and Jo had been arguing again. It was as if he could sense it. She hated to think that she was so transparent. Gormley was the only one in the force – barring Bright – who knew of her intimate past with Jo Soulsby, her own *hidden depths*.

She moved on. 'Lisa, what's the state of play with David Hedley?'

'Lives alone, or so he says.'

'You have reason to believe otherwise?'

'Hard to say . . .' A vague expression crossed Carmichael's face. 'There were no sign of a female presence in his flat, but he was difficult to read. He seemed more than a little nervous around me—'

'It's the effect you have on all men,' Maxwell quipped. ''Specially Andy.'

Maxwell's joke drew a few sniggers and a hard look from Naylor. Regretting his indiscretion, Maxwell stuck his tongue in his cheek and looked at the floor. Andy Brown blushed, avoiding Carmichael's gaze. It was common knowledge that he liked her – more than liked her, if truth be known. Not that he'd ever have the bottle to do anything about it. He was far too shy to make the first move and Carmichael's focus was exclusively on her career. Everyone knew it and so did he. He didn't stand a chance.

Daniels eyeballed Maxwell. He had an attitude problem where female officers were concerned. He'd improved a lot in recent months but occasionally reverted to type, allowing his mouth to run away with him. Time to pull him back in line with a few choice words, let him know she was not remotely amused.

He mumbled an apology and the DCI invited Carmichael to carry on.

'Hedley *was* the first to arrive at the scene but doesn't remember Ivy's car. In fact, he doesn't remember much at all.

He seems genuinely traumatized by the things he saw. Quite raw, actually.'

Daniels understood perfectly. At one point while standing on the hard shoulder taking notes, her attention had shifted from the pad in her hand to the road beneath her feet. Rivers of blood had trickled across the camber and pooled around her sodden shoes. Not just blood either, but bits of flesh and stuff she couldn't immediately identify as human. No autopsy she could recall had been as gory, probably due to the fact that the bodies in the road were still alive – albeit, in the worse cases, barely hanging on. That was what had made it so distressing. For hours afterwards, she hadn't been able to shake those images from her head.

'So, your impression is what . . . ?' Naylor interjected. 'Hedley's on the level?'

'Honestly?' Carmichael hesitated. 'At this stage, guv, I wouldn't rule him in or out.'

'Maybe I can help?'

Daniels knew that voice.

She turned towards it, a smile appearing on her face. Stewart Cole, a handsome man of about her age, was leaning against the wall with his arms crossed over his chest. He had deep-set eyes, chiselled features and a captivating smile. He was dressed casually – jeans, trainers, police sweat shirt. It was the first time she'd seen him out of a flying suit, which these days bore the logo of the police air support unit.

He stood up straight as she addressed the floor.

'For those of you who've not been introduced, this is Stew Cole, Air Support Unit's newest recruit.' She turned back to Cole, her expectations raised. What he had to say must be

important. If not, he'd have called her instead of attending the briefing in person so late in the day. 'What you got for me, Stew?'

Cole moved towards her, taking something from his pocket. 'This is footage taken from the air following the accident.' He handed her an encrypted USB flash drive. 'The images are pretty blurred in view of the appalling conditions on Thursday morning, but I think you'll find them enlightening. I'll talk you through them if you like.'

Daniels took in the clock on the wall. It was nearly eleven. Her team were wrung out. They had been pushed to the point of exhaustion. 'In view of the hour, I think we'd best leave it till the morning. Can you get in here tomorrow, Stew? First thing would be good.'

Cole nodded. It was his day off, but what the hell.

When the meeting finally broke up it was too late to call Jo. But Daniels had a lot to feel glad about. Both briefings had gone well and she was a damn sight closer to a result than she'd been an hour and a half ago.

As the detectives filed out of the MIR, Cole and Gormley hung back. Packing up her things, Daniels turned off the lights on her way out of the door. In the dimly lit corridor, Gormley opened his mouth to speak but Cole got in first.

'Fancy a nightcap at mine?' he said.

'Careful . . .' Daniels made for the stairwell. 'You're not wearing wings now.'

It was a private joke between them. But the warning was real. As a pilot, Cole had had his fair share of attractive women falling at his feet. Some offers he'd taken up, some not. One in particular he wished he hadn't. The tryst had

landed him in a love triangle and a fight with the other man that ended in a prison sentence for Cole as well as the loss of his military career.

'Excuse me?' His brow creased. 'I don't understand. I heard your wheels got stolen.'

'My mistake.' Daniels walked on, embarrassed at having misread him.

'Besides . . .' Cole caught up with her, 'I couldn't be that lucky.'

She punched him playfully. 'You never give up, do you?'

'Give it a rest!' For once, Gormley wasn't laughing. Acting like a jealous husband, he squared up to Cole and said, 'Your patter stinks, mate. The boss is coming home with me.'

50

Gormley's blue Peugeot was parked in his favoured spot near the back door, the one he collared most days on account of the fact that, after Daniels, he was almost always first to arrive at the station. And he was the last man standing too, pretty much. From there he could make a quick getaway at a moment's notice. Though it was getting on for ten years old, the car was his pride and joy. The registration, DS 3459, was the number Julie had bought him when he made detective sergeant, when they were still very much in love – 3459 being his police number.

'Why do we do it, Hank?' Daniels said as they got in the car.

'Do what?' Gormley slammed his door shut, strapped himself in. He put his key in the ignition and fired up the engine. 'Flirt with the wrong people?'

'I wasn't flirting! Neither was he!'

'Oh yeah? He practically had his tongue down your throat!'

Daniels fastened her seat belt as he pulled hard on the wheel, swinging the car right as he reversed. Stopping briefly at the security barrier, he tapped his fingers impatiently on the steering wheel waiting for the red-and-white pole to lift. As soon as his exit was clear, he accelerated sharply, turning

left out of the car park. On the open road he put his foot down, apparently as keen as she was to get the hell away from the office for once. Even *he* had a limit. From the look of him, he'd reached it.

A couple of kids on unlit push bikes crossed the road in front of them within inches of the car. Gormley blasted his horn. They responded with wheelies along the pavement, scattering a crowd of pedestrians making their way home from a local chippy, at least one of them losing their supper as a result. Gormley scowled at the kids as he drove by.

'Give us a clue, boss. I've no idea what you're on about.'

'I meant why do we fuck with each other's lives?' Daniels said. 'Maggie and Mark Reid looked so happy in the photograph I found in his flat. Baby on the way. Everything to look forward to. Then within a few months they've separated. Moved on. Don't people ever stop to consider what they're doing these days?'

'For some the grass is always—'

'Greener, yeah I know. But it isn't, though, is it?'

Gormley glanced to his left. 'You still talking about Mark and Maggie Reid?'

Daniels went quiet. It was late. They were both too exhausted to get into a deep and meaningful. In less than seven hours they'd be making their way back to the MIR for another long shift. Tonight's briefing had signified a move in the right direction and they couldn't afford to lose momentum. If anything, they needed to up their game.

They drove the rest of the way in silence, no more than a ten-minute ride. Pulling up outside her house, Gormley yanked on the handbrake, almost taking it off its ratchet. He

let the engine idle as she grabbed the door handle in readiness to get out. Unusually, he declined an invitation to join her for a quick drink, making an excuse that his wife would most probably be waiting up to finish the argument she'd started at the breakfast table.

'You know Julie . . .' he said. 'Never likes to see anything half done.'

Behind his tired eyes Daniels saw pain. The same pain she'd been feeling since having a go at Jo earlier. She wasn't fooled by his attempt to make light of his marital problems and suddenly felt guilty for keeping him so late. Sorry that another 'perfect couple' weren't getting on. From what he'd told her – which wasn't much – unless he could pull off a miraculous recovery, his marriage was as good as over.

For fuck's sake, what was wrong with everyone?

Daniels got out of the car. Ducking her head, she peered back in and tried not to sound as down in the dumps or as tired as she felt. Late at night things often seemed worse than they actually were. Hopefully, a few hours' kip would see them both back on track. She said goodnight and thanked him for the lift home.

'You wouldn't have got rid of Cole as easy.'

It wasn't like Gormley to be so familiar. Daniels debated telling him to keep his nose out of her personal business, but the dynamics between them had shifted lately. She was no longer simply his DCI, he her DS. They'd grown much closer since she'd confided in him about her feelings for Jo. Or, to be more accurate, since he'd discovered their affair and confronted her with it. At the time he'd taken her silence personally. Hurt by what he saw as a betrayal, he'd accused

her of not trusting him enough to be honest about who, or what, she really was. But Daniels hated labels. She didn't need the distraction that everyone knowing her business would bring. Hell, *she* didn't even know who she was any more. Why should Gormley? Did he think she needed protection from herself now? That she was no longer capable of making the right choices?

She forced a smile. 'What have I told you about acting like my dad?'

'Whatever!' Like a petulant teenager, he stared out at the dark leafy terrace through the Peugeot's front windscreen. Pressing her lips together tightly, Daniels resisted the temptation to laugh out loud and managed to recover as he turned back to face her. But what he said next made her angry.

'You do what you want, Kate. You will anyway.'

'Hey! What is your problem? You're my DS, not my personal minder.'

And still he wouldn't let it go. 'Just don't come crying to me if it all goes pear-shaped.' Looking in the rear-view mirror, he engaged first gear. 'Pick you up tomorrow?'

'No! I'll ride in.'

'Not speaking to me now?'

'Of course I am, you idiot. I fancy bringing my bike, that's all.'

He blipped the accelerator and raced off into the night.

51

Heading down Dog Leap Stairs towards the Quayside, Chantelle followed her usual crowd. Many of the guys were already pissed, their normally smart dress code ignored in favour of jeans and mandatory footie shirts. Their chanting and singing was getting right on her tits. Earlier it hadn't seemed so bad, but now it was reduced to the National Anthem, she'd had enough.

Who *were* they kidding?

England versus Germany was a headline-grabbing game no matter which way it went. But England were *bound* to lose. Chantelle had placed a bet on it. Got reasonable odds too. If only her mates would shut the fuck up, she'd be able to hear herself think and work out what she'd win for her five-pound stake.

Maths was never her strong point.

The girl in front of her tripped and went hurtling down the remaining steps, landing in a heap at the bottom with her cellulite arse on show. Everyone laughed and walked on. Not one of them batted an eyelid or stopped to help her up. Daisy had never been able to hold her drink and would get worse as the night went on.

Chantelle took a swig from her wine bottle as she stepped over her. Winter or summer, Newcastle city centre was always

pretty mad and this balmy Saturday night was proving no exception. World Cup hysteria meant that all her mates had come out to play and were intent on having a good time. There was plenty of talent to choose from and the bars were buzzing with a real party atmosphere.

Every single person she'd spoken to that night had been full of hope and expectation with the big game looming tomorrow. It was to be an afternoon fixture, she was pleased to hear, ample time to sleep off the excesses of tonight's binge before coverage began. Just as well, Chantelle thought. At the beginning of the pub crawl she'd foolishly bragged she'd drink them all under the table. Not the brightest thing to do in view of *her* track record. Even if she managed to stay upright, in the early hours she'd probably find herself plaiting her legs as she fought her way to the nearest taxi rank.

Fought being the operative word.

Not that Chantelle minded that. It was all part of the fun, as far as she was concerned. She always gave as good as she got and rarely came off worst. Only twice had she needed medical attention. Once when she'd had her stomach pumped after trying a different cocktail at every bar in the Bigg Market for a bet. Not the most pleasant of experiences. The other time was when she decided to go swimming in the Tyne at midnight and had to be rescued by the river police when she couldn't drag herself out again. Last January she'd been locked up for disorderly conduct. But that was OK too. A damn sight better than collapsing on a bench somewhere in the freezing cold. She'd created such a fuss during her few hours in the cells at Market Street station the daft bizzies

took her home just to get rid of her. She ended up quids in, having saved on the taxi fare.

Now that's what she called a public service.

Chantelle turned right on to the Quayside itself. Two well-built lasses were staggering towards her, footie shirts on, heavily tattooed forearms around each other's necks. They had short, spiky hair and wore jeans and trainers. Not your usual Saturday-night attire, Chantelle thought. Unless . . .

Fucking dykes.

Chantelle tensed. She'd seen girls like them in Styal Prison and something told her they wouldn't get on. They burst out laughing when they saw her. The tallest, a real bruiser, looked like she could handle herself. Blinking as if she couldn't quite believe what she was seeing, she pointed in the general direction of Chantelle's right thigh, her hand waving around as she tried to focus properly.

'Something I can do for you?' Chantelle asked.

The two girls made faces at each other.

'Maybe . . .' the bruiser laughed. 'Not!'

Now they were *really* taking the piss.

'That was the right answer,' Chantelle said. She stood her ground, the hair rising on the back of her neck, her hand closing on her wine bottle. She'd been rolled in town before and there was no way it was happening again. 'You wanna drink? Get your own.'

Holding her hand to her chest, the bruiser burped. 'Don't wanna drink . . .'

Her mate collapsed in a fit of laughter. Chantelle barged past them, knocking them both sideways like skittles in a bowling alley. The skinny one was no threat. She lurched first

217

one way and then, as Chantelle was sure she'd hit the deck, she lurched the other, almost defying gravity before grabbing hold of a lamppost for support.

As they moved off, Chantelle caught her reflection in the blacked-out window of a restaurant that had recently closed down. She did a double take, embarrassment washing over her as the girls disappeared around the corner. Her classy dress had accidentally got caught in her knickers. It was at least half an hour ago that she'd nipped up a back lane to relieve her bursting bladder. Pulling the dress out, she smoothed down the material and ran a hand through her hair.

Looking good, all the same.

More like Cheryl Cole each day. Chantelle had every reason to feel happy tonight. She was on a promise to a guy called Jason Mountfield, someone she'd had her eye on for quite some time. She knew he'd come round in the end. She didn't feel at all guilty for intimidating his current girlfriend, sending her texts threatening to spread the word that she'd had an abortion when they were both at school.

All's fair in love and war.

Chantelle smiled to herself. Today had been a blast. She'd made her move to flog the images stored on her phone to the local newspaper. It hadn't been as lucrative as she'd hoped. Beer money was all. The stuck-up cow she'd spoken to had promised more, depending on something she called 'content'. *Whatever that meant.* Probably news-speak for quality of the shot or some such bollocks.

Who gave a stuff?

Chantelle sure as hell didn't.

No. What upset her was being talked down to, like she was shit on the woman's very expensive shoes. She felt like marching into that office and decking the bitch. But then her old man's wise words jumped into her head and made her think twice: *Never bite the hand that feeds you, Chantelle. Never look a gift horse in the mouth.* Just two pearls of wisdom from the biggest loser she knew. But she got the gist and decided to zip her lip. That newspaper reporter would get hers when the time came. Probably when her editor realized she'd missed the scoop of a lifetime.

Chantelle turned around. Her mates had moved along the road without her, Jason Mountfield bringing up the rear. He turned, checking her out. She grinned as he mooned at her from across the road and got her phone out to take his picture. Then the smile slid off her face as quickly as it had appeared. The silly fuck hadn't seen the dark van lurking on the corner, two pairs of eyes focused on his bare arse.

Suddenly the van door opened and a couple of cops emerged. Pulling up his strides, Jason legged it. But one of the cops ran faster, and the big bugger brought Jason down in one fell swoop. A rugby tackle Johnny Wilkinson would've been proud of. Chantelle literally stamped her feet as the cop cuffed Jason, dragging him kicking and screaming into the van, pushing him inside with some force, only a cage separating him from a barking Alsatian that looked like it had seen its supper arrive on a tray.

Chantelle swore at them as they went by, swigged her wine and watched the van drive off at speed, her promise along with it.

Just her luck to back another loser.

52

The sheet slid off Daniels' shoulder. She was neither asleep nor awake but in that space in between. The next thing she was aware of was the smell of exquisite perfume and the low flicker of candle light. Then Jo's warm naked body slid into the bed, shuffling up close until she could feel every part of her. Arching her back in response, Daniels lay there savouring the moment. Then she turned, locking eyes with her ex, unable to believe she was really there.

'How did?'

'Shh . . .' Jo put her forefinger to Daniels' lips and followed it up with a gentle, almost imperceptible kiss. 'You never asked for your key back.' She held out both wrists and smiled, the way only *she* could. 'You going to lock me up for breaking and entering? I seem to remember you have before.'

She kissed her again, this time with more urgency.

'*Jesus!* You drive me mad . . .' Daniels pulled away, a sudden rush of mixed emotions. She felt elated and yet forlorn. They had wasted so much time and many harsh words had passed between them. Jo's presence now didn't alter a thing. It certainly didn't make up for the fact that they were about to part company – perhaps for good. 'Have you decided yet?'

'Shh . . .' Another kiss. 'Do I look like I'm going anywhere?'

They made love to the point of exhaustion – the months

they'd been apart drifting away – and fell asleep in the darkness wrapped in each other's arms. But in the morning, Jo was gone. Daniels sat up and listened. Nothing. Leaning out of bed to switch off her alarm, she realized Jo had never been there. It was all a vivid dream – wishful thinking on her part.

Feeling miserable, she got out of bed and drew the curtains back from the window. The sun was up already, another fabulous day in prospect, according to the radio. She dressed quickly, ate some toast and drank orange juice. It was far too early to call Jo, a final attempt at talking sense into her. Besides, it would probably turn into yet another round of aggravation. Daniels needed that like a hole in the head at this hour on a Sunday morning. She wouldn't beg her to stay, why the hell should she? Instead, she went in search of her bike.

Wheeling it outside, she yanked it on to its stand and did a quick BOLTS check: Brakes, Oil, Lights, Tyres, Suspension. Satisfied that all was as it should be, she went back inside and pulled on her leathers ready for the short ride to work. Lifting her helmet off the floor, she opened the front door and was about to leave when the house phone rang, startling her. She picked up expecting to hear Jo's voice, her hopes dashed as Gormley came on the line.

'It's me.'

'Hi, you.' She tried not to sound disappointed.

'Sure you don't want a lift?'

'I'm all sorted, thanks.'

'Was I a prat last night?'

Daniels grinned. 'I think you'll find the answer is in the question.'

'Then I'm sorry.'

'Don't be daft. You at home?'

'Yeah.'

'Last one there buys lunch.' She hung up.

By eight o'clock the MIR was buzzing. Daniels headed for interview room number three for a meeting with Charles Milburn, who had been brought in for questioning by the early shift. Elliot had described his father as nasty piece of work, and so it proved. He refused to help with enquiries, insisting on having his brief present before any questions could be put to him. Exasperated, the DCI had gone to find Stewart Cole so they could view the footage of the A1 crash, only to be told that he'd had to leave the station for an hour or two, a personal problem she hoped wasn't serious.

By the time Milburn's solicitor arrived, her prisoner was insisting on being fed, frustrating the hell out of Daniels who had to wait in line to see him. And when she did eventually get to him, he was totally unconcerned by the loss of his father, even less so with the nightmare his girlfriend was going through.

Nothing he had to say moved the arson enquiry any further forward.

Forced to release him, Daniels returned to her office.

Cole wasn't yet back, so she bent Carmichael's ear about her wasted morning. They had an early lunch at her desk, discussing outstanding actions, the main one being Jennifer Rankin, their prime suspect for the A1 case. There was still no news of her.

Daniels had an idea.

Telling Carmichael she needed to make a call was a heavy

hint for her DC to return to work. As the door closed behind her, Daniels picked up her mobile, scrolling to the number for the analytics team of NFIB. The National Fraud Intelligence Bureau – a police unit set up to combat fraud and funded by the Home Office – held all manner of data on organized crime groups, including aliases of people on their 'most wanted' list.

It was a long shot – but anything was worth a try.

A female DI with a southern accent answered almost immediately. Daniels explained who she was and why she was calling, asking if the name Jennifer Rankin had ever come up on their radar. The DI agreed to look into it, offering to call back as soon as she had a result. Thanking her, Daniels put the phone down, then lifted it again and rang Gormley's desk. His extension was engaged, so she called Stewart Cole's mobile just as the man himself walked through the door, apologizing for keeping her waiting, advising that Gormley was now tied up on a call but would join them as soon as humanly possibly.

While they waited for him to arrive, Daniels made coffee. Cole never mentioned why he had been called away and she didn't pry – not directly.

'Is everything okay?' she asked.

Cole nodded. He didn't look upset or anything, so she let it go. He was supposed to be on a rest day and she felt guilty about encroaching on his free time. *Again.* She seemed to be making a habit of that. Wondering if she'd spoiled a pre-arranged engagement, she told him she'd make it up to him.

'Don't worry about it,' he said. 'Joining the force is the best move I ever made.'

'That's great, Stew. I'm *really* chuffed it's working out for you.'

'I owe you, Kate. Big style. Anything I can do in return, just ask.'

He was standing by the window looking like he belonged on a windswept prairie: a pair of old jeans, a faded checked shirt, a worn brown belt with a brushed metal buckle that had some kind of winged motif on it, his tan cowboy boots all scuffed at the toe. Although he'd never said as much, it didn't take a super brain to deduce that he worked out in the gym. It occurred to her that she knew very little of what he got up to when not on duty. What she knew of his past, he probably wished she didn't. His criminal record might be short, his offence a one-off, but it was doubtless a deep source of embarrassment to him and always would be.

Gormley still hadn't arrived so she suggested they view the footage without him. Daniels knew from experience that 'as soon as possible' was difficult to measure. It could mean a few minutes, an hour, or half a day, depending on what was keeping him. Viewing video recordings was a task she'd normally delegate to a junior member of the squad, but Cole's attendance at the briefing the night before had raised her expectations. He'd told her it contained something she needed to see for herself.

And so it proved . . .

As she placed the flash drive in to her computer, Cole drained his coffee and pulled up a chair. He sat closer to her than she felt comfortable with. She moved away slightly as the footage began. On screen, a bright beam of light from Cole's aircraft illuminated a section of the A1 below. The

direction indicator in the bottom right-hand corner of the screen showed her that he was travelling south. He flew directly over the accident, giving a running commentary of what he could see, highlighting traffic problems to the control room at the same time, no panic in his voice as he relayed the information.

'Can you fast-forward?' he asked.

She looked up, puzzled.

'You won't see anything interesting until after I complete a reciprocal and head back the other way,' he explained. 'It'll save you some time.'

Daniels did as he asked.

Cole's eyes were riveted on the counter, bottom left on the screen. 'Stop it there!'

Daniels paused the recording, then restarted it again. Cole had fixed his beam on the epicentre of the crash, the impact zone, flying in a tight full circle around it, all the while transmitting footage back to the control room via a satellite link. They watched for a few seconds. Then the beam of light stopped moving and the camera zoomed in. Daniels saw herself and Gormley on the ground being pelted with torrential rain. A split second later, the beam flashed off, then on again.

His greeting to her from the air.

This was really helpful as it fixed the memory in her mind, gave her a real sense of time and place. She glanced up as Gormley entered the room, beckoned him round behind her so he could see what she and Cole were seeing. Putting on his bifocals, Gormley approached the desk and moved in close, looking over their shoulders.

'You found anything?' he said.

'Coming up now,' Cole said.

Daniels saw herself again, walking up the line, taking notes. The moving beam picked up Ivy's Honda Jazz, a figure crouching at the rear, their head obscured by the roof of the car. Gormley stepped into shot, paused briefly. He crouched down but didn't approach the vehicle.

'You spoke to them?' Cole said.

'Yeah, I did. I got no answer though. Or if I did, I never heard it. It was mayhem out there.' On the screen, Gormley's attention was taken by another casualty. 'The Home Office pathologist, Tim Stanton, said the old man died instantaneously. But Ivy Kerr was alive then. She actually smiled at me.' He leaned in further, eyes like heat-seeking missiles on the crouching figure next to the car. 'Look at this evil shit . . . unbelievable!'

'Can you get in closer?' Cole asked.

Daniels zoomed in on the car but the nearer she got, the grainier the image became. She ran the recording again, only this time in slow motion, her eyes still glued to the screen. 'I can't distinguish at this range between police, fire and medical personnel.' Pausing the footage, she turned towards the two men. 'I want you both to keep quiet about this for the time being. Hank, I need to see the officer responsible for interviewing scene attendees immediately. And find out exactly what every one of them was wearing at the scene.'

Cole looked flummoxed. 'Why?'

'Look at Hank and me.' Daniels indicated the frozen image on the screen.

Cole said, 'So?'

'I was wearing a police-issue high-viz jacket,' Daniels

explained. 'Hank, on the other hand, was wearing an Arco rip-off.'

Gormley looked at Cole. 'She means unofficial uniform. Stuff gets lost all the time. People replace it with anything they can get hold of. Or should I say, anything they can get away with. No one questions you, so long as it fits loosely with requirements.'

'We need pictures of all official and unofficial uniforms worn that night, Hank. Get *everyone* to identify what they were wearing and then I want itemized clothing verified by at least one colleague who was there. And I want possession of each and every item. No exceptions.' Gormley's attention had strayed. He was staring intently at the screen. 'Oi! You listening to me?'

'Yeah, I heard you. But what's that?' Gormley touched a point on the screen, specifically the rear end of Ivy's Honda Jazz. He glanced up at them, a serious expression on his face. 'There was nothing recovered from the rear of car! I checked.'

Daniels peered at the bright object he'd drawn her attention to.

'Shit!' Her interest grew. 'I know *exactly* what that is.'

53

Cole looked at her, a puzzled expression on his face. Gormley peered at the screen, trying to see what she was getting at. Ignoring them both, Daniels scanned the screen herself, making absolutely sure she wasn't jumping to the wrong conclusions.

'If I'm not mistaken, that's a hat on the back seat, gents. Whoever attended Ivy Kerr was a professional,' Daniels said. 'Someone who knew to take the hat off so as not to soak the casualty. Either they were assessing her injuries, establishing ID, or trying to free her. We're not looking for a civilian here. This is a massive breakthrough.'

'You're suggesting it's one of ours?' Cole queried.

'I bloody well hope not.' Removing the flash drive from its slot, Daniels handed it to him. 'Take this to Technical Support right away, Stew. Tell them I want it enhanced as a matter of urgency. Whatever else they've got on can wait. And while you're at it, tell them this is absolutely hush-hush. We need to keep a lid on it for now. If it reaches the media, there'll be a public outcry.'

As Cole left the room, Robson entered. 'Thought you'd want to know: we have unequivocal proof that Ivy Kerr bought that winning lottery ticket at Tesco Extra, Kingston Park at five past eleven on Friday the eighteenth of June.'

'Time and date Camelot gave us?' Daniels asked.

Robson nodded. 'Exact match. Checked the CCTV myself.'

'And it's in our possession?'

Another nod. 'So, that's motive sorted,' Robson said. 'Now all we have to do is find Jennifer Rankin.'

A worrying thought washed over Daniels. Rankin hadn't put a foot wrong so far. She'd covered her tracks well and it wouldn't be easy to find her. 'Any news on her yet?'

'Not a squeak,' Robson answered as he made for the door.

Gormley asked him if there was any news on team selection for the World Cup game gripping the nation. Robson shrugged, his hand resting on the doorknob. 'You want me to ask Neil? He's had his radio stuck to his ear all morning.' Gormley waved the offer away, but as he turned away DS Robson caught the stony expression on Daniels' face. His shoulders dropped. 'What? You are kidding me! The lazy bastard said he'd cleared it with you. He didn't, did he?'

Daniels gave a wry smile. 'That's classic Neil. He's so bloody sharp he'll cut himself one day. Don't be too hard on him, Robbo. You know how fanatical he is about football. To be honest, I fully expected him to pull a fast one. Pull a sickie even, but he hasn't. That's progress, in my book.'

Feeling a little hard done by, Robson went back to work.

Daniels sent Gormley on an errand and set off in search of Naylor with two purposes in mind. One: she had an idea to run by him. Two: she wanted to ask a favour. On both counts she was out of luck – he'd been summoned to headquarters by the head of CID, which meant she was forced to make a decision without first consulting him.

What the hell. She'd take the flak if it wasn't to his liking.

She returned to the incident room.

Seconds later, Gormley entered from the corridor, nodding conspiratorially as he sat down at an empty desk. Everyone in the room had their heads down, oblivious to both of them. One or two looked abnormally glum today, their minds on the Free State Stadium in Bloemfontein – kick-off for the big game was less than half an hour away. A quick check on the murder wall confirmed no new events requiring their attention. Daniels already knew there were very few calls coming into the incident room today.

'Listen up, everyone!' She waited for them all to stop what they were doing. 'Hank found a big telly in the lost property – we're going to use it for the match.' Her statement was met with cries of thanks – *Yes! Really? Good on ya, boss* – and words to that effect. 'Just the match, mind. No preamble bollocks or post-mortem afterwards, understood? We still have three murders to solve. Maxwell will fill you in on team selection.'

Realizing all eyes were on him, Maxwell looked up and nearly fell off his seat when he saw her standing there. Pulling his earphones out, unsure of what he'd missed, he took in the reaction of the team, curiosity getting the better of him. There were beaming faces all round, in some cases unadulterated joy. In a city like Newcastle, football was a big part of life: players were gods, St James's Park the city's cathedral, supporters the congregation. It was unthinkable that they'd miss out on the biggest game the country had faced for years.

'Lorna – and only Lorna – is in charge of the remote,' Daniels added.

The focus of attention switched to a woman sitting quietly

in one corner, a headset clamped over short cropped hair. Lorna McKenzie had worked for Strathclyde Police for many years until transferring south to Northumbria. Well liked by everyone and possessing a wicked sense of humour, she was one of several call handlers drafted in by Naylor, due to the level of people ringing the MIR.

Until today.

Today, phones had fallen silent. There was absolutely *nothing* going on.

'Lorna, you kill the sound if a call comes in.' Daniels gave the rest of them a pointed look. 'So no jeering or whingeing – or the set goes off! And remember, you lot, Lorna's a Scot – so you better be nice. Any excuse and she'll turn the damn thing off.'

Lorna narrowed her eyes at the detectives, a big smile on her face.

54

The incident room door creaked shut as Naylor released the handle, letting it lock behind him automatically. The room held its collective breath when he asked Daniels to join him in his office right away. She followed him in and closed the door, aware of two dozen pairs of hopeful eyes watching her every move.

Winking at the team through the glass, she turned to face him. 'Guv, I—'

'Handled that well, from what I heard . . .' Naylor walked round the desk and sat down heavily in his chair. 'Good leadership doesn't always mean cracking the whip, Kate. I'd have done the same thing in your position as SIO. Can't see we'll be inundated with calls in the next few hours. There's not a soul on the roads and no chatter on the radio. Same story all over the country.'

'Thanks, guv. They really deserve it.'

'I hope we win,' Naylor said.

'So do I . . .' She made a scary face at Naylor. He was more a rugger fan himself. He could take or leave footie and she appreciated his attempt to lift morale by allowing the squad to watch the match. She pointed through the window at the MIR. 'I'll see to it personally that they work late to make up the time—'

'No need.' He patted fresh air, gesturing that she should sit. 'I know how hard you've been pushing them.'

Daniels sat down and spent the next forty-five minutes updating him on both cases. They were still hard at it when, suddenly, there was an almighty uproar from the room next door. A glut of expletives hit their ears. Neither needed telling that Germany had scored.

'*Jesus!*' someone yelled. 'What the *fuck* was Terry doing?'

'He's on another planet, man!' Maxwell sounded incredulous.

'What a gift!' Carmichael added. 'Where the *hell* were the defence?'

Daniels wondered if letting them watch the match was such a good idea after all. Naylor grinned, telling her to relax. He'd just come from headquarters, which was like the *Marie Celeste*. The place was totally abandoned. Everyone who could do had decamped to the pub or taken leave in order to check out the national team. Except Bright who, like Naylor, was a fan of the funny-shaped ball.

'How *was* my old guv'nor, anyway?' she asked.

'Bright by name, bright by nature, actually.'

'Really? Didn't think he liked it up at Fantasy Island.'

Naylor smiled. Fantasy Island was the nickname for Ponteland headquarters, the home of the Northumbria force. 'I think you'll find things have changed a little since you last spoke to him. There's a certain attraction to the place of late.'

Daniels' face lit up. 'Ellen Crawford?'

'The very same. A PA like no other, apparently.'

'Well, good on him!' she said. 'I suspected they were made for each other from day one.'

And she had. Even so, she had to admit she was surprised how fast events in the romance department had moved. Bright's wife had died relatively recently, though in truth he'd lost her to injuries sustained in a car crash much earlier than that. He'd been driving at the time and had been to hell and back over it.

Her eyes scanned Naylor's desk. There were no framed photographs on it as there used to be when his predecessor had occupied it. No personal memorabilia or knick-knacks she might've expected to see there. She and Naylor were very similar in that respect; work and home lives entirely separate. Baggage was a definite no-no for those intending to rise through the ranks. Maybe that's why they got on so well. Good detectives, from DCs to top brass, had fallen by the wayside because their private lives had got in the way. But it was also true that ambition had killed many a once-happy relationship.

Will you ever forgive me, Jo?

'You think we should bring Jo Soulsby in on Ivy's case?' Naylor asked.

Mention of her name made Daniels blush, this morning's dream flashing into her head.

'Problem?' Naylor said.

'No, guv.' Daniels ran a hand through her hair, aware that he'd noted her hesitation. 'It's Sunday. I think she'll have better things to do, that's all. I'll give her a call later, fix up a meet.'

Her phone rang.

Naylor smiled. 'Maybe that's her.'

The way he'd said it made Daniels feel decidedly uncom-

fortable. Did he know about her and Jo? Had her former boss said something? *No way.* Bright had too much integrity for that. She relaxed. Pulling her phone from her pocket, she checked the display: *Gillian Garvey.* A crime reporter at the *Journal*, a young woman she had a lot of time for, someone with her ear to the ground. It was true they'd had their ups and downs, but she'd given the police good intel over the years.

And she *never* rang just to chat.

Looking up, she said, 'Mind if I take this, guv? It might be important.'

'Better had then.'

'Gillian? What's up?'

'I just had an interesting conversation with a reporter on our news desk. Someone's been on the phone trying to flog a picture of a dying man. Ralph Street was mentioned in there somewhere and I thought you'd like to know.'

'Someone?' Daniels waited.

Garvey didn't answer.

'What do you want, Gillian? I need a name.'

'I'm not withholding evidence. It's—'

'I'll tell you how this works, shall I?' Daniels' tone was harsh. 'You have important information. You pass it to me. Everyone's happy. If you don't, you'd better look for another gig because your days on the crime desk are numbered. No detective on this force will give you shit!'

'And if I still don't?'

'You ever heard of the Press Complaints Commission?'

'OK, don't get your knickers in a twist.' Garvey paused for effect. 'The caller lives across the road from your crime scene – the arson, I mean, not the old lady in the car.'

'Jesus! How the hell—?'

'Don't worry, Kate.' Gillian sounded smug. 'I'm not printing that until I'm informed officially. But I'd like the heads-up ahead of the pack, if that's OK with you. You help me, I help you. Then, as you so eloquently put it, everyone *is* happy. Got to stay one step ahead of the nationals if I'm to keep my crown as reporter of the year!'

Daniels was irritated. Someone had been telling tales out of school. But there wasn't a hope in hell that Gillian Garvey would divulge her source. So Daniels didn't waste breath asking her to. 'This woman flogging the photograph? You do *have* a name?'

'Hang on a sec . . .' There was a shuffling sound on the line and then muffled voices. Gillian had covered the handset but Daniels got the gist of a conversation she was having with one of her colleagues. Then she was back. 'The name's Chantelle F—'

'Fox?' They both said the name at the same time.

'Bloody hell, you psychic now?' Garvey asked.

Daniels smiled. 'You're not the only one with your finger on the pulse. Chantelle and I have already met. Can you email a copy of the photo?'

'No. She's cute. Insisted on being paid – get this – *before* she hands it over.'

'Sounds like Chantelle.'

'Our news desk reporter decided to humour her. Offered a few quid, more if it was a good image. She managed to wheedle an address out of her on the pretext of handing the money over. In person. In cash. When what she was really going to do was pass it to me. She reckons there's a bloody

good story in there somewhere. You want me to hold off on that?'

'Yes, I do. I want to knock on that particular door myself.'

'Take Hank with you. He'll make damn sure you get in. How is he these days?

'He's good . . .' Daniels could see Naylor was getting impatient. 'Look, Gillian, thanks for the information. I've gotta go. I owe you one.'

'Yes, you do!' Garvey sang the words and then hung up.

'Something of interest?' Naylor asked.

'Very much so. Remember the address where we found the fag-end stubbed out in the wall?'

Naylor nodded.

'Chantelle Fox, the girl who lives there, tried to flog a picture of a dying man to the *Journal*. She also happens to own a dark baseball cap similar to the one worn by an unidentified person buying petrol prior to the Ralph Street fire. I haven't seized it yet as I'm still waiting on enhancements and I don't want to tip her off.'

'Then you'd better go and pay her a visit.'

'I'm already there.' A worried look crossed Daniels' face. 'Question is, which dying man are we talking about?'

55

Daniels borrowed Gormley's car keys and left the building. Naylor was right. The streets *were* empty. Not a soul on them as she drove along West Road, normally one of the busiest thoroughfares in that part of the city. But today was not normal. Red-and-white flags were everywhere: draped across shop windows, pinned over pub doorways, even wrapped around lampposts.

The car radio was already tuned to the football. According to the commentator, England had gifted the Germans another goal. Upson had clawed one back from a short corner minutes later. Then Lampard should've – some say he had – equalized six minutes from the half-time break.

'We were robbed,' was the cry in the studio. 'It should definitely be two-all.'

We'll stuff them in the second half, Daniels thought. She drove on, urging the radio presenters to keep the faith, refusing to believe the game was over and done with, hoping her positivity would transfer to the players on the pitch. Traffic lights were on green so she shot through them, turned left and then sharp right into Ralph Street, pulling up directly outside Chantelle Fox's house.

As she got out and locked the car, a little boy approached, no more than five, maybe six years old. His front teeth were

missing and he had elongated bruises on his left cheek like someone had given him a backhander.

'Watch ya car, missus?' he said.

There was a veiled threat to his voice. Daniels was about to tell the little runt to get lost. But she felt sorry for him. The kid had balls, and she liked that. Besides, she had Gormley's pride and joy and not a pool car. She didn't want to risk the damn thing ending up like an etching pad. She threw the boy a quid, promising another if the Peugeot was still in one piece when she returned.

He gave her a gummy grin.

Cheeky little sod!

Daniels rapped on the knocker, secretly wishing she was back at the MIR, watching the match with the rest of the guys. The door was flung open with some force, its tenant poised to remonstrate with her untimely visitor. Chantelle's face dropped when she saw who was standing there.

'Oh, you've got to be joking!' she said. 'What now? I'm busy!'

'Thanks, don't mind if I do,' Daniels said.

'Hey! I never said—'

But Daniels was already inside, taking in the baseball cap still hanging on a peg as she passed along the hallway, that same sweet sickly smell hitting her senses as she pushed on through to the living room. The television was on full volume. The pundits were replaying Lampard's shot on goal, over and over. They shook their heads – unable to believe the referee's decision to disallow it. A blind man on a galloping horse could see it had clearly crossed the line.

Chantelle seemed to find the whole thing hilarious. A

betting slip on her coffee table explained why: her money was on Germany. *Obviously no footy fan.* She looked rough today. Her face was pale, her eyes drawn and she reeked of alcohol. Her hair was scraped back in an untidy mess and, despite the hour, she was still dressed in a pair of silky pyjamas. A camisole top and shorts with drips of hardened egg yolk down the front.

Daniels pointed at her chest. 'You missed your big mouth,' she said.

'Very funny! What d'you want?'

'Can we kill the sound? I need to ask you a few more questions.'

Chantelle didn't move. "bout what?'

Daniels picked up the remote and pressed the mute button. She knew before she got there what to expect from the girl. She nodded towards the television. 'You want to watch the second half here or listen to it along a cell corridor? I want answers, Chantelle. I also want the photos you've been trying to offload.'

Chantelle's colour rose ever so slightly. 'Dunno what you're on about . . .' She looked out the window as if she was expecting company, a supercilious grin on her face. No inkling of embarrassment or guilt at having been caught out in her little scam. 'I want you to go now. Me nana's calling in and I don't want her to find you here. She's not been well.'

'Same nan your father told us died last time we arrested him? Or the one whose funeral he was on the way to when we stopped him for dangerous driving for the third time in a week? Most people only have two. Come on, Chantelle, hand over the camera or whatever device it was you used. The

woman at the *Journal*'s not coming round.' Daniels grinned. 'She sent me instead.'

Chantelle remained silent.

'Do *not* piss me off, Chantelle. I said, give it here!'

The girl looked vulnerable standing there in her summer jimjams, her chunky legs like tree trunks in a pair of skimpy shorts, her knees a bit red from too much sun. But she was as hard as nails. Her eyes, thick with last night's make-up, flicked briefly past Daniels to the sofa beyond, causing the DCI to turn and investigate further. And lo and behold, she spotted a brand-new Mulberry handbag hidden under a cushion, presumably wedged there in a hurry when she'd knocked on the door.

'Well, well,' Daniels said. 'What have we here?'

'Hey! Gimme that!' Chantelle made a lunge for the bag.

Daniels snatched it away. Taking a pair of Latex gloves from her pocket, she put them on. She could smell expensive leather as she examined the contents, eventually extracting a mobile. She threw the bag back down on the couch and then accessed the phone's media files until she came across an image of George Milburn. He was lying on the pavement in brilliant sunshine clutching his chest, but still very much alive. There were other images too, the last one of PC Dixon kneeling on the ground beside the old man, his uniform belt clearly visible as he administered mouth-to-mouth.

If Daniels' calculations were correct, Chantelle must've been standing at least ten feet away from the body as she took the photos, and that bothered her. It was true the girl had form for theft. But would she have taken the old guy's money and then called the police while he was still alive to tell the

tale? Daniels didn't think so. More likely she'd have robbed him and legged it, leaving him dying on the pavement.

It wasn't looking good for the Italian stallion.

Glancing at the image in her hand, Daniels was sickened by what she saw. Happy slapping – youngsters videoing violent assaults – was one thing, a craze she hoped had had its day. But happy snapping? She'd read somewhere that mobile phone subscriptions had reached over five billion globally. Every sale placed a camera in a hand. It stood to reason that the practice of capturing any kind of human disaster on film was a growing trend. But there were limits of acceptable behaviour, unless you had a screw loose, or a cruel fascination with death.

Did Chantelle?

Was she a voyeur?

If so, was she connected to the arson?

Daniels had been in the police long enough to keep an open mind. She decided to rule nothing in or out until she knew which way the wind was blowing. Thankfully, she was on her own today. Had Gormley been with her, she'd have had her work cut out to keep him from rounding on the girl. He had a tendency to tell the unpalatable truth to offenders who pissed him off. But on this occasion she didn't even try to restrain *herself*.

'You're despicable, you know that?' Daniels said. Her words made no impact. The girl looked at her like she was from another planet. 'He was an old man, Chantelle. And this . . .' Daniels tapped the mobile. 'It's just not on! I hope you're really proud of yourself.'

'It's not an offence to take a picture,' the girl said, sheepishly.

'Handling stolen goods is, though.' Daniels pointed to the Mulberry bag. 'Get a pay rise, did you? Been saving up your pennies?'

'Told you, I had a bit of good fortune.'

'Even so, I hope you have proof of purchase because something tells me you can't afford that.'

'Don't keep receipts, sorry. Anyway, it's a knock-off. A copy.'

'My arse. I know quality when I see it. Knocked off more like. What if I take possession and maybe arrest you for . . .' Daniels pretended to think hard on it. 'Theft? Receiving? How does that sound?'

Chantelle's right hand formed into a fist. Her knuckles turned white. But she wasn't about to get violent. Her eyes were back on the television set. With sixty-seven minutes gone, the Germans were celebrating yet another goal. From the way she was behaving, Daniels half expected her to punch the air in celebration. It didn't surprise her that she had a flutter now and then. Her old man would bet on two flies crawling up a wall.

Like father like daughter.

Daniels tried shock tactics. 'Taken any other photographs of dying men recently?'

It worked. 'What d'ya mean?'

'Don't play dumb, Chantelle. You know exactly what I mean. If I find out you're not telling me the truth, you'll lose more than your handbag. Show some respect, why don't you? A man and a child lost their lives across the road. And take that smug look off your face before I do something about it – this is no laughing matter.'

'Hey, wait a minute, I had nowt to do with that! I took those . . .' She pointed at the phone in Daniels' hand. 'But that's all I did, I swear. I didn't take the old man's cash neither. I saw him go down and dialled 999, like I said last time you and the fat fucker were here. I took his picture, then the polis came along and tried to help him. I wasn't going to give the skanky old minger mouth-to-mouth now, was I?'

There was an uncomfortable silence for a moment or two. Daniels stood in the centre of the room, considering her options. The girl had more to tell, she was sure of it. Nevertheless she decided to bide her time. 'I'll see myself out,' she said. 'But mark my words, I *will* be back.'

She walked out with Chantelle's voice ringing in her ears.

'Hey! When do I get my phone back?'

'When I'm good and ready.' Daniels turned. 'By the way, you had better find a receipt for that bag or come up with some information or I'll be knocking on your door from now 'til Doomsday.' She walked to Gormley's dark blue Peugeot feeling the girl's eyes on her back. The gummy kid appeared from nowhere with his hand out. The DCI threw him a quid, got in and drove away.

Chantelle remained on the doorstep unable to keep the smug grin off her face. Her friend Tracy walked up to the front door and asked what the police were doing there. Chantelle ignored her. She was too busy watching Daniels' car drive slowly down the street. *Keep the phone, fuckwit – the photos an' all! I've got more interesting ones than that! And someone dafter than you dying to get her hands on them.*

*

The redhead knew a cop when she saw one. She slid down in her seat, watching Daniels drive away, keeping her eyes firmly on the wing mirror until the Peugeot turned the corner and disappeared from view. Across the street, Chantelle and the other girl lingered on the doorstep for a moment or two and then went inside and shut the door.

Her phone rang: *the Cypriot*, a hint of tension in his voice. 'Did you find it?'

'No. The cops were there.'

'And now?'

'Gone. But she's got company. Did she ring back?'

'No. Maybe she bluffs you.'

'We're in no position to take that chance.'

'Silence her then!'

'No!' The redhead could see Chantelle laughing through the window. 'She dies and we may never find the incriminating evidence she insists she has. I'm not prepared to risk that. There's too much at stake. I'll watch her. When it's clear, I'll make my move. Don't worry. She won't get away with black-mailing me. The girl is greedy for cash. We're safe. For the time being.'

56

The journey back to town didn't take long. At the Swan House roundabout, Daniels took the second exit left on to the central motorway and picked up speed, travelling north away from the River Tyne. University buildings stood like sentries on either side of the four-lane road. She swung sharp left with the city centre straight ahead, arriving at the station minutes later.

There were few vehicles in the car park: a couple of squad cars lying idle along the perimeter fence, one or two belonging to the CID. A mishmash of civilian vehicles too, some smart and well cared for, others rust buckets that didn't look legal. Her own two wheels were parked where her Toyota ought to have been, a niggling reminder that she must find time to sort out a replacement. Had it been a weekday, a prison van would've been backed up to the rear door, waiting to take prisoners from the magistrates court to either HMP Durham or Low Newton Remand Centre, depending on their age. But on this sunny Sunday afternoon, the place was relatively empty.

By the time she'd reached the MIR the England game was over and the acrimony over a bizarre decision by the Uruguayan referee had just begun. Her team were loitering by the coffee machine, their bitter disappointment clearly

visible. Maxwell looked positively pale, shell-shocked, utterly miserable, like a kid whose parents had taken away his toy soldiers. Jacket off, tie loosened, he had dark wet patches under his arms. Daniels stifled a grin. *Probably the first time he'd broken sweat in the incident room for a very long time.*

'Even a fucking octopus predicted that one,' he was saying.

Daniels gave him a sympathetic pat on the arm as she walked by. Gormley looked up as she approached. She threw his car keys at him. 'You need diesel and a car wash. It smells like a brothel inside.'

He didn't answer.

Things were always serious when Hank's sense of humour went walkabout.

Pushing her way to the drinks machine, Daniels dropped a coin into the slot, selecting white coffee, a change from her usual black. Too busy to replenish her personal supply, she was resigned to something a little less palatable and hoped the milk would help. As the drink was being dispensed, she listened to her colleagues' tales of woe, letting them air their grievances and get the match out of their systems before reminding them they had work to do.

After a few minutes, they peeled off and went back to their desks. Even Maxwell agreed there were more important things in life than a bunch of under-achievers who'd let their country down by not rising to the occasion. Leaving them to it, Daniels went directly to her office, shut the door behind her and pulled down the window blind – her way of saying: Do Not Disturb.

Cradling her coffee in both hands, she relaxed back in her seat, put her feet up on her desk and shut her eyes, trying to

rid herself of the noise in her head. Random thoughts of three incidents came and went in no particular order. A confused jumble of concerns. So many questions. Too few answers. No matter how hard she tried to pull them apart and make sense of them, they merged into one bloody big problem that threatened to overwhelm her.

Chantelle Fox knew more than she was letting on – that was a given – but it didn't mean she was lying about everything. The photographs she'd taken clearly showed PC Dixon working on George Milburn, which meant that he was still alive at that point – probably a thousand pounds richer too. What if she was telling the truth vis-à-vis the old man's money?

Am I dealing with a bent cop?

The more Daniels mulled it over, the more convinced she was that the girl was covering up something even more sinister than theft from a dying heart attack victim, as distasteful as that might be. The arson perhaps? During their little encounter she'd slipped up, shown her colours in a way she probably hadn't intended to. If she disliked football enough to bet against her national team, maybe she wasn't at the party on the night of the fire.

Sitting up, Daniels put down her coffee cup. Accessing the HOLMES system, she typed in Chantelle's details and quickly located the names of those reported to have been at the Ralph Street party. Her name wasn't among them. Her house-to-house statement confirmed that she was alone at home that night. Or was she? Daniels knew Chantelle was a smoker. She'd smelled nicotine on her, seen spent fag-ends in ashtrays in her home. A smoker had extinguished a cigarette

at her front door. Was it her? Had she been watching? Was there more than one person involved? Maybe Chantelle started the fire and someone else was keeping toot? Or was *she* the one acting as lookout?

Daniels' mind was in turmoil. She'd yet to discover the identity of Mark Reid's mystery girlfriend, the person whose clothing was in his flat. The person who'd rung his home phone at 01.23 a.m., hours after he was killed. W*as* this the same woman his mates had seen wearing a uniform? A security guard? A fire officer? A prison officer?

A cop?

And what of Cole's footage from the air? Was the item in the rear of Ivy's car what Daniels feared it might be? If it *was* a hat, who did it belong to? A medic? A fire officer?

A cop?

There was a pattern forming here and Daniels didn't like it.

She sighed, frustrated by her lack of progress. She needed results and she needed them now: DNA from the cigarette butt she'd sent to Matt West at the forensic science laboratory at Wetherby; enhancements of CCTV images Maxwell had retrieved from the garage; the same of the object Cole's recording had captured in the back seat of Ivy's car. Technical Support were working flat out, but not fast enough.

The rest of the day was a blur.

57

Four miles away, Jo Soulsby began her Monday morning by scanning the shelves of her local library trying to find a novel she hadn't yet read. Despite working within a related field, crime fiction was her thing. Opting for Karin Slaughter's *Faithless*, a book she'd missed in the Grant County series, she got it stamped and made her way outside into the sunshine. Despite the lovely weather, her mood was grim. Kate Daniels had been on her mind all morning and she wondered what her reaction would be when she confirmed that she was leaving the Murder Investigation Team to take up the job at HMP Northumberland.

Who was she kidding?

Jo knew perfectly well what Kate's reaction would be: disappointment, frustration, regret – all three.

Take your pick.

As if on cue, her mobile rang.

It wasn't Kate.

'Have you told her yet?' Emily McCann said. 'Assuming you've made up your mind.'

'No, I haven't,' Jo said.

'Told her or made up your mind?'

'Don't push it, Em.' The doors to Jo's Land Rover clunked open. Climbing in, she placed her book on the passenger seat,

steeling herself for an earache from her friend. 'I've been really busy and never got the chance.'

Emily McCann was too astute to buy such a pathetic excuse. 'You *must*. You know how she feels about you. If she finds out from someone else, she'll be completely devastated!'

Jo started the engine. 'She's tough. She'll cope.'

'You owe her—'

'I owe her nothing!'

'OK, OK.' Emily sighed. 'But you're in the wrong and you know it. Why can't you two kiss and make up and put the past behind you? Life's too bloody short. I'd give my right arm to have Robert back—'

'That's different!'

'How?' Emily asked.

'You were married, for years. He was—'

'The most amazing person in the world, my soul mate? I seem to remember you describing Kate in exactly those terms not so very long ago. You only get to meet *the one* once, Jo. Believe me, I'm speaking from experience. Isn't it time you started acting like grown-ups?'

'Isn't it time *you* stopped pretending it'll work?'

Jo didn't mean that. She knew it *could* work. One word from her and Kate Daniels would succumb to whatever demands she made, including coming out to the whole wide world if she really pushed it, despite what she'd said yesterday. But Jo wasn't about to ask her to sacrifice her police career, a job she was good at, a job that meant everything to her. It'd always been – and still was – Jo's contention that Kate would rise through the ranks no matter what her sexual orientation. But she'd got it into her head that the opposite

was true. And every time a high-up closet gay was outed by the press and felt compelled to resign from his or her job, it only served to reinforce her perception that ambition and homosexuality were a disastrous combination.

Jo suddenly had that aching feeling, the one she got every time she thought about Kate, the one that began in her chest and worked its way into the pit of her stomach where it ached some more. She didn't need reminding how good they were together, by Emily McCann or anyone else.

'Are you angry with me?' Emily asked.

'No, Emily. I'm angry with *her*! I've been angry with her for months, so angry I could punch her lights out. *She* did this to us, not me!'

'So bite the bullet and put an end to it.'

Jo sighed. Until Kate came along she'd not had much luck in the love department. She'd been married and divorced from a bully who'd since been murdered – caught up in a sinister psychopath's game of revenge against his mother. Jo had actually been accused of his murder by the force that employed her as a profiler, spending several weeks in custody on remand, only to have the charges withdrawn by the CPS before the case reached court. She had Kate to thank for that.

Another thing to thank her for.

'Jesus, Em. Why is life always so fucking complicated?'

'I don't know, it just is . . .' Emily's voice trailed off. 'Have you actually made a decision about the research project? I need to know one way or the other.'

'Yes, no . . . not entirely.'

'You'd be mad not to take it.'

'I know I would.' To Jo's left, the library door opened. A

woman wheeling a shopping trolley with the words *These wheels emit no CO_2* written large across the front emerged into the sunshine glaring at Jo's four-by-four. Turning off the ignition, Jo looked away. 'I need time to think it through, Em.'

'You did apply?'

'Yes, I did.'

'Good . . . then the job's all yours.'

Torn both ways, Jo leaned her head in her hands, her elbows on the steering wheel. She loved working with the Murder Investigation Team. Hell, she loved working with Kate Daniels. But maybe the time had come to make a clean break of it. Yesterday morning she'd lied to Kate for the very first time, stalling, pretending to have too much on when she'd asked her to help with her current murder incidents.

Nasty cases they were, too.

Out the front windscreen, an elderly couple with cotton-wool hair and wrinkled skin strolled by hand in hand, a young couple following close behind, their arms wrapped around each other. The whole world appeared to be in love. The question Jo was asking herself was: *did she want to join them?*

'I'm not taking the job,' she said.

58

The Bacchus was on High Bridge in Grainger Town; a narrow cobbled street that ran between Grey Street and Pilgrim Street. It was very close to the police station, which is why Daniels had chosen it. She rarely drank in the pub herself but it was Gormley's second home. They could be back in the incident room in minutes if need be.

Adele's voice floated in the air as he held the door open for her.

Inside, four men were propping up the bar. Another stood waiting to be served. The young man pulling his pint looked shagged out, a growth of designer stubble on his chin, hair thick with gel. Like any good barman, he clocked the detectives the minute they appeared in the doorway.

'Bit early for you, isn't it?' he said to Gormley as they approached.

'Funeral,' was all Gormley managed in return.

The barman raised an eyebrow. 'Anyone I know?'

Gormley shook his head. 'Daughter of a polis killed in the A1 crash last week.'

'Grim. Want the usual or a short?'

'A half, and pour yourself one, Justin. Second thoughts, make mine a pint.' Gormley turned to Daniels. 'My shout, boss. What can I get you?'

Daniels scanned the optics. 'Famous Grouse. Straight, no ice.'

Froth from the John Smith's spilled over the glass and pooled on the bar as the lad set it down. Gormley paid up and then followed Daniels across the worn wooden floor to a quiet table in the corner of the room. As she sat down, she glanced back towards the bar.

'Justin a new friend of yours?' she asked.

'Wife's nephew.' Gormley took a long pull on his pint and wiped a wet hand on his jacket. 'He's harmless. Bit of a bar-rack-room psychologist, mind you. You know the type. Thinks he can solve everyone's problems across the bar. Jumps to conclusions too. You'll be the scarlet harlot by the time I get home.'

Daniels smiled at his attempt to lift her mood. It was a difficult task with multiple enquiries weighing her down. The Ralph Street enquiry had stalled. Naylor wasn't happy because headquarters were breathing down his neck for a result. Letting out a big sigh, she asked Gormley for his take on it, knowing full well what his answer would be.

He didn't disappoint.

'It's a dog's breakfast, if you ask me.' He pointed out the obvious, that they had begun the investigation with four possibilities: random kids' prank gone wrong . . . right house, wrong person . . . right house, right person . . . wrong house entirely. 'As far as I can see, that remains where we're at.'

He had a point. The investigation was going nowhere, and scratching around for leads was frustrating the hell out of both of them. Mark Reid's mystery girlfriend still hadn't

materialized and Daniels was asking herself why. The identity of the woman was vital. They needed to rule her in or out. But all efforts to trace her had failed. According to her service provider, her phone had gone silent since Gormley tried to contact her.

'We're missing something, Hank. Why has Reid's girlfriend not come forward? She's bound to have seen reports of the fire by now.'

'Not necessarily. Maybe she didn't recognize the address, didn't connect the two.'

'That's always a possibility.'

'He was supposed to be babysitting Jamie at his own house, don't forget. She might've rung late that night because she was going away for the weekend. If she's out of town, she could be completely unaware. It does happen.'

Daniels wasn't convinced and told Gormley why. She'd been going over and over Judy's phone call the whole way through the funeral. There was no mention of a trip when she called him, no 'miss you' message. If she was on the level, why were there no clues to her identity in his flat? They had found nothing written down, no photos, no personal mementos or keepsakes. They had no evidence tying her to him, just a wardrobe full of clothes, if indeed they *were* hers . . .

'You don't think that's odd? Because I do,' she said.

Draining his pint, Gormley set the empty glass down on the table. He had something on his mind. Something he was reluctant to part with.

'What?' Daniels queried.

Gormley shrugged it off. 'Doesn't matter,' he said.

'Yes, it does. You got something to say, I want to hear it.'

'I think it's too early to judge her, that's all. She could be completely innocent. She and Reid might have legitimate reasons for keeping their relationship secret. I'm not having a dig, but you of all people would know about that.' He met her gaze across the table. 'I'm making a pig's ear of this. What I'm trying to say is, it's not only the guilty who have things to hide.'

He meant no offence and none was taken. He knew all about her 'baggage' and was cool with it. She was pleased. It made it easier to talk to him. Besides, she knew exactly what he was getting at. But she wasn't buying it. Even if she was dealing with a clandestine relationship, she'd have expected to find stuff belonging to Judy in Reid's flat. So far she'd found zilch. There was still no clue to Judy's identity – *except a uniform* – assuming she was the same woman Reid's mates had seen him with – and they had no proof of that either.

'Maybe they didn't want to go public until his divorce went through,' Gormley suggested. 'I know a guy whose ex screwed him rotten because of a new squeeze, insisted on having her salary taken into account when the civil courts were working out alimony payments. You said yourself the clothes in his wardrobe were top notch. For all we know, she may have been a high earner too.'

'That's plausible . . .'

'So what's bothering you?'

'There wasn't even a toothbrush of hers there.'

'No DNA, you mean?'

'That too. But people in love send each other daft things, don't they? My relationship with Jo may not have been

common knowledge, but I've got loads of that sort of thing at home. Books, letters, cards she sent me when we were together, all of them signed. Suffice to say, there's plenty there to lead a clued-up detective to her if they looked hard enough. See what I'm saying?'

Gormley shrugged, his eyes darting to his nephew then settling on Daniels.

'Maybe she wasn't that important to him,' he said. 'Maybe he still had the hots for his wife and was waiting to see how the land lay before getting too involved with anyone else.'

Gormley could identify with that. His own marital problems had begun many years ago when he was conducting enquiries away from home. He'd been unfaithful to his wife and got caught, quite literally with his pants down, when she turned up unexpectedly to tell him she was pregnant. The hooker he was with hadn't batted an eyelid, just picked up her clobber and left the room. His wife had never really got past it.

That didn't mean he loved her any less.

Daniels wanted to reach out and hug him, support him like he'd supported her. If he could turn back the clock, she knew he would. But was the same true of Mark Reid, she wondered? It would certainly explain the photograph of Maggie they'd found in his flat. Had he strayed while his wife was pregnant only to regret his indiscretion afterwards? Had Judy got wind of it and taken drastic action to get rid of the competition?

The voice message again. *Hi, babe. Tried your mobile. Assume it's on charge. Hope I haven't woken Jamie. If you get this message, call me.*

Suddenly, a thought occurred that really wound Daniels up. Not quite a Eureka moment, but enough to get her excited.

59

'You know, you might be right, Hank.' She stared at him, her eyes wide with hope. 'For days something's been niggling away in the back of my brain. I couldn't quite nail it. Judy hasn't phoned Reid since the night of the fire or left any further messages, right? *Why* hasn't she?'

'Well, he didn't return her calls, did he? Maybe she's lost interest, hooked up with someone new.'

'No.' Daniels shook her head. 'The tone of her call didn't suggest that to me. I think she *knows* he's dead and therefore knows there's no point calling him again. The questions we have to ask ourselves are these: did she phone him to give herself an alibi initially and isn't bright enough to have kept up the pretence? Or did she really not know he was dead until she read it in the press? You just said it yourself: she thought he was at home with Jamie. If she's the one who set the fire, the target being Maggie, she may not have realized her fatal mistake until afterwards. I want you to be more proactive. Get out there and concentrate on *her*. Talk to Reid's mates again, his neighbours. Someone must know who the hell she is.'

'What you going to do?'

It was a good question, one she didn't answer straight away. Her head was spinning with countless jobs, a long list

of actions for her team. She needed to call Matt West for a start, see how the Forensic Science Lab were getting on, find out how close they were to a result on the cigarette butt. Then she planned to ask Carmichael to exert pressure on the Technical Support Unit for those video enhancements in both murder cases. And set aside some time to analyse the report on the high-viz jackets she'd asked the accident investigators to supply. And re-interview PC Dixon and a whole lot more besides.

Her work mobile rang: a number she didn't recognize. 'DCI Daniels.'

'Is it convenient to talk to you, ma'am?'

Daniels sat up straight. Gormley gave her an odd look across the table. She mimed a puzzled look in return. It was Sergeant McCabe, the officer whose daughter's funeral they had come from. There was background noise on the line. The crackle of a police-issue radio and the familiar voice of a custody sergeant she knew. It was less than two hours since McCabe had buried Bridget and he was already back at work? Surely not.

'Yes, of course, Mick. Sounds like you're at the nick?'

'Custody suite, Market Street.' He paused a beat, then explained that Bridget's twin and his other daughter were with their grandparents, on the way south for a bit of a break.

'So soon? You sure that's a good idea?'

'For them or me?'

'Make your way to the MIR on the second floor. I'll meet you there in five.'

Daniels ditched her whisky and left the pub immediately. Four minutes later, she found McCabe at the top of the stairwell, pale and drawn, slightly the worse for wear, still dressed

in his funeral suit and black tie. She led him along the corridor to the major incident suite and towards her office, stopping on the way to tell Carmichael she wanted some quiet time and wasn't to be disturbed.

McCabe was more than a little unsteady on his feet. She sat him down, offered him coffee.

He declined. 'I don't want to take up your valuable time, ma'am.' He gestured through her office door to the MIR beyond. 'Looks like you've got a lot on. It's just . . . well, I've lost something of Bridget's and wondered if you could help me find it. Me and my girls have looked everywhere. The only possible explanation is that she was wearing it when . . .' He stumbled over his words. 'It definitely wasn't returned with her possessions by hospital staff, I checked.'

Daniels' ears pricked up. 'Go on.'

'My father bought each of the girls a seal ring. I know it sounds stupid, but we have this family crest. He thought it would be nice if they each had one. Bridget didn't often wear hers because it was a bit loose for her little finger and too small for her ring finger. She was terrified of losing it. Thing is, it isn't in the house. I wondered if you noticed it on the night, y'know, when you were with Bridget.'

Ivy's missing lottery ticket leapt into Daniels' mind. She tried not to look alarmed or let her growing anger show. The idea that anyone might steal from – or, in Ivy's case, kill – a person at their most vulnerable appalled her. She knew from talking to Bridget that someone had attended her immediately following the crash, before *she* had come along. The burning question was, who? Emergency services personnel? A member of the public?

Shit! A cop?

McCabe filled the silence. 'I shouldn't have bothered you with this.' He stood up. 'I'm sorry, I'm dog tired and not thinking straight.'

'No. Please sit down. I want to help.'

'It's fine, I'll check with Traffic.'

Daniels could almost feel Bridget's hand in hers. Cold. Wet. Trembling. She could smell the girl's fear. Taste it even. Images flashed through her mind. Slim fingers on young hands. Painted nails: two of which had been torn off in the collision. *A ring.* She *was* wearing a ring, but not the one McCabe just described, she told him . . .

'It was a simple gold band, worn on the middle finger of her left hand—'

'Her mother's wedding ring.' McCabe was losing it, the harsh reality of the day hitting him hard. He cleared his throat before continuing, swallowing down his heartache. 'That one *was* returned. Becci now has it.'

His words hung in the air.

Daniels could see he was a broken man. She leaned across her desk and handed him a tissue, her thoughts very firmly on the missing ring. There was no evidence that a theft had actually occurred, but if the seal ring *had* been stolen then why not the wedding band too? *Or did it?* 'This is going to sound like an odd question,' she said after a while, 'but was the wedding ring a tight fit?'

'Yes, why?'

'Then you could be right . . .' Daniels hated keeping her suspicions from him. 'The seal ring most probably came off during the crash. Why don't you let me look into it for you?

I'll have Bridget's car searched. It'll still be at the recovery garage, it shouldn't take long. I'll get someone on to it right away and get back to you.'

'Thanks, ma'am.'

'It's no problem,' Daniels said. Even as she said it, she knew that wasn't the truth.

Far from it.

60

PC Dixon was desperate to talk to his girlfriend. He'd been calling her for days but she wasn't picking up or returning his calls. He'd gone to her home but there was no answer at the door. The neighbours hadn't seen her either. Completely baffled by her disappearance, and wondering what the silly cow was up to, he'd returned to the station only to run into more bad news. Daniels had called in Professional Standards.

Ray Montagu, a severe-looking detective superintendent, was facing him now, an equally serious female DI by his side. The pair had years of experience under their belts, impressive reputations in their field of expertise. Dixon didn't need telling that his own good name was on the line.

You want a better class of detective, complain about a polis.
Report a rape, you get a numpty.

Those words had come from his shift sergeant as he'd left to face the big guns. He could say that again. Montagu was looking right through him, judging him before he'd even opened his mouth, a cause of deep anxiety for Dixon. A file on the table had his name, rank and number written in thick black pen on the cover. There was no mistake. *He was fighting for his life here.*

Taking her cue from her senior officer, the woman introduced herself as Detective Inspector Jane Trent. Advising

Dixon that she was recording the interview, she then cautioned him, giving the time, date and location of where the interview was taking place. 'You're entitled to have a solicitor present,' she said. 'Or someone from the Police Federation, if you'd prefer.'

'I don't.' Dixon cleared his throat. 'Want anyone, I mean. I've done nothing wrong, ma'am.'

'Then you have nothing to worry about, Constable.' The DI's lips were smiling but her eyes were not.

Dixon kept shtum, so Trent carried on: 'On Saturday the twenty-sixth of June you were spoken to by Detective Chief Inspector Kate Daniels of the Murder Investigation Team with regard to an incident in Ralph Street. An old man, since identified as George Milburn, had collapsed in the street. You left her crime scene to render assistance. Is that correct?'

'Yes, ma'am,' Dixon said.

'Following on from that interview,' Montagu chipped in, 'we have a few more questions for you. You're aware that an amount of money was taken from the old man?'

'Yes, sir.'

'Money which you deny having any knowledge of.'

'That is correct.'

'Have you anything further to say on the matter?'

Montagu waited, searching Dixon's face for clues. There were none. The PC was showing no signs of distress. He sat stony-faced, not a flicker of concern, his expression deadpan. After a moment, he told them that he had nothing at all to add to what he'd already told DCI Daniels when first questioned.

'That's a shame,' the Super said. 'I really was hoping you'd help us out here.'

Montagu looked away deliberately. Opening up Dixon's personnel file, he flicked through a few pages, commenting on his exemplary record, reminding him what he stood to lose should any impropriety be uncovered during the interview. A ploy designed to make him sweat. Closing the file, he looked up.

'I'll get straight to the point then, shall I?'

'If you would, sir. I'm due on at two.'

Cocky shit!

'You allege that a young woman at the scene may have taken the money.'

'That may well be the case, sir.'

'But that's not true, is it?' Montagu said. 'What if I told you we've already established that *you* were the only person within touching distance of the old gentleman while he was lying prostrate on the ground – what would you say?'

'I'd say you're mistaken,' Dixon replied. 'The girl was with him when I got there, sir.'

'We're willing to accept your word on that score,' Trent said. 'That would be Chantelle Fox, yes? The young woman you described as a "gobby cow" to DCI Daniels?'

Dixon's gaze shifted from the Super to Trent. 'Yes, ma'am.'

'Yes, indeed . . .' Montagu let some time pass before moving the interview along. 'We've made extensive enquiries. We've spoken to a number of witnesses to the old man's unfortunate collapse. I have to tell you, the information coming back is fairly conclusive. Everyone agrees that, while Chantelle Fox did take photographs of him lying on the deck, she did not approach him at any time. Therefore she couldn't have removed anything from his person. What have you got to say about that?'

'Not true. She was very close to him.'

'You're saying the people we've interviewed are lying and you're telling the truth?'

'That's exactly what I'm saying. Shit stick together, sir.'

'Do they?' Trent bristled. 'You got something against people living in the West End?'

'No, ma'am.'

'Sounds like you have.' Trent glanced at Montagu. 'The people we interviewed were very cooperative, weren't they, sir?' Taking in Montagu's nod, Trent turned back to Dixon. 'Chantelle may be gobby, but she had the decency to admit taking inappropriate images. Her neighbours back up her claim that she went nowhere near the old man. They seemed pretty genuine to me.'

'Someone's lying.' It was a statement, not a question. Montagu was watching Dixon closely. Making a fist of his hand, the PC propped up his chin, his elbow on the table, all the time insisting that Chantelle Fox was with the old man when he got there. 'So you said. And sit up straight when you're talking to me. You're not in the staff canteen now, son.'

His harsh words had the desired effect.

Dixon sat back, couldn't look the detectives in the eye.

'That's better . . .' Montagu waited until he had Dixon's full attention. 'According to DCI Daniels, you deny having taken possession of Mr Milburn's cash, even for safekeeping. Is that still your contention?'

'I didn't take anything, sir.'

'Very well.'

Montagu had a bombshell to drop. But not yet. Not until he was good and ready. Not until the little shit across the

table denied his career away. For a moment or two he did just that, repeating his claim that Chantelle Fox was the guilty party, insisting he had nothing whatsoever to hide. He was simply doing his job, as always.

Silly boy.

The hiatus proved too much for Dixon. 'I'm not pointing any fingers, sir. Perhaps she wasn't the one who took the money. But I didn't, that's all I'm saying. I'm as clueless as you appear to be.'

Trent had to work hard to keep the smile off her face. Her eyes flicked to the Super. His expression was inscrutable. They had worked together for years and 'clueless' was not something he'd ever been called before. Not by anyone. It was a big mistake on Dixon's part, because Montague had realized he was beginning to crack.

'First she did, then she didn't . . .' Montagu paused. 'You were certain a moment ago. Have you changed your mind?'

Dixon was sweating profusely. 'No, sir. All I'm saying is, I didn't see her take it. She was near him though, whatever her neighbours told you.'

'You're prepared to admit that you may have been mistaken though, yes?' Trent pushed.

'It's possible.'

'Cut the crap!' Montague was angry now and it showed. 'We have you bang to rights, son. For security reasons, DCI Daniels installed covert monitoring equipment in Ralph Street following the arson attack. It proves beyond a shadow of doubt that Chantelle Fox went nowhere near the dying man. Now what do you have to say for yourself?'

'If she didn't take the money, then the ambulance crew

must've. Or the medics when he was in the hospital. I don't know, do I?'

'You're prepared to admit you were the only person near the man having the heart attack?'

'No! Yes, maybe . . .' Dixon was showing classic signs of stress. He'd gone terribly pale and a thin film of sweat had appeared on his upper lip. 'Look, I was on my own and under pressure. I'd left a crime scene unattended and I was trying to save a life. As I told DCI Daniels, I'd never done that before.'

Trent shook her head. She wasn't buying it.

'Chantelle wasn't close enough to take the cash, was she?' she asked.

'Then the ambulance crew must have it. I don't!'

'No need to lose your temper, Constable. I'll ask again, did you or did you not take money from George Milburn following his collapse? Think carefully before you answer.'

'No!'

'Let me recap,' Montagu said. 'You now accept that Chantelle Fox wasn't close enough to take the money, so it must have been the ambulance crew. Is that correct?'

No reaction.

'PC Dixon? There's no point in denying it. We have unequivocal proof, man.'

'Yes.'

'You really aren't as bright as your record suggests, are you, Dixon?' The comment had come from Trent. 'You're obviously unaware that the ambulance service operates a strict protocol for taking patients to hospital, logging them in with a triage team. They also have equipment to protect themselves from outrageous allegations from the likes of you.'

Dixon dropped his head as she waited for a response. None came. It was time to go for the jugular. 'Have you ever been in the back of an ambulance?'

Dixon looked up. 'What's that got to do with anything?'

'Answer the question,' Trent said.

Dixon shook his head.

For the benefit of the interview room's digital recorder, Trent indicated that he'd done so. 'PC Dixon, you are telling *lies!* Throughout this interview you've shown classic signs of a guilty man, shifting the blame, changing the story when it suited you. First you tell DCI Daniels that Chantelle was quote: standing over him . . . with him. Those are *your* words, the ones *you* used when first questioned. You repeated them today and then back-pedalled as soon as you realized you weren't getting away with it. The truth is, Chantelle Fox couldn't possibly have taken the money. Then you tried shifting the blame to the ambulance service. Well, let me enlighten you. There is video recording of what happens to the patients in transit and CCTV inside and outside accident and emergency departments. We've viewed the footage, which includes the transfer of Mr Milburn between the ambulance crew and the trauma team. Guess what? He was searched by a member of the hospital staff – because they knew he was in a bad way – so they could ID him and inform next of kin. Barring a few coins, he didn't have any money on him. We already know Chantelle was telling the truth, so that proves to me you're lying – unless you are suggesting that all the hospital staff are conspiring together to commit an offence? And that doesn't happen.'

Dixon's head went down as the interrogation came to an

end. He was beaten and he knew it. For a moment the room was silent. When he looked up at his superiors he had tears in his eyes and his chest was heaving under his uniform shirt. 'OK,' he said. 'I did take the cash, but I swear to you it was only for safekeeping. I was going to give it back. But when DCI Daniels contacted me, I panicked.'

'Too. Late. Now,' Trent said.

61

'Ma'am, this is PC Dixon. Please don't hang up . . .'

Daniels happened to be standing at the window looking out when she took the call. She'd seen him enter the car park in the pouring rain, a civilian jacket on, a mobile phone stuck to his ear. He stopped short of the station entrance, was just beneath her window now.

'Ma'am? Are you there?'

'What do you want?' Her tone was harsh.

As if sensing the intensity of her gaze, the PC glanced upward, squinting as the rain fell even harder, a look of contrition on his young face as he saw her looking down on him. 'I know you think I'm a piece of a shit. And I am, OK? But I need to see you right away. It's very important . . .'

His voice was lost in a sudden rumble of thunder.

'I have nothing to say to you,' Daniels said. 'Take my advice and keep well away from the station. You're no longer welcome here.'

She hung up.

Dixon checked his phone and redialled. Almost immediately Daniels' phone rang again. She hesitated. The drenched PC looked up at her window, held a hand to his chest, pleading with her to answer and stay on the line – a gesture so pathetic, she took the call. What he said next both surprised

and excited her. Allegedly, he had information pertaining to the Ralph Street fire.

'Station interview suite,' she said. 'Five minutes. It had better be good.'

Putting down the phone, Daniels went back to her desk to collect her mobile before heading downstairs. What the hell was Dixon on about? She'd observed his interview from the viewing room. Her colleagues had done well. Questions had been fired at him in quick succession, each one designed to trip him up. It took Professional Standards less than half an hour to break him, ten more minutes to get a clear admission of guilt. His explanation? He'd taken the money to impress a woman with expensive tastes. She'd since dumped him and was now refusing to take his calls.

So . . . bloody . . . what.

Daniels was curious. There had been no mention of information on Ralph Street at the time of his arrest. Although, now she came to think of it, as he left the charge room following his suspension from duty he'd asked to see her – for reasons she couldn't fathom then. Still couldn't. The custody sergeant refused, telling him that no one, least of all the DCI, was remotely interested in anything he had to say. He was an outsider now. No longer one of *them*. He'd crossed that invisible line and there was no way back.

On leaving court, Trent had called, letting Daniels know that Dixon had been bailed, despite an application from the CPS for a remand in custody. He'd been in the dock less than five minutes – probably the longest of his life – the focus of much press attention, more was the pity.

Daniels sighed. *Bent cops sold newspapers.*

The case had been adjourned so Dixon could seek proper representation. He'd elected trial at the Crown Court. *Good move*. Odds were he'd get a lesser sentence that way. He was young in service, but experienced enough to know that judges tended to be less punitive than magistrates when evidence was presented to them, even in cases where there had been an appalling breach of trust. He was facing a custodial for sure. But, in determining length of sentence, a judge would listen to all the evidence, properly weigh up the mitigating factors and take into account his previous exemplary record.

He'd be counting on that.

There was no longer even a slim chance of a future on the force and Daniels was finding it hard to understand what on earth possessed him to return to the station to face the vitriol of his former colleagues. It wasn't anger *she* felt. It was sadness. Although Dixon had no one to blame but himself, the DCI took no pleasure in his downfall.

Still, the question remained: what the hell was he up to?

Dixon hung his head in shame as he was shown into the same interview room where he'd been questioned earlier. Daniels' way of making a point, he thought. He felt like scum off the street as he sat back down. His eyes scanned the bare walls, the fly-infested fluorescent tube above his head, the digital recorder that had captured his full confession, a soundtrack that would be replayed in a court of law should he choose to plead not guilty. He could almost see the heavies sitting opposite, their wisdom as well as their contempt on show.

Dixon's head was spinning, his face burning up with the heat in the room. His hands were ingrained with fingerprinting ink. It was in the charge room of the custody suite that the realization had dawned when he overheard two officers talking in low whispers about the Ralph Street fire. Not low enough. That snippet of station gossip had hit him like a brick. Daniels was looking for a female in uniform, a classy dresser, by all accounts.

Susan.

What a bloody fool he'd been.

After leaving court with his reputation in shreds, he'd gone home to remove his own uniform before making the most difficult journey of his life. He'd made one last attempt to contact Susan before the shit hit the fan. Then he'd driven back to the station for the final time, plucking up the courage to call Daniels instead.

Flinching as the door to the interview room flew open, Dixon stood to attention, force of habit in the company of a senior officer. Not that it mattered any more. Daniels charged into the room and didn't say a word. She didn't have to. He knew exactly what she thought of him by the ugly expression on her face. He couldn't feel any worse if she slapped him. Utterly ashamed of himself, he pushed an envelope across the table, George Milburn's money inside. He wasn't expecting thanks or sympathy.

Didn't get any either.

'I was duped, ma'am,' he said.

'Where have I heard that before?' Daniels pointed at the cash. 'You're a damn disgrace, Dixon. It was a shameful thing

to do. Whatever possessed you? No, don't answer that. Your girlfriend dumped you. I know, I heard. Get over it.'

Dixon looked at her, his face draining of colour. 'She's a firefighter, ma'am.'

Daniels sat down. He had her attention now.

62

Gormley's car sped up the West Road, dodging in and out of rush-hour traffic. After a long spell of blistering weather, the thunderstorm had been welcome, lifting the humidity and giving the ground a good soaking. The rain was short-lived. Within minutes of the downpour stopping, the sun came out and any surface water completely disappeared.

At the West End Fire Station, where Dixon said his girlfriend was stationed, they were met by the duty watch manager who told them no officer with the name Susan Armstrong worked there.

'Check again,' Daniels' tone suggested an order, not a request.

He eyeballed her. 'I know my officers.'

'Please . . .' she said, trying to placate him. 'We haven't got time to piss about. Can you do another search for Susan and Armstrong separately? She could've been married and reverted to a maiden name.'

Placing his fingers on computer keys, the watch manager searched the personnel database again. Looking up, he shook his head. 'No matches. No female firefighter of either name anywhere in the system – in fact, anywhere in service locally.'

Thanking him, Daniels apologized for her abruptness. He said he understood, but she doubted it. 'I require photo-

graphic records of all female personnel as soon as possible,' she said. 'I have a witness needs to take a look at them.'

The guy hesitated. 'I'm not sure—'

'Oh, don't whinge, man! Give us them. We're desperate to trace this woman!'

This time he didn't argue. He agreed to send the files electronically as soon as he'd cleared it with the appropriate authority. Daniels had a nasty feeling as she walked back to the car and got in.

Gormley put his seat belt on and then took it off again, straining to get the keys out of his left trouser pocket. Turning the car over, he asked Daniels where she wanted to go. Dixon had given Armstrong's address as Wingrove Road – a stone's throw away – and she told him that would be their next port of call. They could've walked there in minutes but, in view of her recent experience of leaving a car unattended, she suggested they take the Peugeot in order to keep a close eye on it.

Wheels squealed on dry tarmac as Gormley did a quick U-turn in a confined space and headed back the way they'd come. 'You think she'll be up for visitors?' he asked.

Daniels gave him a look. 'Why, you want to stop and buy cake?'

'I'm bloody starving, now you mention it.'

'You're always starving. Can you drive any slower?'

Ignoring her sarcasm, Gormley crossed the West Road, negotiated a mini roundabout and entered a wide street of red-brick Victorian houses. It was an area favoured by Asian householders, many of whom owned businesses nearby. Cars were parked on both sides of the road. Gormley braked

gently in order to scan the numbers on the doors, then stepped on the accelerator as he realized he had a way to go.

Lucky for them, there was a space outside the house. They got out of the car, walked up the path and rang the bell. After a few seconds of waiting, Gormley left Daniels on the door-step and took a peek through the bay window. The room was tidy but there were no lights on inside. No personal possessions lying around to suggest its occupant had just nipped upstairs.

He shook his head. *No signs of life.*

'We got grounds to obtain a warrant?' he said.

Daniels stared at the locked front door. 'Bloody right, we have.'

Gormley looked around, braced himself for a shoulder charge. Daniels held him back, preventing an unlawful entry, telling him the last thing they needed was to find their offender and have them escape justice on a technicality. No – if they were to catch this woman it would have to be water-tight.

'Everything by the book,' she said. Taking out her mobile, she called Carmichael. 'Lisa, we're at Susan Armstrong's house. We need a warrant. Get your arse into court with the necessary paperwork and make it snappy. If the magistrates have all gone home, interrupt someone's tea and don't take no for an answer – I need that double-U as soon as I can get it. Ring me when you have it. Better still, meet us here.'

Waiting for the warrant was a pain in the arse. Dead time. Time they could ill afford to waste. Gormley suggested they find a café on the West Road and wait there, but Daniels refused. She didn't want to leave in case Armstrong showed.

Sending him for a takeaway coffee, she went back to the car, ignoring the twitching curtains of neighbouring houses, imagining mobile phone calls criss-crossing the street. Why were the police sniffing around? What had Armstrong done?

What indeed?

When Gormley didn't immediately return, Daniels made a few calls and then lapsed into boredom. The door of the neighbouring house opened. A man walked out into the sunshine dressed in shorts. He sat down on his front door step, eating what looked like a bacon stottie – a large bap that was a favourite in this part of the world.

Daniels left the car.

Approaching the man, she offered up ID. 'Excuse me for spoiling your tea.'

'Breakfast,' he corrected her.

She nodded to the house next door. 'Do you know Ms Armstong?'

'Is that what she's called?'

God! You're a bundle of joy. 'You don't know her then?'

'Hasn't been there long . . .' He took a bite of his buttie and spoke with his mouth full. 'Never speaks to me or anyone else in the street. Keeps herself to herself, y'know. Fine with me, I'm a nightshift worker. Baggage handler at the airport, ten-to-six shift. The less people know I'm here all day, the better I like it.'

'I remember . . .' Daniels smiled. 'I used to work at your local nick when I was in uniform.'

'Nights are killers, the wife says.'

'Yes, they are. Would you know if Ms Armstrong lives alone?'

The man threw a crumb of bread to a bird in the garden. It hopped away, squabbling with another bird who wanted to share. 'Far as I know.'

'Any visitors lately?'

'A bloke, now you mention it.'

Dixon. 'Boyfriend?'

'Didn't get that impression . . .' He stifled a half-yawn. 'Didn't really suit each other, know what I mean? Bit rough for her, I would've said. She was classy . . . bit up herself.'

'Can you describe the man to me?'

'Middle-aged. Big. Swarthy complexion. A scar here.' He pointed to his right cheek.

Not Dixon.

'Hard-looking,' he added. 'You know the type.'

'Thanks. You've been really helpful.' Daniels turned her head away, giving her eyes a rest from direct sunlight. She noticed that the upstairs window of the house the other side of Armstrong's was open, a net curtain billowing out. She turned back to the man on the step. 'Mind if I send someone to take a formal statement, Mister . . .?'

'Caffrey. Anytime after three,' he grunted. 'Come earlier and you'll get no reply.'

'After three . . . I'll make sure it goes down on the sheet.'

As she walked down the path, Gormley arrived back at the car with a coffee in each hand. Just as she opened the door, Carmichael pulled up with a signed warrant and a battering ram.

63

It was an unremarkable rental property, like many in the neighbourhood. Not flash. Not scruffy. Just your average furnished let.

Stepping over unopened mail in the hallway, the DCI led the way, immediately dispatching Carmichael upstairs, telling Gormley to search the ground floor. Leaving them to get on with it, she checked out the kitchen at the back of the house. What she found there led her to believe that Armstrong hadn't been around for a few days. Either that or she'd already done a runner. There were some snacks in the fridge past their sell-by date, stuff Daniels classed as emergency food. There were no dishes in the sink. The bin was empty. The cupboards were bare and there was a thin film of dust on the work surfaces.

Unusual for a kitchen.

'This isn't a home. It's a drop address,' Carmichael said as she walked in. 'There's a change of clothes in the bedroom wardrobe, same size as those you found in Reid's gaff, a few items of toiletries in the bathroom: toothbrush, hairbrush, a bit of slap. The rest of the rooms are totally empty. But this was hanging on the bathroom door.'

She held up a blonde wig.

An exclamation from Gormley reached them from the living room.

'Hey, take a look at this!' he yelled.

They followed the voice. As they entered the room, Gormley opened his hand, gesturing towards an old-fashioned writing bureau in front of him. He looked elated. No wonder. He'd found a stash of incriminating evidence: several European passports, medical cards, bank and credit-card statements, suggesting that Susan Armstrong was more than your average con artist. Using the tip of his pen, Gormley turned over one of the medical cards, revealing a name: Judy Amos.

'Yes!' Carmichael was getting excited.

Snapping on a pair of Latex gloves, Daniels thought it ironic that intelligence on Reid's girlfriend – the elusive 'woman in uniform' – had come from a man who'd be stripped of his within a matter of months. Dixon had been well and truly duped. For a split second, she almost felt sorry for him, until revulsion took over when she thought of what he'd done. His actions were despicable: not only to George Milburn and his grandson, but to Chantelle Fox and his police colleagues too. Why should they be tarred with the same dirty brush? Right now though, that was the least of Daniels' worries . . .

Sifting through the passports, her stomach took a dive as a woman's face stared back at her from the laminated photographs in each. Despite attempts to change her appearance, there was no mistaking *her*. The SIO didn't need to ask Carmichael or Gormley for confirmation. They all knew it was Jennifer Rankin, the woman who'd casually walked into

Lottery HQ with a stolen ticket, passing herself off as a big prize winner. The question was, did she bludgeon an old lady to death – and, if not, who did?

'Hank, get a scenes of crime team down here now!' she said. 'And a uniform to stand guard until the house is secure.'

Gormley didn't move an inch. His face was white with rage and he appeared not to have heard her. There was no doubt in Daniels' mind that he was dwelling on his one and only brief encounter with Ivy Kerr, strapped to her seat in the pouring rain next to her dead husband, mayhem all around her, minutes before she met her end at the hands of a callous and cold-blooded killer.

In an attempt to snap him out of his reverie, Daniels raised her voice. 'Hank! CSIs, pronto! Lisa, get this lot bagged up, the entire contents of the bureau. Log everything meticulously and get it all back to the nick. As soon as it's been processed you're going to be very busy on that computer of yours.'

As soon as they got back to the incident room, Daniels went to brief Naylor. When she returned an hour later, Carmichael had made excellent progress. Susan Armstrong, aka Judy Amos, was already under investigation by the fraud squad, Interpol and the National Fraud Intelligence Bureau. The names were just two of several aliases used in connection with a real estate scam where foreign property was either sold or rented to unsuspecting victims, the proceeds channelled through Internet accounts in foreign banks in Spain, Portugal, Cyprus and other places before disappearing into the ether.

'Her criminal activity is well documented.' Carmichael buried her head in her notes. 'Funds go in and out of dodgy accounts like fiddlers' elbows, at which point accounts are abandoned and the trail goes cold. Investigators have travelled many a blind alley trying to collar her – whatever her name is. Her "businesses" look kosher, but they're far from that.'

Daniels rubbed at her aching neck. The lottery money had disappeared in much the same way, gone within seconds of arriving in the destination account, according to the guv'nor. She had wondered how the woman managed to bury it so quickly, why it left no trail. Now she knew. She'd worked in the fraud squad as a DS. If scams were well set up, it was like chasing shadows trying to follow the cash.

'Have you spoken to any of her victims?' Daniels asked.

'Andy has,' Carmichael said. 'Not one of them had any direct contact with her.'

'Doesn't surprise me,' Daniels said. 'Most business is conducted via email or phone these days. No one bats an eyelid, paying for stuff by electronic transfer without first seeing the goods. That's a gift for someone who's dodgy.'

Carmichael nodded. 'I gather victims turned up on holiday and found that either they weren't booked in, or else there was no dream villa in the sun. Poor buggers. Can you imagine ploughing your life savings into a pile of rubble, or turning up with your bucket and spade with nowhere to stay?'

'They only lost a holiday, Lisa. Or money. I have little sympathy.'

'That's a bit harsh.'

'Is it? Some people ask to be fleeced.'

'Even Ivy?'

Daniels gave her a pointed look. She didn't say as much, but the sad fact was the old lady had been foolish telling a stranger about her windfall.

Carmichael flicked her eyes right. 'Is Hank OK?'

Daniels glanced in Gormley's direction. Carmichael's hero had crumbled and was staring blankly out of the window, deep in thought. A massive breakthrough in a murder case was usually a time for celebration. *But not today.* A vicious killer was out there. He knew it. She knew it. And so did Carmichael. The team couldn't afford to relax. Gormley would have to 'man up' and get on with it. They needed to find this woman before she fled the country. She certainly had the means to do that. But first they needed to find out who she really was.

'It's late, Lisa.' Daniels managed a half-smile. 'We're all exhausted. He'll be OK.'

Responding to the whispering, Gormley turned around. He got up and walked over to join them. 'Did you record the names and numbers on the passports?' He was talking to Carmichael.

Nodding, Carmichael reeled off a list of names from her notebook.

'Gimme a look at that!' he said, taking it from her. He scanned her neat handwriting with Daniels breathing down his neck: Judy Amos, Karen Thompson, Marriane Forbes, Naomi Crouch, Olivia Raynard.

No Jennifer Rankin, Daniels noticed, but then why would there be? Whoever they were dealing with was clever and

sophisticated. She wouldn't risk using the same name twice. Gormley studied the names for what seemed like ages, noting that the capital letters of each first name ran alphabetically. He read them out: Judy . . . Karen . . . Marriane . . . Naomi . . . Olivia.

'The only missing letter is L,' he said, looking up.

'You think that's significant?' asked Carmichael.

He shrugged. 'I'd bet my pension that Judy Amos *is* Reid's girlfriend. His mates say she was shy and never joined them socially. Dixon told me the only reason he knew Armstrong's address is because he followed her home one night. She was cagey about where she lived and refused to have her picture taken. Now we know why. If Armstrong, Amos and Rankin are one and the same, we should alert the press. Every shift should have a copy of her picture. We should publish it on the PNC and in the media too. I want to lock this woman up so badly it hurts.'

Daniels didn't argue. It was nice to have him back.

64

The redhead lay back in the roll-top bath, surrounded by bubbles and drinking pink champagne in the penthouse of a converted printworks with stunning views of the city. She particularly liked the glazed brick walls, expansive windows and industrial architecture, the exposed steel and solid timber beams.

The apartment belonged to a musician who wanted to sell. But she'd talked the estate agent into a short let, pretending it was a 'try before you buy' lease when it was nothing of the kind. She needed the property for a day or two until the Cypriot gave her the nod to move. First, however, she had some unfinished business with Chantelle Fox . . .

Fox knew stuff – dangerous stuff that could be useful to the pigs. While the rest of the morons on Ralph Street had been getting pissed, she was not. She claimed to have photo-graphic evidence of the arson and wanted to cut a deal in return for keeping her big mouth shut. The redhead wasn't having that. She needed to silence the bitch before things got out of hand.

But how? It was risky with cops around and because of that the Cypriot was angry. He didn't understand why Fox was such a threat – why should he? – so she threw him an explanation to keep him off her back, reminding him that in

the early days the girl had been a source of cheap phones. That much was true, but it wasn't why she had to be dealt with.

'I didn't hear you complaining then,' the redhead said. It suited her to let him believe that Fox could implicate them both in serious fraud. 'How was I to know she'd turn on me and threaten us?'

She stressed the word 'us' so he understood that the threat extended to him also, even though that was not the case. She could hardly tell him the truth – that she'd been seeing other men while he was out of the country, one who was going places and knew how to treat a lady, the other an obsessive tosser who'd fallen for her big style – a polis who thought he was God's gift to women. Then he really would go off on one.

'You were a fool to use the girl!' he yelled.

'Hindsight is a wonderful thing,' she bit back. 'Chill out, why don't you?'

His eyes grew dark and dangerous. He hated being told to chill and was sweating like a pig. She didn't need him telling her that they stood to lose everything through her stupidity. She'd been insane to use Chantelle directly in the early days. Hadn't he told her time and time again to employ a go-between? *Always, always cover your tracks when requisitioning hardware. No trace. No way back to us.* No wonder he was spoiling for a row.

Any moment now he was likely to snap. Then he'd fly into one of his rages, guaranteed to last several hours – possibly even days. She was bored with his strops. Bored with him. He'd outlived his usefulness and she had plans to deal with that. In the meantime he was the one with all the contacts, so

she needed him for just a little longer, until she was free and clear of a difficult situation.

She wished she'd never met him. He was older than her, a small-time crook back then, posing as a businessman. A brief fling on the holiday island of Cyprus had led to something more serious before she'd learned what he really was up to. Instead of putting her off, it had the opposite effect. She'd seized her chance to muscle in as the UK arm of his operation.

It turned out to be a lucrative partnership.

Lifting her right leg out of the water, she watched the suds slide off her foot. Admiring her painted toenails, she thought of those early days. They had cooked up a scam to make easy money – and, boy, did they live up to that. People were so obliging. They were asking to be relieved of their hard-earned, accepting anything they were sent because it happened to look right, believing whatever they were told by the posh bird on the phone.

The redhead grinned.

She was good – *really* good.

Learning her scripts came as easy to her as learning the two times table. Before long she didn't need the written version. In fact, she was *so* good, she began believing she was who she said she was: a property developer, a foreign travel agent, whatever the hell she wanted to be. When not in the UK, she spent her time at his home in Cyprus. There was no extradition to the UK from the island, an obvious attraction should she be forced to flee the country in a hurry.

She'd always been clever at pulling the wool, a faulty gene she'd inherited from her father, a two-timing bastard who'd

let her mother down spectacularly. For years he'd lied about working away from home. In reality, he had a whole other life, a second wife too, they later discovered. But lying to her mother was nothing compared to what he had done to *her*.

The Cypriot reminded her of him and it made her skin crawl.

He was staring at her now.

'I teach you *nothing*?' he yelled. 'This girl? She sees. She exploits. She makes the most of every opportunity. We have something in common, do we not? Maybe it is her and not you I should've chosen to share my bed. Every one of us is greedy, my dear. It is basic human nature to want more than God gave us when we arrived in this world.'

He was right.

The bastard was *always* right.

Not that the redhead would ever admit it.

'I'll take care of it,' she said.

'We cannot afford to wait.' The Cypriot puffed on his cigar. 'You said yourself, the girl she is smart. Smarter than you, I hope. If that is true then we must assume she also realizes the information she has is too valuable to share. Pay her off. Do it tonight or we're finished, you and I.' He chucked a large brown envelope on the tiled floor. 'Our escape route. Make sure you study it to the letter. No more mistakes.'

The redhead knew what was inside: fresh passports, airline tickets, new names, new identities. She told him she'd sort it, find out what the girl knew and pay her off. Money talks, she told him, a more permanent solution entering her head. No need for cash to change hands. She'd silence Fox for good. It was that or forever face the threat of life imprisonment with

a tarrif-date of twenty-five years or more. She'd be drawing her pension before she saw the light of day. And she wasn't having that.

65

Daniels had stepped out for some air. It had been a hell of a day, but at least she was finally making headway. There was a way to go though, before catching the woman with the multiple aliases.

Her mobile rang.

Daniels had lost count of how many calls she'd received during the day. She checked her watch. It was five past ten. Maybe this was Matt West with the result on the cigarette end she'd found stubbed against the wall of Chantelle Fox's home. He'd promised it was imminent a couple of hours ago.

'DCI Daniels . . .' She cringed on hearing the voice on the other end of the line. It wasn't Matt West. Not even close. Daniels was tired of silly games. *Tired full stop.* She took the phone away from her ear, put it on speaker, and tried not to sound too interested. 'What can I do for you, Chantelle?'

'Nothing! But I can do something for you.'

Leaning against the wall of the station, Daniels waited for Chantelle to explain herself. She didn't speak right away, but the DCI could tell she was indoors, a TV on in the background, *News at Ten*, by the sounds of it, a programme she'd meant to catch herself. At her request, the BBC were running a piece warning people to be aware of a female fugitive wanted in connection with a murder by Northumbria Police.

And then the penny dropped . . . *Chantelle had seen the breaking news.*

'Has this got something to do with the woman I'm looking for?' Daniels asked.

'Might do.'

'Has it?'

'Just so happens I know who she is—'

The girl's voice was lost as a siren wailed into action close by. A panda car reversed, then shot out of the car park, blues-and-twos engaged. A Traffic car followed it out, adding to the din. Daniels waited for the noise to fade away. For a moment, she thought the girl had had second thoughts and hung up. Then she heard a siren on the other end. A coincidence? Or was Chantelle close by?

'Chantelle? Sorry, I didn't catch that.' Taking out her key, Daniels pushed open the back door and stepped inside. 'Who is she, Chantelle? I need a name.'

'Nice one, Inspector. You think I'm daft?'

'You really want me to answer that?' Daniels said, heading upstairs.

'Well, I'm not as daft as you, am I? 'Cause I know stuff would make your eyes pop.'

'So tell me. And stop buggering about – this is really important.'

'I need assurances.'

Daniels mounted the stairs two at a time. 'Such as?'

'That I won't face prosecution for wasting police time.'

'No deal . . .' Daniels paused on the landing. 'Look, tell me what you know and I'll see what I can do. I really could use some help here.'

'You're not the only one.'

'Fuck's sake! Tell me who she is!'

'You know what, forget it!'

The line went dead.

Cursing Chantelle, Daniels called Gormley but he didn't pick up. Running back down the stairs, she burst through the exit door looking for him. His car was nowhere in sight. He was probably out picking up Dixon – they needed confirmation that the woman he knew as Susan Armstrong was in fact the woman in the passports – or maybe he was in the Bacchus, having called it a day.

No. If that was the case, he'd have rung to let her know.

Daniels called Carmichael instead.

'Lisa, I'm in the station yard. Get down here ASAP. We've got a witness to see. And bring your snips. I've a feeling this one won't go quietly.'

66

Carmichael's old 3 series BMW pulled to the kerb. No kids around at this time of night to lighten their pockets for watching the vehicle. Ralph Street was in semi-darkness, streetlights still missing, despite Daniels' request to the city council to fix them. She looked up and down the terrace as she got out of the car. Some women were gathered in a doorway chatting. They looked over in her direction then went back to their conversation, unperturbed by her presence.

Seeing the law in *this* street was an everyday occurrence.

'Chantelle's obviously expecting us.' Carmichael pointed to an open front door.

'That's handy for us . . .' Daniels smiled. 'No need to knock or wait for an invitation.'

Daniels led the way, Carmichael behind as they passed through the hallway, stopping dead in their tracks as they entered the living room. The place had been trashed, thoroughly ransacked: drawers emptied on to the floor, cupboard doors flung open, the fireside rug lifted, cushions slashed – the stuffing inside removed.

The back kitchen was much the same.

A thud on the ceiling got their attention.

Carmichael froze. 'They haven't found what they were looking for then,' she whispered.

Daniels put a finger to her lip and pointed to the ceiling above. They moved out of the kitchen and back through the living room to the hallway, picking their way over the debris on the floor. The stairs were clear. Steep and narrow. Light shone out from a chink in one of the doors on the landing above.

Avoiding the centre treads, they crept silently up the stairs, keeping their bodies close to the wall. During situations like these, time stood still. It seemed an age before they reached the top. Another thud from inside the room. Carmichael withdrew her snips to use as a weapon. Daniels took a peek through the door jamb. *Nothing visible.* Her heart was punching a hole in her chest. Carmichael was tough, but they could've done with Gormley's bulk alongside them now. His sheer size was enough to put most offenders off.

Listening with her best ear, Daniels tried to identify how many people were searching. *One*, she thought. Reaching into her breast pocket, she took out a Maglite pencil torch and gently pushed open the door to her left, checking that no one was in there getting ready to rush them. Her torch beam panned around the bathroom. *Empty.* Second bedroom. *Empty.* No cupboards to hide in. No nasty surprises in there: a single bed, an old rocking chair, an exercise bike much like the one she had at home.

Her eyes scanned every corner, every shadow, knowing that Carmichael was watching her back the whole time. That was a given, instinctive. Just like the urge to keep moving forward when a civilian's response would be to flee the scene. Daniels listened again, planning to wait until the person inside was physically doing something before entering the

room. Two hands pulling out a drawer worked every time. She nodded to Carmichael and pointed to the floor.

Flattening herself against the wall so as not to get thrown back down the stairs, the DC positioned her foot in such a way to prevent the door being smashed into Daniels' face should someone try and make an escape.

A ticking noise was coming from the room.

Daniels' brow creased. Carmichael heard it too. She looked at her DCI: *What-the-fuck-is-that?* Daniels spread her hands: *No idea.* Experience told her that ticking sounds were not good. She took a deep breath and made her play.

'Shit, shit, SHIT!' Daniels exhaled loudly.

The ticking sound stopped as a black-and-white cat looked up, interrupted in its attempt to lick a creamy liquid off the carpet. As her heartbeat returned to normal, Daniels' eyes locked on to an open can of condensed milk that lay on its side on the floor, knocked off the bedside table, the source of the baby-sick smell that had confounded her from the moment she set foot in the place two long days ago.

'Boss? Over here!'

Carmichael was on the other side of the bed, staring at a point near the floor.

Daniels joined her and bent down. There was blood on the white duvet cover – *a definite hand print* – and a drip or two on the floor. She looked up, considering what might have happened here. Less than an hour ago, Chantelle Fox had admitted knowing the identity of a woman the whole force were looking for, a strong suspect for one murder and possibly more. Chantelle lived in Ralph Street, directly opposite one of the crime scenes and she was handy with a camera. It didn't take a genius to work out the rest.

'You better get the CSI lads down here, Lisa. Whoever killed Mark and Jamie Reid is responsible for this.'

'You think they took her? Why not kill her?'

'It looks like they tried.'

'But why?'

'I suspect Chantelle's been playing David Bailey again. Pound to a penny she's got more photos. Only these aren't of the old man. I think she saw the arsonist and she's been playing silly buggers in order to make some easy money, blackmailing someone who desperately wants to remain anonymous . . . This time Chantelle bit off more than she could chew.' Daniels glanced at the bloody duvet. 'I told you she wouldn't come quietly.'

Her mobile rang, startling them both. 'It's her!' Daniels pushed a button on her phone. 'Chantelle?'

'The name you want is Lucy Laidlaw.'

Daniels registered this was a name beginning with L. 'Chantelle, are you OK?'

'What do you care?' The girl sounded scared to death and out of breath. She was crying now, her distress reaching Daniels via loud sobs in her right ear. 'You make sure you get the bitch. She nearly fucking killed me.'

'Where are you? Are you hurt?'

'I've had worse . . .' Chantelle paused, choking back tears. 'Inspector?'

'I'm still here. Let me come and get you—'

'No! You be careful, OK? She's one fucking psycho!'

The phone went dead.

67

Tuesday. Nine a.m. The briefing room was full. Some detectives were sharing desks, two and three apiece, the rest standing in groups waiting for the meeting to begin, every single person associated with both cases crammed into the room. Carmichael, Brown and Robson had formed a little faction of their own. They'd had the sense to grab a mug of tea before a rush on the drinks machine. To their left, Maxwell and Gormley's conversation was about football, in particular Brazil's three–nil win over Chile that had nudged them closer to a sixth World Cup title. But most of the excitement in the room was work related.

Since early doors, phones had been ringing off the hook. An image of Susan Armstrong had appeared again, not only on breakfast television, but in the headlines of the local papers and some of the nationals on sale in the shops.

It was the biggest story for years.

The public outcry Daniels had anticipated had arrived. People were incensed at such a despicable act of cruelty to such a vulnerable accident victim. The fact that a rogue fire officer might be involved, not only in the death of Ivy Kerr but also in the arson attack that killed Mark and Jamie Reid – had been withheld from the media for the time being. That revelation would come later, when they caught the bastard responsible.

Daniels' phone rang: *The fire investigator.*

She covered the speaker. 'Guv, I should take this. It's Geoff Abbott.'

'Go ahead,' he said. 'I'll start the ball rolling.'

Naylor told the team to get comfy, outlining the need for a thorough case review.

'Things have moved fast in the last twenty-four hours,' he began. 'Yesterday, acting on information received from PC Dixon – who overheard station gossip about a woman in uniform we were desperate to track down – Hank and the DCI attended the West End fire station where she allegedly worked. They found no trace of her. At that point they had no photograph to show the watch manager and the DCI put in a request for personnel records of all female staff to be made available. She and Hank then went to the address of Susan Armstrong and later obtained a warrant. A search of the premises revealed two things. First: the clothing left there, such as it was, is size 14. An average size, you might say. But it matches that found in Mark Reid's house. Second: the search turned up several passports, all bearing the photograph of a woman who'd attempted to disguise herself by changing hairstyle or colour.'

'There was a wig there too, guv,' Carmichael reminded him.

'Yes, thank you, Lisa.' He smiled. 'I'd forgotten that. Even more shocking is the fact that the woman in the passports is the same woman captured on film at Lottery HQ – the one passing herself off as Jennifer Rankin.' He paused a moment. 'Everyone clear so far?'

There were nods all round.

'Good.' Naylor glanced at Daniels, who was still on the phone. It was important to go over events. This case was getting more and more complex by the minute. 'Last night, PC Dixon was shown the passports we retrieved from Armstrong's house. He confirmed that his former girlfriend is the woman in the photos. Therefore we know she is using several aliases. Although we can't yet prove it, I think – and the DCI agrees with me – that Judy, the girlfriend of Mark Reid, the un-ident buying petrol *and* Jennifer Rankin are one and the same woman. Anyone disagree?'

There were no dissenters.

'Not likely, guv,' someone at the back called out.

'The DCI took the unprecedented step of asking the media to put out a picture of the woman on national TV . . .' He stopped talking as Daniels put down the phone.

'Geoff Abbott is on board,' she said. 'He'll get back to me in five. May I?' She took his nod as her cue to take over. 'When the news went out last night, Chantelle Fox rang me, claiming to know the identity of "Susan Armstrong". By the time Lisa and I got round there, the place had been thoroughly ransacked and there were signs of a struggle, an amount of blood on the floor. Chantelle called again. The poor kid was scared to death. She gave the name Lucy Laidlaw and rang off. Now then – and this is important, so get your notebooks out, because I'm going to be putting out actions any minute . . .'

She waited until the team were ready.

'Several names were thrown in the hat this morning, but I think we struck lucky. One witness, a man called Ben Foster, rang in claiming he'd met the woman on a train to London

King's Cross on Thursday the twenty-fourth of June, a matter of hours after Ivy Kerr was killed. She was using the name Laidlaw but not Lucy. She must've fancied Liv that day. I think she let her guard down and gave her real name by mistake. The name Laidlaw has never come up in the Fraud Intelligence Bureau's investigation. Liv is short for Olivia, by the way, which does appear in one of the passports Hank found in the bureau at Armstrong's drop address. Reduces the likelihood that Chantelle may have been mistaken, yes?'

Again there were nods. The team were buoyed by what she'd told them. She could see it in their eyes. They were on their marks and raring to go. Now all they had to do was prove it . . .

'Cherchez la femme,' she said. 'And to help you in that task, I've asked one of our analysts to interrogate HOLMES for unknown females and un-ident females currently in the system.'

'Excuse me, ma'am . . .' A hand went up at the back. An officer assigned to the team on a temporary basis was looking puzzled. 'What's the difference between unknown and un-ident females exactly?'

'That's a good question. Unknowns are exactly that: persons about whom nothing is known. Whereas un-idents are those where there is some information assigned: for example a partial name, an approximate address, a street name, a workplace. Any information we have that might lead to a full identification at a later date.'

Her explanation seemed to satisfy him and she moved on.

'Hair and eye colour is something that can easily be changed with the use of dyes and or lenses. So we're match-

ing physical descriptions here: height, size, shape – character-
istics that are harder to alter or disguise.' She pointed at the
murder wall where the faces of Jamie and Mark Reid and
Ivy Kerr stared back at her. 'We have three victims so far.
Chantelle Fox is lucky her picture isn't up there too. She's in
grave danger and I want her picked up. We need to find her
before Laidlaw does.'

She caught Gormley's eye.

He shook his head, explained to the others that he'd called
at her house on the way in. There was no sign of her and no
indication she'd been back to the property since it was
trashed. 'She's probably keeping her head down until Laidlaw
is picked up,' he said.

'Smart move,' someone muttered.

'Chantelle has my number,' Daniels said. 'So hopefully
she'll use it. If she does call the incident room, try and per-
suade her to come in. Tell her I need to talk to her urgently
and she'll get all the protection she needs. If she won't play
ball, ask if she knows anything about Laidlaw's male friend
and possible accomplice. Caffrey, the guy who lives next door
to the drop address, described him as a "rough-looking
Mediterranean", so another un-ident we know nothing about.
Andy, keep your eye on the incident log. If Chantelle fled in a
hurry and has no money, she'll be up to her old tricks.'

Brown nodded.

Daniels picked up a remote and pressed a few buttons. The
images on the murder wall changed. There were now several
pictures side by side: the passport photos, the grainy shot
obtained at the garage, a photograph Dixon had taken
covertly for a keepsake, and one the team hadn't seen before

– a good facial image Daniels had uploaded from her phone a mere ten minutes ago.

She highlighted it on the wall. 'This is a photograph I obtained from Steven Watkins, the film buff Hank and I came across at the accident. Lisa managed to track him down through a contact she has at the North East Screenwriters' Group. Last night I interviewed Keith Jewitt, the writer who runs it. Nice man,' she said. 'He speaks highly of Watkins, describing his weird behaviour as youthful exuberance. Early this morning, I knocked Watkins up. Jewitt was right. He's not such a prat as I first thought. He apologized for his remarks and promised not to let his passion for manufactured gore get confused with the real stuff in future. He gave me this picture and it puts Laidlaw firmly at the scene. The hat in her hand is the one Cole captured on video from the air in the backseat of Ivy's car, I bet.'

Dozens of eyes were fixed on the image.

'Anyone wish to comment before we move on?' Daniels asked.

'Jesus! Look at the eyes,' Carmichael said. 'Ice woman or what?'

'They're pretty evil.' Brown looked at Daniels. 'Your film guy deserves a BAFTA.'

'You want me to grab a female officer and take some photographs of my own, boss?' Maxwell said. 'I'm happy to.'

Naylor frowned. 'You finding this funny, Neil?'

'No, guv. Perhaps I should rephrase that.' Maxwell glanced at the murder wall. 'Dixon claims Susan Armstrong is five-ten. I'm suggesting I take a policewoman to the garage. Stand her in exactly the same spot and get some CCTV footage for

comparison. It would confirm or dismiss the person's height, man or woman.'

'That's not a bad idea,' Daniels said.

'I'm full of them, boss.'

The DCI's phone rang.

She answered with a bark. 'Yes! What is it?' After listening in earnest for a moment, she thanked the person on the other end and then hung up, her solemn expression placing everyone on alert. She turned to Naylor. 'Guv, that was Abbott again. Remember the fire officer who went sick with post-traumatic stress after the accident?' She paused. 'It's Laidlaw. Lucy Laidlaw.'

68

Thunder rumbled overhead. It had been raining heavily since first light and the windows of the small café were all steamed up. Chantelle shivered. She was soaked to the skin having come out of her hidey-hole to find some breakfast, a place no one would think of looking for her in a million years.

Another rumble of thunder.

Using her hand, she wiped a window in the condensation and peered through it. Outside, people in summer clothes were running for shelter under misshapen umbrellas, cars had their lights on and a small group of shoppers were sheltering in a doorway across the road, waiting for a break in the weather. Chantelle wondered how Rooney was doing at home. Probably hiding under her bed, scared stiff as usual. She loved that cat. He was a stray she'd picked up off the street, the only living thing she gave a shit about. He needed his scran, just as she did, and would probably starve to death in a few days if he wasn't fed.

Depressed by that thought, Chantelle finished her bacon buttie and picked up her tea. But the mug was empty, just cold dregs in the bottom. At the counter, the middle-aged woman who owned the café was serving take-aways to youths from the building site down the road. She had greying hair cut too short for her oval face and was wearing a Harrow

checked tabard type apron fastened at the sides with Velcro.
She gave a young man his change, throwing a concerned look
at Chantelle as he made his way out the door.

'Are you OK?' she asked.

Other customers turned to see who the owner was talking
to, their eyes sliding over Chantelle.

'I'm fine!' Chantelle said. 'So you can all stop gawping!'

The owner wasn't convinced. 'You don't look it.'

'You looked in the mirror lately?' Chantelle bit back.

'Did your mother never teach you manners, young lady?'

Yeah right, Chantelle thought. The only thing her mother
had ever taught her was how to play roulette and how to
apply fake tan.

The woman had come out from behind her counter and
was now standing over her.

'Can I get you anything else before you go?'

It was a heavy hint that she was no longer welcome.

Ignoring the woman, Chantelle dropped her head into a
magazine someone had left on the table, eyeing the lush
watches on the wrists of the stars. One of them was practi-
cally identical to the watch Laidlaw had been wearing last
night. The memory of the encounter made her tremble.
Chantelle had been watching the vicious cow for days and
knew exactly what she was up to: fancy new watch, new car,
new names too, according to the papers. *Well, not any more.*
Not now Chantelle had done her civic duty by tipping off
Daniels and the fat fucker.

The police were lucky there were people like her around.

'You need medical attention.' The loitering owner un-
crossed her arms and pointed at the makeshift bandage on

Chantelle's wrist, the blood-stained fingers poking out from beneath. 'Your face isn't much better. Look at the state of you!' Her voice softened. 'Has something happened to you, dear? Shall I call someone? The police?'

'No! Just get lost and leave me alone. I slipped in the bath, that's all.'

Chantelle's lie was the first thing that came into her head: the excuse women give in prison if they're attacked in the shower block and don't want to snitch to the zombies looking after them. She knew the wound needed stitches but was too scared to go to casualty in case Lucy was watching. She didn't want the café owner's sympathy. She couldn't cope with that.

'Then I'm sorry, but I'm going to have to ask you to leave . . .' The owner indicated the door. 'This is a café, not a waiting room, and you're upsetting my regulars. Besides, it's against health and safe—'

'Bollocks!' Chantelle got up so suddenly the chair fell backwards and landed with a crash on the floor. Two old ladies at the next table picked up their shopping and made for the exit. A bell sounded as they pulled the door open and waddled out into the pouring rain. Chantelle turned back to the owner. 'See . . . you're the divvi upsetting everyone! You could do with a course on customer service. And don't you ever call me *dear!*'

The woman held out her hand. 'That'll be one pound fifty.'

'Bacon was off. Tea was like piss. You can swing for it, *pet!*'

And with that, Chantelle was gone.

69

Now that Laidlaw's description had been widely circulated, the public were on the lookout and the incident room was buzzing with excitement. Call takers were rushed off their feet. Within the last hour, they had received hundreds of calls from people claiming to know her, some adamant that they had seen her recently. It was impossible to say how many of them were genuine, but all sightings were being checked by an outside team as a matter of urgency. Another team were out looking for Chantelle.

Daniels could see hope in the faces of murder investigators. They knew they were closing in on a suspect. Two cases were at stake here, involving three murders, so it was all hands on deck to make an arrest. In a show of unity and inter-agency cooperation the Chief Fire Officer and the Chief Constable of Northumbria Police had agreed that Geoff Abbott could assist them in order to bring Laidlaw to justice as quickly as possible. He'd just arrived at the office looking a little sheepish with her personnel file under his arm.

'Welcome to my world,' Daniels said. Abbott had never been in the new Major Incident Suite before. 'Good to have you on board, Geoff.'

'Tell me that when you've read this.' He tapped the file.

'Is there a problem?' Daniels asked.

'I'd say there might be.' He sighed, handing over the file and watching as she scanned the pages contained therein. 'It's what's not in there that worries me, Kate. It seems Laidlaw may have slipped through the recruitment net. She had a traumatic early childhood and time spent in care, but there's no psychological assessment, no psychometric test score. Need I go on?'

'Why am I not surprised?'

'What d'you mean?'

'Dixon says she's a manipulative looker who knows how to get what she wants.' Daniels shook her head. It never ceased to amaze her how women – even in her own organization – could get on by batting their eyelashes or stroking the egos of the decision makers. More than a smile and you were destined for a meteoric rise through the echelons of the police service. Nobody cared if you could actually do the job. It was whether you looked good that counted. She glanced sideways. 'Hank, get Jo on the phone. Tell her we need her in on this one after all.'

'After all? Something I missed?'

'Don't question me, Hank. Just do it!' Daniels winced as he sloped off in a strop, passing Andy Brown coming the other way. The DC seemed a little out of breath and headed straight towards her, pulling up sharply as her mobile phone rang in her hand. The display read: Matt West calling.

About bloody time. She was keen to hear the results of the samples he'd been testing.

'Matt, what you got for me?' she said.

'You want the good news or the bad?'

'Don't you start!'

'Pardon?'

'Doesn't matter. What's up?'

He hesitated. 'Your fag sample was contaminated by one of my interns.'

'For God's sake! We're running a triple murder case here!'

'I'm so sorry, Kate. We only used part of the sample, so it is possible to do the whole thing again.' He paused – probably feeling her frustration down the line, hoping she wouldn't fly off on one. 'The guy who made the mistake is a good kid. He's shitting himself that you'll make things difficult for him. Can I put his mind at rest?'

Daniels swore, DS Robson's blunder on a serial murder case popping into her head as he walked past her in the MIR. More recently, Carmichael had come a cropper while working under cover. No matter how much care was taken, how much training given, human error crept in from time to time. Abbott and Brown were both still hovering. She mouthed the word *sorry* before going back to her call. The error was hardly Matt West's fault.

'Don't you worry about it,' she said, trying to keep her temper in check. 'To be honest, the pressure we're under, I'm amazed it doesn't happen more often. We're not perfect this end either. But you be sure to kick his arse and tell him I'm not at all happy. This is a murder enquiry not a petty theft and he should take more care. There will be no complaint from me, but leave him in no doubt he owes me – and I *will* collect.'

'Thanks, Kate.' West sounded relieved.

Daniels glanced at her watch. *Five to eleven.* 'How soon can you get back to me?'

'I'll get on to it right away. As soon as I have a result, I'll call you.'

Daniels registered the indirect answer. Matt West was the most meticulous scientist she'd ever worked with. She'd have a reliable result sooner rather than later. She thanked him, hung up and looked at her waiting DC.

'You wanted to see me, Andy?'

Brown nodded. 'A young woman matching Chantelle's description nicked off without making payment at a café in the West End. The proprietor thinks she's seen her before. Said she'd taken quite a beating and was bleeding from an arm injury. It sounded pretty bad, so much so, the owner was more concerned to report an assault than she was about getting her money back.'

'Sounds like a nice lady.'

'She is. Want me to take care of it?'

'No, I'll sort it, thanks.' She turned to Abbott. 'Sorry, this is important, I've got to go. Can you sit tight 'til our profiler gets here? I'm sure she won't be long.' She grabbed Brown before he had chance to walk away. 'Andy, get Geoff a coffee and bring him up to speed on where we are.' On the way out the door, she rang Gormley. He picked up right away and she dropped her voice so she wouldn't be overheard by officers in the corridor. 'Sorry I snapped at you before. Things are difficult between Jo and I. When she arrives, can you pair her with Geoff? They can work in my office. Tell her . . .' she paused. 'Doesn't matter, I'll tell her myself. Oh shit!'

'What's up?'

'I rode in! Forget what I said before. Just meet me in the car park and bring your keys with you. I might need to trans-

port someone to hospital and I can hardly do that on the back of my bike.'

By the time he got there, Daniels had repeated her instruction to Carmichael.

'Where we going?' Gormley asked.

'Café.'

His eyes lit up. 'Brill!'

'Don't get excited. We won't be eating. I'll explain on the way.'

They reached the café about fifteen minutes later and took a statement from the owner, satisfied that it really was Chantelle the woman had seen. Daniels called the MIR and asked Robson to arrange a uniformed presence at casualty at the hospitals in the city: the Royal Victoria Infirmary and Newcastle General Hospital, the latter being the best bet in view of its location in the West End. Then they walked back to Gormley's car.

'If she's injured, where would she hide?' Daniels asked, getting in.

'She'll be bunkered in with a mate somewhere.'

'No, that's too risky, for her and her mates. She described Laidlaw as a psycho, Hank. She wasn't spooked when I spoke to her, she was bloody terrified. Her world is microscopic compared to ours. She's lived in the same house all her life, never goes further than the corner shop, works just a few streets away – although not today. I checked and got a mouthful of abuse for my trouble. Her P45 is in the post, according to her boss.'

'Oh, she'll love that!' Gormley was being ironic. 'What about the neighbours?'

'No chance. Believe me, she'll be as far from Ralph Street as she can possibly get.'

'Unless—'

'What?' Daniels could see he was excited about something. 'You think she's in George Milburn's empty house?'

'Close . . .' he smiled. 'I think I know exactly where she is.'

70

Gormley started the car. Cancelling windscreen wipers left on when he'd cut the engine, he drove out of the side street on to the main road. While they were in the café, the rain had stopped and the sun had come out, the same blistering heat the country had enjoyed in the run-up to the World Cup. Daniels could feel it on her left arm through the passenger window and noticed steam rising from the pavements on either side of the road.

'You going to tell me where we're going?' she asked.

'Benwell Lane.'

'Because . . .?'

'That's where George Milburn's allotment is.'

She grinned. 'You're smart, you know that?'

'You better believe it!' He opened his window, allowing the breeze into the car. His Peugeot had no air conditioning and it was like an oven inside. 'Chantelle may be a wrong 'un but she's smart, boss. She knows Elliot Milburn won't be there. He was so devastated by his Granddad's death, he's hardly been able to bring himself to visit the house, let alone the old man's cherished plot. They spent a lot of time there together.'

'You like him, don't you?'

'Elliot? There's nothing to dislike. He reminds me of Ryan in many ways. Not because they're the same age. He's got a

lovely nature and good manners. He's a breath of fresh air from the shite we sometimes come across.'

Daniels swivelled in her seat, trying to catch his eye. But Gormley kept his eyes on the road, slowing right down as they approached traffic lights where a crocodile of nursery-age children were waiting to cross. He hadn't mentioned his son in ages, or his wife for that matter, and she wondered how things were going at home.

'How is he?' she asked. 'Ryan, I mean.'

'Struggling. Not that he talks about it much . . . I thought we might take off somewhere after we wrap this case up, have a bit of fun, do stuff like we used to. Julie said he's thinking of moving out. Can't say I blame him.'

'Where to?' Daniels closed her window as they arrived at the allotments.

'He's got mates at Northumbria uni he can share with.' Gormley pulled on the hand brake and removed his key from the ignition, glancing to his left, meeting her eye. 'I wasn't too keen at first, but I think it'll be good for him.' He pointed through the windscreen. 'How do you want to approach this?'

'I've got to make a quick call.' She pulled her phone from her pocket. 'Can you contact the council? Find out the number and location of the Milburn plot? There are forty allotments in there. It'll save time.'

They both began dialling. Gormley's call was answered almost immediately. He asked for the allotments officer and was put on hold to wait for a man named Richard Waites. The number Daniels had called was still ringing in her ear. She was about to put the phone down when Sergeant

McCabe answered with his telephone number. She couldn't decide if he sounded drowsy or drunk.

'Mick?' She waited. *No reply.* 'Mick, are you OK?'

'Did you find Bridget's ring?'

Definitely drunk. 'No, I'm sorry. It must've come off at the crash site. Are the girls home yet? I thought—' But he was already gone. 'Damn it!'

'McCabe in a bad way?'

'Wouldn't you be? Come on, we need to find Chantelle.'

They got out of the car and walked through the allotment gates. The plots nearest to the entrance were a riot of colour. A couple of old men were sitting on a bench admiring the view – fag in hand, a mug of tea – brief respite from a hard morning's labour. One fat, one thin, both heads shaded by flat caps against the midday sun. Typical northern males. They wouldn't have looked out of place making their way into a shipyard or to the coal face, if either industry had still existed.

'Fine day,' one of them said.

'Aye, for some . . .' Gormley held up ID. 'We're looking—'

'She's still in there . . .' The thin man gave them a knowing look and held out his hand. 'I'm ex-job.'

'Thinks we didn't notice her sneaking in,' the other man said.

Gormley and Daniels shook hands with both of them.

'Nowt gets past Jake . . .' the ex polis grinned. 'He outranks me by a mile round here. Has held a plot longer than the rest of us. Makes awful tea, mind. I'd offer you a cup but I'm guessing you're not here to chat or they'd have sent a wooden top like me. I never made it to CID, more's the pity. Uniforms

were scratchy and heavy in my day, no short sleeves in summer like the young 'uns you see walking the streets nowadays . . .' He nodded to the shed where Chantelle was hiding. 'It's the one with the horseshoe on the door.'

'We thought we'd leave her be, given George's recent bereavement,' the other man added. 'No need to chase her until the committee is notified. She'll be family, no doubt. Come to pay her respects at his second home.'

'Something like that,' Daniels said.

The octogenarian knew different. Kate could see it in his eyes. He had obviously felt sorry for Chantelle and didn't want to move her on. Conversation over, the old guys put down their mugs and staggered from the bench, regretting the tea-break now their bones and muscles had seized up. As they resumed their digging, Daniels and Gormley walked on, arriving at George Milburn's shed just as Chantelle made a run for it.

71

Chantelle didn't get far. The fences were in good order and she was in no condition to stand, let alone resist being taken into custody for her own safety. She slumped to the ground looking awfully pale, her right cheek so badly swollen it had forced her eye shut. Dried blood covered a shocking pink scarf wrapped loosely around her right wrist and her fingers were twice their normal size.

'Get her in the car,' Daniels ordered. 'On second thoughts, ring the General, Hank. Let them know we're on our way.'

'No chance!' Chantelle pulled away. 'I'm not going to hospital. That's the first place Lucy will look. She knows I'm hurt.'

'No arguments, Chantelle. You need emergency treatment. You could die of septicaemia.' As Gormley turned away to make the call, Kate helped the girl to her feet. 'Quit struggling, will you! You're coming whether you like it or not. No, *listen* to me!' Chantelle went limp. She'd finally run out of steam. 'That's better . . . you'll be completely safe, I *promise* you. You'll get police protection and a safe house if necessary until we make an arrest. If Laidlaw comes within half a mile of the hospital we'll be waiting there to lock her up.'

Emotionally exhausted, Chantelle began to weep.

'Come here . . .' Daniels embraced the girl, hugging her

gently as her tears turned to sobs. She was in a bad way and Kate was determined to catch the sadistic cow responsible. But first she needed to get Chantelle some help. Shushing her, trying to offer reassurance, she said: 'Lucy can't hurt you now. Can you walk or d'you want the "fat fucker" to carry you?'

Chantelle managed a weak smile. 'I can walk.'

'That's the way.' Daniels returned the smile. 'Come on, we need to go.'

The DCI looked worriedly over her shoulder as the car sped up Condercum Road, then right on to the West Road towards the city's General Hospital. Chantelle was lying asleep across the back seat of the Peugeot, cradling her bad arm on her stomach. Her knees were bent, her eyes shut, her breathing laboured. Getting her to the car had proven more difficult than either of them anticipated. Hank had picked her up and carried her the last few metres, laying her gently on the seat, suspecting broken ribs.

Chantelle stirred.

'Lucy's living in the Turnbull Building. I've been following her for days. Stupid, aren't I?' Wincing in pain, she forced her eyes open. Her right eye was blood red, no white visible. She tried to sit up but Daniels told her to lie still. She looked absolutely wrung out. 'Promise me you'll get her. I wanna go home and feed Rooney, my cat.'

'We'll collect him, don't worry,' Daniels said. 'Was Lucy with anyone else?'

'Didn't see anyone.'

'OK, let's get you sorted first and then we'll look into it.'

Turning away, Daniels rang Brown. 'Andy, we've got

Chantelle and we're en route to the General. Send someone to meet us there to guard her while she receives treatment. I doubt she'll be discharged today, but if she is I want her taken to a safe house until further notice, understood?'

'Yep. Anything else?'

'No, yes. Is Lisa about?'

'She's right here.'

'Tell her to find out as much as possible about the interior of Turnbull Building . . .' Daniels didn't need to tell him which building it was. Like everyone else in the area, he knew the landmark well. A Grade II listed former Victorian print-works, it had been converted years ago and was now one of the most prestigious addresses in the heart of the city centre. At the entrance lodge of the hospital, she waved ID at the security guard as they drove through. 'I want a floor plan, if she can manage it. I'll explain when I get back. And get some-one over to Chantelle's place to find and feed her cat. It goes by the name of Rooney.'

Daniels hung up feeling a real sense of excitement. Gormley felt it too, by the look of him.

Laidlaw would have seen the news. In the past twenty-four hours, her face had been splashed over every TV screen and newspaper. She'd be keeping a low profile for sure, biding her time until she could make a run for it. But investigators from the murder squad not only knew *who* she was, they knew *where* she was, if the information from Chantelle Fox was correct. Their suspect had no idea that they were on to her location and that gave them the upper hand for the first time since the enquiry began.

Game on, Daniels thought.

72

'You idiot!' the Cypriot yelled. 'You go back. And this time you do it properly!'

Yeah, right. As if.

Lucy glared at him. There were times when stuff just didn't go according to plan. This whole week had been like that. She was tempted to tell him about her little forays on the side, her relationships with other men, her scheme to leave his sorry arse and go it alone. But this wasn't the right moment. She'd been biding her time for two years, learning the ropes, infiltrating his contacts. Soon, he'd be going the same way as her old man. The same way as—

Lucy picked up her drink and slugged it back. She couldn't bear to think about Mark in that house as the fire swept through it. It was never part of her plan that he should suffer. Or the child – she cringed – *that beautiful, beautiful child.* No, it was *her*: the leech draining his bank balance that she wanted to disappear. Maggie was the one deserved to fry.

Another slug of her drink.

Mark had been good to her. He was the only man who'd treated her with any respect. He was a good man too, as near to a perfect partner as she'd ever come across, the only man who had ever managed to make her feel—

Lucy shut her eyes as her father's hands crept over her

skin. Even from the grave he managed to make her feel dirty. What was she thinking? It would never have worked with Mark. Once he found out what she'd been up to, he'd have cut her loose. No point in crying about it now, was there? No one's fault if people couldn't stick to their bloody babysitting arrangements. And how was she to know that a better scenario would present itself that very same night? But it had . . .

The old gadgie had croaked by the time she reached the scene of the accident. Fortunately for Lucy, the old bird was still alive. Had plenty to say for herself too, letting slip her big secret, the one that would change her life.

Hadn't it just.

Lucy recalled the moment when the silly old woman told her that she'd won the lottery. 'Wow!' she'd said. 'How cool is that?' She'd patted the woman's bony hand, flashing her a winning smile before panic set in. 'Ivy? Ivy?' Lucy had tapped the old woman's face, almost slapped it to bring her round. *Don't you fucking die on me.* 'You need to stay awake, love. Ivy?'

Ivy's eyes strained to focus and then she was back.

'That's better . . . you feeling a bit more comfortable now?'

'A little.' She was being brave, fading fast.

A voice called out: 'Need any help in there?'

Fuck! Out of the corner of her eye Lucy had seen the copper standing there in the pouring rain, his high-viz jacket on and built like a brick shithouse. With her heart banging in her chest, she had remained crouched over, pretended to work the steering column free, willing the bastard to move away from the car.

Breathe. Breathe, she'd told herself, whispering to the old

girl. 'We've got it covered here, haven't we, Ivy? You're a star, aren't you, love?'

'Nice of him to ask,' Ivy managed in return.

'You must be overjoyed with that win, eh? Planning anything? That's if you don't mind me asking . . .' Lucy had tried to sound casual, allowed her voice to trail off. She'd waved a hand in front of her face as if dismissing some ridiculous notion, her thoughts on all that money. Cash that would go to waste on an old codger who'd most probably be dead in a year – a month, a week – if Lucy didn't act. *Unless.* 'Have you out of there in a jiffy, love.'

Ivy turned her head sideways. 'What were you going to say, dear?'

'Nothing . . .'

'Please, you've been so kind.'

'No, it's daft . . .' Ivy was about to let the matter drop, so Lucy added, 'I was going to ask where the lucky shop is.' She grinned, glancing at Ivy's crushed leg. The bleeding was getting worse and worse. 'Thought I might buy a ticket on my way off duty. You never know, I might get lucky too.'

'They say lightning never strikes twice though, don't they?' Ivy said.

Lucy tried for a grin. 'Yeah, you're probably right.'

'Well, it's rubbish. There was a big win there not so long ago. The girl on the lottery counter told me so. You get yourself along there, dear. Tesco Extra at Kingston Park.' Ivy glanced at her husband, who still hadn't moved. 'We play the same numbers every week and get one lucky dip. Neither of us smoke or drink and we don't go out much nowadays. It's a bit of fun really. We like checking the numbers as they're

drawn, don't we, John?' She reached for her husband's hand. 'Can you get him a blanket, dear? He's cold.'

'Course I can,' Lucy said, reaching for her service torch.

It was a lucky dip, all right. Lucy grinned to herself. *Just not Ivy's.*

'You think this is a joke, eh?' the Cypriot barked.

Lucy looked away. Did he really think he was still in control? She was worth a mint, had taken huge risks to get the money without his help. The only reason she'd told him about it was because she needed his help to filter it away quickly. *No trace. No way back to us.* Just as he'd taught her. And now she had no further use for him.

She didn't answer: *at least not in words.*

73

Six days in and things were moving fast. Having deposited Chantelle in the Accident & Emergency department at the General Hospital, ordering a uniformed presence to remain with her at all times, Daniels had returned to the station to meet up with the team. Her phone rang constantly on the way there. Asking the press for help to identify Laidlaw had lifted the profile of the case in the eyes of local and national journalists who wanted chapter and verse on progress and she'd had to fend off their questions for fear of tipping them off.

'So now we know where they are,' Naylor said. 'How do you propose to handle it?'

'Do we need armed response?' Maxwell said, interrupting.

Daniels shook her head, feeling under pressure to bring in Laidlaw and her cohort. 'There's no question that she's violent, but no evidence she's armed. If she had been, Chantelle wouldn't be alive to tell the tale.'

Maxwell was disappointed. Years ago, he'd applied to be part of the armed response unit but was turned down flat: not the right persona and therefore unfit. The powers that be were very careful about who they let loose with a gun and, on this occasion, she thought they had made a good call.

'I'd like to handle this as quietly as possible,' she said. 'But

it'll be hard to observe her in the Turnbull Building when we don't know exactly where she is.'

'I vote we keep observations,' Gormley suggested. 'Inside and out, see if we can spot her before she spots us. Then we grab her and her boyfriend when they're least expecting it. That way no one else gets hurt.'

'You've all seen the pictures . . .' Daniels pointed at the murder wall where images of Laidlaw remained. 'You know she's clever at changing her appearance, so she may not look like any of these. Chantelle told me she's a natural redhead, but bear in mind Dixon's general description: blue-eyed blonde, short hair, oval face, five ten, fit build, edgy-looking. Think Hermione Norris but ten years younger.'

'That won't be difficult.' Maxwell feigned a shiver.

'She certainly floats my boat,' Gormley added.

'Mine too,' Brown joined it. 'Problem is, I don't have an ice pick.'

Everyone laughed.

'No wonder Dixon fell for her charms,' Robson said.

'He's an idiot!' Daniels said.

'An unemployed idiot!' someone added.

'All right, that's enough! We have work to do.' Daniels waited for the team to pay attention before moving on. 'According to Chantelle, Laidlaw was seeing Dixon, Reid and other men, milking them for all they were worth. She describer her as a money-driven arsehole who can twist men round her little finger. Always could, even at school. She was the one poured petrol through the letterbox. Chantelle saw her do it and captured the image on her phone. She was looking to put the bite on her when police activity died

down. A dangerous plan, in my view. Chantelle could easily have come a cropper – and very nearly did. She may not have committed any offence in the eyes of the law but her actions were morally reprehensible.'

'I agree,' Naylor said.

'And if she'd made an emergency call, maybe Mike Reid and his boy would've lived. She swears she didn't know anyone was in there, guv. I'm inclined to believe her and, if it's any consolation, I think she's learned her lesson.'

'Will she be charged?' a uniform at the back asked.

'With what? Failing to make a phone call?' Daniels looked at him, nonplussed. 'I take your point that she might have come forward after the event and that she may have wasted our time. But, given the information she's now supplied, I think it would be harsh to charge her. The CPS would most probably agree. She couldn't have prevented a death if she didn't know anyone was in the house.'

'Boss?' Carmichael caught her eye. 'You can't just walk into the Turnbull Building. It's like Fort Knox in there. Name any security device going, they've got it: secure underground parking, electronic gates, video entry and CCTV, all designed to keep unwanted visitors out. Probably the reason Laidlaw chose it.'

'Is there a concierge?'

Carmichael nodded. 'On duty, eight 'til four. But that doesn't help us. He's a regulations man. Only a warrant gets you inside. Says it's more than his job's worth to allow us into an occupied apartment whether or not we're –' she used her fingers as inverted commas – '"wearing a badge".'

'He's been watching too much telly,' Naylor said.

All eyes were on Daniels. 'I might have a quicker way in,' she said.

'Yeah?' Gormley said. 'How?'

'I happen to know someone who lives there.' She looked at Naylor. 'Can you hold the fort while I check it out, guv?'

Naylor said he'd be happy to. Daniels told Gormley to meet her in the car park. Walking towards her office, she felt guilty for what she was about to do. But what the hell. She'd burned her bridges with Jo Soulsby and now there was no going back. Happy ever after endings only happened in books and movies. It was a pipedream, no more, no less. Time to move on. Sitting down at her desk, she took Fiona Fielding's card from her wallet and dialled the number.

Fielding picked up on the third ring.

'It's Kate,' Daniels said. 'I'm feeling a little peckish.'

74

Daniels felt like a schoolgirl getting ready for a first date as they drove through town, surprised at how excited she was at the thought of seeing Fielding again. She flipped open the vanity mirror and peered into it, pretending she had something in her eye, wishing she'd run a comb through her hair before jumping into Gormley's car in her rush to get a handle on Laidlaw. This wasn't how she would choose to look, but she didn't have time to go home and change. It was now or never.

'Who is this mate of yours anyway?' Gormley asked.

'Oh, no one special.' *Just a little white lie.*

Gormley tried to catch her eye but Daniels kept looking straight ahead.

A moment ago, Brown had phoned. Word had come through that Chantelle had six broken ribs and a deep gash to her right wrist. She was undergoing surgery to repair a tear to the triangular fibro-cartilage which might result in a shortening of the ulna – the bone extending from the elbow to the wrist. There would be some nerve damage but she was expected to make a full recovery in time, assuming she didn't fall victim to MRSA, E-coli, or whatever other bacterium might be lurking within the hospital.

At A & E earlier, she'd let her guard down, all that hostility

and mistrust of the police fading away. Underneath they saw a frightened child who'd never felt loved – a sad case really. She hadn't stood a chance: losing her mother before the age of ten, being left with a father like Arthur Fox, who used to abandon his kids for weeks, sometimes months on end, resulting in separate care homes for her and her brother Todd – until Arthur decided he wanted them back.

Parking the car, Gormley turned off the engine. He took hold of the door handle in readiness to get out, but Daniels held him back, told him to stay put and keep an eye on the main gate, make a note of any vehicles entering or leaving the building. He grumbled for a moment and then succumbed.

Getting out, Daniels shut the door, leaned in and spoke to him through the open window. 'Keep your phone clear. I'll give you a ring if I need you.'

She entered the Turnbull with a sense of trepidation and dread. It wasn't Laidlaw or the unidentified Mediterranean man that worried her. It was meeting Fielding again. Checking the entrance and exit routes on her way in, she found the right apartment and knocked at the door. Taking a big deep breath, she pushed her hair away from her face, hoping she didn't look too bad. It was the best she could do in the limited time available.

Seconds later, Fielding opened the door.

Daniels smiled but couldn't speak.

'Hello, Kate.' Fielding's enigmatic smile seemed to convey so much more than a greeting. Her eyes went straight to the holdall Daniels was carrying. Tipping her head on one side, she stood aside, inviting her in. 'You planning to stay awhile, DCI Daniels?'

Prompted by Fielding's comment, Jo Soulsby's voice arrived in Daniels' head: *What does a dyke bring on a first date?* She hadn't known the answer back then. *Everything!* Jo had told her, making her laugh out loud.

Noticing the private joke from the smile playing round Daniels' lips, Fielding waited for her to say something. But Daniels was too busy taking in the apartment: the solid wood floors, the contemporary furniture, a mini studio in one corner, lots of objets d'art, much as she'd imagined her place might be.

'This is lovely,' she said.

It wasn't lovely. It was awkward. Having ignored Fielding's postcards for months, she didn't know how to explain the sudden change of heart without sounding like a user – which was exactly what she was. In the end, she decided to go for it. Just tell her straight. She wouldn't risk starting another relationship on the wrong foot.

'I won't deny I've been thinking about you, Fiona . . .' Daniels glanced at her feet, trying to find the right words. 'But that's not why . . . look, I'm sorry—'

'I told you once, you apologize too much.'

She had too, in the station, the first time they met.

'Don't look so glum, Kate. I think I know why you're here.' Her voice was low, breathless almost, like she had a permanent sore throat. It was very attractive too. She wasn't hacked off that Daniels had an alternative motive for being there. Quite the opposite: she seemed pleased to see her, whatever the reason or circumstance. 'Don't tell me, let me guess. It's the redhead who just moved into the penthouse with an ape in tow. I knew there was something dodgy about those two.

Your call confirmed it. What have they done? Something wicked, I hope.'

Smart as well as beautiful.

Fielding put a hand up. 'Sorry, I shouldn't have said that. I guess if you're involved it must be pretty serious.'

'It is. Trust me, I'm a detective.'

Fielding bent down and picked up a glass of white wine from her coffee table. Daniels had forgotten how attractive she was, not just physically, although she was certainly that. She had a body to die for, an alluring smile, and the deepest, most penetrating blue eyes she'd ever seen. She was dressed casually today: black leggings, a figure-hugging, thigh-length, skinny grey T-shirt, strappy sandals on her feet. Each strap picked out in a different colour, her toenails painted to match the one that looped round her big toe. Her attention to detail reminded Daniels of Jo. And that intrigued her. But maybe it shouldn't.

Detectives do eat, don't they?

Both women had used those words at the beginning.

Daniels was suddenly ravenous – in every sense. She hadn't eaten since a piece of toast at six and she hadn't had sex for more time than she cared to remember. 'If you knew I had another agenda, why did you agree to see me?' she asked.

'Why do you think?' Fielding was teasing her now, *as only she could.*

'I'm sorr— what I mean is, I really wish it had been different.' Daniels could feel herself blushing again. 'Can we get the professional stuff out the way and start over? I don't expect you to believe me, but I would've called you anyway.'

'Works for me,' Fielding said. 'You sure you're ready, though? I seem to remember—'

'I've never been surer of anything in my whole life,' Daniels cut her off. She didn't want to talk about Jo. Not here. Not now. So she quickly changed the subject in favour of work, reminding them both of why she was there. 'Tell me about the redhead.'

'Smart but unfriendly. And *he* looks like your average thug. Acts like her minder, if you know what I mean. Shifty git. Walks ten paces behind. Always looking over his shoulder.' Fielding watched Daniels take a stab-proof vest from the holdall and pass it over her head. She pulled a face. 'That's a first. I prefer my women to take clothes off, not put them on.'

Daniels laughed. 'Later.'

'Really?'

'Really.'

'Later then.' Fielding lifted her glass in the air. 'You know what she looks like?'

'I've got a good idea.'

'Come over here.' Fielding led her towards her mini artist studio in the corner. Through the window there were great views across rooftops to the River Tyne. 'Would this help?'

'Jesus!' Daniels was gobsmacked and instantly back in the MIR. *Look at the eyes . . . Ice woman . . . they're pretty evil . . . your film guy deserves a BAFTA.* In front of her was a fantastic sketch of Laidlaw, who was indeed a young Hermione Norris. A gifted and highly successful artist, Fielding travelled the world exhibiting her work. And no wonder. Daniels looked at her. 'You did this from *memory*?'

Fielding nodded. 'Trust me, I'm an artist.'

'Fiona, it's fantastic!'

Fielding took a bow. 'She isn't in, by the way. I saw her

drive away like a bat out of hell not ten minutes before you arrived.'

'Shit!'

'She's driving an Audi A5 rental, steel grey, 09 registration, if that's any use to you. I saw the documentation on the dash and the little medallion thingy dangling from the rear-view mirror. Our bays are next door to each other.'

Daniels shook her head. 'You're amazing, you know that? And wasted as an artist.' Looking down from the window on to the road below she took out her mobile and dialled Gormley's number. He answered right away. 'Hank, did Naylor come through with the warrant? OK, I need you up here, but swing by the underground car park first and check if there's a steel grey, 09 Audi A5 . . .' She grinned at Fielding. 'Meet me at the penthouse as soon as you can.' She hung up and headed for the door. Before she reached it, she turned, retraced her steps and kissed Fielding squarely on the lips. 'Thanks, Fiona.'

'For what?'

'For being so understanding.'

That enigmatic smile again. 'The pleasure's all mine.'

'Stay here. Don't open the door to anyone. Wish us luck.'

Fielding's smile faded. 'You think you'll need it?'

Daniels shook her head. 'I have my own minder, remember?' With that, she turned on her heels and left the apartment, closing the door behind her. She knew how to get to the penthouse from the floorplan Carmichael had commandeered from the council – an old planning application. She took the stairs two at a time, her antennae raised for any movement on the floor above.

75

Daniels watched the lift ascending. A bell rang, announcing its arrival. The doors slid open and Gormley stepped out. He too had on a Kevlar vest. He was carrying a police baton in one hand and a warrant in the other, delivered by Robson a few minutes before. Naylor had attended court himself, making an emergency application for a warrant to search the premises of a prime suspect in a triple murder case, telling the bench that he was confident it would lead to the arrest and detention of the person or persons responsible. There were no arguments from the magistrates.

Gormley took the key to the penthouse from his pocket and dangled it in the air.

'Courtesy of a red-faced concierge,' he said.

'Shame it took a court order to bring about his cooperation,' Daniels replied. 'You checked the car park?'

Gormley nodded. 'No Audi A5s.'

Daniels knocked on the door but no one answered.

'How'd you know what vehicle they're driving?' Gormley asked, handing her the key.

Ignoring the question, Daniels put the key into the lock, turned it clockwise and pushed open the door. The apartment was much like Fielding's in size and shape: a high-quality furnished rental with some nice artistic touches, possibly

a musician's pad or, at the very least, someone heavily into music.

There were several framed posters on the walls. One in particular caught her eye. Joni Mitchell: *Don Juan's Reckless Daughter.* Joni was at the mike singing, her inimitable pout clearly visible. An over-sized acoustic guitar hung round her neck from a shoulder strap. The singer was wearing faded blue jeans, a throwback from the eighties, possibly even as far back as the seventies, Daniels thought. Underneath her picture were the words: *Give Joy To The World . . . With Music.*

Gormley moved through the apartment into one of the bedrooms while Daniels remained in the living room. There weren't many personal possessions belonging to Laidlaw in the room, just a man's leather jacket slung over a sofa, a pair of very large shoes on the floor, an open bi-fold leather wallet discarded on a side table, no cash but several credit cards inside.

Daniels wandered into the kitchen, the only sound in the apartment coming from her shoes as she walked over the wooden floor. It was then that she saw him. The shock nearly took her breath away. He was a heavy-set man with jet-black, greasy, shoulder-length hair, hard eyes fixed on her, lips slightly apart. He was dressed in jeans and a white T-shirt that clung to a swollen gut.

'Oh my God!' a voice behind her said.

Daniels turned towards it.

Fiona Fielding had her right hand to her mouth. Her eyes were welded to the floor where the man's body lay, a knife still in his back, a pool of settled blood all around him. Having heard the cry, Gormley came thundering through the

apartment with his baton raised in the air, stopping dead in his tracks when he saw Daniels hugging a woman who had her back to him.

'Can anyone join in?' he said, his tongue firmly planted in his cheek.

Both women turned towards him. 'Hank, this is Fiona—'

'Fielding, I remember.'

'Good, then get her out of here!' As the women parted, Gormley's eyes shifted to the body on the floor, to the knife in particular, a spring-assisted flick-knife if he was any judge, the type often used by the military.

'He must've been to a Superintendent's promotion do,' he quipped.

Fielding laughed at his gallows humour but her laughter turned to tears as the shock of seeing a dead man kicked in. It may have been his way of coping with the macabre side of being a murder detective, but it was completely inappropriate in front of a civilian and Daniels wasn't laughing. Repeating her instruction to lose Fielding, she waited for them to leave and then bent down to check for a pulse, even though it seemed pointless; an automatic response to make sure the man was actually dead.

He was.

She pulled out her phone and rang Robson. Giving him a quick update to pass on to their guv'nor, she told him to alert the outside team that Laidlaw was currently a natural red-head, medium-length hair, well made-up. At least, she was when last seen, a description she assumed could change at any minute.

'She's driving a steel grey, 09 Audi A5,' she added. 'I want a

uniformed officer, a scientific aids team and a pathologist down here right away.'

She rang off.

Seconds later, she heard the front door go.

She swung round, half-expecting to see Laidlaw, steeling herself for a confrontation. As the footsteps drew nearer, her eyes glanced at the knife in the man's back, the only weapon within reach.

'She didn't touch anything on the way out,' Gormley said as he appeared in the doorway. Daniels blew out her cheeks. Gormley held both hands above his head as she yelled at him for not warning her on the way in.

'How's Fiona?' she asked.

'Pretty shaken up. You want to pop down and see her while I hold the fort?'

Daniels growled at him. 'What do you think?'

'I think you want to find Laidlaw, boss.'

'Yeah, like it's that simple!' Daniels said. 'We don't know where to look.'

Gormley grinned. *He knew something.*

'Fielding said to tell you she *is* wasted as an artist, whatever that means. She said she's travelled the world and knows an airport hire car when she sees one. Looks like Laidlaw's going to make a run for it.'

76

The Peugeot hurtled out of the city northwards on the central motorway with a Traffic car escort, its blue lights flashing and sirens screaming for other motorists to give way. Gormley floored the accelerator and took the airport road. As the miles flashed by and they left the city behind, the speedometer climbed steadily. But in the passenger seat Daniels' right foot was pressed down hard on an imaginary pedal, wishing she was driving her own car, urging him to get an even greater move on.

Desperate to apprehend Laidlaw, she got on the radio.

'7824 to control. Any MIT officers near the airport yet?'

Pete Brooks in the control room responded immediately: '3962 on way.'

'ETA two minutes, boss.' Carmichael's voice hit Daniels' ear.

Good girl! 'Reference our suspect. We're fairly certain she's making a run for it, Lisa. No details on flights or names, but the Audi A5 is a hire car.'

'Steel grey, 09 plate, yeah?'

'Correct. Check it out, soon as you get there. Hank and I are right behind you. If you see her, do not, I repeat *do not* approach her without backup. When you're done, rendezvous with us at airport security.'

*

Using the emergency bay to park her private car at Newcastle International Airport was always risky. Carmichael placed her circular police sticker in the window, insurance against being towed away or slapped with a hefty fine. There were five car hire companies to choose from: Avis, Budget, Europcar, Hertz and Thrifty. It was guesswork: a matter of getting round the lot as hastily as she could.

Walking quickly towards the terminal building, she scanned the car park, keeping her eye out for Laidlaw, wondering how soon her boss and Gormley would arrive. Word was, they'd found a body at the Turnbull Building. Carmichael was out and about following up on a lead when Daniels called in. She'd received the news second-hand from Andy Brown. As a result, she was first out of the blocks. And, as luck would have it, in close proximity to the airport when the call went out for officers to assist in the apprehension of their prime suspect.

What a feather in her cap that would be, if she was the one to make the arrest.

With that career-enhancing opportunity in her head, Carmichael could hardly contain herself. She'd learned a lot about Laidlaw from looking into her dodgy dealings while investigating the murder of three – now four – people. And what she'd learned enabling her to build a picture of the kind of woman she was. Consequently, she was able to make an educated guess at which hire company her suspect might choose from the list of those available.

Immediately discounting two – Budget and Thrifty were not Laidlaw's style – Carmichael bypassed Europcar and headed for Hertz: the world's largest car-rental agency,

according to the blurb on the wall in front of her. At the counter, she showed ID to a Chinese woman of indeterminate age, explaining why she was there. The woman consulted her records, then frowned and shook her head, telling the detective that no Ms or Mrs Laidlaw was currently a client of the firm.

'Any Audi A5s handed in today?' Carmichael was trying to read the returns sheet upside down. 'The person I'm looking for may well be using another name.'

'That's a little easier. We only have one A5 in the fleet at the moment. It was handed back at, let me see . . .' The woman ran a long red fingernail down the page and then glanced at her watch. 'About forty minutes ago. It was signed off at three-o-five.'

Bingo!

Carmichael asked for details and wrote them down, conscious that she was running out of time if Laidlaw was catching a flight and not laying a false trail. The A5 was part of Hertz' Prestige Collection. *Why didn't that surprise her?* It had been rented by a woman calling herself Marianne Spencer, a Christian name she knew Laidlaw had used before.

Maybe she was getting sloppy.

The assistant remembered her too: 'Short, dark hair, quite striking in appearance.' She described what Laidlaw was wearing, then added, 'Most of our customers are friendly, even when they are in a hurry. But the lady you're looking for was rather rude, too full of herself to pass the time of day with the likes of me—'

'You've been *really* helpful,' Carmichael cut her off. Taking a business card from her wallet, she handed it over. The

woman studied it: the force crest on the top left-hand corner, the words Northumbria Police written across a thin blue strip, details of where Carmichael could be found, her department, her name and rank. 'Please make sure the vehicle isn't cleaned. We'll need to retain it for forensic examination.'

The woman nodded and picked up the phone.

Carmichael did likewise, arranging to have the Audi collected immediately. As she hung up, Daniels and Gormley arrived, separating as soon as they walked through the door, their eyes scanning the cavernous terminal building for any sign of Laidlaw. The departure hall was crammed with tourists, business travellers and families saying goodbye. At the check-in desks people queued, cases were dumped, tickets checked, hopes raised that flights would leave on time. Carmichael caught Daniels' eye and met her halfway in, hurriedly explaining what she'd managed to learn so far. The DCI was too busy studying the departures boards to congratulate her on a job well done. That would come later: Carmichael was sure of it.

'Any idea which flight she's heading for?' Daniels asked.

'None.' Carmichael's shoulders went down.

Daniels cursed. 'Then you and I have a decision to make.'

77

They headed straight for airport security and couldn't get there quick enough. They were met by several official-looking figures and soon learned that no one by the name of Marianne Spencer had booked in for any flight. Gormley made the rendezvous minutes later. He didn't need to say anything for Daniels to know he'd lucked out too. It was writ large across his face the minute he was shown into the room.

Scanning the panel of monitors, he shook his head, muttering something about needles in haystacks. He wasn't wrong. The airport was approaching its busiest period in the calendar, a rush to get away and back before the schools turfed out and prices soared. The terminal was full, a constant flow of pedestrian traffic making it difficult to pick out any one person in particular.

'What next?' Carmichael asked. 'Do we flood the place with uniforms or what?

'No time,' Daniels said. 'We'll have to do this covertly.'

'What does she look like?' a security officer asked.

'Approximately five-ten, last seen with short, dark hair: I think she's wearing a light, possibly linen, beige dress and jacket,' Carmichael said. 'That's if the Hertz clerk has a good memory.'

'Nowt gets past Ann Chow,' an airport policeman said.

'I wouldn't hold your breath,' Gormley said. 'Laidlaw is a clever con woman and master of disguise. She could've changed clothes a dozen times since she got here.'

'Not possible,' Carmichael countered. 'The Hertz woman told me she had no luggage, just a small brown handbag.'

Daniels hoped Carmichael was right.

Her eyes were back on the monitors, but it was useless. There was no way they were going to ID Laidlaw in time to prevent her escape. Unless . . . the idea came to her in a flash. Reaching into her pocket, she drew out her phone, asking the person in charge if it was possible to upload an image directly on to the airport system.

Gormley and Carmichael both looked puzzled. But all became clear as a good likeness of Laidlaw appeared on the screen in front of them, an image Daniels imagined that scores of eyes would now be viewing on their monitors as a level one security alert. She had no time to explain about the sketch Fiona Fielding had done – or why she'd felt compelled to capture the image on her phone – but it was clear from Gormley's expression that he'd made the leap as they waited for airport staff to respond.

Seconds later, the phone rang in the control room. The receiver was knocked off its station as a member of staff rushed to answer it. Daniels glanced nervously at Gormley and Carmichael as they waited, counting the seconds. The security officer wrote something down, ended the call and turned back to face them, his expression buoyant, his tired eyes filled with hope and expectation.

'A guy working the Thomas Cook check-in desk booked a woman calling herself Penelope Clark on to a flight to

Dalaman about a half hour ago as he was about to shut up shop. She was running late but managed to catch him before her flight was called for departure. She was wearing a headscarf as he rushed her through, but he's fairly certain it was her.'

'Dalaman?' Carmichael had never heard of it.

'It's in Turkey,' Gormley replied.

'Fuck!' Daniels' troubled expression darkened as her brain made an obvious connection. The body she'd found at the Turnbull Building had yet to be identified, but credit cards in his wallet suggested he may be of Greek origin, possibly Cypriot. 'She's fleeing out of harm's way!' Daniels said. 'From Dalaman she can easily get to Northern Cyprus, where there's no extradition treaty. If she achieves that, she knows we can't touch her. We need to stop that plane!' Daniels looked at the security man. 'Well, don't stand there, do something!'

78

Lucy Laidlaw took a long deep breath. Linking her hands loosely in her lap, she relaxed back against the head rest as the Airbus A320 pushed back from the stand ready for take-off. She was home and hosed.

Fifty metres away, in the airport terminal, detectives Gormley and Carmichael were standing anxiously at the window of the departure lounge, a locked door preventing them from going airside. They watched as the aircraft slowly began to move, fearful that Daniels' intervention had come too late, and powerless to do anything about it. But on the flight deck of the Airbus, the captain was receiving a vital call . . .

'Kestrel seven-six-two-bravo, this is the tower. We've got a message for you. Ready to copy?'

'Go ahead, Tower.'

'Kestrel seven-six-two-bravo: go to discreet frequency one, two, seven decimal six.'

Captain Kjell Halvorsen looked at his first officer and said, 'Take over talking to the ground on box one. Keep the push-back going. I'm going to box two to see what the tower wants.' He went to box two, dialled in the frequency and said, 'Tower, this is Kestrel seven-six-two-bravo, go ahead.'

'Kestrel seven-six-two-bravo, we've been advised by

Northumbria Police that you've got a criminal on board travelling under a false passport, endeavouring to escape the country. We'll hand you over to the SIO, who has further instructions for you.'

Daniels' voice: 'Captain?'

Halvorsen again turned to his FO. 'Tell them to hold the pushback.' Then, to Daniels: 'Yes, this is the captain. Go ahead.'

'I am Detective Chief Inspector Kate Daniels, Northumbria Police, Murder Investigation Team. It is imperative that we are allowed on board to extricate a passenger travelling by the name of Penelope Clark. She is wanted in connection with very serious offences. Copy that?'

'That's received. What do you want us to do?'

Daniels could hear the FO relaying information to the tower: *Ground, this is the flight deck. Can you stop the pushback there please? We might have to go back on stand.* 'I'd like you to return to stand immediately,' she said.

'Stand by . . .' Halvorsen looked out of his window. He could see two officers, one male, one female, waiting by the departure gate. 'DCI Daniels, please advise if a remote stand is required.'

Daniels thought for a moment. Before boarding, Laidlaw had gone through airport security. If she hadn't been frisked, she and her bag would've been through a scanner. It was highly unlikely that she was armed with anything that could do much damage, other than a thoroughly disagreeable personality, and the DCI took the view that a remote stand was unnecessary.

'That's a negative, Captain,' she said finally. 'She's going

nowhere. If we do this right, it's unlikely that other passengers will be in danger.'

'OK, if that's the conversation complete, I'm returning to stand.' Halvorsen advised his FO accordingly and then made an announcement to the passengers: 'Ladies and gentlemen, we've got a technical problem. I do apologize. Hopefully it won't take very long to sort out, so when we get back on stand please remain in your seats and leave your seat belts fastened. I will be opening the forward left door of the aircraft, but it's nothing at all to worry about and we don't anticipate a significant delay.'

As the Airbus pulled back on to stand, Halvorsen asked the FO to manage things on the ground while he spoke to the number one cabin crew on board. He pushed a call button twice and a female voice came on the interphone.

'Hello?'

'June, it's Kjell. Would you bring the passenger manifest to the flight deck, please?' Halvorsen checked the video and saw his number one approach the door. He hit a switch, allowing her in. 'Shut the door behind you.' She did as he asked. 'Right, we're going back on stand. You heard me tell the passengers it's a technical problem. It's not. We've got a criminal on board. What we're going to do is shut the aircraft down. I'll open the window and talk to detectives on the ground and negotiate how they want to play this.'

The number one nodded.

Having briefed her fully, Halvorsen asked her to go back to the cabin and await further instructions. He opened the window. Below him, Daniels and Gormley were approaching the aircraft.

'What's the sketch here, guys?' he said.

'Can you get the steps put on?' Daniels asked. 'Front or back, it's your call.'

'It'll be forward, left. You come up to the steps. Just knock on the door. The number one will open it and you're in. I've left the seatbelt signs on, so no one else will be getting up. My number one tells me that the woman you're looking for is in seat thirty-three D, on the right-hand side as you look towards the rear of the aircraft. Fortunately, she's the only person in that row. Soon as you get on board, it's over to you.'

Daniels held up a thumb. 'Works for us.'

'Up the steps, two knocks and you're in,' Halvorsen repeated. 'Everybody happy?'

'Let's do it,' Daniels said.

79

The plan worked like clockwork. As soon as Daniels stepped through the aircraft door she'd clocked Laidlaw in an aisle seat about a third of the way down on the right side. Her head was completely shaved and she was wearing a headscarf tied closely round it, like a cancer patient, her face made pale with the use of make-up. It was the eyes that did it: *pure evil.* Eyes that Fielding had so expertly captured in the portrait she'd painted. Eyes that now looked through the senior investigating officer as she approached.

Not resigned or defeated – just ice cold.

As Daniels walked down the aisle, her professional persona on full show, passengers realized the problem wasn't technical at all and craned their necks to see what was going on.

The DCI held up ID. 'Madam, would you come with me, please?'

Daniels' anger grew as she took in the exquisite seal ring on Laidlaw's little finger. *The callous bitch . . . pound to a penny it was Bridget's.* Laidlaw didn't move. She sat there, staring up, waiting for an explanation which wasn't long in coming. There was no need to arrest her for murder, not yet anyway, that would come later. For now, the DCI was content to use the assault on Chantelle as a way of getting her off the plane without causing distress to other passengers.

'I am Detective Chief Inspector Daniels. Lucy Laidlaw, I am arresting you on suspicion of Section 18 Wounding. You do not have to say anything. But it may harm your defence if you do not mention when questioned something which you later rely on in court. Anything you do say may be given in evidence.'

'I bloody love it!' A man across the aisle said loudly. 'I've always wanted to hear someone say that!'

Daniels glared at him. He was the epitome of the great unwashed: mid-thirties, grossly overweight, wearing a black-and-white nylon football shirt and no deodorant. His complexion was angry and red, like he'd spent a fortnight in the sun with no protection, or been to a studio to top up the tan before his holiday began in earnest. He was half-cut too, she noticed, sun and booze, a lethal mixture for the cabin crew to deal with.

The DCI was pleased to be getting off.

'What's she done, love?' the man asked, his alcohol breath filling the cabin.

Ignoring him, Daniels turned back to Laidlaw. 'Come on, Lucy. Let's not make this more difficult than it has to be, eh?'

'I'm sorry, Detective, but there must be some mistake.' Cool as you like, Laidlaw took her passport from her bag, opened it up and handed it to Daniels. 'My name isn't Lucy, it's Penelope Clark.'

'You tell her, Miss Penelope!' The fat drunk again. He was glaring at Daniels through bloodshot eyes 'She's ill man, can't you tell? And it's bloody ridiculous keeping us waiting like this. We've got places to go, people to see, even if you don't. Get the fucking trolley dollies out here. It's time for a bevvy.'

'Wind your neck in, pal,' Gormley warned. 'Or you'll be next!'

The guy didn't need telling twice. He sank into his seat, minding his own business.

Pocketing Laidlaw's passport, Daniels produced a pair of rigid handcuffs from a clip behind her back. In deference to her, Laidlaw dropped her head and took a deep breath. She pointed at the snips. 'There's no need for those, Detective Inspector. I'll come quietly.'

Pleased to hear it, Daniels put them away.

Taking possession of Laidlaw's bag, she handed it to Gormley for safekeeping, then stepped back to allow the woman out of her seat. Laidlaw unclipped her seatbelt. Placing her hands on the armrests, she eased herself up, her trailing hand already reaching for the iPad she'd placed on the next seat. With full force, she swung her arm round, smashing the device across Gormley's cheek, knocking him unconscious and sending him crashing to the floor.

The DCI fought to get hold of her, but Laidlaw proved too strong and managed to struggle free. What happened next made Daniels' day. The smelly drunk stuck out his leg, tripping Laidlaw up as she tried to run for the open cabin door. Scrambling forward, Daniels made a lunge for Laidlaw. In one swift movement, the snips were on and she stopped struggling.

Relieved, Daniels remained on the floor, trying to get her breath back, high-fiving the drunk as she sat there. Further down the aisle, Gormley was on his feet, holding his head. Helping her up, he winked at her. *Job done.* Taking an arm each, they escorted Laidlaw from the aircraft. As they walked

down the stairs, a huge round of applause rang out from above their heads as Captain Halvorsen asked for the cabin doors to be made secure and ready for take-off.

Laidlaw was silent on the way back the city. At Market Street nick, they lodged her in the custody suite, then Gormley peeled off to be checked out by the police surgeon as Carmichael and Daniels went straight to the incident room. Robson was sitting at his desk, a phone jammed between shoulder and neck, taking down notes as he listened. Maxwell was also busy on the phone, feet up, a much more laid-back approach – but at least he was working. Brown was sitting at Carmichael's computer, updating the murder wall with the fourth victim and Laidlaw's recent arrest. He smiled at Carmichael and held up a thumb as she went off to find refreshments, applauding Daniels on a great result as she passed his desk. But they and the rest of the team knew there was still a way to go: facts to be checked, solicitors briefed, offences put, an interview to conduct.

Naylor added his congratulations as the DCI approached. 'How's Hank?' he asked.

'He'll live,' she said. 'Any news on the Mediterranean?'

Naylor nodded. 'Yusuf Sevket. Stanton lifted his prints in situ and we ran them through the system. He's from Northern Cyprus, a fugitive in several countries. Andy found a Warning–Wanted marker on the PNC too. It seems he jumped bail in Turkey in 2005 during an investigation into the killing of a British woman on holiday. Sounds like he and Laidlaw are two of a kind. Let's put it this way, I don't think he'll be missed. You did a good job today, Kate.'

'I taught her everything she knows,' a familiar voice behind them said.

Daniels' old guv'nor, Detective Chief Superintendent Bright, had a wide grin on his face. He was standing in the doorway, feet crossed over each other, looking the picture of health. He was immaculately dressed as usual: grey suit and tie, white shirt, his signature handkerchief in his breast pocket. 'Still running the show, I see.'

A wide smile spread over Daniels' face. 'Hello, guv!'

'She never looks at me that way,' Naylor said.

'Some people have it, some don't.' Bright grinned at Naylor. 'Get over it!'

'And to what do we owe this pleasure?' Naylor asked. 'Paint dry at Fantasy Island?'

'You should try stand-up!' Bright was enjoying the camaraderie. 'The Chief asked me to pass on his appreciation for a sterling day's work. Thought I'd drop by and deliver the message in person . . .' He turned his attention from Naylor to Daniels, his feelings for his protégé plain to see. 'You know, I reckon you could make Super out of this, if you play your cards right.'

'You keep telling me that, guv. But it hasn't happened yet.' She gave him a pointed look, her ambition for promotion no laughing matter as far as she was concerned. 'Don't suppose you know why?'

Acknowledging a gaffe wasn't Bright's style.

'Patience, Kate. It's just a matter of time.' He couldn't meet her gaze. He'd shaped her career, knew only too well she'd done more than enough to progress to the next rank. Scooping up his briefcase from the floor, he scanned the room,

smiling at Carmichael as she arrived laden with sandwiches, crisps and coffee. 'By the way,' he said. 'The drinks are on me when time allows. A knees up is long overdue. Maxwell can come too, if he can still make it off his arse.'

Everyone laughed.

Daniels walked him to the door. 'I hear things are going well at Ponteland.'

She was discreetly referring to his new PA, Ellen Crawford. But as he turned towards her, there was a hint of sadness in his eyes that he was doing his best to hide. His feelings for her hadn't always been purely platonic or professional. There was a time, during his late wife's illness, that he'd have taken things to another level, had she been willing. But that was before he found out about her relationship with Jo Soulsby who, spookily, had just walked through the door and was heading straight for them.

'Catch you later,' Bright said.

And with that he was gone.

80

Jo smiled. 'Was it something I said?'

Daniels didn't answer. She was angry with Bright for walking away. His relationship with Jo had always swung between bearable and non-existent. But in recent months they'd toned their antagonism down a little, tolerated one another, helped by his move to HQ. It wasn't a personal thing when it began. Bright was old school, always would be. Despite Jo's reputation as an exceptional criminal profiler, he didn't see the need to involve her, or anyone like her, in police work. As far as he was concerned, detectives cracked cases and worked best when left alone to do their jobs without outside influence or interference. But Daniels suspected it *was* now personal, fuelled by his knowledge that the two women had once been an item. She hated that two of the most important people in her life couldn't get along. Bright would probably throw a party when Jo handed in her notice.

Maybe it would be best if she did leave.

Life would certainly be far less complicated.

'I heard congrats were in order,' Jo said.

Too distracted to answer, Daniels was busy watching her former boss make good his escape. He turned as he reached the door, made a telephone with his hand and held it to his ear indicating that he'd ring her later. As she nodded her understanding, Jo waved a hand in front of her face.

'Kate?'

'Sorry, what did you say?'

'Absolutely nothing . . .' Jo pointed to Daniels' office door. 'Shall we get on?'

The DCI led the way. On her journey back to town, she'd been as high as a kite for two reasons. One: she'd collared her suspect. Two: she'd seen Fielding again, and that brought hope of something special for the future. Some*one* special she wanted to get to know. But as she made coffee and sat down opposite Jo, her newfound joy faded and she found herself dragged backwards, memories of their time together crashing in on her, all thoughts of Fielding pushed away.

Torn by mixed emotions, she fought her feelings and dealt with the situation badly. Because of where they were, the conversation didn't escalate into a full-blown row. But for the next few minutes there was awkwardness between them she found hard to ignore. If Jo said black, Daniels said white, treating her former partner like any other business associate, making it obvious she had neither the time nor the inclination to prolong their meeting beyond that which was absolutely necessary.

'You OK?' Jo asked. 'You seem really agitated.'

'I'm fine,' Daniels lied. 'Tired, that's all.'

'We're all tired,' Jo said. 'Doesn't mean we can't be civil.'

Daniels' apologetic smile felt like a sneer on her lips.

'Better get to it then.' Jo slapped a thick file on the desk between them and handed Daniels some handwritten notes, a précis of what she'd discovered. 'While you were out searching for Laidlaw, Abbott gave me access to her Fire Service record. I called in a few favours with my colleagues at Social

Services. Bribery and corruption usually does the trick, I find.'

Her joke fell on deaf ears.

'It's very impressive,' was all Daniels said.

'Ahm, what's with the cold and unfriendly tone?'

'Can you give it to me in layman's terms?'

'Of course!' Jo said. 'Have I done something to upset you?'

'No.'

'If this is about my leaving—'

'It's not!'

'Because, if it is, I've decided—'

Daniels cut her off. 'Look, you must do what you think fit. It's really none of my business, is it?'

Jo looked angry but held her tongue. Grabbing the notes from the desk, she buried her head in them, trying to hide the fact that she was upset. As she began to sum up what she'd found out – *something to do with Laidlaw being mistreated as a child* – her words were drowned out by Daniels' guilty thoughts. She was behaving like a prat and Jo had done nothing to deserve it.

'Are you getting *any* of this or am I wasting my breath?' Jo asked pointedly.

'Child abuse doesn't excuse what she did.'

'No . . . but it goes some way to explaining it,' Jo reminded her. 'Shall I carry on?'

'Please.'

'From an early age, Lucy was living south of the river. She was taken into the care of Gateshead local authority when she was eight years old . . .' Jo paused. 'Is she being processed now?'

Daniels nodded. 'It'll take a while to get her brief down here. I wanted your input so I could work out an interview strategy.' Deciding that an apology was in order, she tried to find the right form of words but they remained on the tip of her tongue and were never articulated because she hid behind the work as usual. 'Naylor's building up a picture of the man she was with. Information is flooding in now we've ID'd him. Con man and money launderer was his claim to fame. I think he'd groomed Laidlaw, who was the Brit arm of a much larger operation of organized crime.' Daniels was still choking on the apology. 'Her living in Gateshead during the early part of her life adds up, though.'

'How?'

'It's another connection between her and Ivy's lottery ticket. She wasted no time collecting the winnings. On Thursday she caught a train to King's Cross and met a man who has since called the incident room. Ben Foster happens to be a linguist and nailed her accent which, he says, she was none too happy about at the time. He also said she was very odd. Dangerous, was the word he used to describe her. Reckons she's got a screw loose.'

'Is that a psychiatric term?'

Daniels smiled. 'He claims she made a play for him that he rejected, then denied knowing him when they met by chance the very next day.' She paused for a moment. 'There's something odd about him too, I reckon. I get the feeling he's not telling the whole truth, only the part he wants us to hear.'

'That makes two of you,' Jo said.

'Look—'

Jo held up a hand. 'I take that back. I can see you're under

a lot of pressure, Kate. I'll do anything to help, you know that. Just let's not argue, eh?' She handed Daniels a set of glossy photographs. 'Take a look at these.'

Daniels' face twisted in revulsion as she flicked through the photographs. They were graphic images: close-ups of cigarette burns on a child's torso. There were more than two dozen of them in total. 'They're disgusting,' she said. 'But then so is what she did to Jamie Reid.'

'Violence breeds violence, you know that.' Jo exhaled as if she had the weight of the world on her shoulders. 'It was too late for Lucy by the time social workers discovered the extent of the problem. A school nurse raised the alarm. Education professionals were concerned but didn't flag her up as they should've, despite the fact that she was displaying classic character traits of an abused child. Had they done so, Lucy would've been picked up by child protection much sooner. According to reports, she was a precocious child from an early age, exhibiting inappropriate and provocative behaviour towards adult males: teachers, social workers, doctors, foster fathers. Each time they found a home for her, she was returned to care.'

'Was anyone ever charged?'

'With the abuse? Not according to Robbo.'

'Why not?'

'Her father worked away a lot and both parents apparently had affairs. He *was* questioned but in his defence he cited multiple partners on the mother's side. Without Lucy's evidence, they couldn't make a case.'

'She never told anyone who abused her?'

Jo shook her head. 'Amazing isn't it?'

For a few seconds the room fell silent, a little girl's torment affecting them both.

It was Jo who broke the deadlock. 'Her father passed himself off as a successful businessman, but health-care professionals expressed doubts about his status. He was a bit of a con man himself, I think. That's probably where she got the faulty gene, the aptitude for reinventing herself.'

'How the hell did she get into the fire service?'

'Kids like Lucy learn to manipulate from an early age. It makes them feel powerful and, from what I've learned from your lot, she's good at it too. She's beyond help, Kate. And she's not going to be easy to interview, that's for sure.'

Her comment prompted Daniels to look at her watch. 'I must go.'

Jo uncrossed her legs and stood up. 'Good luck.'

Daniels stood up too and took the file from her. 'Thanks for this.'

There was a moment of heartache and sorrow between them.

'If you can bring yourself to do it sensitively, play on the abuse . . .' Jo suggested. 'If you find the right trigger, she may collapse and tell you all you want to know.'

'I'm surprised to hear you say that.'

'Needs must,' Jo said sadly. 'I told you, it's too late for Lucy. She walks and she'll kill again, there's no doubt about it.'

81

Daniels didn't need Jo to tell her what she was up against. That much was evident from the moment she walked into the interview room and saw those eyes at close quarters. Studying her suspect closely, a slide show of horrendous burns ran through Daniels' head. She decided that anyone who'd experienced such torture as a child and kept it to herself would have no difficulty facing a few questions as an adult – police or no police.

Nothing could possibly touch her after that.

Having been stripped of her designer clothing, Laidlaw was now dressed in a baggy white disposable paper boiler-suit. She stared back across the table at Daniels, an inscrutable expression on her face, the shaved head and pale complexion highlighting her malevolent streak. Her solicitor, Beatrice Parks, was sitting next to her, a woman of around forty-five years of age whose face was covered in hundreds of freckles made worse by the recent sunny weather. She had shoulder-length, strawberry blonde, corkscrew hair and wore pink-framed spectacles low on the bridge of her nose. She was wearing a pin-striped shirt, the neck and cuffs edged with a frill. A senior solicitor in one of the city's largest criminal law firms, she was an excellent advocate who knew every trick in the book and would be watching for any holes in Daniels' case.

Fortunately for the SIO, the evidence was pretty over-whelming for the Section 18 wounding. But that was merely the tip of this particular iceberg. Other charges, some much more serious, would be put to her in due course: obtaining monies by deception, arson with intent to endanger life, and four counts of murder – such was the confidence of the Murder Investigation Team – each count of murder carrying a mandatory life sentence.

'Is everyone ready?' Daniels asked.

Parks nodded on behalf of herself and her client.

Daniels checked her watch and turned on a recording device housed in a recess in the wall. She made sure it was running and then linked her hands together, placed her elbows on the table and looked across at Laidlaw, whose mood was hard to read. 'This interview is taking place at Market Street Police Station. It is Tuesday the twenty-ninth of June 2010. The time is sixteen-forty hours. I am Detective Chief Inspector Kate Daniels.' She nodded at Gormley, his cue to speak.

'I'm Detective Sergeant Hank Gormley,' he said.

Daniels gestured to Parks. 'And you are?'

'Beatrice Parks, of Thomas Gillespie and Associates, repre-senting Ms Laidlaw.'

Daniels gestured to Laidlaw. 'Please identify yourself.'

'My name is Lucy Laidlaw.'

'Ms Laidlaw, I must remind you that you're still under caution. Please make yourself comfortable, because you're going to be here a while. Earlier today, I arrested you as you were attempting to leave the country on a false passport. Leaving that to one side for a moment, I'd first like to talk to

you about an allegation of assault on Chantelle Fox. She claims that on Monday the twenty-eighth of June 2010 you forced your way into her home and assaulted her. Is that correct?'

'I never touched her.'

'We have a written statement says you did.'

'Chantelle Fox is a pathological liar.'

'You're entitled to an opinion. Never let it be said that I would stifle your right to free speech.' Laidlaw probably had a point, but Daniels wasn't about to debate it with her. 'I'm sure Ms Fox will take her chances and allow a court of law to decide who's telling the truth and who is lying. She's already agreed to testify, under oath if necessary.'

Laidlaw and her solicitor remained silent.

'Maybe we should start at the beginning, deal with events chronologically,' Daniels said. 'It might help you to under-stand the gravity of the charges you're facing.'

'My client understands perfectly,' Parks said. 'And she has nothing to hide.'

Daniels ignored her. 'We have CCTV images of you buying petrol at a garage on the evening of Tuesday, twenty-second June—'

Parks interrupted and drew first blood. 'I think you'll find those images will prove inconclusive.'

'They may do,' Daniels agreed. No need to bullshit. The woman knew her stuff and the likelihood of identification was uncertain at this stage. 'They are still in the process of being enhanced, but we have better images, photographs that caught Ms Laidlaw in the act of arson at number 23 Ralph Street. And that brings us back to Chantelle Fox, who actually

saw her do it.' She shifted her focus to Laidlaw. 'That's why you tried to silence her. Isn't that correct, Lucy?'

Laidlaw rolled her eyes at her solicitor. 'This is pure fantasy.'

'OK, let's move on. I don't want to waste time. Need I remind you that you are also under arrest for the murder of Mark and Jamie Reid?' Daniels said. Laidlaw didn't respond. She sat motionless on the other side of the table. 'Was that a mistake? If so, it was the first of many you made this week. You set fire to Maggie Reid's home, unaware that Mark and Jamie were in there at the time. Were you sick of Maggie, jealous of the hold she still had on Mark?'

No reply.

'I think you were. I think that's why you decided to do something about it. Only, unbeknown to you, arrangements were changed at the last minute. That must've come as quite a shock to you, if your intention was to burn the house down.'

Laidlaw lifted her arms, joined them at the back of her neck and yawned.

'I don't think you wanted to hurt Mark at all, did you? And you certainly didn't want to hurt Jamie. You liked him, didn't you, despite the fact that he wasn't your child? I saw the nursery, Lucy. A woman who cared decorated that room. I bet you spent hours on it . . .' Daniels paused. Laidlaw's body language was giving her away. She avoided eye contact by examining her beautifully painted nails. Then the DCI pushed a little further, her tone harder than before. 'Jamie was only ten months old. He died a horrible death in his cot, having suffered ninety per cent burns.' Opening the case file,

Daniels took out autopsy photographs of the child's body and placed them carefully and deliberately in front of Laidlaw. 'Look at them.'

Laidlaw's eyes were everywhere but the table.

'Look at them!'

Daniels eyeballed her suspect with contempt. 'How could you do that to a child you'd held, played with, loved even?'

The silence in the room seemed to go on and on. Jo had shown Daniels horrific photographs of Laidlaw's own injuries as a young child. But she had no sympathy in her heart for the woman. No amount of abuse, no matter how awful, could justify her actions that night. Whether or not she thought the house was empty, as a firefighter she knew how quickly the flames would spread and yet she'd chosen to go ahead and endanger the lives of Maggie Reid's neighbours.

Still avoiding the gruesome photographs, Laidlaw crossed her arms, glancing at Gormley in the process, her attention prompting him to join in.

'But then things *really* got out of hand, didn't they?' he said. 'In the early hours of Thursday morning a better opportunity fell into your lap. You were called out to an accident on the A1 north of the Gosforth Park Hotel. Ivy Kerr told you she was on her way to Lottery HQ, didn't she? So you killed her as she sat trapped in her car in order to claim the money for yourself.'

'Is money so important to you?' Daniels asked.

'Check my bank account,' Laidlaw was almost smirking as she spoke. 'It's in the red. I have no idea what either of you are talking about. I did attend the incident you're referring to, along with several of my colleagues. In fact, I was so

traumatized by it I'm currently off duty with post-traumatic stress disorder. But I don't seem to recall the old lady you mentioned.'

'I never said she was old.' Gormley threw her slip of the tongue right back at her.

Laidlaw's face flushed up. 'Sorry, I thought you did.'

'No, he definitely didn't.' Daniels smiled. 'Did he, Ms Parks?'

Ignoring the question, Parks jotted something down on a pad.

'Did I mention that we have fabulous CCTV footage from Lottery HQ? We've also searched your locker at work and taken possession of the torch . . .' Daniels let that one float in the air a moment, watching for a reaction. Despite Laidlaw's attempt to show no emotion whatsoever, behind her eyes was a clear message: guilty as charged. 'Come on, you're doing yourself no favours. It's your service torch and it has your number and prints on it. I have one of the best forensic scientists in the country examining it as we speak. A tenner says he'll prove you struck Ivy Kerr with it several times.'

Gormley's face gave nothing away. He tried hard to hide his hatred for the woman they were interviewing. 'How could you do it?' he asked. 'Make us understand, because from where we're sitting you look like a monster. But you're not, are you? We know that you had a tough childhood, but even so . . . It's time to come clean now, for everyone's sake.'

No response.

'DS Gormley's right. We're just not getting this. How could you *do* that to an old lady when you've been the subject of abuse yourself? It doesn't make sense. How you could even

think of setting fire to a place when you were once a burn victim is beyond me, it really is.' Daniels threw the set of photographs Jo had given her on to the table. Like a deck of cards, they fanned out as they hit the shiny surface.

Laidlaw flinched as her eyes seized on them.

'That must've really hurt, Lucy.'

A slight flicker of emotion, then Laidlaw's eyes grew dark again.

'Chantelle Fox was clever, wasn't she? With incriminating photographs in her possession, she waited until the time was right and decided to spoil your plan. How much was she asking for? She didn't say.'

Laidlaw glanced at her solicitor.

'My client denies all the charges and has nothing more to add.'

'What about Yusuf? Did you row with him over Chantelle, is that it?'

'I know no one called Yusuf.'

'He's the man you murdered in the Turnbull Building. We're sure to find traces of his blood on your clothing. You were seen leaving in a hurry, by the way. Another mistake. There's a pattern developing here, don't you think?'

Laidlaw looked through Daniels like she wasn't there. When the DCI told her she was going to prison for a very long time, she didn't even flinch. She hadn't talked about her own abuse in twenty years and she wasn't going to start now, no matter what buttons they pushed. As a little girl she'd been let down by a system that should've protected her. While the burns on her skin had long since healed, the emotional trauma remained. Sadly, the cycle of violence had been

perpetuated. Daniels felt angry about that and didn't feel comfortable adding insult to injury. She had enough evidence to convict and a confession was highly unlikely. She ended the interview there and then.

82

A huge round of applause went up when Daniels walked into the MIR. The Murder Investigation Team were jubilant, the pressure off, the case on target for a successful conclusion. There were the usual slaps on the back, calls to tell family the good news, promises of an early finish for once, a chance to catch up with what really mattered. But Daniels didn't feel like celebrating, or particularly elated for that matter. Laidlaw was a victim as much as she was a killer, and that was always hard to come to terms with. She'd been charged with a string of serious offences and would be held in custody until morning, when she'd appear in court at the earliest opportunity. Any application for bail would be futile. She'd be remanded for sure. And probably spend the rest of her unhappy life in jail.

Depressed by that thought but also relieved that Laidlaw could do no more damage, Daniels called the safe house to let Chantelle Fox know it was OK to return home. Then she shut up shop and took everyone to the Bacchus for a few drinks. It was expected, the way things were always done at the end of an enquiry. Regardless of her wish to go home, the DCI would not disappoint the Murder Investigation Team. After all the hours and hard work they'd put in, they deserved to let their hair down.

At the pub, she tried her very best to join in the revelry, to

push Lucy Laidlaw to the back of her mind. But nothing seemed to work. Not the euphoria of having cracked the case – several cases at once – or the booze, the chat or the music. Something was missing and that something was Jo. Normally the life and soul of any party, for some reason she hadn't turned up. For the umpteenth time, Daniels checked her mobile but there were no missed calls, no texts or voicemails. Every time the door opened, she glanced towards it, expecting her to walk in, a smile on her face that would brighten the room, an unspoken look in her eye for Daniels.

Where the hell was she?

Almost like a missile, an explanation crashed into Daniels' head. Jo had made up her mind. This was to be her very last case within the department. She hadn't shown because she didn't want to put a damper on the celebrations.

'No!'

'No, what?' Gormley asked. Despite his bewilderment, he didn't wait for an answer, just held an empty pint glass in the air. 'Ready for another?'

'Why not?' Daniels lied. 'Make it a double.'

She didn't really want a drink. In fact she wanted nothing Gormley could give her. Not here. Not now. She didn't want to hear his take on the case and she certainly didn't want to laugh at his humour. She wanted to scream and shout. Stamp her feet. Take him into a quiet corner and tell him how pissed off she was. But this was neither the time nor the place, so she held it in.

Taking her glass from her, Gormley fought his way to the bar. Raising his voice above the din, he ordered their drinks from his nephew, then stood chatting and joking with other

detectives as he waited for the barman to hand them over. Daniels looked around her. Near the window, Robson and Carmichael were playing a slot machine, Brown looking over their shoulder. Naylor and Maxwell were talking football, Germany inevitably featuring in the conversation. 'A place in the last sixteen,' Daniels heard Naylor say. Some mention of a game with Ghana at the Soccer City in Johannesburg. She checked her mobile again as Gormley returned to her side. Then threw back her drink, gave him a wad of cash to keep the beers coming, made her excuses and left.

A cab got her home in double-quick time. She set down her bag, then picked it up again and removed her iPod. Unable to choose what she wanted to listen to, she set it to shuffle and then placed it on its station and turned up the volume. Jackson Browne – 'For a Dancer' – began to play, a song about love and loss, but the words depressed her so much she was forced to turn it off again. Picking up the phone, she called Jo's mobile. No reply. She tried her landline. No reply there either.

Fine!

Daniels made her way upstairs and took a long, hot shower. She was drying her hair when the phone rang. It was Fielding: the best thing that had happened to her all day. They arranged to meet at Zizzi's on Grey Street at nine o'clock. Nothing heavy: a pizza or pasta, a few glasses of wine. Daniels put down the phone, dressed quickly in jeans and a blue shirt she'd been keeping for a special occasion and then went back downstairs. This time Fielding might get her wish . . .

I prefer my women to take clothes off, not put them on.

Zizzi's was full when Daniels arrived. It was nine on the

dot. Fielding was already there, drinking a glass of white wine, looking divine and relaxed. Daniels ordered Linguine Gamberi, Fielding the Penne Della Casa and a bottle of Pinot Grigio Sartori to wash it down with. All things considered, Daniels had a good night, much better than she expected. She was nervous at first – but in a nice way – and excited at the prospect of a first date with someone unconnected with her work.

During their meal, Fielding was attentive and interesting, really good company as it turned out. They had plenty in common too: a diverse taste in music, the love of a good book, motorcycling.

'Really?' Daniels said.

'You sound surprised.'

'I never figured you for a biker, that's all.'

'Why?' Fielding smiled. 'I like to live dangerously.' She toyed with her wine glass, tilting the liquid inside, watching it stick to the sides. 'There's a lot you don't know about me, actually. And a lot more I don't know about you, I suspect.' She looked up at Daniels and chanced her arm. 'You still on the rebound?'

'Makes you say that?'

'Detectives aren't the only ones with intuition.' Using her free hand, Fielding pointed at her own temple. 'There's stuff happening up there. You going to tell me what it's like on planet Kate?'

'Would it make a difference if I was – on the rebound, I mean?'

'Hey, I'm not criticizing. I saw her, don't forget. She's very beautiful.'

'Yes, she is.' Daniels went quiet for a while and then changed the subject. 'I'm always distracted at the end of a case. We have your murderous neighbour in custody, but there are so many loose ends to tie up and then the case file to compile. I warn you, I'm a workaholic who never really switches off. I bet you're the same when you're putting together one of your art exhibitions.'

'Nice sidestep, Kate. You didn't answer my question.'

'Or you mine.' Daniels took a sip of wine, meeting Fielding's gaze over the top of the glass. 'I'd rather not talk about Jo, if it's all the same to you. I'm here, aren't I? That should tell you all you need to know.'

'It's certainly a step in the right direction,' Fielding said, flirting with her. 'I think we could have some fun, you and I. As it happens, I also come with a warning. I spend a lot of time abroad, Kate. If we can see each other in between trips, I'd really like that. There's no need to get heavy, is there? Sound like a plan to you?'

'Sounds perfect.'

They left the restaurant and went back to Fielding's place. They drank more wine, put on some music and talked until the small hours. Then, without warning, Fielding took hold of Daniels' hand and led her to an adjoining room, sat down on the bed and kissed her softly on the mouth. She smelled of good perfume. Her bare arms were cool to the touch but smooth and toned. Daniels returned the kiss, feeling the need to have all of her.

The urgency of that kiss made Fielding pull back. 'You sure about this?'

'Shut up,' Daniels said, unbuttoning her shirt.

83

It was almost eight-thirty when Daniels woke. Fielding was still asleep, so she slipped out of bed, picked up her clothes and tiptoed from the room in search of the shower. A text had come through on her mobile, the third from Jo during the night, according to the display. The first two said: *Call me.* She deleted them. The third read: *Call your voicemail, please!* Daniels was about to delete that too, but the frantic 'please' made her change her mind. Instead she dialled her voicemail service, put the phone to her ear and listened . . .

'*Hi, it's me. I've been calling you all night . . .*' Jo sounded stressed to death. '*Look, I'm not sure what's going on, I just know I don't like it. I wanted to tell you yesterday, but you seemed mad at me for some reason. I've had second thoughts about . . . well, a lot of things really: the job, you, us. Is there still an us?*' If a pause could be described as a feeling, this one was desperately sad. '*I suppose what I'm saying is, I'm game to give it another try if you are. I don't care about the other stuff, Kate. Please call me when you get this. We really need to talk.*'

Fuck! What's she playing at? And why now?

Daniels caught her reflection in the bathroom mirror. For a moment, guilt stared back at her. Then she thought of Fielding lying in the next room and quickly forgave herself. She'd done nothing wrong, nothing to reproach herself for.

She and Jo had been history for a long time and she'd had every opportunity to make things right between them. In fact, Daniels had almost begged her to. How was *she* to know that Jo would have a last-minute change of heart? And why did she suddenly feel the urge to get out of Fielding's apartment as quick as her legs would carry her?

She was about to switch the phone off when it rang in her hand: *Jo again.* Daniels panicked, fumbling with the phone in order to switch it off, hell-bent on killing the sound before Fielding woke up. She couldn't speak to Jo until she was clear of the apartment.

Some things were plain wrong.

Taking a long, deep breath to calm herself, she opened the bathroom cabinet, looking for a spare toothbrush. There wasn't one, so she put toothpaste on her index finger and cleaned her teeth with that instead, then took a quick shower. She was nearly dressed when Fielding walked up behind her, slid her arms around her waist and kissed her gently on the neck.

'Morning . . .' It was a mumble rather than proper speech. Her voice was more gravelly than normal – if that were possible. 'I made breakfast, such as it is.'

'You didn't need to do that.' Daniels didn't dare turn around. Fielding was a perceptive, intelligent woman who'd know something was up as soon as their eyes met. Instead, she tipped her head back so that their cheeks came together, sweeping Fielding's hair away from her face. 'But I'm glad you did, I'm really hungry.'

'Again?'

'I meant for food!' Now Daniels turned around.

Despite their late night, Fielding's tangled hair and sleepy eyes made her look even more attractive than she had the night before. She was wearing a black, silk, kimono-style wrap with a dragon embroidered in gold down one side. It looked authentic and expensive, something Daniels presumed the artist had picked up on her travels in Japan. Fielding was stroking her lip, a wicked smile on her face as she tried to coax her guest back to bed.

'I can't!' Daniels said emphatically. 'I've got work today, even if you don't.'

'Spoilsport.' Fielding feigned a sulk. 'You want tea or coffee? I've made both.'

'Coffee. Strong and black, please, no sugar.'

By the time she reached the living room, Fielding was already tucking into her breakfast at one end of an eight-seater dining table positioned in front of a huge window with views over the city. The sun was out and in the streets below people were going about their business: walking, talking, driving in cars that looked like toys from this high up. Daniels ate yoghurt and a little fruit and then asked if Fielding minded if she checked her emails, turning her phone back on when her host yawned and shook her head. She'd missed two further calls from Jo, one from Gormley and three from forensic scientist, Matt West, all of which had arrived in the past fifteen minutes. A typical morning for her, clearly not so for Fielding . . .

Fiona yawned again and said, 'You always this dynamic when you first wake up?'

Daniels smiled. 'That's me, a real dynamo. Why don't you go back to bed?'

'Only if you join me.'

'I'm sorry, Fiona. I need to make an urgent call.' Picking up her phone, she scrolled through her contacts, accessing Matt West's work number. He answered on the fourth ring in his usual optimistic voice. 'Morning, Matt. What you got for me?'

'Quite a lot, actually. The first of the two jobs you gave me . . .' There was a shuffling of papers at the other end. 'Reference KD1 is the cigarette stub found in the wall opposite your arson scene. HG1 is the hair lifted from Susan Armstrong's flat. You'll be pleased to know I've got results on both, finally. I'm so sorry for the delay.'

'Don't worry about it. Hold on a sec.' Daniels excused herself and got up from the table. She found her bag on the living-room floor where she'd dumped it the night before. Removing a pen and pad, she took it to the table, switching the phone into her left hand as she sat, poised to scribble down his findings. 'OK, shoot.'

'The cigarette stub is *definitely* Chantelle Fox—'

'That's no surprise. She admitted having watched the house burn and a whole lot more besides.' Her pen hovered over blank paper. 'And the hair?'

'*Might* belong to Chantelle Fox, but doesn't . . .' West paused, giving her time to digest the snippet of information he'd divulged. He was a man who dealt in hard facts, not speculation. 'There are many similarities, but I'm confident that these two samples are from closely related females rather than the same person. And, before you ask, yes, you can quote me on that.'

Daniels was stunned into silence.

'You still there?' West said after a while.

'Yes, sorry, I got that . . .' Feeling a change in Daniels' mood, Fielding looked up from her toast. But the DCI was now in police mode and didn't seem to notice. She was staring into space through the window, trying to make sense of what she'd heard – a mixture of horror and puzzlement on her face. 'Matt, Chantelle hasn't got any sisters and her mother's dead.'

'No,' he countered. 'She *thinks* she hasn't got any sisters!'

Daniels thanked him and hung up.

'Something wrong?' Fielding asked.

'Not wrong, just very surprising,' Daniels said vaguely. 'I can't tell you about it, obviously. Look, I'm sorry, Fiona. I've got to go.'

84

At Newcastle Magistrates' Court, overnight remands were always heard an hour earlier than the rest of the day's business. The building was adjacent to Market Street police station, ensuring a handy transfer of prisoners. At precisely 9:55 a.m., Lucy Laidlaw left her cell flanked by a female security guard whose heavy uniform shoes squeaked on the tiled floor in rhythm with the keys jangling off her belt as she walked. Laidlaw was still wearing the white boiler suit she'd been forced to put on when her clothes were seized for forensic examination. But that wasn't causing her a problem today.

She might yet have a use for it.

A short journey along a corridor and up one flight of stairs would take her directly into a courtroom where she would face senior magistrates sitting especially to hear her case. Half an hour earlier, her solicitor had visited her in the cells. Beatrice Parks had held her hand, both literally and figuratively, and told her what was about to happen: a brief hearing, followed by a further remand in custody until a date could be set for her trial at the Crown Court in front of a judge and jury. Parks warned her to expect to wait a good few weeks. An application for her release on bail was apparently not an option, given the growing body of evidence the CPS had at their disposal: the photographs, her torch, video

evidence taken from the helicopter that her hat had been on the back seat of Ivy's car at the time she was murdered, and probably by now her DNA.

So bloody what?

Did they think she'd be intimidated by that?

If so, they could think again.

Laidlaw played her part, shuffling along the cell-block corridor with her head bowed deferentially – the picture of remorse for all the cruel things she'd done – her jailer watching her all the time, oblivious to what she was really capable of and what was running through her mind. They were passing a white board fixed to the wall; it was sectioned off in rows and columns, with a space to write each prisoner's details. Across the top, reading from left to right, each column had a heading: cell number, name, relevant times, detention review and other important information. She noticed hers was the only name written on the board and bristled as she read the words *suicide risk* in the last column, a throwback from another time, another life, when she was weak and vulnerable.

It didn't surprise her that she was the only prisoner in detention that morning. There'd been no noise during the night to keep her awake, no drunks or prostitutes in custody to disturb her, no banging on cell doors as she'd been led to expect. Just the constant hum from the light above her head, and nothing to keep her mind occupied as she lay there surrounded by four bare walls on a bed so very different from the sumptuous one she'd slept in at the hotel in London almost a week ago.

Was it only a week ago?

'Keep moving!' the gruff voice behind her said.

Laidlaw felt a nudge in her back propelling her forward along the corridor, past a free-standing fire extinguisher she'd examined the last time she was there, an old-fashioned one she'd advised them to replace, a slight smile forming on her lips as an idea jumped in her head. She knew what to do now as she mounted the narrow staircase, taking in every detail, planning her escape when all appeared lost, just as the Cypriot had taught her.

Despite his faults, she had a lot to thank him for.

The courtroom was large and relatively empty as she was led into the dock. Eight people in total: a reporter from the local press; a woman wearing a badge she assumed was a probation officer; two female magistrates on the bench; and a male court clerk sitting in front of them. Directly in front of Laidlaw, facing the bench, was Beatrice Parks. Next to her, a Crown Prosecutor and a young woman in plain clothes who identified herself as DC Lisa Carmichael, representing the Murder Investigation Team should the magistrates have any questions that might need clarifying.

Not a uniform polis in sight.

The hearing lasted less than three minutes in total. Laidlaw stood passively in the dock and spoke only once to confirm her name and the fact that she was of no fixed abode. But that wasn't how she wanted her court appearance to end. She wasn't going down without a fight.

She had absolutely nothing to lose now.

As soon as the magistrates had adjourned the case, she doubled up in the dock, retching as if she was going to vomit, a little show of contrition perhaps for those who gave a damn about a Cypriot fugitive, an old lady with one foot in the

grave and a good man who'd had the misfortune to fall in love with her – *and Jamie.*

Laidlaw swallowed down her shame. Her life had been one long list of regrets, not least of which was losing Mark and his child. He'd come so close to her ideal, almost made her believe that an ordinary life was possible. Or was that another pipedream? Daniels was right, though: father and son were never part of the plan. But what was done couldn't be undone.

With her head bent low, she watched out of the corner of her eye as the magistrates got to their feet and left the court via the back door. The guy from the press and the probation officer walked out through another door. Both solicitors followed. But as Beatrice Parks reached the door she turned around, a concerned expression on her face as she looked back at her client. She pointed at the floor, held up a hand and spread her fingers, gesturing that she'd see her in the cells in five minutes. Then she too disappeared. Only the young DC remained, making absolutely sure she wasn't going to leap over the barrier and make good her escape, which would have been possible had it not been for the funny suit she happened to have on. It had a thick, starchy feel to it and was degrading to wear. She could hardly flee looking like a walking talking fucking J-Cloth. *People might notice.* The sooner it was off, the better . . .

Her heart was thumping out of her chest. Five minutes wasn't very long. Was it long enough? Her arm was yanked upwards by the security escort. She didn't struggle. She just stood up straight and was led back to the cells like a lamb. They were out of Carmichael's sight now and heading back down the narrow, winding stairs to the cell block below.

Her eyes scanned the corridor – *no one in sight* – but Laidlaw could hear voices and laughter coming from an office at the very far end.

It was now or never.

She had one shot.

One shot.

Groaning as if she were in pain, she doubled up again. Before the guard could call for assistance, Laidlaw picked up the fire extinguisher and smashed it into her face, knocking her out instantaneously. Catching the guard as she fell, Laidlaw replaced the fire extinguisher exactly where she'd found it, lifted the escort over her shoulder and carried her into cell number three, the door of which stood open ready for the next poor sod the coppers happened to drag off the streets.

Laidlaw grinned as she laid the unconscious woman on the floor. She knew all that training wouldn't go to waste. There was no time to lose: Parks would be ringing the bell any minute, demanding to see her client. Ripping off the paper suit, she undressed the escort and put on her uniform. It was a good fit too. She'd always been able to carry a uniform. Then she took a deep breath, grabbed a cap off a peg on the wall and walked calmly along the corridor, back up the narrow staircase and out through the remand court as large as life to freedom, keys jangling from the uniform belt as she strolled away unperturbed.

85

With no rush to get into the office, Daniels called a cab and headed home to get changed. On her way she tried to contact Jo several times, but the phone rang out unanswered. Asking the driver to keep the meter running, telling him she wouldn't be long, she unlocked her front door and let herself in. There was a handwritten note from Jo on the hall carpet: *I guess I have my answer* was all it said.

Daniels' heart sank.

At some point during the night – the only night she'd stayed out since they'd split – Jo had come round to find the house in darkness and no sign of her. She reread the note, not knowing whether to laugh or cry. She was about to call Jo again when, right on cue, the house phone rang: the MIR.

What the fuck?!

Was this a conspiracy to keep them apart?

Carmichael sounded cheerful: Laidlaw's case had been adjourned with no application for bail, as Daniels had anticipated.

'Any problems?' she asked.

'None. You never said what an evil shit she is close up.' Carmichael paused. 'Cocky, too, until she was remanded in custody. Almost threw up then. But those eyes . . .'

Carmichael's voice trailed off.

Daniels could tell she'd turned her head away from the speaker. Not surprising given the raised voices in the background. There was a lot of swearing and blasphemy going on. Naylor wasn't a happy bunny by the sounds of it. He was yelling instructions that Daniels only heard snippets of. Something about getting a team together . . . full forensics . . . the whole works. Another murder incident? Then why the rush? Dead bodies were usually pretty patient souls.

'Lisa? Lisa, what's going on?'

'Not sure, but it sounds serious. Call you back.' She hung up.

Seconds later, although it seemed like hours, the phone rang again. 'Boss, you're not going to like this. Laidlaw escaped, seriously injuring one of the court security guards. She's in a really bad way, she might not make it. All units have been alerted and are looking for Laidlaw.'

Jo's words echoed around Daniels' head: *She walks and she'll kill again, there's no doubt about it.* 'Put Hank on, Lisa,' she said calmly.

Chantelle left the General Hospital after an early out-patients appointment to have her dressing changed. The number 684 bus was already at the stop when she arrived, so she hopped on board for the short ride home, paid her fare, and threw herself down on a seat near the front. When she got off, a few minutes later, she had the distinct impression that she was being followed. It was a strange sensation, like heat burning a hole in the back of her head. She looked around, searching the faces of those who'd got off the bus with her.

But there was no one she knew.

She walked on for a bit, glancing over her shoulder before turning the corner. *Daft cow.* It wasn't like her to let her imagination run wild like that. But since Laidlaw had done her over, she couldn't be too careful. As she reached her front door, she swung round again, expecting to see someone for defo this time, but the street was deserted, except for a few idiots riding their bikes up and down trying to impress her by doing wheelies.

Chantelle ignored them. She was too busy scanning the cars lining the pavement. With the sun glinting off windscreens it was hard to tell if anyone was sitting there or not, watching, waiting to jump her. Then a thought suddenly occurred. Maybe the bizzies were keeping an eye on her. Unless . . . were they following her? Was Daniels?

Nah, Daniels was a top bird under all that authority.

She hadn't condoned what Chantelle had done but neither had she made too big a deal out of it. She'd rescued her, sent a cop to guard her, made sure she was treated as an emergency at the hospital. There was no waiting in the queue like the rest of the divvis in A & E – not with Daniels on her side. That didn't mean some other stupid fucker wasn't still barking up the wrong tree though, did it?

Chantelle could tell all along the police didn't believe her about George Milburn's money. She wouldn't deny she knew he *had* some, or that she'd have nicked it had she known where it was hidden. Now she came to think of it, his grandson had given her a hacky look on Monday morning when she left for work. He was round at George's gaff, clearing it out, although what the fuck for was anyone's guess – his possessions weren't good enough for the charity shop. Elliot

was probably the one who accused her in the first place. What an absolute tit he was.

'I want two teams, Hank. You take one, Robbo the other. Chantelle is your priority, Laidlaw his. Her phone is constantly engaged so I'll head over there now. She'll be milking all the attention, no doubt. Some things never change. Before you join me, have Lisa dig off the system every possible location those two girls could be.' A car horn blasted outside. Daniels looked out of the window and held up a thumb to her driver. 'Tell her I want those jobs actioned immediately and put out to the relevant team. No duplication, obviously, we don't want people turfing up at the same place. It's imperative we find them quickly.'

'You think Laidlaw will go after Chantelle?' Gormley asked.

'Don't you? Chantelle is a prime mover in her downfall. If I'm any judge of character, she won't let that lie. By the way, forensic results are in. That the fag in the wall sample is definitely Chantelle's—'

'So?' Gormley shrugged. 'We already knew that, didn't we?'

'Yes, but what we didn't know is – and this has been checked and verified by Matt West – the hair we lifted from Laidlaw's drop address was genetically very similar to Chantelle's—'

'She'd been there, at Laidlaw's place?'

'No, I queried that possibility with Matt. Although the samples are close, he's confident that they are from two different people. It's familial DNA: the two girls are related, probably sisters. Hard to believe, isn't it?'

Gormley stared at the floor, trying to get his head around what he'd been told, his detective brain working overtime. When he looked up, his eyes were wide open. 'Jesus Christ! You're not telling me Chantelle's been playing us all along? That she and Laidlaw are in this together?'

'No, but I can see where you're coming from. Besides, we have too much evidence on Laidlaw for it not to be her. I know Chantelle's a wrong 'un, but I can't see her involving herself in murder, can you?'

'You sure about that? Remember the cap in her hall? We've still to ID the petrol buyer.'

'She'd hardly blackmail Laidlaw if she was involved, though, would she?'

'She had the photos for insurance. Easy to pin the blame on her if we came calling.'

'It would be more than her life was worth . . .' With that worrying thought lingering in the back of her mind, Daniels checked outside. Her driver was still waiting with the engine of his panda running, his arm lolling out the window, a fag-end held between two brown-stained fingers. She turned back to Gormley. 'You know what? I find this whole episode quite sad. I don't believe Laidlaw and Chantelle know they're related. Arthur Fox was a bastard to his women, Hank. It wouldn't surprise me in the least if he has illegitimate children all over the place. Anyway that's not important. We've got to find Chantelle before Laidlaw does. Meet me there as soon as you're done here.'

86

Lucy Laidlaw stepped from the shadow of the upstairs hallway, the sound of a radio and running water reaching her as she crossed over the threshold and into the steamy bathroom. The opaque shower curtain was drawn. Apart from the tips of swollen fingers holding on to the top of the curtain rail, Lucy couldn't see Chantelle. She could hear her though. The bitch was actually singing along to Lady Gaga's 'Telephone'.

Not a bad voice either: *shame in a way to silence it.*

Lucy had entered the house via the back kitchen, forcing the pathetic lock on the back door, lifting the phone off the hook as she passed through the empty living room. Sliding the bolt on the front door in case Chantelle attempted to escape, she crept up the stairs and waited. No reason to rush. By now Northumbria Police would have flooded the city centre with uniforms. They would be combing the area looking for her, not worried about Chantelle bloody Fox.

Lucy grinned. Never would they think she'd have the neck to return to Ralph Street, or that Chantelle would be stupid enough to return home with *her* on the run. Which meant only one thing: *she didn't know.*

On the other hand, Lucy knew exactly where Chantelle would be. The girl had no imagination. And no reason to

hide, if she'd been led to believe that her nemesis was under lock and key. Pathetic really. She was a sitting duck . . .

And she'd picked a fight with the wrong person this time.

The sound of running water ceased.

A hand reached out from the behind the curtain, grabbing a towel from the top of the adjacent wash basin. Seconds later, the curtain was ripped open. Chantelle didn't notice her standing there at first. The steam was thick and her head was down, one corner of the towel held between her teeth as she struggled to wrap it round her body with her one arm. Her right arm was fucked, encased in a plastic bag to save it from getting wet.

As Chantelle's eyes fell on Laidlaw, her mouth dropped open and the towel slipped to the floor. Her face drained of what little colour she had following surgery. Lucy was impressed. She didn't scream or shout for help, just stepped calmly from the shower cubicle, eyeballing Lucy in the process. But beneath the bravado there was a mixture of terror and defeat, as if she was somehow resigned to her fate.

Let's face it, she didn't have a whole lot to live for.

Lucy smiled. 'Hello, Chantelle.'

Fuck! The sight of Laidlaw produced a cold sweat all over Chantelle's naked body. For a moment she was paralysed with fear. She made a sudden lunge for the door. Lucy countered, grabbing for her arm, but her hands slid off wet skin and Chantelle managed to slip from her grasp. She only made it as far as the landing before being yanked back by her hair. Shoving her hard against the bathroom wall, Lucy

pinned her there with her right arm across her throat, blocking off her airway and making her choke.

In desperation, Chantelle fought for breath but none arrived. With her left hand, she tried prising Lucy's arm from her neck but she was far too strong. Their faces were inches away from each other. Lucy's eyes flashed with hatred and Chantelle knew it was useless pleading with her. Kneeing her hard in the crotch with force sent her flying backwards, unbalancing her for long enough for Chantelle to dash past her. Taking the stairs two at a time, she ran for her life. If she could get to the back door she had a weapon there.

Her father's axe.

Time slowed as Lucy thundered down the stairs after her, closer and closer, until she was practically on top of her. As Chantelle ran from the hallway into the living room, she was felled like a deer as Lucy hurled herself at her legs, sending her crashing to the floor on to her injured arm. Unable to move, unimaginable pain shot through Chantelle's body. She didn't recognize her own voice as she begged for mercy. She wanted it over with. She wanted to die.

The attack was sudden and brutal. As the girl continued to beg, Lucy lifted the axe and smashed it into her head, sending a spray of blood right across the room. Lifting the weapon above her head for a second time, Lucy hesitated, her eyes fixed on the raised marks on Chantelle's back. Marks she was seeing for the very first time. Marks that made her whole body shiver. Lucy almost threw up.

She lowered the axe. *Dear God, what had she done?*

*

It was like déjà vu when Daniels saw the open door as the panda car turned into Ralph Street and pulled up outside Chantelle's house. She told her driver to call for backup immediately. She ought to have waited for Gormley, but that was never really an option. She was a police officer with a job to do and she'd make damn sure she did it. And this time it would be done properly. If necessary she'd escort the prison van personally all the way to Low Newton until the gates clanged shut and there was no possible avenue of escape for Laidlaw.

Chantelle heard the thud of a car door. She was lying face down on the floor, her injured arm beneath her body. But that was the very least of her problems. The side of her head felt like it was moving, like someone had poured a pint of warm custard over it, making sure it covered the entire surface of her face. And she was cold – *so cold*. She opened her remaining eye as Daniels stepped through the doorway, the DCI's hand going straight to her mouth, her eyes filled with genuine grief. It was nice to know someone cared. Then crimson liquid covered Chantelle's eyeball. Her heart pumped just once more. And stopped.

Gormley arrived before Daniels had a chance to bend down and check for vital signs. He stood over the naked body, clearly having difficulty reading the scene. There was so much blood the head was unrecognizable. He looked confused, his eyes telling him one thing, his brain something else as he stared down at the burn marks on the young girl's back and came to rest on the seahorse tattoo on her

upper arm. Matt West was right: Chantelle and Laidlaw *were* sisters.

A serious offender had escaped justice and gone to ground. Daniels let herself into the Turnbull penthouse with a heavy heart, knowing that a woman as clever and calculating as Laidlaw could evade the law for years, living off her ill-gotten gains. An all ports bulletin had been posted, but the DCI feared she might con her way through the cordon before the authorities had a chance to apprehend her. She was in the living room when she heard the noise. She swung round on full alert but no one entered. Investigating further, she found the source: an express-delivery package, addressed to Laidlaw, dropped through the letterbox by the concierge who'd signed for it that morning. Daniels ripped it open. Her eyes grew big as she realized what it was.

87

'Tango 318 to Control: I'm parked at Tebay Services, south-bound. Stand by . . .' The Traffic officer looked out of his window as another Traffic car passed him on the northbound carriageway, the driver making a circular motion above his head and pointing in a northerly direction. 'Tango 318: Cumbrian officer travelling north to take the Penrith roundabout in case target vehicle exits the M6, over.'

Thirty-five miles north, Daniels and Gormley were also in a Traffic car – him in the rear, her in front – with one of Northumbria's finest advanced drivers. They were travelling at high speed across the A69, one of several vehicles in pursuit of Laidlaw. Ordering her Porsche 'fully loaded' had been a fatal mistake. In a bizarre twist of fate, the documentation for the vehicle dropped through the letterbox of her rented penthouse at the most opportune moment for the Murder Investigation Team, delivered by the concierge who was unable to hand it to her as she left the building in a hurry.

Of course she was in a bloody hurry: she'd killed the Cypriot.

The radio again, another call-sign: 'Tango 512: direction west on the A66 at Penrith.'

And another, a female voice this time. 'Tango 3529: heading east on same road, over.'

Daniels caught Gormley's excitement through the rear-

view mirror. There was nothing like the adrenalin rush of hunting down a killer. At the A69/M6 junction, their car picked up speed. As the countryside flashed by, Daniels looked out of the window. An hour ago, she had been in a bad place as she entered the Turnbull Building. Not only was Laidlaw a dangerous fugitive with the skills, wherewithal and means to avoid capture, but Chantelle's death had affected Daniels greatly, making her feel inadequate, despondent, and unworthy of the title of SIO. She'd failed in her promise to protect the girl and was wracked with guilt.

Not just guilt . . . sorrow.

Chantelle sure as hell wasn't perfect – there was no doubt that she'd brought trouble to her own door – but she was vibrant and funny and had been through such a lot. She didn't deserve to die at the hands of a psychopath. Hope of apprehending her killer was restored in a flash as Daniels tore open the envelope containing documentation for a new vehicle. A car enthusiast herself, she realized its significance immediately.

For the first time since the enquiry began, the DCI knew something Laidlaw didn't: a tracker device had been fitted to the car, a system ironically designed to prevent theft, consisting of covertly placed transmitters which, when activated, would send a silent signal to every police force in the country, pinpointing the exact location of the vehicle. A quick phone call giving the unique reference number proved the turning point.

The Porsche was mobile.

Within seconds, Traffic officers were dispatched and put on alert across three counties. The police helicopter – India

99 – was also made available. A few minutes later, Stewart Cole was in the air and Daniels was leading a manhunt, hoping to form a rolling road – box Laidlaw in – and make an arrest.

Her car slowed . . .

The driver pointed out the front windscreen. He'd spotted the target vehicle in the distance, a shiny new Porsche in the inside lane, India 99 directly above it, keeping aerial observation, high enough not to be noticed. Laidlaw was sticking to the speed limit, seemingly in no particular hurry.

Good move, Lucy. Don't want to draw attention to yourself.

Calmly lifting a radio handset, Daniels began to transmit: '7824: All officers engaged in Operation Tracker, I have the eyeball. I'm travelling south on the M6 some distance behind the target vehicle. I've got lots of car cover. The vehicle is doing about seventy on the inside lane, a few miles north of the Penrith turn-off. Stand by.'

Keeping her eyes on the Porsche, the DCI gave instructions for other police vehicles to slow the traffic behind her. 'Approaching Penrith turn off . . .' she said. 'Target making no attempt to take the slip road. No physical indication from the vehicle. No, no, that's fine. This is perfect. No deviation, still southbound on the M6. Copy that?'

Glancing over her shoulder, Daniels could see traffic falling back. The units behind her were doing their job. 'Tango 318: Prepare, please. I want you slowly on to the M6 travelling south from Tebay services. Tango 512, I want you behind as the last man. Tango 3529, you're our side man. Take the south M6 also. When you're a few miles away, let

me know what the tale is. I'll maintain my position for the present time. All other units, continue to slow the traffic behind us and give these guys some room. We're not sure how she'll react when we attempt the rolling road. Tango 318, have you got sight of the target vehicle yet?'

'Negative. No sign yet. Allowing traffic to pass—'

'India 99 to Control: Looks pretty good up here. Target has three-car cover plus an Eddie Stobart truck bringing up the rear.'

Daniels again. 'Roger that, India 99.'

'Go on!' Gormley was getting excited in the back. 'We've got her, boss.'

'Bet you my pension she doesn't come quietly,' Daniels said.

'Tango 512: I also have the eyeball!'

The urgency in his voice caused both fear and delight in Daniels' vehicle: fear that an officer might get hurt, delight because a mass of police vehicles had converged on the road and were closing in. It was too early to celebrate. At excessive speeds the risk of serious injury to those involved was high. Tango 512 gave his position. He still had the eyeball as well as eight-car cover. Traffic was busy. At least four very large lorries bunching in the inside lane behind the target vehicle . . .

'Maintaining speed,' he said. 'Target vehicle doesn't appear conscious of us yet. 3529, when you're ready to go, I'll get in position.'

'3529: Roger that and ready to go.'

A split second later, 3529 came screaming past Daniels' vehicle at 140 mph.

'318, how are you in front?' Daniels asked.

'318: I can see vehicle. I'm engaging a blue light and moving to stop her.'

'That's received,' Daniels said. '318, hold your position in front of her, please.'

'512: I'm making up car cover. Have her in sight . . . I have one female in the car, no passengers.' His voice went up an octave. 'She's now changing down and – she's away, boss.'

'7824 to all units, I'll give the commentary. She's clocked us . . . eighty . . . ninety . . . hundred and ten miles an hour . . . she's flooring it, weaving in and out of traffic.' Daniels flinched as something hard hit the windscreen. The Porsche had rammed the lead police vehicle from behind, smashing the offside light, sending debris flying. '3529, big speed up, please. We need to get this sorted! 512, how are we?'

'3529: We've got a rolling road. I repeat, we've got a rolling road. Attempting a stop, but she's not having any.'

Up ahead, Laidlaw floored the accelerator and then braked hard, forcing the following car to take avoiding action. In the back of the Traffic car, Gormley consulted the map on his knee. 'If we can stop her before Langdale Fell, all the better,' he said. 'Less chance of her taking off to Kendal. The last thing we need is her hurtling through the town at rush hour, putting civilian lives at risk.'

Daniels agreed – it would be their best opportunity. 'All units, we're going to try and stop the vehicle parallel with the Langdale Fell. It's very quiet there and we don't want this pursuit to go any further. India 99 has us in observation. Stop, stop, stop! Target vehicle is trying to force them off the road. She's ramming the side vehicle.'

The side Traffic car swerved. For a moment, Daniels

thought the officer might lose control. She hoped 3529 was holding her own, but this was no time to be holding her hand. She was there to stop Laidlaw and that is what she would do. Laidlaw threw the Porsche to the right, ramming her a second time, sending 3529 careering towards the central reservation. There was a pause in the transmission. In Daniels' car, they held their breath, relieved when she regained control and retook her position in the rolling road. When she came back on the radio, there was a telltale high pitch to her voice. Laidlaw had her rattled, but the officer wasn't giving up – not without a fight she wasn't.

'3529: Jesus! I can see the whites of her eyes now. We're going to have to prevent her from disappearing into a built-up area . . . she's not stopping, boss. She's thumping the steering wheel in a temper. She's punching at the window, totally out of control. She's screaming off her face.'

'Silly cow . . .' Daniels mumbled under her breath, wishing she was at the wheel. No reflection at all on her driver but, in situations like these, it was nice to have something to hang on to. Lucy Laidlaw had nothing to lose. She had two choices: keep going or go to prison for life. *A no-brainer then.* '7824 to all units: we need to take positive action. We can't let her any-where near traffic or public. Whoa, stop, stop. She's pulling off. She's trying to bail the vehicle. Bailing the vehicle. We've got a runner! She's out of the vehicle and running south-east across the Langdale Fell.'

Five Traffic cars pulled up simultaneously. Daniels got out of hers and started running, arms like pistons. Laidlaw was way ahead, four officers in pursuit. India 99 dropped out of the sky in front of her. Laidlaw changed direction and so did

Cole's helicopter – once, twice, three times – coming so close it nearly blew her and those pursuing her off their feet.

Exhausted and fighting the lashing downdraught from the helicopter, Daniels closed in as Laidlaw dropped to her knees. Raising her eyes to the heavens, she let out a roar of anger no one could hear for the thwacking sound of rotor blades above them. Daniels launched herself, shoulder-charging her, knocking her flat. As she struggled to get up, the DCI pulled her arms behind her back and slapped the snips on.

'You're nicked,' was all she had breath for.

88

Daniels got out of her new Audi Q5 at Newcastle International airport, lifted the tailgate and removed a suitcase from the back. Pulling up the collapsible handle, she locked her vehicle, made a note of its position, and strode towards the terminal feeling a little sad despite the sunshine. As she walked through the revolving doors into the departure hall, a shiver went down her spine. The last time she'd been here she was looking for Lucy Laidlaw as she tried to flee the country. And now, as Daniels joined a long queue at the check-in desk, she recalled that anxious wait at the control tower and the slightly bizarre conversation with a Norwegian pilot through the flight-deck window of an enormous Airbus A320 destined for Turkey.

The fact that Laidlaw had managed to maim and kill since that day weighed heavily on Daniels' mind. Not that she was at all responsible. *But still.* It was a death that could've – some say should've – been prevented. There would be an enquiry, of course. There always was. Lessons learned and all that bollocks when the report was made public. She could almost hear the Chief Constable waxing lyrical on the subject as he sat in front of the force logo, making sure he got his sound bites in. But that wouldn't help the female security guard, a mother of three who, sadly, had suffered permanent brain

damage in the cell block at Market Street police station and would never work again. Or poor Chantelle, whose unhappy life had come to such a brutal and abrupt end in the home where she was born and brought up – a home that held secrets of unimaginable brutality.

One way or the other, June 2010 had been a hell of a month. The hottest on record, it should also have been the most joyous with England winning the World Cup for the first time since 1966. But it wasn't. Instead it was depressing and sad and any other negative adjective you cared to attach to it, a time of deep sorrow for a great many people: Maggie Reid, Annaliese Ridley, Elliot Milburn, Sergeant McCabe. And also for Todd Fox, a soldier repatriated to England by his regiment for his sister's funeral.

Twenty-seven people were directly affected by tragedy that month. And that was just close family. If you were to add in all the friends and colleagues of the victims and Daniels' own staff in the Murder Investigation Team, that number would run into the hundreds. Gormley had been particularly affected by the death of Ivy Kerr.

It was scant compensation, but Daniels had returned Bridget's seal ring to her father and George Milburn's money to his grandson, Elliot. She'd also managed to find a new home for Rooney, Chantelle's cat. In time, with the help of the National Fraud Intelligence Bureau, she hoped to trace Ivy's lottery win and return it to her estate. Annaliese planned to use some of the money to make that trip to Austria on her father's behalf, to find the place where he'd been held captive during the war. Who knew? Maybe she'd even trace the

people who'd looked after him and kept him safe for a sweetheart waiting back home.

For the Murder Investigation Team, the victory of catching Lucy Laidlaw was bittersweet. There was no doubt she'd been badly treated by Arthur Fox. But she'd shown no remorse for her despicable acts of cruelty; not for the inferno that had claimed the lives of a devoted father and son, or for her actions at the crash scene on that hellish night in the pouring rain. Following her re-arrest she'd shown her true colours. 'The old witch was practically dead already,' she had said, as if Ivy Kerr's life was of no consequence whatsoever. 'Her legs looked bad, really bad. I've seen enough crashes to know a probable amputation when I see one. I gave her a helping hand, that's all.'

Daniels sighed, looking up at the departures board.

Laidlaw had learned one lesson though: those who played with fire did sometimes get burned. She'd always wanted a sister, someone she could share her troubles with. If she had one regret in all of this it was that she'd finally found a sibling and would serve life for her murder.

DCI Kate Daniels was glad the investigation was over, pleased that she was finally able to close the file and concentrate on the future. Her love life was still uncertain. Her timing had always been crap. And so was Jo Soulsby's; her wish to start again had come at a particularly awkward time. If it wasn't so serious it would be funny, a typical scenario for a romantic comedy. Jo had now left her post as Criminal Profiler with Northumbria Police's Murder Investigation Team to take up the research position at HMP Northumberland, promising to keep in touch. There had been no fanfare or

leaving do. She'd slipped away with no fuss and tears in her eyes that Daniels didn't see.

'All set?' Daniels asked.

'I'll send you a postcard.' Fiona Fielding smiled, tucking passport and tickets back into her bag. Her trip to the Far East was due to last a month and she hoped to be back in Britain by Christmas. She hugged Daniels and kissed her gently on the lips. 'Call her,' she whispered before walking away.

ACKNOWLEDGEMENTS

Thanks again to my dream team at Pan Macmillan: especially my fabulous editor, Wayne Brookes, and also his assistant, Louise Buckley, who kept me on track throughout the edit of *Deadly Deceit*. Also, to the entire staff at Blake Friedmann Literary, TV & Film Agency who look after me in so many ways. A special mention must go to my friend and agent Oli Munson who makes writing so much fun. Lastly, to my wonderful copy-editor, the woman from whom I have learned so much along the way, Anne O'Brien.

Appreciation to my friend Dave Willis (pilot extraordinaire, now also known as Kjell), who helped Kate Daniels climb aboard an enormous Airbus A320 destined for Turkey in this book. To New Writing North who support and promote my work – I am very grateful.

To my whole family, a constant source of feedback and encouragement: Paul and Kate, Chris and Caroline. Also to the A-team of helpers, Max and Frances, who inspire me to do my very best every single day. Lastly, to my partner Mo, who somehow manages to keep all the other balls in the air while I play with words. I could wish for no more.

extracts reading groups
competitions books new
discounts extracts
competitions
books
new
events books
extracts
new reading groups
interviews
events extracts
discounts
new books events
events new
discounts extracts discounts
www.panmacmillan.com
extracts events reading groups
competitions books extracts new

reading groups
events
reading groups
events
books
events
interviews new
books